JET AND
BLAST CASTLE

By

Jeanie Doyle Singler

authorHOUSE®

AuthorHouse™ LLC
1663 Liberty Drive
Bloomington, IN 47403
www.authorhouse.com
Phone: 1-800-839-8640

Cover Art by: Wyatt A. Doyle

Published by AuthorHouse   07/16/2013

ISBN: 978-1-4817-7393-5 (sc)
ISBN: 978-1-4817-7394-2 (e)

Library of Congress Control Number: 2013912067

To My Three Sons

who have inspired and made possible many of the characters in my books by sharing, demonstrating, and explaining their thinking, motivations, actions, and dreams to me.

CAST OF CHARACTERS

JET

Jessica Thompson-Sayre—(Jet Sayre) Young woman who learns just before her mother's death that the man she believed was her father may not be and now she wants to know who is.

Mona Sayre Thompson—Jet's mother

Roger Thompson—Mona Sayre's ex-husband and the man Jet grew up believing was her father.

Tana Capucine Rosen—(Latte) Jet's friend and former college roommate.

Landon and Logan Rosen—Latte's twin sons

KINSEY

Parkinson Sayre II—(Kinsey) Young man who wants to save the family mansion from its bad reputation and demolition.

Parkinson Sayre I—(Park) Kinsey's father, who has no love for the family mansion.

Nathan Berendt—Kinsey's friend from childhood.

Evana Sayre Stevenson—Kinsey's widowed sister.

Patricia Barnes—(Pat) Kinsey's aunt and the woman who raised him.

Daniel Barnes—Kinsey's uncle and Pat's husband.

OTHER

Lieutenant Davy Sarkis—Pierce County Sheriff Department's homicide detective.

Agent Elaney—United States Treasury Secret Service Agent.

Susannah MacFadden—Nathan's co-worker.

Billy Monk—renter at Blast Castle.

Chapter One

In retrospect the worst of times are often the best of times.

Jet Sayre considered the clothing heaped on the queen-sized bed, wondering why she was the one moving out. "He wouldn't move if I put bombs under it and lit his clothes on fire," she mumbled, catching a glimpse in the dresser mirror of her small face nearly lost in the bubble of black hair crowning her head.

On the closet shelf she found two hanger bags into which she managed to stuff all of her hanging clothes. With boxes from the supply room at work, another stack from her friends, and Brad Westfield's book boxes, she had enough space for her personal possessions, which had multiplied with reckless abandon while she lived with Brad. She packed the Bose sound system she had purchased with her last year's Christmas bonus, the designer set of dishes, and the Le Creuset pots from the hallway kitchen. Brad wouldn't know designer from Walmart.

"What's going on?" the sound of his voice at the bedroom door startled her. She hadn't expected him home yet.

"I'm moving." She turned to face him.

His bewildered glance assessed the room. "Were you moving my things or just going to tell me where to bring them?"

"You can stay here." Jet sighed. "I'm moving away from you."

His mouth opened, but no words came out.

Struggling for a way to explain her decision, Jet watched his stunned disbelief with an attack of guilt. She had no explanation to satisfy him. She didn't want to argue; she had made up her mind.

"How can you leave me?"

Literal minded, Jet began explaining her arrangements then realized that wasn't what he meant.

"I love you," he said.

"You love you. I'm just convenient to have around." When had he last looked at her even when she was talking? After all he could see her any time, but he might irretrievably miss the Seahawk's touchdown.

"What does that mean?" Her retort made him defensive.

Jet arched her eyebrows. "Do you love me enough to get married?"

Apprehension flooded his expression. "Well—."

"No need for marriage when you have everything you need with no commitment, inconvenience, or risk."

"And it's different for you?" He bit out the words.

As far as it went he was right. Maybe that was why she had been willing in the first place. Starting out perfectly content with their live-in arrangement, she hadn't wanted to marry Brad. What had changed? With a pang of intense grief the answer came. *My mother died.* How could she explain to him what she couldn't resolve for herself? She had attempted the night she came home from the care center after her life-shattering conversation with Mona Sayre Thompson. Three weeks later her mother slipped into the coma from which she never returned. Jet could still recall that scene like replaying a video.

It had been one of her mother's better days. When Jet entered the room Mona was seated upright in bed, clear-eyed and peaceful. She beckoned her daughter to the wooden chair beside her, announcing she needed to explain a few things.

Jet sat, overtaken with apprehension. Her mother never explained anything and a lot of things in Mona's life needed explaining.

"I'm making my end-of-life confessions," Mona said with a wry smile. "You need to know some things and Pastor Ansgreth convinced me it would be better if you heard them from me."

Apprehension elevated to alarm. Jet had met Pastor Ansgreth leaving when she arrived. The empathy in his crystal blue eyes triggered her anxiety. She had encountered the pastor only once before visiting her mother. Mona wasn't exactly a church-goer. Jet wasn't certain how she had even made his acquaintance. Religion had played no part in their lives to this point.

"This isn't easy for me to do," Mona confessed, brushing her light brown hair away from her face.

At some level Jet knew her mother was dying, but she hadn't come to terms with it. It never seemed real, especially when she looked at Mona who had retained her lovely youthfulness into her mid-fifties. Tiny crow's feet accented her gray eyes, but she had no facial lines or sagging skin, no gray in her hair. Her mother had been beautiful when she was in good health, something Jet had never been in health or out.

She stared at her mother's bruised hand on the bed sheet reaching for hers.

"I realize, Jessica, you believe Roger Thompson is your father."

Jet narrowed her eyes and searched her mother's expression. "What do you mean I believe he's my father?"

"Well, he could be. I'm not saying that he's not."

"What are you saying?"

Mona took a deep breath, watching Jet's face. "There are others also who could be."

"Others?" Jet's voice rose an octave. "Others?"

Mona lifted her chin and stared at the blank television on the ledge across the room. Glittering amusement in her eyes and the impish curve of her lips reflected the pride she took in her male conquests. Jet looked away, torn between revulsion and rage. Her mother was dying of cervical cancer, one of the many consequences, as the pamphlet put it, of multiple sexual partners.

"So who is my father?"

"That's the point, dear, I don't know."

Jet felt like screaming or crying, shaking her mother or pulling her hair, something to get her attention, make her take some responsibility. Instead she sat very still, staring at Mona's scarred hand. It was too late for anything to be done according to the doctors.

Lifting her gaze to her mother's face Jet asked the question to which she wasn't sure she wanted the answer. "Who are the possibilities?"

"Well, Roger Thompson, of course. Although we were divorced at your conception we did spend a long week-end together then considering reconciliation."

Jet sighed. "Who else?"

"I worked with a nice man with who was lonely and frustrated. We dated a few times."

Which meant they went to bed not a movie. "What was his name?"

"He's happily married." Mona's expression pleaded.

"Name?" Was her mother trying to protect a conquest?

"Jesse McFadden." Mona said then quickly continued, "But that's not all. My second cousin Park Sayre spent a week staying with me after his wife died."

"And you consoled him?" Jet remarked sarcastically. Mona Sayre, the therapist. "Are they all the possibilities?"

Mona pressed her lips together. "Not quite." She cast Jet an apprehensive glance. "One night I got sloshed at a party and ended up with someone whose name I never knew exactly."

"And that's probably my father, Mr. Unknown." Jet covered her mouth, stifling the scream of fury welling inside.

"It sounded like Otto Lane, but I'm not sure that was it."

Jet sat in the chair, tears rolling down her face while her mother made excuses for her behavior. A month later Mona was dead, but the tears were still there every time Jet thought about her. She could not explain to herself or to Brad why she no longer wanted a live-in relationship. But she didn't and that was it.

❧

"You can't sell it," Kinsey Sayre roared at his father. "It's part of the Sayre heritage."

"Like death and taxes, you'd just as soon avoid both." Parkinson Sayre I stood in front of the massive wood-carved mantel, his hands behind his back. Pressed into a thin line his lips confirmed him the immovable object. "In fact that's all you'd get with this place is death and taxes."

Adamant, Kinsey glared at the tall gentleman with a touch of gray in his dark hair. "It's not the house's fault." How could his father be so obtuse?

Parkinson Sayre always reminded Kinsey of Gregory Peck. However the comparison broke down when Kinsey faced his own reflection and his resemblance to his father.

"Taxes, maybe," Park conceded, "but the deaths are."

Kinsey faced his father across the expanse of hardwood floors, shining in spite of the dust. "Houses don't kill people."

"This one does."

"That's just superstition." Kinsey refused to believe the rumors spread about the castle-like mansion that had been in his family for decades.

"The last two renters are dead. It's not superstition. They're really dead." Although restrained Park's voice carried a bite. He stood with his feet planted apart as if daring Kinsey to budge him.

"But it's not the house's fault." Kinsey raised his voice, enunciating each word.

"Convince the public. I'll be lucky if I can unload this place on anyone for another fifty years. The media calls it Blast Castle."

Kinsey wandered to the leaded-glass windows set in dark wood panels. He gazed into the landscape, bright green beneath its blanket of orange and yellow leaves. The last wisp of fall had shaken the foliage from the trees while Thanksgiving approached like an oncoming train.

Blast Castle or not, he loved this place. It represented his dreams of legacy, tradition, and the interwoven connection of family and values, lending continuity and stability to life. He wanted to be the kind of person who belonged in Blast Castle, someone with character, significance, passion and strength. In spite of his existence in the technology generation his heart lived in King Arthur's court.

Kinsey turned back to his father. "So you're putting it up for sale?"

Parkinson sighed, lifting his winged eyebrows. "The only other option would be to exorcize its reputation."

"Don't you have to do that before you can sell it?"

"Not if the buyers want to demolish it."

"Demolish it!" Kinsey was horrified. "You can't let that happen."

"I don't have another option."

You would if you weren't scared to death of it, but Kinsey couldn't say that to his father. "There must be another way."

Park paced the parquet to the grand piano covered with enough dust to draw out the building plans.

Shoving his hands into his pockets and watching with apprehension Kinsey fought for an idea to forestall his father's intention. "What would it take for you to keep it?"

Park continued pacing without a reply.

Kinsey waited, feeling like a prisoner before the bar.

Pausing, Park turned to his son. "If you could prove what's happened here has nothing to do with the house and clear its reputation, I'd quit claim deed it to you. Provided you could afford to live here and keep it up."

"Are you serious?" Kinsey held his breath. Would his father really hand over the mansion that easily?

"I know this place means a lot to you. But I don't have a lot of time and honestly I don't think you can clear its reputation or afford it."

Whatever the price, it was worth a shot. "How long will you give me?"

Park stroked his square jaw. "Taxes are due again in six months. I'll give you until then."

That wasn't much time, but more than Kinsey had expected. "I'll move in tonight."

Alarm leaped into his father's expression. "I'd rather you didn't stay here."

"If I'm going to find out what's going on I'll have to." Park's irrational apprehension of the mansion always mystified Kinsey. He couldn't align it with his father's otherwise strong and confident resourcefulness. His father felt the house was bad luck. Kinsey couldn't buy that, but he was unable to explain what he had heard about it either. "The renters weren't attacked by ghosts, Dad."

"No? One fell from the second floor balcony in a fevered delirium and broke his neck."

Kinsey glanced at the magnificent staircase angling its way to the second floor. "They said it was an accident. He was a sleep-walker and ill."

"The other one was electrocuted."

"Ghosts don't electrocute people." Kinsey fought his rising frustration.

"This one did."

No point in arguing. His mission was to clear the mansion's name without endangering himself. Maybe he could get someone to join him, in fact the more the jollier. It might help shake things loose. He voiced his idea.

"Who do you think would want to live in this death trap?"

Kinsey loved his father, but Park's chronically negative perspective was a bitter pill. Kinsey returned to the tall windows and their view of the formal approach. "Do you know anything about the renters before they came here?"

"Just what was on the applications."

"Are they available?"

"I can probably find them." Park ran his hand through his hair. "What good do you think they'd do you?"

"I don't know, but I have to start somewhere."

Chapter Two

Kinsey drove an older seven series BMW, black with dazzling aluminum rims. His friends called him "grandpa", laughing at his love for the old car, given to him by his uncle. It's perfect symmetry and graceful lines made it one of the most beautiful cars he had ever seen.

"You can afford better than this," Nathan Berendt chided when Kinsey arrived to pick him up. "At least one of the Z cars." Nathan drove a gussied up Mustang with the attitude of a race driver in a Lamborghini.

Nathan had been Kinsey's buddy since before they were old enough to separate their esses from their tee-aiches. Kinsey's Aunt Pat used to ask him what a "nasanssouse" was.

"And your point is?"

"Be a little adventurous, man. Get yourself a girlfriend."

Frowning, he drove the winding boulevard through a tunnel of trees to the bar and grill perched above a newer building in Steilacoom, Kinsey realized he never understood the reaction he got from women. He had no idea what it was about. He found staying on the move his best protection from aggressive females.

Nathan made friends easily, especially with women, who never seemed intimidated by him or interested in smothering him. Kinsey would have gladly traded places, but he didn't figure the BMW made the difference.

After being escorted to a booth with glimpses of the sparkling bay, ordering sandwiches and beer, Kinsey launched into his proposal. "You're always spouting off about adventure, Nathan, how about plunking down your assets where your jabber is?"

Nathan cocked his bushy head, leveling his emerald gaze at Kinsey. "What have you got in mind?"

Kinsey described the conversation with his father and the bargain he made. "You can rent a spot in the house for half what you're paying now."

Nathan laughed. "I live with my mother."

And I'm supposed to be impressed? "You pay her to do that." Kinsey was well aware of his friend's resources and line of reasoning. Nathan probably still had his Life Saver Book from first grade.

"It helps her out."

Yeah, right. "Your mom has plenty of money. Maybe she'd like you to move on."

Nathan grimaced, running a freckled hand through his bright red hair. "What's in it for you?" Nathan always had an angle, enlarging his portfolio or his sphere of influence. His ambition was to break through the glass ceiling into a high income and flashy lifestyle.

"Dad thinks the house is dangerous." What inducement could he offer for Nathan's cooperation? "I thought if I wasn't alone it would keep him from laying on his philosophy of doom."

"Two of us in that huge mansion?" Nathan shook his head.

"I'll get more renters than you." Kinsey's sister, Evana, who accused him of illusions of grandeur might help out. In spite of her mockery she also loved the old castle. It would only take five more to fill it.

After the waitress delivered platters with grilled sandwiches and piles of fries, Nathan lifted a fair eyebrow. "What kind of renters?"

Kinsey frowned. "What do you mean?"

"Women?" Nathan flashed a toothy grin.

Kinsey shrugged. "We can probably get a couple female renters, but you'd better keep your feet on the ground or some frilly will raid your bank account."

Nathan shrugged.

"I know a bunch of young people trying to make ends meet and keep an apartment. I can offer space at a bargain and they could help provide protection. Then we might figure out what garbage is going on there."

Nathan pointed an accusing finger. "You think the house is dangerous too."

"Not the house." Kinsey hadn't bought into his father's superstitious fears, but he wasn't prepared to ignore the evidence. "Something is wrong though and I have to find out what."

"You want a sleuth?"

The way Nathan's expression lit up gave Kinsey second thoughts. "Are you volunteering?" he challenged his friend. "You're the one who's always talking about taking risks to accomplish something."

"Okay, what the heck. I don't have anything to lose."

Not so sure that was the case; Kinsey wasn't going to argue his success.

"How soon do you want me to move?" Nathan put his elbows on the polished table and held his sandwich up for scrutiny.

One thing about Nathan, he jumped from decision to action with jackrabbit speed.

"I still have to get a cleaning crew in and have the place put in shape. No one has lived there for a year or so." Kinsey shook ketchup onto his fries. "But I'm letting the rooms first come first served."

"Furnished?"

"Basically." He would have to figure out a way to price them fairly. "On the second floor I've got two suites and three bedrooms with private baths. I'm taking the suite at the south end with the 180-degree view. I figure it'll help me keep an eye on things."

"Are there differences in rent amounts?"

On the back of a napkin Kinsey scribbled figures related to what he knew of the cost of running the castle. Adding a percentage for ignorance and dividing the numbers by the eight possibilities for lodgers he came up with a rental fee.

"What's the cheapest?"

"Third floor. There's a suite and a couple bedrooms, but they have lower ceilings and less windows."

"Give me a great big room. No kitchen, I don't cook much." Nathan spoke around his sandwich. "I'd need space to store some chemicals. Samples, you know, that kind of thing."

Kinsey hadn't considered storage space. Probably others would need that too. Since the house was nearly 30,000 square feet it shouldn't be a problem.

"Why don't you hire a cook and we can live like royalty?"

Kinsey snorted, but it probably wasn't that crazy an idea. He also realized he had plunged into the scheme without giving much thought to the details.

Nathan signaled for the check. "I can do that—after Thanksgiving though."

"It'll take me a week at least to get the cleaning completed." In the midst of his excitement Kinsey had forgotten about Thanksgiving. It would slow matters down, but it might give him a chance to put his proposition to Evana. "Do you know anyone else who is looking for a place?"

Nathan squinted across the room. "A girl in the office was complaining about her situation the other day. She might be interested. Do you want me to ask?"

Although preferring a man, Kinsey agreed. "At least you can ask."

"You going to your aunt's for Thanksgiving?"

"Yeah. The whole crew will be there. I want to be able to tell Dad I've got things moving." A dumpster load of disasters had befallen his father over the years. Although Kinsey resented Park's negative perspective, it wasn't like he had no reason to be pessimistic. Both his parents had passed away, his wife died when Evana was a year old, his firstborn son had been born too early and did not survive. He had inherited Blast Castle for which he had no great love and promptly had to deal with two deaths there and its plagued reputation.

"You think he'll renege?"

Kinsey shrugged. "No sense taking chances. I was blown over when he made the proposal."

❦

14

Jet steered the big SUV into the driveway of the lodge-like duplex her friend Latte Capucine Rosen rented, parking behind her own yellow Saturn. Jet and Latte had gone to college together, sharing a dorm room their first year. Latte had shortened Jet's name, Jessica Elaine Thompson-Sayre, to JET Sayre. In response Jet called Tana Laurain Capucine, Latte Cappuccino. Latte had agreed to let her use her third bedroom until she found another place to live.

As she got out of the SUV Latte's six-year-old twins came roaring out of the duplex shouting. "Mom says you're going to have to find another place."

Jet considered Landon, the friendly outspoken one, processing what he said.

Logan, his more reserved brother, added, "We all have to find another place to live."

Mildly apprehensive, Jet followed the bounding, curly-headed pair into the story-and-a-half townhouse. Latte, her blonde braids sticking out from under her headband, sat at the knotty pine table with the classified ads, her computer, and a cell phone.

"What's going on?" Jet observed the evidence with anxiety.

Latte's wide-eyed grimace told Jet circumstances had gotten beyond her control. "The landlord decided to renovate and sell the duplex. We have to move out."

Jet sighed. "How soon?"

"The end of the month." Latte huffed with frustration while her eyes checked out Jet's expression. Latte wasn't as innocent as she sounded.

"That's a week and a half." Jet's voice squeaked. "Don't they have to give you more notice than that?"

"I agreed to be out if he'd give back the advances and deposit immediately, no questions asked." Latte sounded pleased with herself in spite of her concern for Jet's reaction.

Jet sat in the chair at the end of the table. "Why did you do that?"

Latte had a habit of running to the end of the high dive before she decided whether or not to jump. Her big brown eyes shot Jet a reproachful glance. "It would give me more money to get a better place."

At least her reasoning made sense. Jet figured her own precipitate decision didn't give her room to criticize. "Should I unpack the SUV or just leave my things there?"

Latte squinted thoughtfully. "You'd better unload. I don't think we can find something that fast."

With the boys help Jet moved her possessions to the small extra bedroom, stacking most of it along one wall. Anatuviak, Latte's Labrador retriever, ran back and forth barking as if in charge of the operation. When they had completed the task and Jet had unpacked enough necessities to make it through the day she returned to where Latte sat.

"Any luck?" Jet envisioned the four of them preserving their lifestyle in a tent under the bridge.

Latte made a disgusted gesture. "No one allows pets."

"What exactly are you looking for?"

"Well, I thought if we could find a place we both could live that would be good." Latte consulted her friend with a glance.

Jet nodded, gratified to be included in Latte's plans. "I could use the company right now."

"Are you missing Brad already?" Latte leaned back twisting a pen in her hands.

Jet made a face and shook her head. Brad was so wrapped up in himself all their conversations had been about him, his work, his ambitions, his frustrations and his health. He never asked about her and if she volunteered any information it served only to remind him of something he wanted to say and off he would go on another tangent. She almost felt as if she didn't exist. "I need to get my mail taken care of."

"Go ahead, we can fix dinner when you get back."

Jet transferred to her roadster and headed for the Post Office where she rented a box and picked up what had accumulated; noting with curiosity a small blue envelope with a return address sticker indicating it came from another Sayre.

After returning to her car Jet opened the envelope.

Dear Jessica,

Since your mother has passed away I wondered if you would be alone for Thanksgiving. We would love to have you join us on Thursday for dinner at about three o'clock. An assortment of family members will be there and you would be most welcome. Let me know if you can come.

Love, Aunt Pat

Jet stared at the note trying to recall her exact relationship to "Aunt Pat". Her mother had relegated the Sayre side of the family to the outer reaches of the stratosphere. In fact, as far as Mona was concerned she was a free spirit born of the vapor that blew in with the marine air. It increased Jet's surprise at her confession to spending time with her cousin, Parkinson Sayre.

Jet tossed the envelope onto the pile of mail in the passenger seat and drove back to Latte's duplex. Before answering Aunt Pat's note she needed to find out Latte's plans.

Fussing around the one-person kitchen, Latte prepared dinner while Jet set the table, listening to her grump about the difficulty of finding a rental that allowed pets. Anatuviak lay on the floor oblivious to the difficulty he presented.

"I've three places to look at, but the ads make me suspicious." Latte described the possibilities, absentmindedly stirring the pasta sauce.

"Did you make appointments to see them?" If Latte didn't control the splattering sauce she'd soon pass for a dish of pasta herself.

"Yes, for tomorrow."

As they cleaned up from dinner, Jet asked Latte about Thanksgiving.

"I promised my parents we'd come. They're sending tickets."

Jet explained her letter from Aunt Pat. "I'm not even sure who she is, probably a cousin rather than an aunt. I may have met her at Grandpa Terrence Sayre's funeral." A teenager then Jet had little concept of who he was either, probably not her grandfather. Although who could say? "I think I'll accept the invitation."

"Will Park Sayre be there?" Latte spun the dial on the dishwasher and set it in motion.

Jet shrugged. "Probably. If he's my father and Mom was a Sayre by birth that would make me a Sayre double over."

"Wouldn't you be mentally handicapped then?"

Jet smacked her forehead. "I knew there was a reason I made these stupid decisions."

Latte scowled then shot her a mischievous grin. "Well, you can see if you look anything like him?"

Chapter Three

After a restless night, dreaming she was an English princess secluded by her father in a western state for safety until the enemies of the land had been deposed, Jet rose Thanksgiving Day unaccountably excited for its potential. Late the previous afternoon she had driven Latte and her crew to SeaTac International, seeing them off to California.

Spending the week dutifully driving by every remote rental possibility, they failed to find another place to live. Apartments were available for Jet alone, for Latte and the kids, but a spot to handle all of them plus Anatuviak, no deal. Those they inspected turned out to be grungy, surrounded by homes in shrieking disrepair, sporting kamikaze vehicles and graffiti, or simply too expensive. Even the pricey ones fell short of their criteria.

Alone with Anatuviak for the holiday Jet figured the weather with its bank of clouds hovering along the horizon was having sufficient difficulty making up its mind to allow time for their morning run. The background of evergreens and bare deciduous trees etched on the eastern sky shot with streaks of pink captured her mood with its dark side and brightness, portraying the misgivings and hopefulness teeter-tottering for control of her emotions. She felt remorse for her precipitate move yet excited for future possibilities.

In her travels Jet had noticed Pastor Ansgreth's Thanksgiving service on a church reader board. Feeling an undefined connection to him, perhaps the only person who knew the ugly truth regarding her heritage, she was drawn to it. Even her father, Jet thought bitterly, probably wasn't aware he had a daughter. She fought tears of loneliness and betrayal. At thirty did it make any difference?

After securing Anatuviak in the fenced back yard, she dressed in the red sweater with white snowflakes and black slacks she had set out the night before then headed to the church.

Not only a stranger to the congregation but to church period, Jet chose a back pew, tucked herself into the corner, and followed the service on the overhead while endeavoring to recall how her mother had become acquainted with the pastor. As the service proceeded through the confession of sins Jet wondered if Mona ever saw her behavior as sin. Although far from clear on the concept Jet felt her mother's behavior resulting in Jet's undetermined paternity was wrong. She was certainly offended. She figured God ought to be too.

The sermon addressed thankfulness, not only because God deserved it but also acknowledging God's provision eased one's anxiety. The whole principle left Jet vaguely uneasy.

"Happy Thanksgiving, Jessica," the pastor in his reception line greeted her. "I'm glad you came today."

"Happy Thanksgiving," she said, feeling gratified and a little less abandoned when he remembered her name.

During church the wind kicked up, pushing a bank of clouds over the sun and peppering her windshield with a fine drizzle. Heading to the Sayre Thanksgiving dinner with gratefulness not to be alone on the holiday, Jet hoped for enlightenment regarding her family. Her mother's aversion to them still puzzled her. Mona never seemed to bear any grudge; she just ignored them.

The circular driveway to the Tudor brick home overlooking Commencement Bay was crowded with cars when Jet arrived. She parked on the street next to a brick balustrade enclosing the property. Multicolor leaves rested in precarious positions along the top and against its base. More leaves scattered the brick walkway with which Jet approached the arched wooden door.

Taking a deep breath, she willed herself the courage to face this aspect of her life. A magnificent evergreen wreath fresh with the scent of pine and cedar hung on the door. Jet pressed the bell then listened to it chime.

A pudgy older man with mild brown eyes and a fringe of gray hair circling his shiny forehead opened the door. His green sweatshirt with a turkey begging for mercy gave him a slightly comical appearance. The quizzical expression on his face meant he had not recognized her. Not that she could blame him.

"I'm Jessica Sayre."

Blushing, he apologized, opening the door wider. "I'm Daniel Barnes." Which made him Aunt Pat's husband.

Assaulted by the aroma of roasting turkey, Jet stepped into the wide foyer, paneled in light wood from which the mahogany stairway wound behind her to the floor above. Ahead she noted people gathered in conversational groups. She followed Daniel into a sea-green room where individuals representing various ages lounged on colorless sofas, ornate French chairs, or perched on the window seat. Panic seized Jet; she recognized no one.

From amidst the company a beautiful young woman with wedged black hair approached. "You must be Jessica." She offered her hand with a warm smile. "I'm Evana Stevenson. I used to be Sayre, which makes us cousins."

Jet extended her hand, willing her lips to smile.

"Aunt Pat's in the kitchen. She should be around in a minute. Let me introduce you." Evana led Jet farther into the room where she went around the group giving names and explaining relationships. One person stuck out as Evana said, "This is my father, Park-Parkinson Sayre." She introduced a tall, aristocratic man to whom she bore a strong family resemblance.

It flashed through Jet's mind that Evana might actually be her sister.

To her father Evana said, "This is Jessica, Mona's daughter."

Park's sculptured lips formed a tight line while his eyes regarded her gravely, but he offered his hand and smiled. "Welcome and happy Thanksgiving."

"Thank you." Jessica could feel the eyes in the room examining and appraising as Evana explained her presence there.

"I'm sorry about your mother." Park's gaze was direct enough to indicate sincerity.

Why had all these people been excluded from her life?

❧

By the time Kinsey left for Aunt Pat's on Thanksgiving Day the western monsoons had returned to the Pacific Northwest sweeping through the area in waves. Commencement Bay had disappeared into the mist leaving the Barnes' house sitting on the edge of the world. He recognized most of the cars in circular driveway and along the street except for the yellow roadster.

He had been staying at the castle, having conveyed his readily hauled possessions there. A cleaning crew had transformed it, impressing him with what dusting and moping could do. In spite of its lack of habitation the mansion had never fallen prey to deterioration or neglect.

The scent of roasting turkey almost transported him physically into the kitchen when he pushed open the large wooden door. However, his great aunt Tansy waylaid him in the hall. Shaking her bony finger at his dripping coat, she pointed to the antique coat tree. After shedding his trench coat he encountered Cathy and Mary May, his cousin Jordan's two daughters, on the French settee giggling. They both jumped up demanding a hug, which he obliged, picking them up together and whirling them around. By then, spotted by the majority of his family, he was persuaded to join them in the living room.

"Kinsey," Evana's refined voice hailed him. "Come meet Jessica-Jet." Although her words invited, her expression warned. "This is Mona Thompson's daughter."

Kinsey raised a questioning eyebrow, as Evana turned to a half-pint woman whose elfin face was nearly lost beneath her heap of dark hair and ebony rimmed glasses. To Jet she said, "This is my brother, Kinsey."

Considering the libidinous rumors about Mona Thompson, Kinsey found Jet an anticlimax. She hardly looked the saucy dish Mona would have raised. Offering

24

his hand, he noted that her kaleidoscope eyes studied him with undisguised interest. Her hand was small but her grip strong.

"Welcome to the clan." Although he must have seen Jet before, he didn't remember her. She looked like a twelve-year-old boy with a few small curves and a trace of poise.

"Are you living in Tacoma?" Evana asked her.

"Lakewood, until the 30th. We have to find a new place."

Aha, Kinsey realized, an opportunity. "What sort of place are you looking for?"

"One large enough for my friend who has two kids and a dog, and me. Most are either too expensive or won't take the dog."

"I've a huge house with suites I'm renting. We don't mind a dog or kids."

Jet's eyes lit with interest. "How much?"

"Depends on how much space you want. After dinner we could run over and take a look." Kinsey glanced at his sister whose narrowed eyes suggested disapproval. "You, too, Evana."

Aunt Pat, looking the warm-hearted hostess with an apron tied about her large frame and gray-brown hair slightly askew, appeared in the doorway, winked at Kinsey then announced dinner. From around the room people arose to make their way to the dining room. Evana led Jet to a seat beside herself across from Kinsey.

He still had to engage Evana in his plans. Although she knew he was staying at the estate he had not approached her to join him. Ever since her husband died she and Kinsey had supported each other, spending a good deal of time together.

After the blessing they passed plates of turkey, dressing, potatoes, gravy, cranberry sauce, corn casserole, sweet potatoes, and rolls. Kinsey tested Evana's interest in the mansion.

"What do you think you're going to do there?" Her words challenged, her tone proprietary. She sounded like his mother might have.

"Transform *le* Blast Castle into *une maison elegante.*" He flashed her a cheesy grin, hoping he wouldn't have to deal with more skepticism. "You know I've always wanted to live there. So have you," he reminded her.

Evana's marine blue eyes met his with a grave nod and a knowing smile. "Ever since the last renter died it's been a taboo subject around here."

"I'll make you a deal."

She gave him a sidelong glance, offering her don't-try-to-schmooze-me smile. "Better than free?"

"That wouldn't do me any good. Think about it though. Here you have people who mind your business for you, invade your privacy, make demands on you. There you could come and go as you please, socialize if you want or keep to yourself.

Evana cocked her head. "I'll think about it."

❧

Kinsey's description hardly prepared Jet for the sight when leaving Gravelly Lake Drive they came through the trees. This isn't a house; it's a hotel. She gazed in awe at the immense stone mansion with tall arched windows and rows of chimneys, trying to imagine what it might be like to live in such place. Her imagination failed her, but an injection of excitement sent a thrill up her spine.

The circular driveway, embracing an inoperative fountain, deposited the trio at an arched passageway to the castle entrance. Kinsey unlocked and opened the door. Orange scented furniture polish greeted them as they stepped into the chilly anteroom.

While Evana and Kinsey bickered over their father's attitude about the mansion, Jet followed into the grand parlor, shadowy in the light of a half dozen arabesque wall sconces, making the oak floors gleam and wood furniture shimmer.

"You need more furniture than this." Evana stood between two sofas facing each other over a faded Aubusson rug, pointing to the wide-open spaces in the room. A couple Queen Anne chairs shared a heavily carved table next to the leaded-glass windows while across the expanse a grand piano stood in lonely silence.

As Kinsey turned to Jet she noted the same blue eyes and chiseled face as Evana.

He beckoned to the huge oak staircase. "Let's go see if there's something that would work for you." When they reached the top, he waved his hand to encompass the rooms across from where they stood. "The four doors you see there include a suite with kitchenette, plus two other bedrooms with baths. That might work great for you and your friend with the kids."

Dollar signs waved warning flags. "How much?" She steeled herself against getting attached before she had any idea they could afford it.

"Why don't we leave price to the end?" Kinsey headed to the door left across the hall then stood back while the girls entered.

Jet stopped just inside the dusty blue kitchenette with cabinets painted a cheerful lemon color. From there the three wandered through the rose-colored bedroom containing a double bed and a Queen Anne sofa. Jet was in love at first sight. Tears came to her eyes as she stared at the fireplace then turned to note the sweeping bay windows. Oh how much she would like to live here.

Leading them back to the hall Kinsey continued a couple doors further, to a sea-green room with antique twin beds, a velvet loveseat, and walnut armoire. Jet nodded her approval, realizing its suitability to Latte's twins. After a quick look at this room they moved to the next, another bedroom with a four-poster bed, lavender wing back chair and a floral printed loveseat sitting in a bay window alcove.

"What do you think?" Kinsey faced Jet, his winged eyebrows raised. "Would that arrangement work for you?"

She bit her lip. "I'm sure we can't afford it."

"Don't be a pessimist." Kinsey turned to Evana. "How about something on the third floor? No more suites on this one."

Evana shrugged, consenting to follow Kinsey as they turned right to a staircase at the south end of the hall. Their shoes made muffled sounds on the carpeted stair runner. Arriving at an open area from which a long passageway led to the rest of the floor, Jet noted two doors to the right and one to the left. Kinsey led them to the farther right door and a suite tucked under the eaves with angled ceilings and wedge shaped rooms furnished in polished black walnut.

Evana wandered around peering in the closet and bath, opening kitchen cupboards and drawers.

Kinsey came to stand beside Jet. "I only saw your mother a few times at family events, mostly funerals."

Jet searched her mental database for an image of Kinsey at family gatherings. His leading man looks, tousled dark hair and dressed as if he had just stepped out of GQ brought no recollection to her. "You don't look like anyone I've ever seen before."

Kinsey frowned at her frank dismissal.

"I've always wondered why my mother wanted nothing to do with the Sayres."

Kinsey's eyes widened as if she'd just slapped him. "The family tossed around theories. Her lifestyle wasn't exactly seven pounds sterling." He shot her a reproachful glance. "The contrast may have made her uncomfortable."

Jet frowned, discomfort wasn't Mona's style. She would have been in their faces, laughing at their antiquated morals and stodgy life styles. "You live with your aunt?" During dinner she had tried to piece together the family situation.

"Ever since my mother died, Aunt Pat's been my mother in effect."

"How old were you when your mother died?" Jet's brain began formatting a family tree.

"Three," Kinsey replied.

Jet hadn't realized there were others in her family with tragic beginnings. She felt a twinge of compassion for him.

He cleared his throat. "Evana and I lived with Aunt Pat. Dad lived on his own until after she inherited the house they now live in. Then Dad joined us."

"Did he ever live here?"

"Hardly." He sounded as if she suggested his father presided over the real estate division of Madoff's empire. "He's never cared for this place." Kinsey's frown questioned her interest.

"And the others your age?"

"Jordan and Francine are Aunt Pat's actual children. We all grew up as brothers and sisters, although they're really our cousins."

"How much?" Evana returned to Kinsey's side.

"Let's go put something together." As he moved to turn out the lights a muffled blast of music sounded across the room.

Evana shot Kinsey a suspicious glance. "What was that?"

"Neil Diamond."

"*Cracklin' Rosie.*" Jet suddenly realized.

Kinsey crossed to the window and opened one of the panels. All was quiet.

"It sounded like it came from over there." Evana pointed across the room at the blank wall.

Kinsey closed the window. "I haven't figured out how to get into that area."

"What do you mean?" Evana sounded alarmed.

"Beyond this there should be more space."

She put her hands on her slim hips. "And you want me to stay here?"

Kinsey looked apprehensively at Jet. "That's why it's a bargain. Something is going on and I have to find out what. The price compensates for the risk."

On the main floor he led the way into the dining parlor where a massive table capable of a medieval feast occupied the center of the room. Beckoning the girls to be seated, Kinsey drew a piece of notepaper from his breast pocket along with a tiny calculator he spent a few moments consulting. On the paper's edge he wrote a couple figures. One he showed to Evana and the other to Jet.

"Come on Kinsey, I deserve a better deal than that," Evana protested. She gave Jet a sly wink as Kinsey reviewed his figures.

Jet smiled. It was just possible she and Latte could afford it.

Kinsey glanced at her as she watched him redo his amounts. "If I lower it for Evana then I probably need to do the same for you, right?"

Jet wasn't going to snub a better deal. "Whatever the amount I still have to consult my friend."

Kinsey nodded. "When can you do that?"

"She won't be back until Sunday night. But we have to move by Tuesday."

Kinsey took a business card out of his wallet and wrote a number on it. "That's my cell phone. Let me know as soon as you can, okay?"

Chapter Four

Friday morning Kinsey found Jet's message on his cell phone and accepted reservations on the suite and two bedrooms. That afternoon Nathan called for an appointment, indicating his friend Susannah from work was also interested. Taking Evana for granted would leave only one more room to rent. Kinsey was vaulting over the finish-line. He could have given the monster from the black lagoon a high five.

While waiting for Nathan, he descended the grand staircase. Midway a leaded glass window provided a view of the lush landscaping descending to Gravelly Lake lying tranquil in the overcast afternoon. While he watched a green panel-wagon sped around the bend leading to the garages. It wasn't Nathan's and Kinsey didn't expect he would have come with his friend from work. Perhaps one of the neighbors, but they rarely used that road.

On Thanksgiving Day his father gave him files on the two renters who died at the house. Lounging in front of the parlor fireplace, Kinsey read the applications. The first, a man named Harvey Brittmeier collected rare books.

Single, in his fifties and highly educated he had come from Chicago to the Pacific Northwest as a professor at University of Puget Sound where he taught English literature. He declared his intension of using the house for storage, display, and exchange of his collection of rare books.

Before he got to the second renter Kinsey heard the mansion's melodious chime. He slid the paperwork into its manila folder and went to the door.

The hazy mist, scattered in patches among the trees, made Nathan's bushy hair stand out like a cartoon fraidy-cat. He escorted a Betty Boop young woman with dark spiral curls and eager eyes into the house. "This is Susannah McFadden."

Kinsey extended his hand into which she placed warm limp fingers, gazing at him with a gleam in her liberally shadowed eyes and tilting her amply funded figure toward him. He felt his early warning system go on alert.

While young and naïve he had fallen for a diabolical enchantress intent on claiming a scalp. More entranced with his family's money than him, she took him for a lively spin on the love-them-and-leave-them merry-go-around. The whole episode left Kinsey cautious. No way was he putting his hand on that stove again. He retreated a couple steps.

Nathan, gawking like a teen-ager in a car dealership showroom, wasted no time getting to the point. "Show us what you've got."

"Upstairs," Kinsey pointed to the staircase, snagging a wad of keys from the table near the door. "I've received a few reservations since I talked to you." He took them first to the second floor, a spacious chamber with white moldings and navy wallpaper.

Susannah bounced around the room in her short skirt, black tights and clunky shoes oohing and aahing as she checked out the four-poster bed, the brocade loveseat, carved armoire and marble tiled bath. "This is just too much, Nathan." She landed a few steps from Kinsey, gazing at him with puppy dog eyes.

Nathan maintained his cool. "Pretty fancy, Kinsey. Did you get a cook?"

"Everything but." He had arranged for The Maids once a week, but still hesitated regarding a cook.

Nathan shot him an admonishing glance.

Kinsey moved to the far wall in the bathroom and studied the ceiling, figuring there must be a way to reach the far north end of the third floor. This bathroom had to be beneath that closed off area. Also, if he wasn't mistaken he had just heard a footstep above. Naw, that couldn't be. He sighed; he couldn't live in denial. He needed to investigate every incident.

"How about we look at the other room?" Nathan prodded.

From the top of the third floor staircase Kinsey beckoned to the first door on his right. Much less ostentatious than the last, a textured shade of yellow paint brightened what could have been a dark room. Heavy squat pieces of furniture made it appear more masculine.

When Nathan saw the huge bathroom with its heart-shaped spa tub he declared, "I'll take it. Susannah can have the other one."

Kinsey turned to her.

"Okay," she declared, "I'll take it."

At the advice of his father, Kinsey had obtained a traditional rental agreement he had Nathan and Susannah sign, each agreeing to pay rent on the day they moved in.

"I still need a place to store things," Nathan reminded him.

Kinsey needed to solve that problem. "Let's go see what's in the basement."

Susannah looked as if they had just suggested bungy jumping.

"You can stay here if you want."

"No, I'll come." She vaulted from her chair, swinging the black cape she carried over her shoulders.

Kinsey led the way from the dining room through the butler's pantry into the kitchen where next to the backyard exit was the basement door. They descended into an oblong stretch with stone walls and tiled floor. It contained a water heater, the boiler for the hot water heat, the breaker box, a workbench with household tools, and a sizeable walk-in freezer. A wall of shelves loaded with storage boxes faced them. However, though capacious, the area was not as big as Kinsey would have expected.

Wandering toward the wall at the far end he imagined the rooms on the floor above. Somewhere in the vicinity of the grand parlor he ran into a brick wall, literally. Uncertain where the wall was located relative to the expansive room above he, nonetheless, figured the extent of the basement they had found thus far failed to encompass the amount of space that should have been there.

He roamed the perimeter as it formed an L. The long leg of which was too narrow to make sense given the size of rooms above it. However, the solid, unbroken walls gave no appearance of closed access to other space. It made no sense. "How do we get to the rest of it?" he mumbled to himself.

"You're sure there is a rest of it?" Nathan came to stand beside him.

Kinsey studied the wall at the far end. "This wouldn't make a good place for storage." He led the way back to the main floor then outside where they wandered along the foundation analyzing it for additional basement. The windows at the north end gave evidence of the cellar they had just left. However, farther south it appeared different.

"Are you sure about this?" Nathan challenged.

Doubt about his assumption had attacked Kinsey by the time they reached the south end and the covered terrace over which was the balcony opening off his suite.

"Isn't this cool?" Susannah whirled around on the brick floor of the patio where an assortment of wrought iron furniture presented a cozy outdoor living space.

Kinsey rubbed his chin, staring at the floral cushions. Why, given it was November and the house had been uninhabited, was this alfresco asylum intact? He examined the concrete pots located at either side of the stone archways. "Cigarette butts."

Nathan stood at the edge of the terrace where archways joined the facade of the main building. To the right of the French doors into the music room he pulled away a section of the stone façade with a rusty squeak. "What's this opening for?"

Made of the same beige bricks as the house it was almost unnoticeable. Employing a notched brick with handle-like leverage Kinsey gave it another pull. Creaking noisily the wall moved a couple more inches. Together they pulled until it came far enough to let a person through.

Nathan stuck his head into the cavity. "Pretty dark in there."

"I'll get a flashlight." Kinsey opened the French doors to the music room where he crossed to a cherry hutch. In the top drawer he found a tiny electric torch.

"It's a stairway," Nathan declared as Kinsey waved the beam around.

"Shall we?" Kinsey started down the steps. At the bottom he turned the knob on a wood door and pushed. It didn't budge. He examined his ring of keys then took one and tried it, then another. An old skeleton key did the trick. More darkness greeted them, but using the flashlight he located a string hanging from a bare bulb. When he pulled the space lit up exposing a long wide hallway ending in a solid brick wall.

"This is creepy," Susannah breathed moving closer to Nathan.

"No it's not." Nathan grinned at her. "It's great storage space."

Approximately fifteen feet wide, the hall was made of concrete with the floor joists visible above it. "We'll have to have some way to divide up the space and secure it."

"Well, dude, I need to get going. Susannah said she had to be back by 7:00. I know a guy who does carpentry and sheet rocking. He could help you turn this into storage area."

"Okay, give me the name." Kinsey held out a business card he took from his wallet.

❧

Latte's flight arrived at 7:30 p.m. Sunday night. She came charging out of the arrival doors, her carry-on duffle bouncing and handbag sailing behind her as Jet maneuvered the SUV into a slot next to the curb. The two boys trailed behind, each dragging a brightly colored roll-on. When Jet came around the end of the vehicle to assist with loading the luggage, Latte grabbed her by the arm. "Let's go see it."

Jet backed up a couple steps, "Welcome home."

"Mom says we get to live in a castle," Landon chimed in collapsing his handle and handing the bag to Jet.

"Do you think we could see it tonight?" Latte asked as she fastened her seatbelt.

"Let me call Kinsey and see what he says." Jet located her cell phone as Latte moved the SUV into the traffic lane.

When he answered Jet explained the situation and Latte's impatience to see the rooms.

"Great, come on out." Kinsey had a deep melodious voice.

"Mom's bugging me to move back to California," Latte explained when Jet assured her they could look at the house. "She doesn't think we can make it on our own."

"Were they planning to help you?" Jet dropped the phone into her handbag. Parents often entertained unreasonable expectations of their children. Jet figured Mona would cheerfully have exchanged her for a sassy sexpot with a PhD. in political science. Jet's MBA was an affront to her mother's social conscience.

"No." Latte shot her friend a frustrated grimace and stuck out her tongue. "They want me to get back together with George."

"Did you see him at Thanksgiving?"

"Mom wanted to invite him, but I told her I wouldn't come to dinner if she did. As it turned out he was going to his family on the east coast."

Although Latte appeared to handle her divorce with equanimity, Jet knew she had been desperately in love with George Rosen when she married him. Was Jet in danger of choosing an unsuitable mate? Her limited experience with the opposite sex was fairly neutral. Mostly they ignored her.

"Do you think he wants to get back together again?" Jet couldn't help but wonder how George felt about their separation.

"It wasn't his idea to leave in the first place. If he's properly married to a good Jewish woman that keeps all the relatives in line and lets him do as he pleases."

"But you aren't Jewish."

"Mom is. Apparently that's enough to be acceptable." Latte laughed, a sarcastic hack. "Besides it crimps his standing in the family to be divorced."

"And being married doesn't crimp his dating schedule?" Like Mona, George found it difficult to confine himself to one woman.

When they reached the Gravelly Lake exit from the freeway, Jet explained how to reach the Sayre estate. Mist clinging to the trees created little stars in the headlights. Dots of illumination somewhat larger drew the girls as they approached the opening in the forest.

Latte gaped at the mansion silhouetted against the golden gray sky. "Holy cow, you weren't kidding."

"Is that it?" Landon asked, straining to see.

"Wow," Logan breathed. "Cool."

Two other vehicles sat in the driveway. Latte parked behind a small KIA and they all piled out.

Leaded-glass windows at the front of the house blazed with light providing a welcoming aura. Kinsey in a turtleneck sweater and Dockers opened the door and met them with a blank stare.

Jet, lost at the back of the group, moved forward. "This is my friend Latte-Tana Rosen."

Kinsey smiled, opening the door wider and allowing the group to enter. Landon and Logan stood close to the exit apparently intimidated by the immensity of the grand parlor. On a sofa near the fireplace a young man with bright red hair sat beside a curly headed woman laughing. They turned to observe the newcomers.

"They're also renting space here. I'll introduce you later." Kinsey beckoned toward the central staircase across the room. "Let's look at the suites first."

He followed Jet, Latte and the boys to the rooms he had shown Jet on her earlier visit. As he stood back to allow them into the suite he said to her, "Most everyone is moving in Tuesday. Evana is coming on Wednesday."

Jet noted the way his gray and royal blue sweater brought out the deep navy in his eyes. "Is there really space in the house you can't get into?"

Kinsey sighed, looking toward the end of the hall. "If you look at the outside of the house you can see where Evana's suite is on the third floor. But a good quarter of the house goes on beyond that to the north."

"You don't think the extra space is simply attic?"

Kinsey wrinkled his nose skeptically. "There should be more room than just an attic." He ran his hand through his hair. "There's a balcony visible outside on the third level."

Jet abandoned Kinsey to follow Latte into the third bedroom and watch her examine it. After she conversed with Kinsey regarding arrangements for the dog she said, "Could you let us have a conference?"

Kinsey shot Jet an anxious look. "Sure, I'll be downstairs."

"This works for you?" Latte asked when Kinsey had gone. "By rights I should pay at least two thirds. But I think that would be hard to do. If you could afford half then you could have the suite, if we could borrow the kitchen."

Jet did a fast calculation regarding the amount she would need to pay. "I can do that." One look at Latte told Jet she was containing her exuberance with difficulty.

☙

Swallowing his anxiety, Kinsey left the girls in the upstairs bedroom. Nathan stood at the foot of the stairs, examining the boom-box Kinsey had brought down figuring some music on the main floor would jazz up the creaking stillness of the old mansion. "Are they renting?"

Kinsey rocked his shoulders.

Nathan flashed a thumbs up. "Women! A man of your word."

Kinsey shook his head. "The blonde's a packaged deal. The kids are hers. The other one's my cousin."

Nathan resumed his investigation of the music machine, successfully producing a charge of jazz marimba from the Spyro Gyro CD Kinsey had left in it.

A sound on the stair alerted Kinsey as Latte and Jet descended.

"I've a question." Latte came to stand beside him. Her big brown eyes gave away the excitement she tried to control. "Is there a laundry?"

Kinsey led them through the cavernous dining hall and adjacent butler's pantry into the kitchen. "My aunt Bernice remodeled this before she died."

The girls gazed in awe at maple-paneled walls with cabinets finished in high gloss paint. Granite counter tops

41

and professional grade appliances gleamed beneath canned lights. A huge crystal chandelier hung over the center island. On the west wall one of two doors opened into the laundry room equipped with giant sized washer and dryer.

Latte examined them. "Any charge?"

"No." A missed opportunity Kinsey realized when Latte gave him a curious glance. "You need your own soap."

As Latte opened cupboards an unexpected clatter lasting a few seconds stopped the three. Kinsey realized the sound came from the other side of the wall.

Jet shot him a suspicious glance. "What was that?"

"Birds, or squirrels?" He had no clue, might as well bluff. However, his voice rose at the end, betraying him.

Jet pointed to the far end of the laundry. "What's behind there?" She had the judge-and-jury-are-out-but-you're-as-guilty-as-sin look in her eye.

Kinsey sighed. "Let's go have a look."

Latte had wandered into the second room off the kitchen when Kinsey and Jet left through the butler's pantry. Instead of returning to the dining hall they passed through a side door into an L-shaped expanse boasting a powder room and filigreed circular stair.

"This is the morning room," Kinsey indicated the long leg of the L. Windows facing south and west surrounded it. A round glass table was accompanied by four painted antique chairs.

Jet paused half-way into the space. "What did you do in the morning room?"

"Eat mostly, breakfast and lunch if there were just a couple of us here." Kinsey moved to a set of double doors opening into another chamber with two walls of windows. "And this is the solarium."

Jet stood at the door between the two rooms gazing at the assembly of sofas and chairs in slipcovers of oatmeal canvas.

Kinsey crossed the slate floor to stand next to an expanse of wood paneling and shelves on the east wall. Was this where the sound came from?

"Have you always lived here?" Jet joined him running a finger down the grove in the paneling as if suspicious it wasn't genuine.

"No. I never lived here until just before Thanksgiving. But I visited my great grandfather here and then my great uncle Terrence." That's when he fell in love with the place, playing cavaliers and swords in the hall, imagining adversaries hiding in the alcoves.

"So who actually owns the house?" Jet had moved to the French doors in the north wall where she looked out on the stone patio there.

"My dad inherited it from Uncle Terrence. The house where we had Thanksgiving belonged to Terrence's brother Thomas, who was my grandfather." These people were Jet's family, too, although she appeared to know nothing about them. "He died a couple years ago. Since Aunt Pat was to inherit that house, Terrence left this place to my dad."

"Your family has a fixation with big real estate?" Jet observed, looking at him from the corner of her gray eyes.

Kinsey raised his eyebrows. Unsure the description fit his father who seemed to have neither any love for this place, nor the Barnes house in which he lived.

"Do you have the building plans?" Jet inquired.

"I can ask Dad, he may know where they are." Focusing on her, he asked. "Is this going to be a problem?"

She lifted her shoulders.

Kinsey faced her squarely. "I didn't initially plan to rent to women and kids."

Jet crossed her arms over her chest. "What's that supposed to mean?"

Kinsey touched the top of his head as if the fiery darts her eyes shot would set his hair on fire. "Several people have died in this house already. My father thinks it's dangerous." And his father probably wasn't the only one.

Jet lifted her small chin. "More dangerous for women than men?"

Woops, he stepped in the trap that time. He'd be better off hiding behind the dragon than slaying it for feminist Mona's daughter. "No."

"Then what do you mean?" Jet's voice could have cut steak.

"They aren't as strong as men." Undoubtedly a stupid arguable statement. How was he supposed to get out of this? Contending with tough women was about as productive as flapping your arms and trying to fly off the roof and about twice as deadly.

Jet crossed her arms over her chest. "Men *think* that."

Obviously, Kinsey shrugged. "Shall we return to the group?"

After she and Latte signed their rental agreement and made out their checks Kinsey brought them to the parlor and introduced them to Nathan and Susannah.

The reverberating chime of the doorbell interrupted. In the portico stood a wide-shouldered, pudgy young man with a pretty face, black upswept eyelashes, and shaggy dark hair. At the sight of Kinsey his face lit with an easy-going smile. "I understand you have a room to rent."

Kinsey frowned. "I don't believe it's been advertised."

"A friend of mine knows a friend of yours and told me about it."

Likely story, but since Kinsey actually did have a room to rent he stepped aside, allowing the man to enter.

"Billy Monk." He offered his hand.

Kinsey shook hands. "I only have one room left, but I can show it to you."

Kinsey led him upstairs to the remaining third floor bedroom. This, the smallest of the ones Kinsey was renting, contained a double canned bed, a painted desk and walnut armoire.

After a quick once through Mr. Monk announced he would take it before Kinsey could even explain how much he would be charging. This left Kinsey feeling vaguely uncomfortable.

Chapter Five

Considering availability advisable, Kinsey took his renter's moving day off work. Between bouts of assisting them to lug personal cargo upstairs he examined the papers his father left regarding the second dead resident.

The name Matthew Markovich surprised him, unaware the renter had been the well-known interior designer. His lease of the mansion intended to display the man's talents as well as provide space for handling clients. His file included the lease application, references, and some financial information. A receipt indicated who had claimed the belongings left behind. Kinsey fingered one small item, a newspaper clipping describing the mysterious death.

"Tuesday, October 19, Matthew Markovich was found dead, electrocuted in the basement of the vast mansion he leased on Gravelly Lake Drive in Lakewood. The police are puzzled by the death where it appeared Mr. Markovich was attempting to remedy a bout of electrical disturbances the house had experienced recently. Efforts to locate his wife Carmen have been unsuccessful."

The article went on to describe the decorator's career and achievements, continuing with a listing of his wife's activities as a wedding planner.

Gushing precipitation compounded problems for his new boarders, creating a grimy mess in the reconditioned mansion. Anatuviak reminded him that he told his father he would get more dogs. Anatuviak wasn't much of a watchdog, wagging his tail and begging to be petted. The security system check verified its operation although its effectiveness remained doubtful. Having given the code to his renters, Kinsey shut it off for the day considering all the traffic.

Mid-afternoon, as if summoned by Kinsey's concern, Park appeared in the library where he dropped into the fan-back easy chair. "How's it going?"

"Great." Kinsey refused to share frustrations with his father, explaining instead the progress he had made taking care of the financial end of their agreement. "Do you know where the building plans are for this place?"

Park focused on the bookcases. "Not offhand."

Kinsey rocked back in his office chair. "Would you know another way down from the third floor than the stairs at the south end?"

Park rubbed his chin. "If I recall both north and south ends had stairs from the main floor to the third."

"All I found was the circular staircase in the morning room, but you can't get from there to the remainder of the third floor." Kinsey shrugged. "Or the second for that matter."

"Then something's wrong. You know about the staircase from the music room to the second floor suite above it?"

That was Jet's suite. Kinsey grimaced, moving to his next concern. "What exactly happened to that decorator who leased this place?"

Park sighed, looking harassed. "He electrocuted himself on some wiring in the basement." Then added, "That's why it's called Blast Castle."

"He grabbed a live wire?" Surely he wasn't that stupid.

"There shouldn't have been any live wires to grab." Park sat up straighter. "Something had been going on here though."

His father's troubled expression puzzled Kinsey. "Like what?"

"He called every other week to complain. First it was rats."

"Rats!" That's all Kinsey needed with four women in the house.

"I had an exterminator in. They found a couple but it was odd. We'd never had that problem before." His father scowled. "Then it was the sewer backing up into main floor bathrooms."

Kinsey wrinkled his nose. "But you got it fixed?"

Park nodded. "Then the water problem that shut down the heat."

"It's a wonder they didn't leave."

"Carmen . . . the guy's wife wanted to," Park shot Kinsey a quick glance causing him to wonder what he had missed. "But Matt was determined. After that there was a six month break before the electrical stuff started up."

"Electrical?" Ghosts didn't do electricity, or for that matter water, sewer or rats.

"At first Matt complained the lights would come on and go off without anyone around. Carmen . . . Mrs. Markovich made it sound like a light show with lights going on and off throughout the entire house almost in a sequence." Park ran his hand through his hair. "I had an electrician in but he found nothing wrong."

"Did the problems stop?"

Park shook his head. "Matt got paranoid, but refused to be run away. After the electrician came things stopped for a week or so then started up again."

"You've no idea what caused it?" It sounded pretty fantastic, but not supernatural.

"None." Park made a rueful face. "After the guy died it all stopped and hasn't started up again. It makes me think he was the cause of it."

"What about his wife?" Was she the cause?

"She disappeared." Park crossed his legs, studying the toe of his shoe. "No one knows where she is."

"Frightened off?"

Park flinched as if Kinsey had struck him.

"Did the problems stop when he died or when she left?" He watched his father fight an internal battle, noting the haunted look on his face. What was that about? Kinsey must have touched a nerve. "According to the news article she left the night he died and hasn't been seen since; makes it hard to say if things stopped because of him or her. What were they like?"

Park shrugged his eyebrows. "The guy was hoity-toity, wrapped up in his decorating business."

"And his wife?"

Park crossed his arms over his chest with the look of one who might refuse to answer, but he said, "A beautiful woman."

What did that mean—exactly?

☙

Like a bad omen, moving day brought with it the Pineapple Express producing unrelenting rain. Latte, her hair in pigtails, and the boys in new rubber boots blasted forth with enthusiasm. Occasionally Anatuviak shook the moisture off his coat, sharing it with anyone in striking distance, adding offense to misery. By the time Jet had assisted Latte with five loads in the SUV and one of her personal possessions she looked like a soggy cat. She stifled her irritation at each slippery mishap, pressing her lips together to prevent a stream of ugly words from escaping.

After successfully relocating their possessions to the new residence they flopped on the sofa in Jet's suite. She felt like crying, but burst into hysterical giggles instead. Latte joined and they laughed until they cried. In spite of the hassle, to have gotten successfully transferred was an enormous relief.

Kinsey appeared at the door, his hair a tousled tumble. "I've arranged a cook to come in and do evening meals on week nights. Although we'll need to discuss paying for it, tonight is on the house."

"What time?" Latte sobered up enough to ask.

"Six o'clock." A smile flickered across his face as he glanced around the room.

"Thanks." Jet stood up. "He probably thinks he just rented to Tweedle Dee and Tweedle Dum."

Latte looked at her watch. "We can get this straightened up in a couple hours."

The boys moved their prize possessions to their assigned room while Jet helped Latte with hers. In the process Jet realized Kinsey's suite was across from hers and the stairs to the third floor were just outside her door. She heard Nathan and Billy carrying luggage up the staircase.

"You know any of the women?" Billy's voice was high-pitched for someone so stocky.

"Only Kinsey's sister, Evana. She's moving in tomorrow."

"Does she look as good as the others?"

"Better. She's beautiful, but . . ."

As their voices disappeared up the stairs Jet wondered what the "but" was.

The enormous dining hall, already dark with cherry paneling and burgundy wall covering, became even darker as daylight escaped with the sun. Dinner was served on the gigantic table set for eight, occupying less than half the length of it.

Kinsey presided with Nathan to his left. Susannah maintained a stream of chatter resembling a critic's version of the social column while Nathan made eyes at Latte, seated beside Jet.

"What are you doing with a courier service van?" Susannah questioned Billy seated across from her.

Jet noticed his intake of breath. "I work for them." He plunged into an old familiar line. "You look familiar. Where did you live before this?"

"In Olympia with my dad. He works for the state."

Mona's position at the state provided Jet with some acquaintance of personnel there. "What's your dad's name?"

"Jesse McFadden."

The name penetrated slowly, leaving Jet frozen in disbelief. Staring at Susannah, who had moved on to a new topic, Jet realized Jesse McFadden was the nice guy with a family, one possibility for her father. Undoubtedly her name Jessica had been for him, Jessica for Jesse McFadden, Thompson, for Roger Thompson and Sayre for Park Sayre.

That would be typical of her mother's sense of humor. And what about her middle name? For whom had she been given that? Mr. Unknown?

She felt cold and hot at the same time. Her stomach summer-salted. She set her fork down until the feeling passed, casting a quick glance at Susannah seated across from her. Was there any likeness between her and the bushy headed brunette? Jet detected no specific similarity. Not that it signified anything. With the Sayres to whom she knew she was related and whose pronounced features appeared dominant the lack of resemblance had greater consequence.

"What's wrong?" Latte asked on the way upstairs after dinner. "You look like you saw a ghost."

"Do you think there's any family likeness between Susannah and I?"

Latte frowned. "What are you talking about?"

"One of my possible fathers is Jesse McFadden."

Latte put her hand on Jet's shoulder. "At least you won't have to hunt him down."

Jet sighed. "Maybe if I wait long enough they'll all come to me."

Chapter Six

"Hey." One of Latte's twins addressed Kinsey from the doorway. "What about a Christmas tree?"

His brother was right behind him. "Mom said we should ask you."

With Thanksgiving past they were careening toward Christmas at break-neck speed. Kinsey recalled what a tree had meant to him at that age.

Landon turned his palms up and spread his arms. "No tree, no presents." They echoed his boyhood belief.

"Well we'd better get one then." Kinsey ushered the boys back into the parlor and pointed to the front entry. "Meet me over there in an hour and we'll see what we can find."

On his way to the kitchen he met Latte.

"Should I have run out of hot water after two loads of clothes?" She flipped her long French pigtail over her shoulder, implying he was purposely frustrating her plans.

Kinsey followed to the kitchen where he found the water from the hot water faucet not even lukewarm. To his recollection the only appliances using that water heater were the laundry, kitchen, main floor powder rooms and butler's pantry."

"I did two loads on warm. When I touched the water for this load," she lifted the washing machine lid and put her hand in the water, "it was cold."

With a quick plunge of his hand Kinsey verified her report. "How was the water in your room this morning?"

"Fine." She stood hands on her hips as if still convinced he was the culprit.

"I think all the suites have separate water heaters so they shouldn't affect this one, but let me check with Susannah." Her suite was closest to the kitchen on the floor above.

Kinsey took the stairs to the second floor. Susannah answered in a silk striped robe and fluffy slippers, carrying a bottle of nail polish. With her hair still wet from the shower and none of Stygian shadows on her eyes she appeared years younger.

"You're just in time." She held her robe loosely, allowing a tempting glimpse of cherry lace and cleavage.

The parade of expressions crossing her face reminded Kinsey of a boa constrictor. He took a step back. He didn't relish getting squeezed to death. "Did you just take a shower?"

She cocked her head and raised her eyebrows. "I heard funny noises on the other side of the wall in my bathroom." She shuddered. "Gives me the creeps."

"Was the water hot?"

She frowned as though he had missed her point. "Of course, you can test it if you want."

Kinsey backed up another step.

Susannah moved into the hall losing grip on her robe a moment before clutching it together with one hand and waving the nail polish in the direction Kinsey had just come. "What's back there?"

"Stairs to the kitchen." Kinsey pointed out the route he had just ascended, opening the door to prove it. "You think you heard something there?"

She shrugged. "I heard someone moving, but it sounded higher than those stairs, like inside the wall."

Kinsey frowned as he moved along it, noting more space beside the stairwell than he could account for. When he tapped on the wall it sounded hollow.

"Could I come into your suite a moment?"

Susannah waved him in with a toss of her head.

"I'm still unpacking," she informed him, following to the far end of her bathroom, which still held the steam of her shower. "I'd like to do some decorating. I bought a lamp and some candles. It can be dark up here at night."

"Just don't start any fires." Kinsey stood opposite the door where a linen closet held shelves loaded with toilet articles. He tapped on the back wall of the closet, which also gave the hollow sound.

"A hidden room?"

Kinsey shrugged. "So far it's just unexplained space." After thanking Susannah he returned to the kitchen by the back stairs.

Latte was in the laundry room unloading the dryer.

"I'll have the water heater checked out," he informed her. "Why don't you wait an hour and try again. Let me know if it's hot."

Latte agreed both to his request and a plan to take the boys out for a Christmas tree.

Checking his watch, Kinsey returned to the parlor where he found the twins waiting for him on a deacon's bench next to the door. "Let's go."

They bounced up.

Traversing the main drive to a stone building close to the entrance gates, Kinsey considered Susannah's complaint. Attributing it to female heebie-jeebies would be simple, but he too had heard the scuffing. Even her theory of a hidden room was not beyond possibility. Dissecting the blueprints raced up his to-do list.

When they reached the gardener's shed Kinsey handed Logan a hatchet with instructions on carrying it, Landon a pruning shears, and grabbed a chainsaw. They returned part way back to where a low boxwood hedge surrounded a grove of evergreen trees planted in orderly rows.

Anatuviak followed, running from tree to shrub and back. At times tearing across the grounds until he was at the opposite end then racing back to wag his tail.

"Do you see one you like?" Kinsey stopped at the edge of the garden to survey the prospects.

"Let's get a really big one," Logan declared eying a fifteen-foot spruce.

"Where do you think we'd put it?"

Landon scratched his head. "In the big room at the bottom of the stairs."

"That'll work," Kinsey agreed, locating a tall noble fir with well-placed branches. "How about this one?"

The boys eyed it analytically, walking around slowly, patting branches and examining its height. After which they turned to Kinsey, nodding their approval.

"Okay guys, put those things here and go stand over there." Kinsey indicated where Anatuviak had stopped his running to dig in the soil between rows of trees. "I don't want this to fall on you."

While the kids moved to where Anatuviak worked on his hole, Kinsey put the saw to the base of the tree. Once he had it over half sawn he checked to see where they were, noting that Anatuviak had hold of some dark substance and was pulling it out of the ground. When the tree came down with a whoosh the boys came running to examine the results. Anatuviak came galloping to join them carrying a dark piece of leather in his mouth.

"Come here, boy." Kinsey coaxed, inducing the dog to drop it at his feet. He picked it up, a leather jacket with zippers, metal studs and extensive topstitching, an expensive woman's coat. "Let's see where you got this."

The kids raced Kinsey to the hole and stood staring into it. More fabric, less substantial than the leather, appeared to cover a stiff object. Kneeling he examined the cloth, realizing that beneath it were bones, neatly arranged in the form of a rib cage.

❦

Saturday's rosy dawn teased Jet awake. While packing to move she came across the pouch of items her mother had entrusted her to distribute after her death. One envelope was addressed to Roger Thompson, giving Jet an excuse for calling him.

She had always dreamt of a father who cared what happened to her; was interested in who she was and what she did; someone who would call to have lunch or invite her to do things. She envisioned him stopping by the bank to say "Hi", asking if she needed anything, giving her a bad time because she wasn't married and he had no grandchildren. Maybe he would have a pet name for her, not something that sounded like a fast airplane.

She never had an easy relationship with Roger even though he was the only father she knew. She always felt like a nuisance. With her mother gone and knowledge he may not actually be her father she was even more hesitant to approach him. Nonetheless, he was the best place to begin her hunt. So it was time to buck up and contact him.

Collecting her wool coat and a pair of slacks for the cleaners, Jet contemplated the call, wondering how to address his fatherhood or lack of it? It wasn't like he would know.

What would it take to have DNA testing done? Obviously DNA. And how to obtain his, she shrugged. Ask for it? That was something she truly dreaded doing.

Jet met Latte, her arms full of laundry, in the hall at the head of the main stairs. "Can I help you?"

"Open the door to the kid's room."

Jet followed as she dumped a stack of shirts onto her son's bed.

Latte turned wide eyes on Jet. "There are some spooky things about this place." She shivered. "I heard shuffling noises from the wall in the laundry room."

"I heard that the first night we were here. Kinsey said it might be squirrels or birds."

Latte shook her head. "It sounded like someone running down a set of stairs." She divided the shirts and put them in the tallboy.

"But there aren't any stairs." Jet gathered the used clothing scattered around the room. "We went to the backside of the laundry. It's a solarium with bookshelves on that wall." She dropped the clothes into a basket near the door.

"Maybe it has one of those hidden doors. You know, the bookcase turns around and opens into a secret room."

"That wouldn't explain someone going down stairs."

Latte shrugged.

"I'm going to the cleaners then I think I'll see Roger Thompson if I can."

The garages sat south of the house, necessitating a hike over bright green lawn, whose returning color after the August drought presented a deceptive impression for the declining days of the year. Even the roses, still blooming with the deep color and scent of summer, told a lie on this December day, flimflamming her into discounting winter's approach. Nature's deceit made her feel light-hearted enough to believe she could actually face Roger.

Occupying number four in a long rectangular building with eight doors, Jet's bright yellow car shimmered in the sunshine. After backing it out she headed for the strip mall where she dropped off her cleaning. Then with her cell phone she called the number she had for Roger.

"How about Nordstrom coffee bar?" he suggested when she reached him. "I've got to stop at the mall to pick something up."

Jet agreed. Taking Gravelly Lake then Lakewood Drive she parked near Nordstrom's and entered through the upscale store, glittering with discrete golden lights, frosted evergreen boughs and silver reindeer. A romantic Christmas song played in the background.

After noting Roger had not arrived, Jet ordered peppermint mocha and took it to a table in the mall concourse.

Her nerves felt jangly. This is probably a stupid idea. Why even bother with who my father is? How would knowing help? It might just make matters worse.

She focused her attention on a window display picturing holiday clothing in winter white with snowflakes and sparkles. Green gifts tied with red and white ribbons were stacked beside a tinsel tree.

"Good morning." Roger slid out one of the chairs and set his shopping bag down. "I'll get coffee."

His light gray slacks and charcoal sweater gave the elegant sophisticated appearance she had always associated with him. His conscientious attention to apparel helped make up for his thinning black hair, squinty dark eyes, and pudgy cheeks. He pulled a third chair over from the adjacent table and sat down. Flipping the lid off his coffee, he added a couple packets of sweetener and stirred it. "So what's on your mind?"

Jet removed the envelope from her handbag and held it out to him. "My mother left this for you."

Roger lifted an eyebrow, eying the envelope as if it might contain anthrax.

Jet laid it on the table so he could see his name in Mona's handwriting. "She said I was to give this to you after she died."

Making no comment, he picked it up and dropped it in his shopping bag. "How is it going for you since she passed away?"

Jet swirled her coffee cup. "Okay. My friend Latte and I moved into an old mansion on Gravelly Lake Drive."

His eyes widened. "Not the Sayre estate?"

Jet nodded. "Have you been there?"

Roger crossed his arms over his chest. "Your mother's cousin owns it." His eyes became slits through which he scrutinized Jet.

"Kinsey Sayre is renting out suites there." Jet noted the invisible shield that slid across his expression. "His father agreed to quit claim deed the estate to him if he can clear its reputation and prove he is able to afford it."

"He thinks he can do that?" Roger looked like a bank loan officer impressed with his client's balance sheet.

Jet shrugged. "I've no idea." She took a deep breath and plunged into her quest for information. "My mother said Park Sayre could be my father."

Roger crossed his legs and adjusted the crease in his slacks. "How does that strike you?"

"I grew up believing you were." Jet studied her hands realizing she needed to redo her nails. "I didn't know it was possible you're not." Taking up her courage she returned her gaze to Roger's face.

"We weren't married when you were conceived, or even living together." He sounded neither apologetic nor disturbed.

"Did you ever meet the men my mother dated?" Jet noted a trace of frustration in his expression.

"Some of them. Your mother always had an entourage." Roger leaned back in his chair holding his coffee in both hands as if he would like to shake some sense into it. "That I'd know who could be your father." He shook his head. "She had plenty of affairs but didn't confide in me. She liked having power over men. In fact, that's all it was about with her."

Hearing this was difficult. Jet felt sad, disappointed and orphaned. "But you could be my father."

Roger released the hold on his coffee cup, placing it back on the table. "Apparently. She put me on your birth certificate."

Jet detected a trace of compassion in his tone of voice. "Just before she died." Jet took a deep breath and willed herself nerve to continue. "She mentioned that you and Park, plus a couple others I don't know were the possibilities. One of them she didn't know; didn't even have a name."

Roger squinted at the diamond advertisement in front of the jewelry store. "That was like her. Don't take it personal."

"Don't take it personal," Jet burst out, tears rising. "It's my identity." She paused to regain her self-control. "You couldn't say who might know the other person?"

Roger considered, frowning at her. "What did she say about him?"

"She was out on a drunk and spent the night with him. She said his name sounded something like Otto Lane."

"There was a group she partied with. A couple people from the state, some she worked with on the campaign."

"Would any of them know who the other person was?"

"I can give you their names."

Jet nodded dubiously, not sure if she would have the courage to contact them. But it wouldn't hurt to have the information.

Roger took out a business card and wrote four names on the back then handed it to Jet. "How do you like living in the mansion?"

"It's magnificent, but strange things are happening."

"Like what?" He shot her an alarmed glance.

"Noises, like they're coming from behind a wall."

"I might come out and pay Kinsey a visit one of these days."

After some time chatting about the holidays Roger emptied his cup and rose. "Call me if you need anything."

His offer brought a catch to Jet's throat. Brusque as it was, it was still an offer to be there for her.

Chapter Seven

"What's that?" Logan demanded.

"A lady's jacket." Kinsey laid the coat beside the hole.

Landon peered down at it. "Whose is it?"

Kinsey shook his head. Anatuviak moved to pick it up again.

"Leave it alone," he commanded.

"Anatuviak," Logan scolded the dog, grabbing his collar.

"Take him back to the house?" Kinsey told Logan. "Landon and I'll bring the tree."

Logan dragged the dog away from his hole. Although Anatuviak kept trying to look back Logan held him securely.

After pruning a few of lower branches, Kinsey took the tree from the bottom, instructing Landon to pick up the top. Together they carried it to the house's front archway where they leaned it against the wall.

Logan came running from the south terrace where he had put Anatuviak on his leash. Once inside the house the boys ran in search of their mother.

Kinsey called the police. Crummy luck. What would this mean to his redemption plan?

Latte came out of the dining room with questions inscribed on her face. "What's this about something Anatuviak found?"

"The dog might have dug up a body."

"You're kidding." Latte's brown eyes widened "Human?"

"Animals don't usually wear clothes."

The cell phone jingled. The Lakewood Police, inquiring about Kinsey's report, informed him they would send a detective and forensics within the hour.

Kinsey's logic raced through his mental data bank searching for a clue to Anatuviak's find. Who was to say the body hadn't been there for decades? Speculation was hopeless.

When the door chime reverberated through the house in less than an hour Kinsey opened it for a man several inches taller than himself, wearing a trench coat over his slacks. He regarded Kinsey with close-set brown eyes from behind a pair of wire-rimmed spectacles.

"I'm Lieutenant Sarkis." He put out his hand. "Kinsey Sayre?"

Kinsey nodded as he shook hands.

"Why don't you show me what you found?"

Ever since the change back from daylight savings dusk appeared without warning. Already the sun, descending toward the edge of the southwestern horizon, shed a feeble light. Noting the large white van parked behind a black SUV, Kinsey led the lieutenant across the lawn to the grove of evergreen trees, explaining the discovery. On reaching the hole, Kinsey stopped to point out the jacket, still lying where he left it. In Anatuviak's hole other fabric, dulled from its burial, lay exposed.

Crouching on his haunches Lieutenant Sarkis peered at the evidence. "I'll get the guys up here. They'll know how to take this apart without losing any evidence."

Kinsey's gaze followed as the lieutenant spoke to the driver of the van then returned across the lawn. The van lined up then backed into the site. Two men in coveralls climbed out and came to examine the hole.

"I'll get Sweeney, he's the bone specialist." The van driver removed the cell phone from his breast pocket.

In the meantime a police officer strung crime scene tape along the periphery of the tree garden.

"It's hard to determine the crime scene at this late date," Lieutenant Sarkis grumbled. "Anyone you know missing?"

Kinsey shook his head. "Those of us who live here just moved in a week ago."

Lieutenant Sarkis frowned. "Who owns the property?"

"My dad. But he's never lived here. He usually leases it."

"How long has he owned it?"

Kinsey calculated. "My great uncle Terrance died in '98 and left the estate to my dad."

"When did he rent it out?"

Having recently read the lease agreements Kinsey knew that. "The first one rented it in 2001 and died in 2003."

Arching an eyebrow, the lieutenant shot Kinsey a suspicious look.

"The next one rented it in 2005. He died in 2009."

Lieutenant Sarkis scowled. "Don't sound too healthy here."

Kinsey grimaced. "The media calls it Blast Castle. The last guy was electrocuted."

The lieutenant laughed, staring at the huge mansion. "Awful big place for a guy to rent. What did they want with it?"

"The second guy was a decorator, used it for display and business in addition to living here. The first guy was a book collector."

"What about you?"

"I've wanted to live here ever since I was a kid. My dad agreed to let me have the mansion if I could clear its reputation and afford it."

The lieutenant eyed Kinsey as if he had difficulty believing he could do either. "What do you do?"

"I'm comptroller in the family business."

"Why don't you go back to the house? We'll let you know when we're done."

Although preferring to stay, Kinsey figured he was being politely dismissed and lack of cooperation would produce more than a suggestion.

❧

Following a white SUV off the freeway, Jet slowed for the castle driveway, noting the SUV made the same turn. Approaching the mansion she noticed someone standing near the road, beckoning to the driver, hand-signaling it toward the evergreen grove. Among the trees she could see a larger truck. Another SUV sat in the circular driveway where she stopped her car. What's going on?

In the house near the grand staircase Latte stood holding a tall noble fir slightly off kilter while Nathan fastened it to the tree stand. Landon and Logan, positioned a few feet back, made hand and arm signals for straightening it. When Jet entered they came running to her.

"Someone's buried in the woods," Landon informed her.

"We found it." Logan finished.

Jet glanced at Latte for confirmation.

"Apparently," she nodded, the tree becoming further askew.

"Dead?" Jet asked the stupid question.

Nathan stuck his head out from under the boughs. "Naw, someone just misplaced a few bones. We'll give them back as soon as we find out who they belong to."

Latte shook her head and rolled her eyes.

Jet shuddered. "I'm going to take these upstairs then go put my car away." As she descended the stairs Billy Monk came through the door.

"What's all the fuss? There's a boatload of police in the driveway."

Outside Jet verified his observation. One in the driveway directing traffic, another stood guard near the crime scene tape strung around the grove of trees.

To put her car away Jet needed to return to Gravelly Lake Drive then take the next passage to the west and circle the estate. Flagging her down, the policeman took her name for his record before allowing her to leave. With her car in the garage she returned to the house along the path through the rose garden, where blossoms bobbed in the breeze.

She met Kinsey in the entrance passage, looking like Garfield-the-cat-met-the-dog with his hair frazzled and a thwarted expression on his face.

"Do you know who it is?"

"No," he barked. "It's probably been there longer than I've been alive."

Wishful thinking she figured. "What are they doing?"

"Digging."

"Are you worried?"

"Why should I be worried?" Kinsey scowled. "I didn't bury someone in the yard."

You wouldn't know it from the looks of you, Jet thought, but wisely kept her mouth shut.

He held the door open for her. "I'm going to call Dad. I think he needs to hear about this before the police jump him."

The moment they entered the house, the twins came running to Kinsey.

"Where are the decorations?" Landon demanded.

Kinsey paused to survey the tree. "That's a good question. Why don't you give me until after dinner? The tree needs to rest a while anyway."

"That long," Logan complained.

Kinsey patted him on the head and turned to Jet. "Dare I ask if you'd be interested in coming with me later to get some things?"

"Sure." She didn't have anything better to do.

Chapter Eight

Dinner in Jet's suite was an animated affair. The twins expanded their buried bones story, working out a whole mystery with Ninja warriors and dead princesses. Latte finally shushed them, ordering them to eat.

Although Latte had brought candles from her collection to dispel the gloom and Jet had closed the shutters on the window over the sink, eliminating the black hole effect, the early evening brought with it a depressing obscurity that neither the tiny candelabra bulbs nor the candles could eliminate.

"How did your interview with Roger go?"

Jet drug her linguine through the pasta sauce considering. "Not bad, but I still have no clue to my father."

"He didn't think it was him?"

"He didn't seem particularly interested one way or the other." Jet didn't know what she had expected. If Roger had been angry, denied any claim to fatherhood, at least it would mean he had thought about it. Instead he was perfectly indifferent. Was it worth having someone like that for a father?

Latte put her hand on Jet's arm. "I'm sorry. I know it means a lot to you."

"He did give me some names Mom used to party with. I just don't know how I'd go about approaching them." Jet cleared the table. She was losing confidence in the viability of her aspiration. "I told Kinsey I'd go with him to get Christmas decorations."

"That'll make the kids happy." Latte was rummaging in the refrigerator. "Can I use the kitchen to make cookies? We can have a tree decorating party when you get back."

The boys were playing with Matchbox cars on the hall floor's black and white squares when Jet stuck her head out wondering when Kinsey wanted to go. He opened his door about the same time stuffing his cell phone into his pocket. "You ready?"

She grabbed her rain jacket and handbag, letting Latte know she was leaving.

Kinsey stood in the glow of an arabesque sconce looking distracted when she reached the grand parlor. As he led the way across the driveway toward the garages she noticed the SUVs and van had gone along with the police, leaving only the crime scene tape to divulge the day's discovery.

"Dad was pretty squeamish about my staying here. This might jettison my plan." Kinsey sounded frustrated. "He'll be over later."

Intermittent ground lights illuminated the path, covered in loose gravel. The clear night sky was dotted with stars, or perhaps helicopters. Jet could see the landing lights of an airliner as it made for McChord's airfield. A trace of wood smoke, reminding her of autumn, floated on the cold night air.

She struggled to keep up with Kinsey's long-legged stride. "It was a body they found?"

"Skeleton, a woman, they figure."

Jet shivered. "Do they think it has anything to do with you?"

"Not yet, but they'll get around to it. They've never located the wife of our second renter." Kinsey pointed to the first garage on the end. "The lieutenant said it'd be a few days before they'd have any information."

Jet waited while he backed his car out then jumped in before he had a chance to open the door for her.

With raised eyebrows Kinsey's glance accused her of unladylike behavior.

"Does a woman have to be helpless?" she defended her action.

"Does accepting a kindness deem you helpless?" He shifted to a forward gear.

"My mother believed it was a sign of weakness to have a man help you. She said they'd take advantage of it."

Kinsey frowned. "How exactly do they take advantage?"

Taking the road around the mansion they headed for Gravelly Lake Drive.

Discussing Mona was a road leading nowhere. "Maybe she wanted to maintain control."

Kinsey turned to Jet when they paused at the stop sign. "Of what?"

Jet took a deep breath. "Herself?"

"She never struck me as giving fig's pit about self-control."

Jet didn't know what being taken advantage of meant to her mother. Nonetheless she felt compelled to defend her against Kinsey's criticism. At an impasse she changed the subject. "What do men want?"

Kinsey laughed in his mellow baritone. "A princess."

"A princess?"

"They want to win the princess." Kinsey gave Jet a big grin.

"You're teasing me." Jet scowled at him.

"Why would I do that?" Kinsey protested. "It's part of my dream."

She raised her eyebrows.

"To be the prince in his castle." Kinsey flushed as if he had just been caught reading fairytales.

"I can understand that." She smiled at him. "I used to play I was the princess."

"Real life doesn't match up very well, does it?"

She shook her head. "My mother always came out the wicked witch."

Kinsey laughed. "Sometimes I think my dad is the troll under the bridge."

He slid the car into a parking space in front of the Walmart on Bridgeport.

"If you'll risk being controlled and wait a moment, I'll open the door for you."

Frowning, Jet opened her door and leaped out before Kinsey could reach her.

In the store the greeter informed them Christmas decorations were at the south end.

Kinsey eyed the isles of trims. "What do you think we should get?"

"Lights to begin."

"Okay, I'll work on lights if you'll figure out what else we need."

Jet wandered along the shelves of Christmas tree bulbs, ornaments, garlands and ribbons. Her artistic sense kicked in and she began to analyze possibilities for color combinations. Once they succeeded in filling their cart and checking out, Kinsey pushed it to the car.

Once the cart was empty, Kinsey grabbed the passenger door, holding it open for Jet with a big showy grin. Ignoring him, she got in.

࿇

Returning to the mansion, Kinsey wondered how Jet had survived being raised by Mona. Given her early flower-child life style, her in-your-face disregard of propriety, she invited both twittering fascination and disgust. She had spurned the family standards and ideals as ridiculous, even worse accused them of being used to manipulate others.

Jet was such a bristly little snippet, yet so perceptive and relatable. He shrugged not sure what to make of her. In the past she had hardly ever been mentioned. Even now, in spite of his acquaintance with her, Jet remained a shadow of her mother, behaving like a prickly brier snagged off Mona's bush.

Dreading the results of the tree garden discovery, Kinsey feared, no matter how unconnected to the castle, it would produce bad publicity. Would his father withdraw the offer?

After helping Jet remove their purchases and transport them inside the house he drove to the garages. On the path back the breeze that had cleared the skies ran its fingers through his hair, promising another Pacific storm.

Approaching the south terrace he noticed a shadowy figure moving toward the road between the house and lake. Although unable to recognize the individual, he could see the person carried a duffle bag of some size. As if shot with adrenaline Kinsey took off in pursuit. However, the individual quickened his step, passing between a group of huckleberry bushes and a western hemlock. Kinsey doubled his pace in pursuit but the person vanished. Although he wandered around the trees and shrubs for a time Kinsey found no evidence anyone was there.

On entering the grand parlor and counting noses, he noted the whole group had gathered around the Christmas tree. Latte had brought fresh cookies. Evana had made hot chocolate and coffee. Jet was stacking their purchases by category and Susannah was instructing Nathan in putting on the lights. Landon and Logan gravitated from one person to another, chattering like magpies. Billy Monk hovered on the edge of the group as if uncertain about getting involved. So who was out walking on the grounds?

When Nathan had finished arranging the lights to suit the girls he approached Kinsey.

"Has anyone been here besides our group?" Kinsey questioned him. "I saw someone walking away from the house toward the lake just before I came in."

Nathan raised an eyebrow and shook his head. "Police?"

Kinsey shrugged. Possible, although it would help if someone had let him know.

At the piano Evana began playing Christmas carols. Everyone joined in singing as they continued to decorate the tree. Kinsey helped himself to a cookie and a cup of hot chocolate then dropped onto the sofa. Gradually as the tree became covered in red and white, with crystal and silver accents twinkling under the golden lights he recognized Jet's talent at picking trims.

Plunking herself down on the Chesterfield beside him, Susannah waved her hand to encompass the room. "You need more decorations than just a tree." She gave him the hey-sugar-daddy look from beneath her heavy black lashes.

Kinsey was no fool. "I'll veto anything inappropriate."

Susannah snorted her disdain. "What Christmas decorations could be inappropriate?"

"Whirling dervish Santas with body jewelry and tattooed angels."

Susannah rolled her eyes as the door chime reverberated throughout the main floor. Nathan answered it allowing Kinsey's father to enter, abashed by the crowd in the parlor.

Kinsey rose attracting his attention.

Park approached carrying a large white envelope. "What was that message about?"

Nodding in the direction of the library, Kinsey led the way through double paneled doors into the adjacent room and closed the door. This wasn't a discussion he was hot to have. "This afternoon the kid's dog found a body buried in the tree garden."

Park stared uncomprehending. "What kind of body?"

"A people body." How many kinds of bodies were there? "Well not a body really, just a skeleton and some clothes."

"What did you do with it?" Park set the envelope he was carrying on the desk.

Kinsey frowned at his father. Obviously he hadn't connected to reality. "Dad, the police were here. They took it."

Park's face froze in disbelief. "Could they identify it?"

"Not yet. They're checking for missing persons." Kinsey watched with dismay his father's internal battle for comprehension. Considering the flush on his face, he wondered if his father would faint.

"Are the police still here?" Park dropped into the purple velvet chair where he stood.

"I don't know." Kinsey sat across from him. "Did you see anyone when you came?"

"Someone crossed the road toward the other side of the driveway to the garages." Park ran his hand through his hair. "I don't think you should stay here, nor all these people either."

Kinsey shook his head. "It's a little late for that."

"No one has died."

What did that mean? Someone out in the yard was dead. "You can't continue to let this place be a monstrosity of rumors and haunting."

"Why can't I?" Park barked, his distraction turning to indignation. "Let someone else deal with it."

Did he know something he wasn't talking about?

"Like who?"

Park pursed his lips and glared at Kinsey. "The police."

"All they'll do is figure out who was buried in the garden." Kinsey recalled Lieutenant Sarkis' skeptical look when he asked about missing persons. "Did you ever find out what happened to that renter's wife?"

All the color left Park's face. He shook his head.

"Do you think she could be buried out there?"

"Lord have mercy." His father shuddered, looking dismal.

That would certainly explain some things. "You don't know anything about this do you?" If his father knew about the body it would go a long way to explaining his aversion to the place.

Park shook his bowed head.

Chapter Nine

Sunday morning Jet stepped out of her suite, stumbled over Anatuviak and fell into Kinsey's arms. He steadied her with the surprise of a third baseman catching the fly ball.

"Not only am I really sexy." She pushed the sweatband up on her forehead. "But I'm light on my feet and very graceful." She managed a mock pirouette.

Kinsey laughed.

Besides the fact his normally tousled hair was neatly arranged, he wore a dress shirt and tie. "You going to work?"

"Church."

She blushed, embarrassed not to have thought of it.

"Is that so strange?" He frowned at her expression.

She shook her head. "I suppose people do it every Sunday. I just never knew one."

"Want to come along?"

Jet hesitated. "When are you leaving?"

Kinsey consulted his watch. "In an hour or so."

"Sure. I can do that." She shrugged. What was the big deal anyway?

Loose gravel crunched as she ran toward Gravelly Lake Drive. The crime scene tape encircling the garden of trees was more florescent than the golden leaves drifting to the ground. She continued to the lane bordering the property on the west then along the lake and onto the drive to the garages. Retracing her run she noted a green van pass, continuing on the road to the east.

What had possessed her to accept Kinsey's invitation? She never went to church; at least she didn't used to. Somehow she connected her visit on Thanksgiving to her mother's relationship with the pastor. It was so atypical of Mona that Jet sought answers for the phenomenon.

Needing to shower and dress to keep her appointment, she returned to her suite where Latte was fixing pancakes for the boys. They sat on her heart-shaped footstool watching cartoons on television.

"I'm going to church with Kinsey," Jet informed her.

Latte raised her eyebrows and cocked her head, giving Jet a suggestive glance as she flipped a cake that partially missed the pan. "What's got into you?

Jet shrugged.

Squishing the batter back into place, Latte patted it down. "I really need to get the kids into Sunday School. Believe it or not I'm a Christian," she declared. "In spite of my partial Jewish background."

Jet remembered in college Latte had gotten up early to go to church, even attending some Christian group off and on. Jet had paid little attention at the time.

Religion was a foreign country to her, something like Mexico where they spoke a different language. She was never sure what they were talking about even when she could understand the words. I can handle it, she told herself as she pulled a long wool skirt out of her closet and put it on with a turtleneck sweater, chain belt and high-heeled boots.

Logan and Landon stared as if they had never seen her before. Even the look on Kinsey's face as she descended the grand staircase was gratifying. He actually gazed at her as if she were a woman not some idiotic annoying child.

"I'll bring the car around and pick you up." He started for the door.

"I can walk."

Kinsey stopped and turned. "Why?"

Jet stared at him. "Because I can."

"But you don't need to." His gaze challenged her. "Maybe you should get your car, come around and pick me up."

Parry, parry, thrust, she thought. Taking a seat on the deacon's bench, she declared, "I'll wait."

Traveling Gravelly to Bridgeport Way she observed Kinsey was headed for the same church she had attended on Thanksgiving. "Is this where you usually go?"

"For the last few years. Why?" Kinsey parked and they got out of the car.

"The pastor of this church came to see my mother before she died."

"Did she go to church here?"

"Are you kidding?" Surely he knew her mother was a raging infidel.

"I thought Pastor Ansgreth did her memorial service."

"I keep wondering how she got to know him." Jet noted the people nodding to Kinsey or greeting him. "And why?"

"Maybe she was concerned about eternity." Kinsey ushered Jet into a gold padded pew about the middle of the church.

Jet snorted contemptuously then changed her mind. "Maybe."

While Kinsey opened his bulletin and read Jet did the same. Not as uncomfortable as the first time, she knew the service would be projected and how to find her way around in the hymnal. This gave her an opportunity to glance around at other people. To her astonishment she noticed all of Kinsey's family seated a couple pews ahead Aunt Pat, Daniel, Park, Evana, Francine, Jordan with his family and even little old Aunt Tansy.

"Your family didn't go to church on Thanksgiving?" Or had Jet been so self-absorbed she hadn't noticed them?

"Most of them did. Aunt Pat usually cooks. Francine and Evana help her."

Jet realized at that time she would not have recognized them.

Pastor Ansgreth's sermon seemed to be about Jesus, some woman the Jews wouldn't associate with, and living water. Jet followed with difficulty until he quoted Jesus' words to the woman, "You are right when you say you have no husband. The fact is, you have had five husbands, and the man you now have is not your husband." Then he quoted the woman, "Sir, I can see that you are prophet."

Jet's mind went on a journey. Did God know about all her mother's men? Did he know who Jet's father was? And the big question, could He, would He help Jet find her real father?

When the service ended Kinsey's family gathered in the wood-paneled vestibule to chat. Aunt Pat hugged Jet, expressing her pleasure at seeing her again. Park appeared preoccupied. The half smile frozen on his face looked more like a grimace.

In Kinsey's car as they were leaving the parking lot, Jet asked, "Do you pray for whatever you want?"

He drew his eyebrows together. "What do you mean?"

"If there is something you want God to do, do you just ask?"

Kinsey shrugged. "Pretty much."

"Is that what praying is about?"

"Partly." He shot Jet a questioning glance. "There's more to it than that, but if there's something you want, ask. He's promised to answer our prayers."

While waiting at the light to turn onto Gravelly Lake Drive, Jet contemplated. It sounded too simple; there must be a catch. "Has He given you what you ask for?" During the time it took Kinsey to reply, Jet concluded there must be a difference between theory and practice.

"Usually what He gives me is better than what I ask for, but I don't always recognize it right away."

What does that mean? Jet scowled at the deciduous trees ablaze in shades of gold and fuchsia. Was it reasonable to ask for God's help in locating her true father?

"Okay." She sighed inwardly. "God, would you help me find my father?"

She cast a guilty glance at Kinsey. He seemed absorbed in driving. What did she expect? A gong would sound and God would strike her down for daring to address Him? Words from the sermon returned to her. Even Jesus was kind to the woman of Samaria with all the husbands.

⁊

Driving back to the estate, Kinsey contemplated his father's feverish appearance. What mental monster molested his peace of mind?

82

Kinsey dropped Jet off at the mansion then took his car to the garage. Instead of returning to the house he turned toward the formal landscaping, walking the paver patio along the balustrade. Here deep green lawn still provided a setting for the remaining marigold, asters, and chrysanthemum. The waterless fountain pool was a bowl of potpourri filled with colored leaves.

He crossed the main driveway and stood outside the boxwood hedge beyond the crime scene tape examining the area. The sun, ducking in and out from behind scattered clouds, cast alternating shadows and patches of light. The excavation site stuck out like an open wound. Why did Anatuviak bring the coat out first? When Kinsey looked into the shallow grave the bones had still been covered. Obviously the jacket had not been on the buried body. Did that mean the jacket would identify the corpse?

Next question, how did the dog detect where to dig? An odor? But the body had been there long enough to totally decompose. Had the ground been disturbed in a way that attracted him? Wondering if anything else was buried there, he wandered along the perimeter studying the ground. With his suspicious mindset and the shadows he could imagine burial sites everywhere. He needed to zip his imagination or dig up the entire plot to quell his doubts. He headed back to the house.

Enough renter problems had arisen during the week to keep him handcuffed to the grindstone indeterminately. With hot water first on his agenda he knocked on Latte's door, but received no answer. Wondering if she were with Jet, he knocked there and was met by one of Latte's twins.

"Mom," he yelled, "that Mr. Sayre is here."

Latte stuck her head around the door in the west wall. "Come in, Kinsey. Have you had lunch?"

"No, I thought I'd check and see how you came out with the hot water?" He stepped into the room.

Jet appeared at the door. "Come have a sandwich with us."

Kinsey followed into the kitchen. On the painted wooden table sat an assortment of sandwich fixings, four plates, two glasses of milk and two cups of coffee.

"Have a seat," Latte waved him to a chair. "When I went back for the next load the water was fine."

Kinsey frowned. "That doesn't make sense."

Latte sat down to make sandwiches for her boys. "Are you really serious about cleaning up the reputation on this place?"

"I have to or give it up." Kinsey decided to take advantage of the opportunity and accepting a plate began building a sandwich.

Latte continued, "I'd swear there are stairs behind the laundry room. I could hear someone going up and down."

"Dad brought me a copy of the blueprints. After lunch I'll get them and we can take a look."

When they finished Kinsey went to the library and grabbed the white envelope his father had brought. He took it to the dining room where he spread the plans on the dining table, arranging them by floor.

Latte and Jet arrived shortly after. Latte concentrated on the first floor. However, Kinsey noticed something else.

Jet came to stand beside him. "Did you find something?"

He pointed to stairs going all the way from the basement to the third floor in the northwest corner, which made sense to him. "But where are they?"

Latte stood by the main floor plans. "It doesn't show anything here, but I'll swear there's a stairway right there."

She pointed to the spot on the blueprints behind the laundry room.

Kinsey sighed. "Let's get the measuring tape and see what we can find." In a kitchen drawer of odds and ends he found a contractor's tape measure, a pencil and notepad. "Let's go outside."

Through the kitchen door, into the garden and around the north side of the house he led the girls. Handing Jet one end of the tape measure, he instructed her to go to the other end of the house. Since the tape wasn't long enough to measure it in one long shot, they measured it in sections. Latte recorded the numbers on the pad Kinsey gave her.

He looked up the side of the house. The second floor would mimic the first, but the third, although it appeared to do the same would be smaller because of the sloping roof. "Now we have to measure inside."

In the house Kinsey and Jet measured the north wall in the kitchen, pantry, and solarium. Then they went to the table to add up their figures.

"It's short," Latte declared in an ah-ha voice.

"We have to add some for the walls."

"How much?"

"Let's give each wall a foot. That's overkill but we won't make a false assumption." Kinsey searched the plans for plumbing or heating in the space.

Latte recalculated her footages. "That still leaves three feet."

Kinsey lifted his shoulders. "Tight, but possible."

"How do we find out?" Jet asked.

"I hate to go tearing into walls unless I have more evidence than this. If the plans indicated a stairway it would be different, but anything could be there including empty space."

Kinsey noted Latte's disappointed sigh. "Let me talk to my dad about it.

"How about the other one you mentioned?" Jet pointed to the plans.

The group picked up their tools and headed back into the kitchen, golden-hued in the late afternoon light. Kinsey opened the door to the second floor stairs and ushered the girls ahead of him up the wooden steps, ending in an L-shaped open area at the end of the second floor hall. A painted daybed, a tiny glass table, and parlor chair did little to keep the area from appearing bare.

"Here should be a stairway to the third floor." Kinsey wandered along the wall in the L portion of the room. He had already paced Susannah's wall. The missing square was too long to be consumed by her bathroom. The plans indicated stairs from the basement to the third floor here and here he needed them to be. But there was no opening into any stairway. "I can't figure it out."

Jet came to stand beside him. "Maybe it's been walled up."

As they stood an unmistakable clatter came from the other side of the wall. Latte turned wide eyes on Kinsey. "What was that?"

The sound's duration was momentary, ending without further noise, although the three stood for several minutes waiting.

"What if you dug a hole in the wall?" Latte pounded in different spots with her fist.

"I might have to." Kinsey grimaced. "My dad may have an idea. I don't want to start tearing the house apart willy-nilly."

☙

When Jet returned to her suite and Sunday afternoon's tranquility settled on the mansion, she took the leather bag containing items Mona had entrusted to her off the closet shelf. Since her mother's death she had become apprehensive of what the bag might contain. Only God, and maybe Pastor Ansgreth, knew what Mona hadn't told her. What secrets would leap out of some note, letter or picture to upend her universe?

Delivering the envelope to Roger, she had been so apprehensive of speaking to him she had given little thought to its contents. His suspicion then dismissal made her curious to know. For all Jet knew Mona could be bribing, extorting or blackmailing him, even from the grave.

She flipped on the gas fireplace then took the bag to the brocade sofa where she removed a folder of old pictures. Some were of Jet as a baby and growing up, some of parties and social events Mona had attended. Most were pictures of Mona posing, Mona at the state caucus, Mona in Hawaii, Mona at the governor's ball, Mona on the boardwalk at Commencement Bay, Mona in a convertible, Mona in a bikini. Mona was fond of her own picture and made every effort to appear glamorous, incongruous, given her mother's contempt for anything smacking of feminine display. Jet wondered how her mother succeeded in rationalizing her scorn for womanhood with her avaricious sexuality.

Intrigued by the backgrounds, Jet was less interested in her mother than her companions. Were there clues to her father here? She found a 5x8" manila envelope with Parkinson Sayre written on it. She manipulated the packet, which was thick in the middle, guessing it was photographs also. Having forgotten, she realized she needed to deliver it. The other one Mona entrusted to her said "Otto Lane?" which Jet assumed was the phantom possibility for a father. Delivering that constituted an absurd puzzle.

Why was there none for Jesse McFadden? She searched the bag again in case she had missed it. When her mother had told Jet about him, she had sensed Mona didn't want to involve him. On the whole that seemed as odd as everything else.

One more packet included several smaller envelopes marked Ethel, Theresa and Aunt Jane. In handling the packages Jet took them to be filled with jewelry or other small treasures. Although Jet knew these people to be her mother's sisters and aunt, they were just names. Would Kinsey know them?

As she contemplated the stack of dubious treasures there was a knock on her door.

"Come in," Jet called, expecting Latte.

The door opened carefully and Evana stuck her head in. "Are you busy?"

"No." Jet stifled her surprise. "Come in."

Stepping in with her customary grace, Evana sent her gaze around the room as if committing its contents to memory. "I didn't mean to interrupt what you were doing."

"I was just putting it away." Jet stood. "Would you like soda, or tea?"

"Tea would be great." Evana's voice had the same musical quality as Kinsey's.

Evana followed Jet into the kitchenette where she poured tea from a red teapot into black and white mugs and heated them in the microwave. "Milk or sugar?"

"Just milk." Evana accepted the cup.

When they returned to the sitting room Jet replaced the envelopes and pictures in the leather bag wondering what brought Evana to her suite. "Are you all settled in?"

Evana slid her feet out of her Birkenstock's and tucked them underneath her as she sat in the corner of the French provincial sofa. "Mostly. Living so close I keep thinking of things I should bring over."

As Jet considered Evana, her sharply bobbed black hair and dark blue eyes, she thought of the comment she had heard Nathan make to Billy on their way upstairs, "beautiful but . . ." She wasn't simply pretty or attractive, Evana was beautiful in the way an art master's portrait was beautiful, full of color and emotion. A thought popped into Jet's head. Evana had a different last name than Kinsey.

Jet hesitated to ask the touchy question, but figured she might as well get it over with. Eventually she would stumble over it anyway. "Were you married?"

"Yes." Evana's expression made Jet feel suspected of ulterior motives.

She found the look intimidating, making her hesitant about continuing. "What happened?" she ventured to ask.

"He was killed in a helicopter training incident."

"I'm sorry."

"Everyone thinks I should get married again." Evana stared into the fire. "But I believe there's only one love for a lifetime."

"You don't think you could ever love enough to remarry and be happy?"

"Not that way." Evana's gaze rested on Jet as if assessing feeblemindedness.

Jet had fancied herself in love numerous times, probably ever since she was big enough to realize boys weren't girls. Nothing ever came of it. She always fixed her affections on someone totally out of reach, hop-scotching for the moon.

"I believe there is only one true love for each person. If something happens to that person there'll never be another."

"If that's what love means I don't think I've ever been there." Jet was shocked by Evana's theory.

"Kinsey seems to attract a lot of women, but he'll never love again."

Jet's astonishment must have shown in her face since Evana narrowed her eyes as if daring Jet to contradict.

"His girlfriend dumped him a few years ago and it took him a long time to get over it."

Was Evana warning her off Kinsey? Jet figured she might as well save her breath. She knew Kinsey could be her brother. For one brief moment she was tempted to tell Evana, but thought better of it and remained silent.

"Your friend." Evana's gaze moved to the cherry end table and a picture of Jet and Latte taken when they were in college. "She's divorced?"

"That's right."

"She's very attractive, the Scandinavian kind of good looks."

Jet laughed. "You'd never know she was part Jewish."

Evana raised an elegant dark eyebrow. "No, you wouldn't. She's not really Kinsey's type."

Jet frowned. What did that mean? Was Evana building a shield around Kinsey?

Chapter Ten

Monday morning brought Blast Castle a ponderous layer of dark clouds and Lieutenant Sarkis. Even before dawn could hint at day the sound of door chimes reverberated through the main floor catching Kinsey in the kitchen with a quickly scrambled egg.

He looked up as Nathan waved the lieutenant in to the room. "Kinsey Sayre, sir."

Kinsey heaved a deep sigh at his day's auspicious beginning. "Coffee, lieutenant?"

Sarkis didn't look that put together himself. His red-brown hair lifted in a cowlick above his ear and his spectacles had slid to the lower slope of his nose. Tempted to ask if he'd had a rough night, Kinsey cancelled that thought, figuring tact was the greater part of valor since he was the one with the corpse in the yard.

The lieutenant bobbed an affirmative nod, helping himself to a stool at the kitchen island.

"Have they identified the body?" Kinsey handed him a cup of coffee then pushed the milk and sugar his direction.

"Not yet." Sarkis plopped a shot of milk into his. "We do have some information however. Female, middle aged—forty or fiftyish—Caucasian. Nice set of teeth." The lieutenant's hawk-like expression warned Kinsey he was waiting for a telltale reaction.

"How did she die?" Could they tell from the bones?

"Shot."

"Shot?" What had he expected? You don't bury Aunt Bea in the garden after her heart attack. "When?"

The lieutenant shrugged. "At least a couple years."

Oh, great, just the right timing to be the renter's wife.

"You think you know who it is?" The lieutenant read Kinsey's mind.

He grimaced and repeated what he had read in the newspaper article, giving the lieutenant the details on the electrocution. "After that his wife was never found."

Sarkis retrieved his notebook. "Name?"

How much of a calamity was this going to trigger? "Markovich—Carmen Markovich."

"Who would know her?"

"My dad, Park Sayre." A visit from the police, that should thrill his father.

"I've an appointment with him later. No one else here would have known these people?"

Kinsey sighed. "My sister could have but I doubt it."

The lieutenant wasn't interested in Kinsey's doubts. "Is she here?"

Kinsey shrugged. "I can check." He put his plate in the dishwasher and headed upstairs.

Answering his knock dressed in a charcoal pantsuit and bedroom slippers, Evana agreed to come as soon as she grabbed her shoes and bag.

Returning to the kitchen Kinsey found the lieutenant at the window staring into the landscaping.

"Where does that road go?" Sarkis pointed to the street running along the lake.

"To the properties on either side," Kinsey told him, wondering what had attracted his attention.

At the sound of Evana's step in the kitchen, Kinsey turned to introduce her, noting Lieutenant Sarkis stunned expression. She moved across the room, gliding with the grace of a ballet dancer. Kinsey had grown accustomed to the dazed male's reaction to his sister.

She glanced uncertainly from one to the other. "May I help you?"

"The lieutenant wanted to know if you knew the last renters here."

Evana set her bag on the counter and moved to the refrigerator. "Sort of."

"What does that mean?" The lieutenant crossed his arms and leaned back against the counter.

"I met Mr. Markovich once. Also I had coffee once with Dad and Carmen. Other than that I saw her a couple times in the yard when I brought something here for Dad." She opened the refrigerator and took out a paper bag.

Impressive, she knew more than Kinsey realized.

The lieutenant fired another question. "You haven't seen Mrs. Markovich since her husband died?"

Evana tossed Kinsey a bewildered glance, shaking her head.

Lieutenant Sarkis turned to Kinsey. "What happened to the renter's possessions?"

"I've a receipt upstairs from the person who accepted them"

"I need a copy of that."

The encroaching fog extended misty arms as Jet stepped onto the terrace from the library. Even sheltered there the density of the haze told her it was pointless to use an umbrella. Moisture didn't fall out of the sky, it dangled in the air as if uncertain whether to proceed or withdraw, giving her hair volume that reduced her face to the size of a big-eyed rodent.

The national bank where she worked was so close to the mansion if public transit had been reasonable it would have made a better choice than driving. In good weather she could have walked.

She enjoyed the peacefulness of the bank before doors opened for customers. The phone didn't ring, no one bothered her, making it possible to jump start the day's work. She had a lot on her mind; none of it related to her occupation. She took a moment to look up the names Roger had given her on the computer, checking facebook. com and the city directory online. Jesse McFadden, Susannah's father, was the only name she could recall her mother mentioning. No name even remotely resembled Otto Lane no matter how she spelled it.

If she got a chance to talk to Jesse through Susannah it would be less intimidating than calling him out of the blue. However, first she needed to decide what she wanted to know. Obviously Jesse wouldn't know if he were her father. Did he even suspect the possibility?

Every time she visited the difficulty of obtaining the truth, she reevaluated proceeding. What difference did it make? She could never quite answer that question.

The tinkling sound of her cell phone alerted her. "This is Roger Thompson. You busy for lunch?"

Recovering from her astonishment, Jet glanced at her day planner. "No." After agreeing, Jet spent the next hour and a half on her work, trying to imagine what he could want. Nothing in her personal database provided a clue. To the utmost of her recollection Roger had never made any overture toward her. He had to want something.

Full of suspicion, she met him in the lobby at 11:45. His debonair costume failed to hide anxiety's imprint. He drove her to the Mexican restaurant in the Lakewood Town Center in his silver Mercedes SLK 320, making light-hearted small talk all the way.

When the waitress left them in a colorfully painted booth with water, chips, salsa and menus, Roger tossed out carelessly, "I hear they found a body at the estate."

Savoring the salt and spice of her dipped chip, Jet eyed him. "Just a skeleton."

"Do they know who it is?"

"They figure it was a woman." She met Roger's beady eyes, pinched in the corners casting doubt on his nonchalance. "Lieutenant Sarkis was at the house this morning."

Roger examined his menu. "Did they say how long they thought it had been there?"

"It must have been a long time since it was only a skeleton." Jet decided on a combination plate since Mexican food came in quantities befitting a famished football player. She could save part of it for the next day's lunch.

Noting the rosy tinge to Roger's cheeks and the feverish light in his eyes, she suggested airily, "Someone you know missing?"

He made a half-hearted attempt at laughter ending in a coughing fit. "A couple people, but I don't think they'd end up there."

After giving their orders to the waitress, Jet ventured a question. "What was in the envelope my mother gave you?"

Roger choked on a chip then grabbed his water to ease it down. "Just a matter between her and I, something to do with her work, nothing personal."

Interpretation: it's private and I'm not telling you. Jet shrugged.

"I heard Kinsey had questions about stairs at the mansion," Roger continued.

As she explained Jet wondered how he knew about that.

Roger pinched the end of his nose with his thumb and forefinger. "Maybe the contractor eliminated them for some reason."

"Wouldn't that be illegal? According to fire codes I'd think there'd have to be more than one staircase for the third floor."

Roger gave her an indulgent smile inferring lots of things people did were illegal. "What is he doing about it?" Roger gave his nose another pinch. Maybe he kept unwanted thoughts from escaping that way.

"Making inquiries."

When their meals were delivered they ate in silence for a time. Roger wore indifference like a raincoat as if preventing penetration of emotion. Although he had never married again there never seemed to be another woman about. Not that he'd confide in Jet. He maintained a large home, lived an upscale lifestyle, and traveled perpetually, often out of the country. According to Mona his family had a lot of money, although she had never been interested in his family or their money, unfortunately for Jet.

"What went wrong in your marriage to Mom?"

He shot her a rueful smile. "Believe it or not I was too much of an idealist."

"And Mom wasn't?"

"Different ideals. Tritely enough, I believed in country, motherhood, and apple pie."

"You left out God."

Roger shrugged. "I never quite got that far."

"And Mom?" Jet could guess. She had never felt sorry for Roger figuring he and her mom probably deserved each other, but suddenly she realized that might not have been the case.

"She believed in women's rights, bleed the rich to pay for the poor, government should have the control and responsibility, and free love."

"You were a conservative and she was a liberal?" Jet hadn't known that either.

"Libertine was more like it. I believed in freedom, capitalism, responsibility, and patriotism. We clashed."

He had her mother pegged right. "Are you still a conservative?"

"As far as it goes, I suppose." He took a deep breath and let it out slowly. "Just no longer an idealist."

His had succeeded eliciting Jet's compassion and respect. When they finished lunch Roger returned her to the bank. "Are you getting along okay without your mom?"

Jet sighed and nodded.

He asked her to keep him informed regarding the castle skeleton. "I realize it's a problem if Kinsey wants to keep the house." Then he left; his sports car sprung into traffic and disappeared.

Chapter Eleven

Delayed by the lieutenant's morning visit and hit by a barrage of untimely urgencies, Kinsey remained in his office past his normal quitting time. Then, entangled in the rush hour traffic mess, he arrived at the estate just as dinner was ready, prepared to bark at anyone obstructing his path. A fact obviously clear from his expression for when he entered the house Evana, her eyebrows peaked over her nose, approached as if fearful he'd shatter into a thousand pieces. "Dad called. That lieutenant is meeting him here tonight."

"Great." Kinsey grimaced. "Didn't Sarkis see Dad earlier today?"

Evana shrugged, still treading on eggshells. "Maybe he postponed it. Isn't most of what's he's questioning Dad about here?"

She had a point.

When the group had moved into the dining room, taking their customary places, Kinsey asked the blessing. The way he figured, whether the others liked it or not, they needed all the help they could get and prayer was his first line of defense, God being the only security and protection he could count on.

Nathan piped up. "When I came home around noon there was a green van with a flat tire pulled off to the side of the road between Gravelly Lake Drive and the shore road." He grabbed a roll from the basket in front of him. "It was gone when I got done." He gestured for the butter. "Do you think someone on the other side of the estate owns it?"

Kinsey recalled noticing the same vehicle. "It doesn't sound like something a Mercedes broker would own."

Nathan went on talking. "I've seen someone walking on the property when none of these people were around."

"No law against taking a walk is there?" Billy joined the discussion.

"On private property there is."

Returning to his suite after dinner, Kinsey heard Latte instruct her boys to take Anatuviak for a walk.

Summoned by a loud rap on his door he found Billy. "Some guy downstairs wants to see you."

Stepping into the hall Kinsey watched Billy climb the stairs to the third floor, still wondering what had brought him to Blast Castle out of the blue.

When Kinsey reached the main floor, Park was standing in front of the Christmas tree staring. His hair fell over his forehead, his trousers were rumpled and his shirt had lost a button. If he didn't clean up his act he would soon look like a homeless person.

"Nice tree." Park shoved his hands into the pockets of his dockers. "Did you get it from the property?"

"Out where they found the body." His father already knew that. What was the matter with him?

Running his hand through his hair, Park left it worse off than before. "That detective is meeting me here."

Noting his father's expression Kinsey wondered what was eating him. He looked like he'd jump off the Narrows Bridge if someone shouted "Boo".

"He wanted to see us together." Park moved toward the library like a man headed to his own execution.

Suspecting his father possessed more information than he would willingly part with worried Kinsey although he wouldn't bet it had to do with the skeleton. Something connected to the house and its history was devouring Park's peace of mind.

He slumped into the purple velvet chair facing the fireplace.

Kinsey debated confrontation. He had to step up; his future depended on it. "What are you not telling me?"

Park's mouth dropped open, but he drowned his surprise in self-discipline.

Before Kinsey could get off another question the doorbell chimed. He went to let the lieutenant in then led the way to the library and motioned him to the fan back chair.

The lieutenant sunk into it, took out his notebook, flipped over a few pages then dropped his bomb. "We have a tentative identification on the woman in the grave. It appears to be Carmen Markovich."

Park's face turned white and the area around his eyes turned red. "Are you sure?"

"We don't have a positive, but the skeletal features fit and evidence we found in the grave indicates it was her body."

Considering what he had seen in the grave Kinsey asked, "What evidence?"

"Her cell phone for one thing." Lieutenant Sarkis addressed Park. "How well did you know Mrs. Markovich?"

He swallowed like he had a mouth full of frogs. "I saw her sometimes when I came to make sure the people I hired were doing what they were supposed to be." He lifted a hand and set it down. "Occasionally I ran into her at Starbucks and we had coffee."

Kinsey was amazed. What bushel had he been hiding under to know so little about his father's relationships? Frowning at the lieutenant he wondered how he came to know so much about Park and Mrs. Markovich.

The lieutenant still addressed his father. "Your name was on her cell phone contact list, if "Park" means you." He kept his eyes fixed on Park's face.

What did he see? Park's expression appeared more regretful than alarmed.

The lieutenant went on, "When did you last see her?"

Park moved his gaze to the woodwork arch above the fireplace. "I'm not sure after this long I can give you dates."

"Let's say her husband was electrocuted on the 19th. Working back could you calculate it?"

Focusing on his fingers, Park counted. "Then it would have been Friday the 15th at Starbucks in Lakewood, on 100th. I'd gone to Lowe's to get some moss killer and ran into her there."

"What time?" The lieutenant was on a roll.

Park lifted his shoulders. "Ten o'clock, or thereabouts."

Kinsey wondered at the significance of his father's memory after that long.

"Did she give you any idea of her plans for the day?"

Here the lieutenant lost Park as his attention drifted back to the fireplace. "Not that I recall."

Sarkis stayed in pursuit. "You never saw her again after that?"

Park shook his head.

"Were you surprised . . . not to see her again?"

Park's gaze darted to the lieutenant's face. "Yes . . . I guess I was."

What had the lieutenant picked up that eluded Kinsey?

"What do you think happened?"

Fearing his father was being led into a trap, Kinsey interrupted. "I don't think my dad should be asked to surmise what happened in someone's death."

Park ignored him. "I didn't know what to think."

Sarkis shot Kinsey a how-far-can-I-push-this glance then tossed his question. "What about after her husband was found dead?"

Zipping his lips shut Park shook his head.

"You didn't wonder if there was a connection?" the lieutenant prodded.

Opening his eyes wide, Park turned to him. "You think she had something to do with her husband's death?"

Lieutenant Sarkis raised his hand halting the presumption. "Not necessarily. Electrocution wouldn't be a woman's way of getting rid of someone."

"You think Matt was murdered?" Kinsey hadn't considered that.

"No one is taking that position. I just wondered if you'd thought about it at the time."

Park did not respond.

"Did you see Markovich's body?"

"They'd removed it before I arrived." Park grimaced. "It was mostly over when they called me."

The lieutenant flipped over the page in his notebook. "What is your understanding of how the electrocution occurred?"

"I was told he stuck a screwdriver in the bus. They figured he'd become the ground. He was in stocking feet plus near the plumbing pipes." Park heaved a long sigh. "The doctor told me Matt must have had some health problems that made him unable to withstand the shock."

"Fits with forensics." The lieutenant nodded. "Why do you think he was fooling around with the breakers?"

"The lights had been behaving strangely." Park sat up straighter. "I'd had an electrician come and check the wiring but he found nothing wrong."

"Not even the ungrounded breaker?"

"Apparently not." Park ran his hand through his already unruly hair, giving him a frazzled appearance. He looked like someone who would pay a premium for the ability to give a conclusive answer to the lieutenant's questions. "Matt called me earlier the day he died to tell me the lighting thing had started up again."

"What did you do about it?"

"Nothing."

Kinsey could see the end of his father's patience coming.

"I was trying to figure out what I could do about it. Actually I'd begun to suspect Matt of funny business."

The lieutenant raised an interrogative eyebrow.

Kinsey's father shook his head.

When Lieutenant Sarkis left, Kinsey worried his father was holding something back, but what and why?

&

After hearing the door chime and wondering if Park had arrived, Jet descended to the parlor. Pausing near the library she listened for voices but the doors were too heavy.

Sprawled on the sofa near the fireplace, Nathan read a science fiction book. "Looking for someone?" he asked without lifting his gaze from the page.

"Did Park come?"

"Yeah, he's with Kinsey and the lieutenant."

Thinking it strategic to wait rather than miss him, Jet sat on the opposite davenport. She placed the envelope for Park in her lap then stared across the room at the leaded-glass windows, gaping black holes reflecting the sprinkling of Victorian lamps and arabesque sconces that failed to illuminate the room.

A pair of headlights approached from the left, moved around the circular drive then came to a stop. Shortly after that the doorbell rang again.

"Do you want to get it or shall I?" Nathan queried, still focused on his book.

"I will." Jet opened the door to a teddy bear of a man with fuzzy brown hair framing a round face on top of a chunky middle-aged torso.

"Is Susannah McFadden here?" he inquired with wide glassy eyes.

Jet stepped back, holding the door open. "Her suite is on the second floor. Did you want to go up, or shall I get her?"

"I'm her father," he declared. "I suppose I could just go up."

Jet pointed to the staircase, "Up one floor and take a right, her suite is the first door."

Once he had started up the stairs, Jet chastised herself. This man could be her father. She needed to get to know him. Returning to the sofa, she resolved to remedy that when he returned. However, at that moment the library door opened and Lieutenant Sarkis appeared in the parlor.

Turning back to Kinsey, who followed him, he said, "I need to get hold of the person who claimed those renter's belongings. I'll probably be back tomorrow or the next day."

Jet entered the library where she offered the envelope to Park. "My mother left this for you."

Park's eyes widened in surprise.

She perched on the bold-printed Chesterfield opposite him.

Fingering the package, he said, "I'm sorry about your mother." Sympathy made a quick appearance in his expression.

Jet figured Mona probably deserved what happened to her. In spite of missing her mother she still resented her lack of responsibility. All of a sudden it hit her, here was her opportunity. If she failed to speak she may regret it interminably. "My mother said you could be my father."

Jet held her breath while Park stared at her as though considering whether or not to accept such a slight specimen for a daughter.

He smoothed his hair with his hand, sighing. "I realized the possibility when you were born. Since your mother never talked about it I thought she knew it wasn't me."

"Roger Thompson is also possible." Jet transferred her gaze to the toes of her shoes. "He agreed to be on the birth certificate since he'd been married to her." Glancing up she caught the flash of incredulity in Park's expression.

"Your mother didn't know?"

Jet's eyes smarted and her nose ached. Pressing her lips together she worked to maintain her self-control. "Apparently there were a lot of possibilities." She wiped away a couple tears that dropped on her arm.

Park watched her in agonized sympathy. "If it makes any difference, I'd be happy to be your father."

Jet took a deep breath and cleared her throat. "You're probably the least likely. I think I'd look more like Kinsey and Evana if you were."

His gaze shot to her face. Undoubtedly he could see the lack of resemblance.

"Would you," Jet ventured, "would you mind taking a DNA test to see?"

Frowning, Park peered at her as if inspecting her suitability. "Sure. What could it hurt?"

Since his frown continued, Jet figured some things it could hurt had occurred to him. Nonetheless, she was grown up. It wasn't like she would hit him up for a college education, or to pay for a wedding, or sue him for neglect. To the best of her knowledge she wasn't retarded either.

He must have read her mind for he said, "We're quite distant cousins by blood."

A noise at the door indicated Kinsey had reentered the library. He sent a questioning glance to his father then Jet.

To avoid explaining, she stood up. "I need to get going." As she returned to the parlor, Latte's boys burst in through the anteroom door.

"Look what we found." Landon waved a twenty dollar bill.

Logan was holding another, but keeping a lower profile.

"Where did you find that?" Jet asked Landon.

"Outside, over by the road." He waved an arm.

Nathan had abandoned his reclining position to observe the conversation. "The one that goes to the garages?"

Logan shook his head. "The other one."

"You're going to have to see if they belong to anyone here?" Nathan informed them.

The boys looked disappointed.

"Come on guys, let's go talk to your mom." Jet ushered them up the stairs.

Latte was on her way down. They waved their find for her to see. She agreed to make inquiries and if no one claimed the money she would let the boys have it.

Chapter Twelve

Monday morning's gloom became Tuesday's raging wind and flying rain. Jet traveled to work with windshield wipers flapping. Putting up her raincoat's hood, she sprinted for the shelter of the bank-building's overhang.

Inside tranquility prevailed. The storm's fuming kept people home, hoping for a better day. Jet wouldn't have minded a cozy fireplace and her Ipad either, but had to settle for a print out of repossessions and bad loans. Losing herself in work she was startled when her cell phone rang.

She noted Latte's number. "Hi, what's up?"

Latte shrieked, "We're going to jail for passing illegal money. Those twenties the kids found were counterfeit." Her voice still came in a high pitched rush. "I couldn't get anyone to claim them so the kids took them to Toys R Us. They called the police."

"Where are you?"

"At the police station." Latte sounded as if Jet insinuated she was rushing through Toys R Us filling her cart.

"Didn't you explain?"

Latte harrumphed. "How would it sound to you if someone said they found counterfeit twenties lying beside the road?" Latte's voice began to calm down. "Can you come and get the kids?"

Jet noted it was nearly quitting time anyway. "Sure. Was this your one phone call?"

"They haven't taken away my cell phone . . . yet."

After logging off with her, Jet called Kinsey. Obviously Latte wasn't counterfeiting, but since the kids found the bills on the estate, he should be warned.

After a moment's silence he sighed. "Great, next we'll find this is where D.B. Cooper stashed his money. Where are you?" He sounded resigned. "I'll pick you up and we can go see what kind of trouble your friend is in."

"Why don't I just meet you there?"

"Right, I forgot," Kinsey's pique was perceptible. "You're too independent to have someone pick you up."

That's not fair, Jet thought. She would still have to get the car home.

Typical of Latte she had constructed a tower of calamity from a few bricks of adversity. When Kinsey and Jet reached the station they found her and the boys in an office waiting to speak with the Secret Service.

Jet gave her friend an encouraging hug.

"They wouldn't let us go home." Latte crossed her arms over her chest, glaring as if Jet were the offending officer.

"It sounds," Kinsey said, "as if they're just looking for information."

"I don't know anything," Latte squealed. "I never even saw where they found the money."

Turning to the twins Kinsey asked them to describe their discovery.

Landon took a deep breath as if he had already explained it to the Washington State Court of Appeals and the Supreme Court. "You know where the road goes by the lake?"

"They were right there," Logan added. "Beside the road."

"How far off?"

Landon spread his arms. Kinsey cast Jet a dubious glance.

"You're sure?" Kinsey glanced at each of them. "It was lying on the grass?"

"Not together," Logan said.

"How far apart?"

Landon spread his arms again.

Latte added, "They don't budge from that story."

Kinsey shrugged. "Then it's probably the truth regardless of how unlikely it sounds."

The office door opened and a uniformed policeman ushered a corporate executive type into the room. "This is Agent Elaney."

Jet studied the man who was medium height, with thick dark hair and fine boned features as he listened to Latte explain what had happened. Although he spoke very little, his glance jetted around the room at the other occupants. His intense expression resembled the concentrated silence of the computer tabulating and organizing information.

After posing a few questions about the property to Kinsey Agent Elaney suggested, "How about we take a ride out there?"

"Are we under arrest?" Latte demanded.

He frowned. "I want to see where they found the money."

Jet watched the agent usher Latte and the kids to a black Acura parked in the station lot. Kinsey's BMW was parked behind her Sky Roadster and they all pulled out in procession.

Confident Latte wasn't passing counterfeit money Jet wondered what it all meant. Kinsey appeared worried. His problems with the property were already enough to keep him beset in perpetuity.

When the procession arrived, parked in the circular driveway was the SUV Jet had seen previously, probably another shot of bad news.

The three cars lined up behind the SUV. Landon and Logan tumbled out and ran toward the north end of the house, disappearing around the bend. The agent followed with Latte, Kinsey and Jet not far behind. Rounding the end of the house Jet could see the boys heading in the direction of the lake. Unrelenting rain had so drenched the lawn the boys splashed water to their knees with every step, making Jet thankful she had worn boots.

Before reaching the lake road the boys stopped. Simultaneously they pointed then ran to stand at the edge of the lane, declaring this to be where they found the bills. Frowning, Agent Elaney rotated taking in the surrounding territory. Where could the money have come from? The whole story sounded phony as a three-dollar bill.

❧

Moving away, Agent Elaney methodically canvassed the edges of the road as far as the rhododendron garden then paced back and forth across the grass. At one point near the low growing herb beds he bent to pick something off the ground. Kinsey couldn't see what it was, but the agent spent time examining it before wrapping it in a handkerchief and sticking it in his pocket.

After returning he asked about a time to come back. "I need to meet the people who live here."

"Everyone is usually around for dinner at 6:00."

"Then 7:00 should work?"

Nodding, Kinsey walked with the agent back to the cars. The kids had gone to the house. Latte and Jet had taken refuge from the rain on the south terrace where Kinsey joined them, sitting in wrought iron chairs surrounding a matching table.

"Whew!" Latte made an exaggerated swipe across her forehead. "After this, if the kids find money they'll put it right back where they got it."

"And if someone else finds it pretend they never saw it before?" Kinsey continued her thought.

"Exactly!" Latte made a chopping gesture.

Placing her elbow on the table Jet rested her chin in her hand. "Do you think someone here is holding counterfeit money?"

Kinsey ran his hand through his hair. "Well it didn't sprout on the end of a stem like a flower." What a mess! Every time he thought he had solved a problem two more showed up in its place.

Latte rose. "I'd better see what the kids are up to."

"After you check on them we can go pick up your car," Jet told her.

Kinsey followed Jet into the grand parlor where they came face to face with Lieutenant Sarkis who shot Kinsey an aggravated glance. "Where have you been?"

"Looking for counterfeit money."

Sarkis' expression declared he wasn't amused.

112

Although Kinsey would like to forget the whole deal he figured the lieutenant would stumble on the situation anyway so he explained the money and the Secret Service Agent.

Pinching his nose Lieutenant Sarkis peered over his spectacles as if about to dive into water over his head. "I should talk to him."

"He'll be back at 7:00." Wondering if that meant the lieutenant would be back too, Kinsey wandered into the kitchen where he found the cook preparing to put dinner on the dining room table. A sprightly woman, wiry body and unruly dark hair, she spoke in quick concise sentences informing him supper was ready.

"I think I'll fix a plate and eat in my room." Kinsey wasn't prepared to face the crew at his table.

"Suit yourself."

When he entered the dining room to remove his place setting he noticed Jet outside the door and called to her. "You want to have supper in my suite with me?"

From the look she shot him one would have thought he'd suggested eloping.

"We can see what theory fits the facts we have." It would have been more appropriate to invite Nathan, but he needed a listener. Evana would listen then scold or pressure him to do something for which he wasn't ready.

Jet hesitated momentarily then as if throwing caution to the wind agreed.

Maybe she figured he had a hidden agenda. He was too worn out for ulterior motives. Besides that she was his cousin.

Chapter Thirteen

Surprised at Kinsey's invitation but aware of his problems, Jet followed him back to the kitchen where she helped herself from the dishes being prepared for the table then took the back stairs through the second floor hall to his suite, which she had never seen.

Ushering Jet ahead of him, Kinsey opened the door and flipped the switch igniting a number of table lamps scattered throughout. Painted a deep emerald green it held a bed big enough for an average sized family covered in a satin quilt shimmering in the soft light. The brass headboard glimmered as did the embellished corner fireplace. Jet stood enchanted by the gilded opulence of the room and its romantic ambience.

Kinsey put his hand in the middle of her back and pushed her forward enough to close the door. "Dinner, food, kitchen," he hailed her attention pointing at a door to the right.

Larger than the one in her suite, it was furnished with a glass top table and metal chairs. French doors led to a terrace.

While he pushed aside a pile of paperwork and took a couple basket weave place mats from a drawer nearby Jet examined the view from the terrace doors. Daytime might provide abundant sunlight to the kitchen. However, its retreat left only a soft glow within and gloomy obscurity without. Night's blackness allowed no relief of stars, moon or even city lights. The gathering mist prevented Jet from detecting any sign of the residences across the lake, creating a ghostly haunting like an old black and white horror show. Peering into the fog, she failed to notice until Kinsey barked "What the heck" and she turned around that all illumination in the suite had been extinguished. Remaining still for fear of losing her balance, she called out, "Where are you?"

"By the frig," Kinsey responded.

"What happened?"

"I don't know. I'm going into the hall and see."

Jet could hear him moving, bumping things as he made his way through the bedroom. Gradually her eyes adapted to the blackout. Dark shapes in the room took form and she was able to move away from the table toward the kitchen door.

"Everything's out on the second floor." Kinsey called. "It sounds like the same thing on the main level. I'm going to the electrical box in the basement."

Jet remained at the door between the kitchen and the bedroom. "Do you have a flashlight or any candles?"

"In the drawer next to the frig."

She groped her way along the counter to where Kinsey indicated and located a cylindrical object. She pushed protrusions on it until suddenly a beam of light lit the room. Before taking it to him she searched the drawer, locating a four inch stub of candle and a packet of matches. After lighting the candle she brought him the flashlight.

"In the parlor are big tapers," he said. "And an old kerosene lamp is in the billiard room if you can get that far."

She followed him out of the suite. As he continued toward the back stairs Jet descended the grand staircase. Meeting Nathan half way down, she handed the matches to him and he lit the tapers on the credenza against the north wall.

Latte stood at the dining room door. "What's going on?"

Landon and Logan came running from the other set of dining room doors shrieking, pursued by flapping wings.

Nathan crossed his arms in front of his face to ward off a low flying gull. "Where'd the birds come from?"

The boys ran to their mother for protection while two seagulls flapped around the room, moving from table to ledge.

"Is the door open?" Jet headed back to the kitchen. The basement door was ajar, which she figured meant Kinsey. Cold air had met her in the dining room. Checking the kitchen's outside entrance and finding it closed, she proceeded to the solarium. Her candle allowed her to see the French doors to the north terrace had been flung wide and a couple more seagulls trotted around like enthusiastic tourists. After shooing the birds out and closing the doors she noticed another fowl perched on the window ledge.

Suddenly the lights blazed on in full force. Although still unlit, the solarium gathered light from the remainder of the house. Jet blew out her candle, pursuing the gull as it dropped from its perch and hopped into the morning room.

Realizing she was in pursuit, it hastened into the kitchen just as Kinsey came up the stairs from the basement.

"What was the deal?"

"Something blew the breakers." Kinsey stared at the seagull as if he considered disowning his vision. "All of them."

That didn't sound normal. Jet frowned. "There are birds all over the house."

Kinsey eyed the gull as if it hardly qualified.

"The solarium doors were open." She lifted her hands in a gesture of perplexity.

Kinsey scowled. "None of this makes any sense."

All of a sudden the lights were out again, plunging the room into total blackness. Jet stood still not wanting to stumble.

Disregarding caution, Kinsey moved, stumbling over the seagull who squawked, flapping its wings. "Blast that bird!" he cried as he lost his balance, toppling into Jet who managed to keep him upright.

"Sorry, should have waited." Regaining his equilibrium he headed for the basement door. "I'm going down again. Tell the guys to turn off everything in the house except the lights."

Returning to the parlor Jet found Latte, the boys, and Nathan still looking befuddled. She communicated Kinsey's message, noting birds trotting along the plate ledge near the dining room door. "Where are Evana and Susannah?"

"They left the table before everyone else." Latte dived for a gull, which jumped from its perch with flapping wings, landing on the piano.

Jet waved her arms at the fowl. "Would you tell the others to turn everything off in their suites too?"

"Sure." Latte responded. "Come on boys."

Jet returned to the kitchen, wondering how Kinsey faired. Once again the lights blasted on in full force. Fearful of another relapse she remained still. As she waited she could hear what Latte had described earlier, noises like someone going up or down the stairs, not the back stairs Kinsey had taken, but ones behind the wall in the laundry room. The movement came quickly and staccato, like someone ascending. However, it ceased instantaneously and even though Jet waited she heard no more.

Descending the basement stairs, Jet located Kinsey near the electrical box. "What are you doing?"

"I just wanted to see if it blew again." He flicked a glance at her then returned to his observation.

"I thought I heard someone running up those imaginary stairs between the kitchen and the solarium."

Kinsey grimaced, scowling at the electrical box. "Come on," he said, heading for the stairs.

Reaching the kitchen they paused a moment to listen, but heard no sounds except voices from the parlor. Kinsey led the way out the kitchen door into the back yard.

❧

The overcast had backed off to a loftier spot in the sky apropos for plopping fat rain pellets on unsuspecting passersby which Jet and Kinsey discovered as they emerged from the overhang above the kitchen steps.

"Let's make a trip around the outside of the house." Kinsey had to figure out what was going on but couldn't decide if it came from within or without. "Look for how someone could get in or out and not be seen."

Moving quickly from the back stoop through the herb garden with its brick pathways and onto the lawn surrounding the castle, Kinsey observed the construction protrusions along the exterior of the mansion. Foundation shrubs obscured the groundwork in most locations although lights from the basement where Kinsey had observed the electrical box were reflected in patches on the lawn.

"Do you think someone is making things happen?" Jet scrambled after him.

"I know someone is," Kinsey declared with more certainty than he felt.

"But why?"

Still possessing the flashlight, he extinguished the beam. "I could make a few guesses." He stopped to peer into the darkness where he had seen the individual previously.

Jet paused beside him and whispered, "Do you think someone is trying to get rid of us?"

"That's one possibility."

They made their way to the south terrace as the lights of a car rounded the bend and headed toward the garages.

"A sports car," Jet breathed, "It looks like . . . ." She stopped, staring. "Roger's Mercedes."

Kinsey turned, catching the wide-eyed expression on her face. "What would he be doing here?"

Jet shook her head.

They continued their reconnaissance across the south end and on to the circular drive. Rain pellets made Jet's hair look like a moussed alpaca. Kinsey wiped the water from his eyes.

"What's that?" Jet pointed to a square object sitting on the edge of the fountain.

Kinsey examined what appeared to be a cage or wire trap.

"There's another one." Jet pointed to the concrete bench near the driveway. "Maybe someone brought the birds in those."

"Someone's pulling a stunt," he mumbled. Okay, if that's the deal I can handle it. "Come on."

Continuing to the north end of the house, they crossed the terrace and reentered through the solarium. Kinsey could hear the door chime and voices from the parlor he didn't recognize. Following the sound they went from the dining hall into the front room. At the door stood Agent Elaney and Roger Thompson.

Roger formatted his face to a smile. "Playing hide and seek in the rain?"

"Just seek," Kinsey grumbled. "Someone else did the hide."

A sociable seagull dropped in front of them and ran around in a circle. Elaney frowned at Kinsey, glancing at Jet with lifted brows. "Pets?"

"Hardly," Kinsey huffed. "We're having an adventure." Kinsey explained the lights and Jet the birds.

Agent Elaney appeared confused. "Are the two people you mentioned earlier here?"

Kinsey turned to Jet. "See if Billy and Susannah can come down to talk with Mr. Elaney?"

She frowned at him, but left on her errand.

"I'll send them to the library." Kinsey motioned toward the double doors across the room. "Do you want to speak to anyone else?"

"How about your sister and your friend?"

"Nathan's right there," Kinsey pointed to where he stood by the fireplace, coaxing a seagull from the mantel.

He made a preemptory dive for the gull. It leaped to an end table nearby. "Gotcha," he cried grabbing the bird by its legs. The seagull let out a fierce squeal and pecked at him, but Nathan held on. "What can I do for you?" he asked as he headed for the anteroom to put the gull out.

"Agent Elaney wants to talk to you."

Once they had disappeared into the library Kinsey turned to Roger. "What brings you here?"

Roger drew himself up to his full height, putting him eye to eye with Kinsey. "I heard you were having problems."

Kinsey snorted, "That's an understatement. How did you know?"

"I'm not talking about tonight. I wanted to be sure you didn't go digging into walls without checking to be sure it wouldn't pull the support out from under the house."

A whole raft of caustic replies sailed Kinsey's direction. Instead he asked, "Were you around when that renter was electrocuted?" Roger's alarmed expression made him instantly suspect.

However he retrieved his nonchalance. "Not really, but I heard some things." He leveled a warning glance at Kinsey. "He had started taking the electrical box apart. Another good reason not to fool around with things you know nothing about."

Kinsey ignored the uninvited admonition. He wasn't backing off that easy. "We're having electrical problems again tonight."

Roger appeared bored with the irrelevance of it. "What's the deal with the birds?"

"You tell me," Kinsey huffed. He watched Roger exit, wondering what inspired his visit. Could he be involved with the lights and birds?

&

When Agent Elaney released Nathan from the library, Kinsey hailed him. "Come on let's get these birds out of here."

The two went on a feather-flying rampage chasing gulls, snatching them off their perches on plate rails and mantels, scooping them off the furniture. When they had expelled half a dozen and ceased to find any more they retired to the sofas near the fireplace.

Kinsey ran his hand through his hair. He needed to process, but things kept moving too fast. What was the significance of the evening's events? Someone had planned this little charade. But who? And why?

"What did that agent want from you?" Kinsey retained a hostile suspicion regarding the Secret Service.

"Name, rank, and serial number." Nathan flopped his feet over the arm of the sofa. "He asked some questions about you, the house and your dad."

Kinsey scowled. "What about the money the kids found?"

"He asked, but all I knew was what I heard from you."

Nathan gazed at the painting above the fireplace. "I got the impression finding counterfeit money here didn't come as a big surprise."

Kinsey followed Nathan's gaze to the English hunting scene. "What do you mean by that?"

Nathan shifted his glance to Kinsey. "His questions assumed the existence of counterfeiters. All he needed to know was which of the group he ought to suspect."

"Great," Kinsey growled. "As if a body in the garden isn't enough. By the way, where did Sarkis go?" Kinsey glanced around the room without setting his eyes on the lieutenant.

As if summoned, Lieutenant Sarkis came through the anteroom door his hair damp, raindrops beaded on the shoulders of his jacket. Pulling a parlor chair over from the arrangement near the staircase, he sat down. "Did you find the cages?"

Kinsey nodded and explained his sojourn with Jet.

Lieutenant Sarkis grimaced. "Did you handle them?"

"Briefly."

"I'm taking them with me," the lieutenant declared, removing a handkerchief from his pocket. He wiped his face and patted the top of his head.

"Do you think this deal tonight is significant?" Kinsey felt frazzled from the constant bombardment of unexplained events.

"Everything's significant," the lieutenant barked, favoring Kinsey with reproachful scrutiny.

He noticed Jet descending the stairs escorting Susannah, Evana, and Billy.

"I'll be back in the morning," the lieutenant informed them.

"Do I need to be here?" Kinsey figured if he didn't get some work done at the office it would end up his final resting place.

"Not unless I find something." Lieutenant Sarkis put his chair back and let himself out of the house.

Chapter Fourteen

Kinsey was on a roll tabulating a column of figures when the jingling of his phone made him lose his place. Grumbling he grabbed the receiver.

Lieutenant Sarkis barked in his ear, "Who's been digging around your trees?"

Kinsey still saw pillars of numbers.

"I came out here today," the lieutenant explained in his modulated tone of patience, "and found a new mound of dirt a few feet from the other."

"I know nothing about it."

Sarkis' voice mocked, "You know so little about this place it makes one wonder if you actually live here."

"You were there last night," Kinsey snapped. "Who had time to be digging?"

"Who says it was last night?" The lieutenant's voice was pregnant with insinuation.

Abandoning his column of numbers, Kinsey mentally walked through the estate. "There'd been no digging on Sunday when I checked."

"So who's been around since you saw it?"

Roger Thompson immediately popped onto Kinsey's mental monitor, but he wasn't hot to sic the law on him without cause. "Is there a hole?"

"Not now. It's all covered up again."

"I know nothing about it." What more could he say?

"I'm getting forensics out here." The lieutenant didn't sound pleased.

Kinsey sighed. "Do you want me to come?"

"Bring your lunch."

Kinsey hung up wondering when it would ever end. He might have been better off to . . . no, that wouldn't make any difference. No way around it, if he wanted the property he would have to pay the price, whatever that meant. Kinsey stared at his column of numbers without seeing them. His earlier reconnaissance although creating suspicion in his mind offered nothing in the way of recent burial. Anything he saw would have been in the tree garden for years, which meant someone had disturbed the area after the body was removed. But who? And when?

By 11:15, too anxious to accomplish anything, Kinsey left for an early lunch. The clouds managed the sky, allowing a peak at the sun from time to time, making the day seem warmer than it actually was, much better for digging holes than the night before.

Kinsey swung by Burger King and picked up a whopper and fries. Proceeding from Gravelly Lake Drive he saw the lieutenant's SUV and another vehicle parked near the tree garden. Apprehension hailed him as he pulled his BMW in behind them.

The lieutenant stood beside an oblong hole some feet from where the previous grave had been. "What does this look like to you?"

Kinsey shoved his hands into his pockets. "A hole in the ground."

"It was another grave." Lieutenant Sarkis fastened his gaze on Kinsey's face.

"How do you know?" Kinsey surveyed the expanse of earth searching for evidence of their find. "Was there another body?"

"No," the lieutenant conceded. Nodding his head in the direction of the forensics van, he added, "But there's evidence one had been here."

What did that mean? Kinsey frowned. "So where is it?"

"That's what I'd like to know." The lieutenant's tone accused Kinsey of playing skeleton hide and seek.

"I know nothing about it." He felt like he'd been caught with a smoking gun.

The lieutenant shrugged. "I'm getting a team in here to dig up this whole place."

Kinsey opened his mouth to protest.

"You got a problem with that?" Sarkis eyed him over the rim of his spectacles.

"It's not my property . . . yet."

"Then tell your dad or whoever owns it." The lieutenant turned toward the van, then back. "I'll get a court order if that's what it takes."

Walking back to his car, Kinsey called his father's cell phone. "Dad, there are more problems here." He explained the lieutenant's project.

"Let him do whatever he wants." Park's voice sounded resigned. "They found another body?"

"No." Kinsey sighed. "Just evidence there'd been one buried here."

"Which is even worse," Park grumbled. "They'll think we're moving it around."

"Yep." Kinsey realized that was exactly what the lieutenant thought.

"Let them dig up the whole thing. We'll never get rid of them otherwise."

Returning to the hole in the ground Kinsey informed Lieutenant Sarkis there was no objection to his digging. "But let me know before you dig anywhere else."

That turned on a light bulb. Sarkis wheeled on Kinsey. "Are there other places this could happen?"

Kinsey took a minute to think. "Other garden plots, but the plants are much closer together. It wouldn't be as easy to bury a body."

"You'd better tell me about them."

Kinsey explained the locations of the rose beds, the rhododendron and formal gardens.

"Okay, we'll take a look. If there's no sign of disturbance we'll leave them alone."

"I'd appreciate that." Kinsey didn't have money in his budget for a new landscape. "Maybe it's buried money. That Secret Service Agent could have been trying to find more counterfeit money."

The reproving look in Sarkis' piercing eyes shot down Kinsey's hope, admonishing him for trying to divert his attention. Kinsey resigned himself to the inevitability of more dead bodies on the property.

☙

Jet was tired, finding concentration on her work difficult. The previous night's falderal had inspired her imagination with a hurly-burly of disturbing possibilities parading Technicolor through her dreams. Feeling she had already put in a full day's work, she was concerned for

Kinsey who appeared stuck in a pot with the heat rising. All his efforts to salvage the family estate from infamy only shoved it further down the road to ill repute. Continual exposure had increased her respect for him; even worse she had begun to adopt his concerns.

Captured by an unexpected flash of guilt, Jet could hear her mother's admonition. "Honey, you need to be careful. Men just take advantage of you." What did that mean . . . exactly?

Had Roger profited from Mona? He had married her, put his name on Jet's birth certificate without even knowing if she was his daughter. Who had taken advantage of whom?

Reflecting on her belligerent responses to Kinsey's gallantry, Jet realized she was behaving like her mother. Did she really want to do that? What was the feminist thing about anyway? Equality with men? Mona never pretended equality. She considered herself infinitely superior. On the other hand Jet didn't feel superior, just different, maybe even complementary. Even as the idea passed through her mind, she felt a traitor's guilt. Mona would have squashed her in a verbal corner over a thought like that. Complementary implied working together using different abilities, strengths and weaknesses. As far as Mona was concerned men had all the weaknesses and women all the strengths. Men were only fit to be dominated, but with subtlety of course. Mona certainly did it with finesse. One thing Jet did not doubt, she had no finesse where men were concerned.

Jangling of the phone pulled her back from her reverie to the work on her desk. Plodding through the loan papers in front of her, she watched the tellers trim the Christmas tree, looking forward to the holidays with more enthusiasm than she had in a long time.

Possessed by the romantic spirit of the season Jet detoured to the mall where she found Macy's Holiday Lane a magical inspiration and purchased decorations for her suite.

Turning off Gravelly Lake Drive on her way to the mansion, she contemplated Christmas with undefined hopes soaring into the space beyond reality. A new gathering of police cars and ominous white vans canon-balled the spirit right out of her. What was going on now?

Following the lane she passed several squad cars, the coroner's van, a white panel truck and an SUV to park in the circular driveway where she unloaded her purchases.

Latte, looking like a Highland Barbie with a braid-trimmed apron over her miniskirt, was in the anteroom when Jet opened the door. "What's the deal now?"

Latte shrugged, snatching her son's backpack off the floor before Jet could stumble on it. "Apparently they found another burial site."

Sounds like the family graveyard," Jet grumbled as she deposited her packages on the deacon's bench near the door.

"The family better say something or the police will dig up all the relatives."

"Maybe they could dig me up a father," Jet mumbled to herself.

"I heard that," Latte declared with a laugh. "What did you buy?"

Allowing Latte a peek into her shopping bags, Jet explained her impulsive trip to the mall. Latte offered to transport Jet's things to her suite while she put away the car.

A movement caught Jet's eye as she crossed from the garage to the rose garden, hardly more than a shadow against the hedge; perhaps the breeze in one of the arborvitae scattered among the roses. However, another movement as if someone passed through the opposite corner of the shrubbery caught her attention. Anyone heading to the house from the garages wouldn't go that way. With considerable misgivings she moved to the corner of the rose garden where she had seen the movement. A strategically positioned shrub covered a small opening in the boxwood hedge. Pausing by it, she looked toward the road running along the lake. A man was just disappearing into the greenery that bordered the driveway on the far side. While searching for a sheltered observation spot she heard the start up of an engine and moved to a cluster of escallonia in time to watch a dark panel truck pull onto the lake road heading for Gravelly Lake Drive.

Although she intended to mention the incident to Kinsey it flew out of her mind the moment she stepped into the parlor and spotted the Secret Service agent. He stood near the dining room doors looking as if he had just been beamed aboard the Starship Enterprise. Finding Lieutenant Sarkis roaming around the house in search of evidence had become an accepted nuisance. Jet wasn't ready to accede to the Secret Service as if they would find counterfeit money in the cookie jar.

After glancing his direction, she dismissed him, continuing to the staircase. But as she reached the grand piano he hailed her, "Ms. Sayre."

Jet turned to face the deep, commanding voice.

"I'd like to ask you a few questions."

What would she know the Secret Service would be interested in?

The agent's dark eyes challenged her reluctance.

"Maybe we could go in there." He pointed to the library where he had held his inquisition the night before.

Since she had not been previously subjected to interrogation Jet realized it must be her turn. He followed as she diverted her steps toward the dark room.

Switching on the antique chandelier, Agent Elaney pointed to the fan-back chair near the fireplace. "Sit down." Taking a seat in the purple velvet chair, he continued, "Kinsey mentioned you've seen someone in the landscaping around the mansion."

Surprised at his beginning Jet nodded.

"Could you tell me about it?"

She took a deep breath. "Actually I think I just saw someone in the rose garden heading toward the driveway when I came from the garage."

"Just now?"

Jet nodded.

Elaney sprang from his chair and left the room.

Shocked by his reaction Jet gazed through bay windows across the room where the sliver of moon made a shimmering path on the water. It sent a shiver of premonition through her.

Within five minutes the agent returned to take his chair. Given the few moments to recall times she saw someone Jet related succinctly her observations and concerns.

"You're convinced Kinsey Sayre is on the level?" Agent Elaney aimed his dark eyes at her with an intensity that induced her to carefully control her facial expressions. "He's not running something on the side and covering it up with all this rental stuff."

A flash of anger on Kinsey's behalf attacked Jet. "What sense would that make?"

Agent Elaney raised an eyebrow.

"Kinsey wants to clear the house's reputation so he can own it. His father wants to demolish it because of all the problems."

"Maybe he's part of the problems." The agent widened his eyes. "Someone here is producing counterfeit money."

"And you think it's Kinsey?" Jet felt helpless rage at her inability to deflect the agent's suspicions.

"I have to consider the possibility." The Secret Service agent settled back in his chair with a sigh.

She took a deep breath, making an effort to control her defensiveness. "What do you mean by here?"

"Lakewood."

She frowned. "Why settle on this estate?"

"The money the two boys found was here." Agent Elaney changed his tactic. "You're name is Sayre. You're related?"

Jet nodded. "Cousins." Did that nullify her defense?

Agent Elaney crossed his arms and chewed on his fingernail. "It's possible in spite of the owner's best efforts something is going on here."

"Kinsey figures that's the case and intends to find out what." Glancing apprehensively at the agent she explained the light show, the birds, what had happened in the past, the dead renters, and the house's bad reputation. She also told Agent Elaney about the extra space that couldn't be found, the noises in the walls and the missing stairway. When he left she figured she had sunk Kinsey's boat.

ও

Returning to the castle after work Kinsey found the courtyard full of vehicles again forcing him to return to

Gravelly Lake and circle the property to the garages. A glance at his car clock told him he was on the point of being late for dinner. Did the police never eat?

Approaching the terrace he noticed through the undraped windows lights on in the library and Jet seated with the Secret Service agent.

After dropping his coat and briefcase off in his suite Kinsey returned to the main floor as Jet and Agent Elaney emerged. The expression on Jet's face worried him. With a nod to Kinsey, Elaney departed.

"Had you on the hot seat?"

Jet grimaced. "I might have told him too much." She explained her defense of Kinsey and the additional information she had donated.

They walked together toward the dining room.

"Don't worry about it." Kinsey felt vaguely pleased at her concern for him. "They're better off with the truth. I wouldn't know what to hide if everything in my life screamed 'guilty'."

"Why don't you guys get in here so we can eat?" Nathan barked from the table where everyone was seated except for Jet and Kinsey.

After taking their places Kinsey said the grace, refraining from any reference to the day's events making no explanation of the continued presence of the police. When someone broached the subject he parried it with denial of any information.

"What is everyone doing for Christmas?" Nathan took a visual survey.

"Do you think we could have a Christmas party?" Latte suggested.

"A real party," Susannah qualified it, "not on Christmas Eve or Day."

"Before the last few days," Latte added. "I need to go to California for the actual event."

After glancing at Evana who nodded, Kinsey said, "I'll let you girls plan it." He had to choreograph ravaging the interior walls.

After dinner he withdrew to his suite where he perched on the chaise and telephoned his father.

A moment of silence occupied the other end of the line. "Kinsey, this isn't going to work." His father sounded frustrated. "Things just get worse and worse."

Kinsey exploded, "That's not my fault, Dad. You gave me six months. It's just been one. Give me a chance."

Park sighed. "I'm afraid the police aren't going to give you one."

"Let me worry about them."

"Don't be a fool. They'll make trouble for all of us. You don't own the house yet. I'm still the one who has to pay the price."

"The price of what, Dad?" Kinsey stared across the room. "Do you know something about this you're not talking about?" He made no effort to keep the accusation out of his voice.

"I know nothing except things will continue to get worse."

"I can deal with it," Kinsey declared. "Eventually we'll figure it out."

"Okay, deal with it." His father sounded as if he were tossing his checkbook off the bridge.

A big help that was; obviously his father had no answers.

Chapter Fifteen

Lieutenant Sarkis shucked Kinsey out of bed before his eyes could open on their own, informing him the police had returned with a forensics crew. Kinsey told them to do whatever they wanted, turn it into a cemetery, build a shopping center, construct a skyscraper, what the heck! What could he do about it anyway? But don't kill the rhodies, he made his illogical plea.

Back in the house he fixed a bowl of cereal, grabbed one of Nathan's rolls, and retired to the library. Seeking a clue to the skeleton he found, Kinsey examined the former renter's paperwork in detail, entertaining little optimism. From the rental applications he made a list of references and family members.

What had the police done to search for Carmen Markovich? Had they contacted these people?

On the first renter's application Harvey Brittmeier listed his mother, his sister, and a friend. The second renter held more promise. For personal references they had listed a previous landlord, their banker—presumably not for financial information—and Carmen's sister, Rosa. Since

Markovich could have pulled off a list as long as his arm what was the significance of those he chose? In addition, Kinsey noted a different individual as his in case of emergency person, a woman's name, designated a friend. That might be worth looking into—although the police probably thought so too.

Kinsey figured his father may know what, if anything, the police had investigated. Pestering Park wasn't his favorite diversion, especially since the man resembled a zombie.

As Kinsey gathered up his paperwork a rap on the doorframe interrupted him. *Oh joy*, Lieutenant Sarkis. The grim set of his jaw and the way his eyebrows drew together over the glinting accusation in his eyes pushed Kinsey's stomach to his throat making it difficult to invite him in. "So what did you find?" Kinsey croaked, not that he had any burning desire to know.

The lieutenant perched on the edge of the settee, squinting at Kinsey's pile of paperwork.

Should he plead his innocence now or wait until charged. "Did you find another body?"

"That's a good question." The lieutenant aimed his laser eyes at Kinsey. "We found two halves of a body, or bodies."

"What does that mean?" Kinsey held his breath.

Lieutenant Sarkis folded his hands, staring at the ceiling as if in prayer. "We have two holes in your rhododendron garden. In one was an upper torso skeleton and head of a body in the other was the lower torso and legs."

"Of one body?" Kinsey frowned.

Davy Sarkis shrugged. "One would presume, although at this point I couldn't guarantee it."

Lord, have mercy, Kinsey thought and meant it. "How did it die?"

"Cracked skull." Lieutenant Sarkis scrutinized him over the top of his spectacles. "You couldn't guess who this might be?"

Kinsey shook his head, unable to conjure up a word in his defense.

"Would your father?"

Horrors, I hope not, Kinsey grimaced, recalling his own doubts about his father. "You'd have to ask him."

"Have you seen anyone around those areas?"

"I've seen people I don't think belong on the property but I don't know who they are or where they come from. Others reported the same thing."

After jotting a few notes in his little book Lieutenant Sarkis left.

Kinsey stacked his paperwork, slid it into a manila envelope, and took it to his suite. After snagging a jacket and his list of references he headed for the garage. The breeze pushed leaves across the lawn like a broom. No longer intermittent the clouds had closed gaps where blue sky showed, reneging on its promise of a lovely day. He drove to the north end where the Barnes' house overlooked the bay. With no trees or buildings to obstruct its path the breeze had morphed into a full-blown wind, sending a shiver up his spine. He parked in front of the garages and entered the house from the side door to the kitchen.

"Welcome home stranger," Aunt Pat greeted him with a hug.

"Is Dad around?"

"In the study."

Saluting his aunt Kinsey left the kitchen and cut through the foyer. Perched on a straight back chair facing the library table where he had spread an arrangement of papers, his father greeted him with a frown.

"The police found another body." Kinsey didn't see any point in sneaking up on the problem.

Park straightened his back as if bracing for a blow. "Where?"

"With the rhododendrons." Kinsey settled into a chair next to the bookcases. "Although the lieutenant thinks it was in the tree garden to begin and moved . . . recently."

Park abandoned his paperwork to scowl at his son. "Who would move it?"

"Who would put it there?" Kinsey figured first things first.

A shadow passed over Park's face. "Do they know who it is?"

"It may be they," Kinsey barked, venting his frustration then adding what enlightenment he had received. "I get the feeling you know more about this than you're saying."

Park shook his head. "I know nothing at all."

His assurances did little to mitigate Kinsey's concern. He took out his list of references from the application. "Do you know if the police went through the renter's paperwork?"

"They questioned me about the applications a few years ago when they were looking for Carmen."

"Did they speak to any of these people?" Kinsey waved his list.

Park lifted his shoulders. "Carmen's sister came to see me about the house, closing it up and removing things that belonged to the Markovichs."

"Is she the one who signed for their possessions?"

"No." Park sighed. "She only took her sister's personal things. Someone else came and got the valuable stuff. A banker, I believe."

"The one on the application?" Kinsey realized he had forgotten to cross check the one who signed for Markovich's possessions with names on the application.

"I suppose. I wasn't thinking about it at the time."

What had his father been thinking about at the time? "Have you seen Carmen's sister since?"

Park stared at Kinsey with a troubled look on his face.

"She couldn't be the other one buried on the property?"

Park waged his head, looking as if he'd opened a can of tuna and found worms. "I called her when the police told me it was Carmen in that grave." He ran his hand through his hair. "I didn't think it was good for her to hear it from them." He returned to his documents, moving papers from one stack to another.

Observing his father, Kinsey contemplated possibilities that could render his father so tight-lipped. Perhaps what he thought was fear and superstition about the house was actually something else. But what?

The day passed tranquilly with the usual boisterous family gathering for dinner. His cousin Jordan's daughters teased Kinsey while little Aunt Tansy pestered him about getting married and having kids of his own. Kinsey caught Evana's attention on him as he parried these remarks. Her expression gave him cause to ponder her state of mind, but decided a head in the sand beat sock in the eye.

After dinner, Kinsey crossed into the kitchen searching for his aunt who was unloading the dishwasher.

"You leaving?" she asked him.

"Yeah," he said. "What's with Evana? She's been giving me the hairy eyeball."

Pat put her hands on her hips. "That young woman adopted a false premise and is trying to fit the world into her hypothesis."

Kinsey raised an interrogative brow.

Pat removed another armload of dishes from the dishwasher. "She lost her husband, her love and she is trying to put everyone else in the same boat."

Kinsey followed Pat into the caramel-colored dining room. "I haven't lost any love."

"That girl you were dating a couple years ago."

"Good grief! That was a stupid infatuation. If she's going to . . ." Kinsey couldn't finish the sentence the idea was so preposterous.

"What's this about Jessica?" His aunt shot him a searching glance.

"Evana seems to have taken a dislike to Jet."

"You need to watch your step young man. She is a cute little thing."

"And about as accommodating as a briar patch."

Aunt Pat laughed as he said goodnight, but Kinsey noted the look of concern in her eyes. What the heck was the matter with everyone? Couldn't a person be friends with his cousin without the world making a big stink about it?

❧

Jet's eyes popped open as the sun peeped over the horizon, not that early in December. As she opened the curtains to invite the sunlight in she noticed Anatuviak galloping across the driveway chasing a silver cat. Moving to the south windows, she noticed Nathan's bright red hair as he came from the rose garden carrying a baker's box and grocery bag.

After gathering her laundry she descended to the grand parlor where quiet reigned. In the kitchen she found Nathan and Billy frying eggs and bacon.

Recalling the police intention to excavate the additional gardens searching for a second body, she wondered what would they conclude if they failed to find one? On the other hand what if they did? She figured Kinsey's goose was stuffed and baked regardless. His efforts to clear the mansion's reputation boomeranged on a daily basis.

She pushed her anxiety for Kinsey's problems out of her mind, not wishing to delve into what motivated her concern. She figured it more appropriate to concentrate on nailing down the identity of her father.

When she returned to check on the progress of her laundry Jet met Latte regarding the occupation of the washer and dryer with chagrin.

"I need to do some shopping," she declared. "Would you mind keeping an eye on the kids while I'm gone? They'd be as useful as a pile of ants."

"Sure," Jet agreed. "If you're leaving right away, I can start your clothes when I'm done."

Contemplating her options, Jet gazed out the arched windows to where a trio of young maples bowed in deference to the wind. She had noticed Lieutenant Sarkis in the library with Kinsey as she crossed the parlor. What black beast had he brought this time? Jet vacillated between caustic irritation, grudging respect and empathy for Kinsey. She preferred to be indifferent.

Although skeptical of her mother's attitude Jet could not help but be affected by it. Having been taught self-sufficiency and the irresponsibility of men she struggled with Kinsey's gentlemanly assistance. He treated her like some fragile china doll, a dangerous enticement. Something she needed to resist at all cost.

More blustery than cold, the wind propelled moisture in a fine spray when Jet went to check on the twins. Braving the spitting breeze, she located the boys chasing Anatuviak around the empty fountain pool. Scattered about were concrete planters empty now of their summer blooms.

Waving to her, the boys came running.

"We found something," Landon shouted.

"Yeah, over there by the trees." Logan pointed in the direction of the escallonia edging the lawn.

Jet frowned, wrapping her arms around herself against the breeze. "What sort of thing?"

"I'll show you." Landon waved a come-on. The two boys took off for the brick patio that lay in the shelter of the balustrade. Halting abruptly near an Alberta spruce, he indicated an urn-shaped planter.

"There, look at that." Logan pointed at an oblong black object.

Jet studied the item without picking it up.

"What's a remote control doing out here?" Landon demanded, lifting his palms.

Although resembling a television remote, variations convinced Jet it was not. "Don't touch it. I'll talk to Kinsey. It might be important."

Both boys took a deep breath, standing a little taller.

"Don't move it. It may be important for Kinsey to see where you found it." She glanced at the threatening sky. "If it starts to really rain, you need to come back to the house, okay?"

They both nodded.

Considering the object lying in the urn, Jet figured she would tell Kinsey when she returned to the house. However, he was not on the lower floor and when she knocked at the door of his suite she received no answer.

Chapter Sixteen

Unable to make contact with Lieutenant Sarkis on the weekend Kinsey had left a message. Just after arriving at work Monday, Kinsey got a phone call from him. "So what's up?"

Kinsey explained the object Jet had shown him the night before.

The lieutenant's deep sigh was audible. "I'll drop by your castle at lunch?"

Just before noon, Kinsey got his car and headed to Gravelly Lake.

He found the lieutenant's SUV in the circular drive as before, but noticed him approaching from the north end of the mansion. "I took another look at your rhododendron garden. I didn't want to miss anything."

"Or anyone?" Kinsey frowned. Crummy to think the police suspected buried bodies all over his property. "Why don't I show you what we found?"

The lieutenant followed Kinsey into the grand parlor where he parked on the piano bench and picked at the keys while Kinsey went for the remote. Opening his handkerchief, Kinsey spread it on top of the piano, displaying the oblong black object.

"What makes you think it's not for a television?"

"The buttons are different. How would you operate the TV with this?"

Using the handkerchief Lieutenant Sarkis picked it up. "You said something about having problems with the lights." He looked around the grand parlor, his gaze moving from one fixture to another. "This looks like a remote to control electrical fixtures."

A pop-up in Kinsey's mind gave him an idea. "You mean someone could use this to turn lights on and off?"

The lieutenant narrowed his eyes. "It would take more than just this to accomplish that."

"Like what?"

Sarkis shrugged. "A module. Something this signals to operate the appliance."

"Could that explain weird light sequences?"

The lieutenant shot Kinsey a suspicious glance. "Have you found something like that?"

"Not yet." He hadn't been looking for that. It put a new task on his list.

"Check your outlets, especially where your lamps plug in."

Perhaps the lighting mystery had a simple solution. Kinsey chastised himself. Why didn't he think of that?

"I'm surprised they didn't find anything when your renter died." Sarkis' expression accused Kinsey of holding out on him.

Kinsey grimaced. The lieutenant had a point. How could Markovich have been persecuted by electrical nonsense, die trying to rectify it, and yet no evidence be found?

"I'll look around. Maybe someone removed it before the emergency people arrived." He sighed. "I'll talk to Dad, too."

Lieutenant Sarkis looked down his long nose at Kinsey, a likely-story expression on his face. "And let me know?" It wasn't a question, but an order.

"Of course," Kinsey mumbled, who else would I tell? Keep it a secret just to annoy you?

ↁ

Invasion by the Pineapple Express drove police persecution underground for the next few days. Driving rain and the wild swirling wind would have made forensics' poking around the mansion's grounds tantamount to setting up camp on a quagmire in a hurricane. Five inches of rain fell in 48 hours making Kinsey wonder if they were going to wash out to sea for real. Lakes had formed in the low spots in the landscaping and a river of watershed ran in the ditch along the road. Had it made puddles of the open graves in his gardens? He had neither sufficient curiosity nor willingness to brave the elements to check. With his luck the rain would wash away the soil and uncover another set of bones.

The girls had planned a Christmas Party for the following night, coercing the guys into name drawing for gifts. Having gotten Latte's name Kinsey considered it strategic to consult Jet regarding a gift. Assuming she had arrived home ahead of him he knocked on her door.

Still dressed in her skirt and boots, she recovered her initial surprise with a smile. "What can I do for you?"

"I drew Latte's name and am looking for suggestions."

Jet opened her door wider. "I brought home Chinese if you haven't eaten yet. Latte is taking the boys out for pizza." When Kinsey hesitated she added, "I have more than enough."

"I drew Nathan's name." She said as she led him to the kitchen. "Have you any suggestions?"

Kinsey sighed. "I could come up with a few, although you might not want to be the giver." Noting her expression, Kinsey added, "Not so bad as that. Nathan's looking for a woman."

"Latte's not looking for a man, but it probably wouldn't hurt her to find one." Jet set out plates and utensils then took the boxes out of a sack.

An idea popped into Kinsey's mind. "How about sending them on a date? We could get them each a ticket to something."

She raised her eyebrows, considering the idea.

"The Pantages has a big Christmas night with music and comedians. How about that?" She handed him soda and a glass with ice.

"Perfect, I can get the tickets tomorrow." Kinsey poured soda into the ice. "Agent Elaney found more money here."

Jet paused in filling her plate. "In the same place as before?"

"Apparently." Kinsey sighed as he helped himself to the Chinese food. "That reminds me, how about doing a house hunt with me?"

"What for?" Jet handed him the remaining steamed rice on which he dumped the extra princess chicken.

"Something for the remote control you found to signal." Kinsey visually checked out the outlets along the tile in her kitchen.

When they finished Jet stacked the empty boxes and put them back in the sack. Before leaving the suite, they agreed to meet again in an hour.

Kinsey started on the third floor. Ascending the stairs between his suite and Jet's, he examined the outlets in the area at the top of the stairs, but found nothing.

He accosted Nathan returning to his room and together they searched, also unsuccessfully. From there Kinsey went to Evana's where she greeted him in surprise when he knocked on her door.

On the third floor her suite occupied a section of the house from front to back, containing a plethora of nooks and crannies with angled ceilings and jutting walls.

Following Kinsey as he searched, Evana said, "You seem to have made a hit with Jet." It was an accusation not a compliment.

Kinsey frowned, glancing at his sister. "What are you trying to say?" Evasive insinuations annoyed him.

"She has a fascination for you, always following you around, running to you for advice, looking to you for assistance."

Kinsey paused in his examination of outlets near her marble fireplace and scowled at Evana. He figured her comment wasn't even worth a reply. He started for the kitchen.

Her voice pursued him. "Come on, Kinsey. She's always there doing things for you, goes to church with you, tags along after you. It's plain to see she has a thing for you."

Kinsey turned to face Evana. "I invited Jet to church. I invited her to come and eat with me the other night. I asked her to help me with the tree decorations. If anything I have a thing for her."

Color drained from Evana's face. "Do you?"

"Don't be silly," Kinsey barked, "she's my cousin. What's it to you anyway?"

Evana opened her mouth then shut it again. "Nothing."

While he continued along the perimeter of Evana's suite, Kinsey battled his frustration. What had Aunt Pat said? Evana worked to fit the world into her mold because she had lost her love. Kinsey recalled his sister's inconsolable grief at the death of her husband and times when the family had worried about her health, physical, then mental. He had to concede her husband had been a great guy, but not the only one in the world surely. Perhaps he should dissuade Nathan from pursuing Latte or Susannah and encourage him with Evana.

Considering what Aunt Pat had said, Kinsey battled Evana's perception regarding Carol. When he reached the door he confronted his sister.

"When did you ever date anyone else with such intensity?" Evana leaned against her wing back chair and crossed her arms. "She dumped you, remember?"

With the vague sense he was stepping on his own feet, Kinsey retorted, "I was lucky to get out of that deal." He shuddered at the thought. "I want a real relationship. I'm not sure what she wanted. Obviously not me."

Finding no electrical devices in Evana's room, he would have liked to complete the perusal of the third floor by tackling the balcony and tower room. However, no access was available from this location.

જી

Jet made a systematic examination of the walls and outlets in her rooms before leaving. Assuming Kinsey would check his own she eyed the walls in the hall as she continued to the boy's bedroom. Aware they were out with their mother, Jet examined their space, picking up stray toys and articles of clothing.

Waiting for Latte to return before inspecting her suite, Jet knocked on Susannah's door. "Kinsey and I are searching for some funny electrical thing, checking everyone's rooms."

Susannah lifted an eyebrow and cocked her head, but opened the door wider. "Come in." She wore black leggings and a long purple sweater with her feet tucked into a pair of fluffy white slippers. Her four poster bed looked like the clearance table for an after Christmas sale with tinsel garlands, candles, and silk poinsettias. "I thought we needed more decorating for the party tomorrow."

Jet smiled realizing Christmas decorating gave her a rush of optimism. Mona had been more interested in New Years Eve, leaving Jet with a sitter or alone. The one time her mother took her on a New Years Eve bash convinced Jet to be happy at home alone.

"Go ahead and look." Susannah moved back into the room. "I bought some mistletoe," she announced as if declaring a *coup d'etat*. Her eyebrows danced. "Where do you think I should put it?" Pushing her Christmas purchases aside she bounced onto her bed.

"Depends on what you want to accomplish." Jet moved from one outlet to another figuring she could guess.

"Where it gets some action of course." Susannah's giggle contained a trace of resolve.

"Did you have someone particular in mind?" Jet paused to glance at her.

Susannah's hesitation belied her mumbled, "Not really." Her wistful tone of voice failed to convince Jet of her disinterest.

"It looks like your room is clear. Thanks for letting me look."

As she left Susannah's suite Jet could hear Latte's boys on the grand staircase. She waited for them at the top then announced her task to Latte.

"Come on in," Latte invited. "You guys go get ready for bed."

After describing her search, they perused the suite. Latte agreed to assist as they moved to the far end of the hall. Jet sat on the daybed to look behind it; nothing there. From her initial exploration with Kinsey she recalled a long empty room plus one full of antique furniture on the second floor. However, no access was available from where they stood.

Facing the unbroken west walls Jet suggested, "Let's see if we can get into the other side of this from the morning room."

Taking the back stairs, they crossed through the kitchen and the butler's pantry into the morning room where the filigreed railing of the circular stairway wound to the floor above.

"Why don't you check here and I'll look in the solarium?" Jet opened the double doors into the adjacent room.

As she started her search Jet heard a shriek and the clang of something metal hitting the tiled floor. "What happened?" she called, returning to the morning room where Latte in a heap on the floor pointed toward the stairs. When Jet looked she saw a pair of big black boots disappearing up the staircase.

"Go get him," Latte squealed.

Jet scrambled up the stairs without considering who it might be or what she would do about it if she caught him. Smaller and lighter, she traveled faster than her quarry, but he was continuing to the third floor as she reached the second. She could see black pants above the boots as she clambered up. Before she reached the third floor she heard a click and arriving found no one and nothing.

Standing in the rain on the enclosed balcony where the stairs left off, she turned around and eyed the dark corners. She went to the edge of the brick balustrade and looked over. Too short to see immediately below the wall, she gazed to where the yard lights illuminated the circular driveway. All was quiet.

Returning to the second floor she met Latte on her way up. "Who was it?"

Latte shook her head. "I didn't see him, except his legs and boots. He knocked me down."

"Did you see where he came from?"

"I'd say that little powder room to the right of the stairs. We came through the kitchen and butler's pantry and no one was there. Where did he go?"

"Just disappeared." Jet raised her palms. "He could have gone over the balcony wall, but it's three flights up."

"That's really suspicious. Are you going to tell Kinsey?"

Jet nodded.

"Should we do what we came to do?" Latte suggested.

Once glance indicated there was nothing in the long narrow room in which they stood. Jet led the way into the one adjacent crowded with wall to wall furniture. Upended chairs covered tables; on the brown and white striped sofa small occasional tables sat upside down. Lamps had been corralled in the corner next to a row of headboards and foot pieces. Against the opposite wall box springs and mattresses were stacked.

Initially looking for electrical gadgets, Jet and Latte wandered the periphery through an obstacle course, moving pieces to gain access to an outlet.

Their task completed, Latte began inspecting furniture. "I could use one of these little stands beside my bed."

"Pick one? I'm sure Kinsey wouldn't mind. It's not like you'd be taking it out of the house."

Latte sorted through the collection.

"How about this one?" Jet suggested, pointing to a small apothecary cabinet with two drawers that sat on top of the sofa.

Latte stood back to study it. "I like the looks of this one better." She pointed to a wider one with a single drawer. The wood was lighter and decorated with floral carvings.

"We have to move this to get to that." Jet pointed to a tufted bench upended on a square end table. "Move it over there." She indicated a leaf-printed bergere near a stack of dining chairs.

"We also have to move that table." Latte pointed to the one on which the bench had rested.

Constructed of hardwood it had a lower shelf in addition to the drawer, making it heavier. Moving the end table away from its spot they could hear a rattle from the drawer.

Latte widened her eyes. "What's that?"

After setting it down Jet opened the drawer. For a moment both girls stared.

"Is this what Kinsey was talking about?" Latte lifted one of the half dozen or so square objects from the drawer.

"You'd better not touch it," Jet cautioned. "Fingerprints might be important."

Latte dropped it like a hand buzzer. "What are they?"

"Modules." At least they answered the description Kinsey had given Jet.

Latte took a deep breath. "Shall we get out that little table?"

"Maybe we'd better check it before we do."

Latte opened the drawer, but it was empty. Lifting it out of its resting spot, Latte indicated she could carry it herself if Jet cleared the way.

Stepping out of the room Jet noticed Kinsey on the stairs.

Chapter Seventeen

After completing his investigation of the accessible portion of the third floor Kinsey climbed the circular stairway to the open balcony and inspected the room adjacent. Gray walls with wood slatted ceilings and a single bed tucked under the eaves left the room so sparsely furnished a quick glance ended his search.

Heading for the main floor he heard a door open just as he reached the second. Pausing in the empty room, lit by two hanging lamps reflected in the tall windows to the south, he noticed Jet step out of the adjoining room.

"Did you find anything?" he jumped her as Latte came out carrying a small oblong table upended. A guilty look streaked across her face when she saw Kinsey. "Swiping furniture?" He gave her a fierce scowl.

"Caught." She laughed nervously, her charm bubbling to the surface. "Do you mind?"

He shook his head. "If there's anything in there you can use, help yourself."

Crooking her finger Jet led Kinsey to the end table and opened the drawer, pointing to the stash residing there.

"Whoa," Kinsey was impressed. "I think that's what we're looking for. Too bad it's here. I'm sure they didn't signal it in this drawer."

"You found nothing?" Jet's gray eyes were charcoal in the dim lighting.

Kinsey shook his head.

"Would this be enough to do the whole house?" Latte perched on a nearby wooden rocker.

"Depends where they were located. Careful placement might make it seem the whole house was affected when it was only a few fixtures." Kinsey reached to take one from the drawer then changed his mind. "We'd better leave them and have Sarkis take a look."

Jet pushed the drawer shut with the back of her hand. "Someone knocked Latte down and ran up the stairs when we were in the morning room."

Shocked, Kinsey frowned at Latte. "Where did he go?"

She shook her head.

"I followed him to the third floor but he just disappeared." Jet lifted an open palm.

"Disappeared?"

She nodded. "Unless he jumped over the edge."

"There's a three story drop and nothing to break the fall."

When they had moved the end table to Latte's room, Kinsey spent a moment staring out the west windows of his suite into the dark landscape where rain swept by the yard light in sheets. Watching, he saw someone move through the fan of illumination, head bent against the wind, heading south across the circular driveway. Kinsey concentrated to determine if it was one of his renters. Too short to be Nathan, too trim to be Billy, it could be one of the girls, but he had just left Jet and Latte upstairs.

Who kept crossing the estate at night? Seized by a thought he dashed down the stairs and across the parlor, where he noted Evana seated at the piano. He passed through the library and out the French doors onto the terrace. Stopping for a moment to allow his eyes to adjust, he concentrated on the place where he had last seen the individual heading. Had he gone to the garages? Kinsey caught a glimpse of movement near the rose garden. Keeping an eye on the surrounding area he stepped through an arch in the hedge. Noticing a figure dart into a break in the shrubbery, Kinsey reversed his direction. Leaving the rose garden and circling it toward the drive that ran along the lake, he endeavored to stay in the shadows, moving from one trunk to another of the enormous fir trees. Longer legged than his quarry, he reached a vantage point allowing him a glimpse as the figure crossed the driveway.

Kinsey could see it was a man, considerably shorter and slimmer than himself, moving with the confidence of someone who knew exactly where he was going. Taking off in pursuit, he crossed the drive to the garages where he saw the individual continue to the adjacent lawn. Having delayed his pursuit too long, Kinsey lost the man as he vanished in the bushes.

Although Kinsey followed all he found was a paved turnout, about thirty feet long, ending in another patch of shrubbery. It went nowhere and belonged to no structure to give cause for existence. There was no sign of the individual and although he waited as the night moped with constant rain, he saw and heard nothing.

Soaked to the skin, he continued south for a few more feet where he was confronted by a wooden fence. Although the road went on this was obviously the end of the estate. The adjacent property belonged to someone else. The lights of a residence beyond wavered in the precipitation.

Time to go back and dry off.

⌘

Christmas party preparations were perfectly synchronized when Kinsey descended to the parlor the next morning, each of the girls occupied with a related activity. Even Nathan had been commandeered, standing on a chair in the doorway to the dining room attaching something to a garland swag hanging there. The grin Nathan shot him gave Kinsey all he needed to guess what it was. Nathan could use it to his advantage. Kinsey intended to steer clear.

Susannah and Jet were arranging garland and candles on the mantel while Evana with broom and dustpan swept away stray pine needles. Latte and her boys sat on the rug in front of the arched windows with red and green tissue paper and silver bows wrapping packages.

Although the festival spirit pervading the room beckoned him with heartwarming anticipation, Kinsey clung to his misgivings, certain annoying surprises lay ahead. He put on his rain jacket intending a trip back to the spot he had noticed the night before. Exiting through the library he took the gravel path across a brilliant green lawn.

The storm had taken a break, leaving behind an atmosphere heavy with suspended moisture. The light breeze jiggled branches on the fir trees, spraying him with a wet kiss as he crossed through the rose garden.

Cutting across the garage lane, he used the road instead of the lawn to reach the abandoned driveway. Standing in the middle he rotated a full circle. Surrounded by huckleberry bushes and several smaller western hemlock the space was neatly paved as if intended as a building approach. Across the road the lawn descended to the lake. Kinsey paced the twenty by thirty foot space tossing up ideas then shooting them down in an effort to recall what might have been there in the past.

Abandoning the pavement he circled the shrubbery searching for a clue something had previously resided there besides lawn. At one point he stumbled across a hard spot, which appeared to be rock beneath the surface. However, unless he dug he couldn't be sure, and even then what would it mean? He found a similar spot a distance farther to the south. Footings for a building? But what building? Nothing had ever resided there in his recollection. Would his father know?

He needed to pay another visit to the gentle man who preferred peace and tranquility. Kinsey figured his father was far more involved in the estate mysteries than he acknowledged. Any mention of Carmen Markovich brought on an emotional reaction Kinsey couldn't account for. What was that all about?

Should he interrogate his father rather than have the lieutenant go after him? Kinsey didn't think Lieutenant Sarkis was fooled by Park's reticence and he had ways of learning things unavailable to the laity.

After checking his pockets for keys Kinsey got out his car. Having laid in wait through the morning, rain commenced hostilities as he traveled to downtown Tacoma and Schuster Parkway. Opening with a bombardment of bullet-sized drops then moving to a wall of spray, it reduced visibility to cars immediately surrounding him. The heavy rain and fog ended the world at the edge of Commencement Bay, leaving nothing beyond but the dismal gray reminding Kinsey enough of a white Christmas he sang along with the radio playing *Winter Wonderland*.

He found Park in his study as usual. The "oh no not again" on his face confirmed Kinsey's impression he was not his father's favorite visitor, indicating they both needed to toughen up.

Kinsey dropped into the fern printed-easy chair facing his father's library desk.

"What can I do for you now?" Looking up from his laptop, Park managed to keep frustration from tainting his tone of voice, ever the polite passive man that he was.

"How could I find out about the driveway that goes nowhere at the south end of the property?" Kinsey described the space he found.

Park focused on Kinsey's face considering. "It was part of a larger estate." His gaze shifted to the bookcases flanking the window near them. "There used to be a book around here, a historical record of that plat." He squinted at the shelves. "Probably over there with that group next to the vases."

Kinsey rose and moved to the spot Park indicated. Between a pair of pottery urns was a stack of larger books which Kinsey examined, an assortment of encyclopedia, history book, and *voila! A chronicle of Interlaaken Platt, Pierce County*. Why would anyone bother to write something like that, Kinsey wondered as he removed the book from its resting place?

Setting it on the table near his father he pushed his chair closer. The book was divided into chapters relating to the various landowners at the time, the very early 1900s.

"Do you know who the original owner was?

"It used to be called," Park closed his eyes. "Harvey Mansion."

"Before Blast Castle?" Kinsey snorted. He located a chapter entitled "Harvey Mansion" where he found pictures of the ground breaking, various photographs of the construction progress and a picture of the newly completed manor house.

One photograph was entitled "carriage house" depicting construction on another building. Kinsey studied this, which bore some resemblance to the gatekeeper's cottage at the entrance to the estate. Since the work was not far enough along to positively identify the building, Kinsey examined the background. One hint in the picture caught his eye.

Pointing to the photograph he asked, "Would you be able to see Gravelly Lake from the gatekeeper's cottage?"

Park frowned. "I don't think so. Even with no trees or shrubs I don't think the lake would show up."

Kinsey turned the book so his father could see. "Could this carriage house be on the property just south and east of the rose garden?"

Park tilted the book and squinted at the photograph.

"What I'm looking for is a way someone gets into the house and those stairs without going through a wall."

Park wiggled his eyebrows. "Those ghosts you don't believe in."

Kinsey explained to Park the discovery of the modules.

"You'd think Markovich would have realized something like that since he lived there." Park sounded defensive. "I couldn't tell. I never saw the lights in action."

Kinsey didn't believe Markovich knew what was plaguing the house or he wouldn't have been fiddling around with the breaker box. "Dad, what's with you and Carmen Markovich?"

Watching his father's face was like observing a huge wave roll ashore then recede leaving behind a collection of sea debris including embarrassment, regret, even fear.

Park took a deep breath, considering Kinsey. "I suppose it'll come out one way or the other."

An attack of foreboding captured Kinsey, but he needed to listen now that he had asked.

"You know I loved your mother passionately, always."

Kinsey frowned. What did his mother have to do with it? He nodded.

"Something about Carmen reminded me of her the first time I met her. She called regarding the flowers in the formal garden and I went out to meet her. She loved working there, planting things, and trimming. She had an artistic eye for landscaping."

Kinsey said nothing.

"One day I ran into her at Starbucks in Lakewood not far from Lowe's. We had coffee and got to talking. After that it became something of a habit. Several days a week we would meet for coffee." Park stopped to regard his son, assessing his expression.

Kinsey made an effort to keep it bland, fearful of where they were headed.

"Her husband was a high-falutin sort of guy, totally wrapped up in his work. He didn't seem to care one way

162

or the other what Carmen did as long as she was home when he wanted her."

Kinsey's mind jumped ahead to the conclusion. His father had an affair with the renter's wife. "Dad," he said, both shocked and hurt.

Park made a stop signal. "We spent time together talking, just talking. But gradually, since both of us were lonely and we had a lot in common, more than just loneliness . . ."

"You had an affair with Carmen Markovich."

"No, I didn't," Park snapped. "Not that I wouldn't have. I was in love with her. I'd have married her if that had been a possibility."

"What about her?"

Park met Kinsey's eyes squarely. "She told me she loved me too."

"And Matt?" Motives were piling up like snowdrifts.

"He didn't know anything about it."

"You're certain?"

Park shrugged. "I wasn't the one who could be certain, but Carmen assured me he didn't."

The implications assaulted Kinsey, sending his thoughts reeling in different directions. "What happened to her?"

Park grimaced and shook his head. "I don't know."

"When did you see her last?"

"I had coffee with her several days before her husband was electrocuted. He was supposed to have clients in that evening, but didn't need her there." Park took a deep breath. "She . . . I . . . We agreed to meet that night."

Kinsey stared at him. "You were planning an affair."

Park pressed his lips together. "I'm not making excuses, Son. I'm telling you what happened."

"Okay," Kinsey made a patting motion in the air. "Did you meet her that night?"

"We agreed to meet next to the entrance of the formal garden. I went, but she never showed."

Kinsey was stunned. "And you never saw or heard from her again?"

Park nodded.

It was going to take time to digest this information.

Chapter Eighteen

Jet was in the dining room helping Latte set the table when Kinsey returned. She noted the rigid set to his lips and his distracted expression.

The girls had spent the day preparing for the Christmas gathering, decorating the grand parlor, library, dining and music rooms with lights and candles, frosted glass balls and glittering ribbon. Heavy hors d'oeuvres and holiday goodies available at the party could be made into dinner if one had not eaten. Susannah tasked herself with preparing party games, the gift exchange, and arranging a spot for dancing in the music room.

Kinsey's forbidding appearance evoked reluctance to pester him. However, Jet need to know before the party began if he had picked up the tickets for Latte and Nathan, which forced her to take up her courage and trek upstairs to his suite.

He opened the door with a frown, his hair falling over his forehead. "What can I do for you?"

She took a deep breath. "Did you get those Pantages tickets?"

"Oh, yes, I did." He held the door open wider. "Come in." He removed the tickets from his wallet. "I've got a couple jewelry boxes if you could wrap them."

"You look like you had a rough day." Jet said, accepting the tickets.

"Just learned some things I need to think about." He opened a drawer in the lamp table and took out a couple flat square boxes he handed her. "Dad was here the night Markovich's wife disappeared."

"But he didn't have anything to do with their deaths." Surely Kinsey didn't suspect his father.

Kinsey gave her an exaggerated grin that would better pass for a grimace. "At least not that he told me." He ran his hand through his hair. "It's just so hard to get information out of people it makes you wonder, especially when you find out what they should have told you earlier."

Noting his agonized expression, she figured he had learned more than he told her.

In her own suite Jet took out enough wrapping paper to cover the two small boxes. When she had completed the project she took one back, reentering Kinsey's suite since he had left the door open, and handed it to him. He stood in front of his fireplace staring into the gas lit flame.

She felt the urge to offer encouragement or consolation but hesitated, unsure of what to say.

"Do you think we'll ever get this mess cleared up?"

Jet laughed. "I have confidence in you."

"That's more than I have," he muttered.

For a moment they stared at each other, Kinsey in frustration, Jet in sympathetic understanding. Suddenly realizing this wasn't going the right direction, Jet dropped her gaze and moved away. "We're close to having everything ready for the party."

"I'll be down shortly."

When she stepped back into the hall Jet observed Susannah returning to her suite, which ignited an idea. At least the girls would probably dress up for the party. Jet returned to her room and, perching on the bed, stared into the wardrobe.

A knock on the door interrupted as Latte stuck her head in. "What are you doing?"

"Figuring out what to wear."

Latte stepped into the room. "Why don't you put on that sparkly thing with the ruffles you got at the sale after Thanksgiving?"

That was an idea. "What can I do for you?"

"Do you think it's all right for the kids to be at the party?" Latte's eyebrows rose to meet her bangs.

"Of course. They live here too. It's supposed to be a nice Christmas party not a bash." Jet noted Latte's jeans and hoodie. "What are you wearing?"

"I bought a dress in California."

That decided it. When Latte left Jet spent extra time dressing, putting on the chiffon skirt, glitter top, and high-heeled sandals. It seemed a long time since she had gotten so dressed up. She hadn't realized how nose-to-the-grindstone her life had become. In one of her frivolous Christmas moments she had bought a pink poinsettia headband with feathery black leaves. Poking and pinning she managed to get her bouffant hair tucked behind her ears and set it on, producing an almost unrecognizable image in the mirror. She almost looked like an adult woman instead of a little boy. If Latte had trouble getting her boys into the party, she could dress them in skirts and flowered headbands. It did wonders for Jet.

Stepping out of her suite Jet noted Susannah in the hall. Although Jet had succeeded in transforming herself into something feminine, Susannah made her look like a thirteen-year-old. She wore a form-fitting red dress with a small flounce at the hem. It left her arms and neck bare except for an array of silver jewelry. Her curly dark hair was swept into a pile on top of her head. In addition, she wore high spiked heels which made her curvy figure wiggle in all the right places. No amount of height to her heels would make anything on Jet wiggle, unless it was the overabundance of her hair.

Susannah eyed Jet with a tinge of uncertainty. "You look great, Jet."

"They won't be able to take their eyes off you."

"That would be good."

Latte's door opened about that time and the boys came roaring out in sweaters and cords. They stopped short at the sight of Susannah and Jet. "Wow," they exclaimed.

Latte followed them in an elegant black sheath. She had braided a string of crystal into her French braid. With her pale hair and long legs she looked like she had just stepped off the cover of *Glamour Magazine*.

❧

Whoa, Kinsey realized when he stepped out of his suite and observed Latte and her boys. He had given too little credit to the seriousness of the Christmas party. Clean Dockers and a sweater might fail the dress code. He returned to his closet and examined it for something more festive.

A teal shirt Evana gave him for his birthday captured his eye to which he added a pair of gray dress slacks and his black corduroy blazer. Changing clothes and spritzing on *Cool Water* lifted the cloud of gloom that had taken possession of his sense of humor.

The second time he opened his door he met Nathan coming from the third floor rubbing his hands together in gleeful anticipation. His violet shirt made a striking contrast with his bright hair.

A romantic melody floated up the stairs like a Ghost of Christmas Past. Kinsey pushed his emotional fantasy into a mental closet and locked the door on it. However, flickering votive candles on the mantle, on occasional tables, window ledges and the piano almost unhinged it to send him down a road of poignant longing. He sucked in his breath as he noted the Christmas tree's multicolor lights reflected in the arched windows across the room. The gas fire's glow touched him where his desire for the castle abided in his imagination. In that moment he realized it was about more than a mansion or even tradition and family values, but he could not have explained what it was about.

Nathan beckoned toward the doors to the dining room where a festive spread of edible delicacies covered the massive table. However he was distracted by the girls having an animated conversation near the fireplace. Kinsey wondered how Lieutenant Sarkis would feel if he saw Evana now, her blue-black hair set off by the royal blue dress.

It was Latte who caught Nathan's eye. "Vavavavoom!" Nathan declared, as they reached the bottom of the stairs.

Susannah tottering on five-inch stilettos was the first to notice the guys and wiggle their direction. But it was Jet for whom Kinsey was unprepared. He might not have recognized her had he seen her in a crowd. Her bouffant hair pulled away from her face and her glitzy outfit gave her an entirely different appearance. Her newly exposed femininity both appealed and intimidated. He realized he had become accustomed to her prickly stubbornness and her boyish self-reliance, which allowed a relationship free from complicated emotions and sensual undertones.

Susannah waved her hand in the direction of the dining room. "The buffet is ready if you'd like to eat."

Kinsey followed Nathan who cast a wistful glance in Latte's direction then turned his steps toward the dining room. Recalling placement of the mistletoe over the doorway, Kinsey slipped through as quickly as possible, eliciting a disappointed frown from Susannah who stood to the side of the door as they entered.

Arriving a few minutes after them, Billy was caught in the doorway and pulled into Susannah's embrace. He looked bewildered when she released him, casting a doubtful glance at the guys. Nathan pointed to the mistletoe hung above the door.

After selecting a healthy plateful, Kinsey followed the girls to the Chesterfields in front of the fireplace where a couple of the parlor chairs had been added. Landon and Logan sat cross-legged on the floor in front of the hearth.

Kinsey commended the girls on their décor and cuisine. "This place never looked so good except in my imagination." Encountering Evana's gaze, he wondered at her indignant expression.

Nathan had snagged a spot on the sofa beside Latte and was passing food items her sons disliked from them to her.

"I should have fed you hot dogs in the kitchen and sent you to bed." Latte scowled at them.

Billy sat between Susannah and Evana on the opposite sofa looking self-satisfied. Kinsey still questioned where he had come from and why.

"Did everyone bring their gifts for the exchange?" Susannah inventoried each face, receiving nods all around.

Susannah rose. "I'm going to put on the music for dancing." Leaving her plate on the coffee table she headed for the music room.

"How about a dance?" Nathan addressed Latte.

She agreed with a smile, then told her boys to go ahead and let Anatuviak in.

"Let me take your plates?" Jet held out her hand.

Billy relinquished his and followed Susannah into the music room. Jet accepted Kinsey and Evana's plates as she retrieved Susannah's from the table.

When Jet had gone, Evana challenged Kinsey. "So what was that look about?"

"What do you know about Dad's relationship with Carmen Markovich?"

Evana crossed her arms over her breast and narrowed her eyes. "What relationship? He used to see her once in a while when he was working in the garden. They had coffee once when she was shopping for plants."

"Dad was in love with her."

"He was not!" Evana declared vehemently. "Mother was the love of Dad's life."

Kinsey stared at Evana. "Mom died *thirty* years ago."

"What difference does that make?"

"Good grief, Evana, can you be that obtuse?"

"There is only one real love for a lifetime, like Jeff for me and Carol for you. Jet will never be your love."

"Jet!" Was she nuts? "Jet's my cousin."

Evana gave Kinsey a studied stare. "At least you remember that."

Chapter Nineteen

After garbaging the paper plates, checking the refreshment table, and adding another supply of soda, Jet returned to the parlor. The boys lay like arrows on the floor pointing to packages beneath the Christmas tree. Anatuviak had assumed a similar position with his head resting on his extended front legs. In the music room she could see Nathan dancing with Latte and Billy with Susannah. Kinsey rose with a scowl from his spot in front of the fireplace next to Evana and moved to watch the dancers.

Jet joined him at the music room door. "You don't look much like a Merry Christmas," she observed.

He snorted his disgust then wiped it off his face declaring, "How about a dance?"

She noticed him shoot Evana a defiant glance as he took Jet's elbow and guided her to the floor. The Chinese rug had been rolled up against the French doors; the peach loveseat and blue striped chair moved to positions along the walls. The boom box played a Christmas rock song as he pivoted her into swing position.

When the piece ended Kinsey cocked his head and grinned. "You swing."

"Ballroom dance lessons in high school." Jet laughed.

Kinsey raised his eyebrows. "Doesn't sound like the usual pursuit for a liberated woman. Or," he amended, "her daughter."

"Mom was making time with the instructor."

Kinsey laughed. "So you waltz?"

"Of course."

"Come on." He led her to the confiscated credenza on which the boom box had been installed and searched the CDs for one labeled popular waltzes.

When the music began Kinsey took Jet into formal dance position. He was a graceful dancer with a strong lead. Effortlessly he guided her through the turns and spins of the waltz. It was exhilarating. For that one moment in time she felt like Cinderella at the ball. After a spin and a dip the piece ended and another began.

"Do you think you can cha-cha to this?"

Jet laughed and nodded.

They had a good time synchronizing their steps. When the piece ended Nathan sprinted to the boom box and selected a languid blues song. Jet remained beside Kinsey for a moment expecting him to bag it. However, he appeared to be working out the timing.

"Shall we?" He opened his arms and took her into a position much closer than the other dances had either required or allowed.

Jet found her body interested in things that her mind refused to consider. Kinsey's cologne was intoxicating and she found the strength of his arms a temptation to surrender, not physically as much as emotionally. His chin rested against her hair and as they turned she caught a glimpse of Evana in the doorway, thunder and lightening on her face.

Jet's conversation with Evana from a few weeks before leaped to her mind, suffusing her with guilt. She took a deep breath and rallied her defenses. When the dance ended, she avoided Kinsey's eyes. "Evana looks upset."

"It'll do her good," Kinsey declared uncharitably.

Evana approached Nathan and Latte after which Latte declared it was time for the gift exchange. Susannah put a Christmas CD in the player and the other dancers retired to the parlor.

Retaking their former positions on the fireplace sofa and chairs, Nathan suggested the two boys play Santa Claus and bring packages. They gleefully obliged, grabbing an armful each. Unable to read the tags they brought the gifts to the adults to decipher.

Jet looked over Logan's shoulder as he tried to read one on the small flat box she had wrapped. "That's for Nathan."

After delivering his package Logan returned with another similar one, which Jet informed him was for Latte. Then Landon handed Jet a flat package.

Amid exclamations, laughter and thank yous, Jet opened her gift from Evana.

Kinsey peered over her shoulder. "What did you get?"

"A family picture." She held it out so he could see.

"It must have been great granddad's funeral judging by who is and isn't there." Kinsey leaned closer. "There's your mother." He pointed to Mona standing in the middle of the group trying to be the center of attention. Jet was in front of her with Evana on one side and

Francine on the other. Beyond them were Kinsey and Jordan.

"You look thoroughly disgusted." Jet laughed.

"I probably was. I hated picture taking. It took so long to get everyone lined up. There's Ethel and Teresa, your mother's sisters, and your great aunt Jane."

Jet stared at the picture remembering the envelopes in her briefcase upstairs. Glancing up from the picture she noticed Nathan and Latte standing by the fireplace staring at her and Kinsey. "Oh, oh," she muttered.

Kinsey followed her gaze. "Will Latte be upset?"

"She'll get over it."

The group dispersed, moving back to the music room. A dance rhythm replaced the Christmas carols. Jet noticed Billy approach Evana, saying something to which she shook her head.

"How about another dance?" Kinsey held his hand out to Jet.

She placed her hand in his and they returned to the music room. Nathan gave Jet a wink and a discreet thumbs-up.

"At least we don't have to worry about Nathan." She murmured, nodding to where he stood.

As Kinsey turned her in a circle she noticed Evana approach to tap him on the shoulder. Kinsey made another circle to face his sister and stopped.

"Dad's on the phone." She spoke to Kinsey but glared at Jet. "He wants to talk to you."

Kinsey, an arm still around Jet, gave Evana a frown and asked which phone.

"In the kitchen."

When he had left, Jet thanked Evana for the picture. "I don't think I've ever seen a copy of it before."

"Your mother should have gotten one. But then with her appreciation for the family, who knows what she did with it." Evana sounded irritated. "You shouldn't take advantage of Kinsey like this." She leveled her lustrous eyes on Jet.

"Take advantage?" Jet was stupefied. What did that mean?

"After Carol there hasn't been anyone for him."

Jet couldn't believe her ears. "We're cousins and . . . ." She stopped. She couldn't say they may also be brother and sister.

Evana's eyes flashed. "Do you think that makes a difference?"

"Of course it does." Even as she said it Jet recalled the temptation Kinsey had awakened in her.

Evana snorted. Jet turned away fighting the temptation to defend herself. What was Evana trying to say? Even brothers and sisters can dance together. Kinsey was fun; she enjoyed his company, which was no crime. If anyone could be accused of tempting Kinsey it would be Susannah with her voluptuous cleavage and tight dress. The way she hung on his words, working to get caught under the mistletoe with him.

The music stopped. Nathan and Latte came to stand with Jet and Evana.

ɔ

When Kinsey reached the kitchen the receiver lay on the counter. "Dad?" No answer, the dial tone sounded in his ear. He redialed the number. No response, what did that mean? He figured he knew and he didn't like it.

Returning to the parlor, he noted Latte and Nathan, Jet and Evana in the music room standing together. Nathan was talking while the others listened. As Kinsey drew closer, he noticed the flush on Jet's cheeks and the grim look on Evana's. His first impulse was to jump Evana on the spot but realized he could embarrass Jet in the process. Pausing in the doorway, he failed to heed Susannah until she attacked him, reaching up to pull his face down and kiss his lips.

Nathan and Latte laughed. Kinsey backed up noticing the flash of anger on Evana's face and Jet's sigh of relief as she moved closer to Latte, confirming his suspicions. In spite of his aversion to female attacks he realized Susannah had done him a favor.

He raised his hands to ward off another assault. "One point for you," he said to Susannah, who glazed him with a sultry stare from beneath her shadowed eyelids then sidled back to where Billy stood next to the boom box. Let Evana ambush Susannah, probably a better match for his sister than Jet.

Evana retired to the piano where she played Christmas carols with vehement force. The group drifted to the upholstered bench and parlor chairs near there. Gradually Evana turned down the intensity and the others sang along. After an hour, Latte sent her boys upstairs to bed. Evana abandoned the piano also heading up the stairs. Jet and Latte launched into cleaning the dining room, while Kinsey sat with Nathan and Billy by the fireplace, keeping a low profile.

It was nearing one o'clock when Kinsey set out for his suite. As he reached the door, Jet stepped out of Latte's, her bouffant hair escaping the headband and her gray eyes smoky in the dim lighting.

He approached. "Did Evana give you a bad time?"

Assorted expressions vied for control of Jet's face.

"She has an electric fence around me."

"She accused me of tempting you." Jet shook her head, rolling her eyes as if the idea were preposterous. "I told her Susannah would be a better candidate for her concern."

"Then Susannah attacked me." Kinsey laughed, leaning against the wall next to his door. "I'm sorry about Evana. She has a problem."

Jet met his eyes with an assessing stare. "She told me you've had your one love for a lifetime."

Kinsey snorted his disgust. "I had a stupid infatuation for a female dragon who just about set me on fire and burned me up." He grinned. "I got over it." Kinsey turned toward his door and then back to Jet. "Do you want to go to church tomorrow?"

"Sure. That would be good." But once Jet had opened the door to her suite, she turned back to him. "Maybe you'd better invite Evana too."

He grimaced and sighed. She was right, although he didn't like the idea. He would rather invite Evana to go home and stay out of his business.

Once inside his suite, Kinsey set the paperweight Susannah gave him on the coffee table and sprawled on his sofa. At this point he regretted having asked Evana to join him at the castle. She would be better off home keeping his father company. Although he loved his sister he had no intention of spending his life as her male companion.

Considering the situation he dropped off to sleep, waking a couple hours later with a cramped neck and throbbing leg. After stretching his ill-positioned appendages he unbuttoned his shirt. As he crossed to the fireplace and turned toward the bed he noticed a light outside the window. While he continued to undress the light plagued him. He stood at the window examining the landscape. Illumination came from the motion-detecting spotlight at the south terrace and the coach lamp positioned near the garage driveway spread a dim circle of light. However, the one he noticed was at the entrance to the rose garden, where no outside fixtures existed except for landscape torches among the shrubbery, which he had turned off before going to his room.

Kinsey put his shirt back on and grabbing his jacket headed down the staircase, through the parlor and out the library doors. Once outside he realized the spotlight at the south terrace would not have been on had it not detected motion. Hearing a noise behind, Kinsey spun around to face Nathan in his robe and pajamas.

"What are you doing here?" Kinsey barked his surprise.

Nathan put up his hands. "I heard a bang like a shot."

"Just now?"

"Ten minutes ago or so." Nathan put his hands in the pockets of his robe and scrutinized the darkness. "Did you hear it?"

Kinsey shook his head. "I spotted a light that didn't belong."

Together they crossed the lawn toward the rose garden searching. It wasn't visible again until they reached the hedge. The light turned out to be a small flashlight, lying on the ground shining into the black grass, visible only because of the pitch blackness of the night. Nathan reached to pick it up.

"Don't touch it," Kinsey warned. "Is there something around to mark this spot?"

Nathan grabbed a couple evergreen branches torn off in the last windstorm. Together they made an X-marks-the-spot by shoving the branches into the ground.

"Whose do you think it is?" Nathan asked.

Kinsey shook his head, removing the handkerchief from his pocket. He picked up the petite flashlight. "Maybe we should check around some."

Wandering the perimeter of the rose garden then crisscrossing the space between there and the road along the lake they found nothing and no one.

"I don't like this," Kinsey said as they headed back to the house. Too many eruptions of unexplained horrors had intensified his sensitivity. What spirit of the dark hole would arise now?

Chapter Twenty

As it turned out neither Jet nor Kinsey went to church. Arriving on the main floor for her daily run Jet encountered Kinsey, Nathan and Lieutenant Sarkis gathered near the grand piano in the gray morning light. The pine scent of Christmas saturated the chilly air.

The lieutenant arched an eyebrow, peering at her over the top of his spectacles. "Did you hear anything last night?"

What provoked this confab? They stared as if she were the Wizard of Oz and could endow them with heart, courage and a way back home. "When last night?"

The lieutenant turned to Kinsey who lifted his shoulders consulting Nathan with his eyes.

"Three-ish," Nathan estimated. "I'd been asleep a while."

Jet shook her head. "I heard nothing." She entertained wild dreams, interspersing events from the evening before. However, she was persuaded that melodrama played in her subconscious without interruption from reality.

"You'd better check your inmates and be sure you can account for all of them."

"I'll check on Latte and the kids," Jet volunteered.

"Susannah too?" Kinsey suggested.

"I can see about Evana and Billy on the third floor," Nathan offered.

Although unsure what the question was, Jet knocked on Latte's door. A floral fragrance drifted into the hall when she opened it dressed in robe and slippers, her hair wound in a towel.

After Jet explained Latte went to check on the boys. Jet knocked on Susannah's door and received no answer. She knocked again louder, still no answer. She turned the knob, but the door was locked. Latte, having remained in the hall watching, wandered toward the north end where the stairs came from the kitchen. "She's in the shower. I can hear it running."

After returning to the main floor Jet reported her findings. Nathan descended the stairs slowly as if the Monster of the Black Lagoon awaited him at the bottom. "Evana's fine, but I couldn't get an answer out of Billy."

"Where's his room?" Lieutenant Sarkis took off like a shot.

Jet trailed behind as the guys ascended to the third floor. At the top Kinsey pointed left then led the group to a door on the right.

"Locked," the lieutenant declared after trying the knob. "Do you have a key?"

"In the safe downstairs."

"Get it," he ordered.

After Kinsey left, Jet asked the lieutenant, "What happened?"

He shot her a scowl indicating he didn't explain police business to female twits.

Kinsey returned with a large ring of keys, holding out one segregated from the others. "I think this is it."

The lieutenant tried it in the door and Jet could hear the lock snap across. "Okay," he said, "I'll go in. You stay here."

The three exchanged glances as the lieutenant left. It didn't take more than couple minutes for him to return. "No one there."

Jet exhaled, suddenly aware she had been holding her breath. Visions of bloody Billy, sprawled on the floor like a NCIS victim, had overtaken her imagination.

Kinsey shuffled through his ring of keys. "I also have one for his garage. Maybe we should check if his car is here."

Like The Pied Piper they all trailed the lieutenant down two flights to the parlor and then to the garages. Kinsey unlocked the door to Billy's stall and the lieutenant lifted the door. The dark blue Toyota pickup sat undisturbed. Lieutenant Sarkis walked around it, peering into the interior and box.

Returning to the group, he shrugged. "What do you think?"

Kinsey and Nathan exchanged glances, each shaking his head.

∽

As the caravan began the trek back to the house Nathan asked Kinsey, "Did you show him where you found that flashlight?"

The lieutenant directed Kinsey a probing glance.

Detouring from the path Kinsey led the way along the garage driveway as it turned onto the lake road. A coach lamp sat at the corner where the two roads met. At that point Kinsey headed into the lawn, unsure of the exact location. Things appeared different in daylight. Studying the ground then looking ahead, he searched for the marker he and Nathan had left the night before.

Nathan spotted it first, pointing past the end of the shrubbery. The two broken branches shivered in the breeze. Kinsey raised his hand stopping the group while the lieutenant visually swept the lawn as far as the south terrace. Turning back to face the direction from which they had come he continued his survey.

What did he see, or not see? What blast from the blue would descend on them now? The rest of the group stood watching, fearful to move lest they disturb the lieutenant's concentration.

Kinsey noticed the spot as the lieutenant moved toward it. In the grass on a line with the yard lamp was a dark blotch on the brilliant green. The lieutenant crouched to touch the grass, bringing his hand back wet with a pink tinge.

"What do you think?" Kinsey figured he probably didn't want to know.

"I'm going to get forensics out here." The lieutenant rose. "You need to make every effort to locate your renter."

Kinsey must have looked like a kid with no clue for Sarkis peered at him over his spectacles, reciting a list of instructions. "Look up your records on him, give me a copy, then contact everyone he mentioned. I'll work from my end, but you might have better luck with people you know or who might have known him." The lieutenant took out his cell phone and fingered in a number. "Make sure no one disturbs this area until the team gets here."

Walking slowly in the direction of the yard lamp he studied the ground, calling back to Kinsey, "Let me know if you find your renter alive and well."

Kinsey's faith in finding Billy Monk safe and sound had sunk beneath subterranean.

Nathan, Jet and Kinsey all moved in the direction of the south terrace.

"Do either of you know anything about Billy? Where he works or what he does?" Kinsey wondered if he even had a place to start searching.

Jet shook her head. The empathetic concern in her expression made Kinsey feel like a wimp; time to buck up and stop acting as if the world had formed a conspiracy against him.

Kinsey figured Nathan was his best bet for information since he had spent more time with Billy.

"He worked for a courier service with an office in Lakewood, up by the town center. I got the idea he has family in this area," Nathan said as Kinsey held the library door open for him. "He mentioned an uncle who lives in town."

"Hopefully his application will help."

Kinsey unlocked a cupboard and drew out the folder with the rental agreements. He flipped through them until he came to the one for Billy Monk.

Nathan read over his shoulder as Kinsey perused the application. Nathan was right; Billy worked for a courier service at the Lakewood Town Center.

Kinsey turned to his friend. "Do you want to see if he's there or if they've heard from him? I'll call the people on this list." There were only three and the phone numbers appeared local. Kinsey began with Patricia Monk, his mother, who answered the phone with a smoker's rasp.

"Yeah, hello?" Her belligerent tone of voice made Kinsey wonder why she even bothered to respond.

"This is Kinsey Sayre, Billy Monk's landlord. Have you seen him today or last night?"

"Naw, what do you want him for?"

What excuse could he give and not raise an alarm? "We're planning a get together tonight and wanted to be sure he knew."

"Naw, I haven't seen him. He never comes around here unless he wants money."

"Does he have an uncle in the area?"

"That rat fink." She broke into a coughing fit.

"Would Billy have spent time with him? Or would he know where Billy is?"

She took a gasp of air. "Like I say, if he wanted money."

"Do you have a way to reach his uncle?"

There was a moment of silence. "He has an apartment off Veterans Drive. I've never been there."

"What's the name?"

"William Krick."

"Does he have a phone number?"

She made a disgusted sound. "He don't want no one to call him."

What did that mean? Kinsey thanked her, figuring he had gotten as much data as he could. Her grungy attitude and references to Billy's uncle caused the probability of Billy's entanglement in enterprises of which no one at the house was aware to shoot up the likelihood list relative to events from the night before.

Kinsey received no satisfaction from the other two numbers on Billy's application. One, a young woman's voice, took a message on the recorder. The other number switched him to a cell phone answering service. He debated calling Lieutenant Sarkis to report his lack of results, but decided to wait to hear from Nathan first.

Chapter Twenty-one

When Jet returned to her suite she determined time had come to make a DNA test appointment for herself and Roger. Minimal risk was attached to that, since he believed it possible she was his daughter and had agreed to the test.

Although Park agreed to participate, the specifics remained undefined. Jet had no idea how to approach Susannah's father and the one lost in obscurity was still there. However, since she had mustered the resolve to make the appointment for Roger she figured she should move ahead with the next onerous task before her determination took a powder.

Sucking in her breath, she fingered in the number of the first name on her call list, Barbara Baker. She could almost bring to mind a face belonging to the name. Her mother had chattered regularly about "Barb", to Jet's recollection a short dark haired woman with a matronly figure, a black pantsuit and a hairdo shorter than Kinsey's.

Once Jet had identified herself Barbara burst out effusively, "Little Jessica, how are you?"

The "little" reduced Jet to the essence of a sniveling child, but the cheerful greeting made it easier to continue. "I'm fine. I wanted to ask a couple questions about my mother and wondered if you would be free to have coffee later."

"I'd love to. I have some Christmas shopping to do and I'm meeting Rita Walden at the Mall. If you'd like we could meet you there at say, 2:00."

Relief washed over Jet like a hot shower. Rita was the other name on her list, which meant one call had nailed both of them.

After a stopping a moment to inform Latte, Jet left determined to do some shopping before her assignation. She needed gifts for Latte and the boys before they left for California.

The morning's discovery near the rose garden pulled her gaze that direction. Had Kinsey been able to locate Billy? Jet had a bad feeling about him.

The gray day with low clouds draped over the city inspired impressions of drifting fairy-like through an unreal world waiting for the drama to begin. Evergreen swags intertwined with crystal lights, sugary snowflakes dangling in store windows, *I'll Be Home For Christmas* in the background, and the cheerful chatter of people around her conjured up dreams residing as obscure impressions in her subconscious, making the mall an excellent escape from the parade of disasters plaguing the castle.

After wandering through Nordstrom and Macy's looking for ideas she bought Latte a pastel blue sweater with crystal snowflakes on it, which would be lovely with her fair-haired coloring. At the game store she purchased one for the boy's Nintendo DS, which she was aware Latte had gotten them.

Stepping out of the store she bumped into a woman only slightly taller than herself, looking backward over her shoulder. As she opened her mouth to apologize the woman grabbed and hugged her.

"Jessica, you're so grown up." It was Barbara Baker, appearing just as Jet had remembered her. "I have to pick something up here. I'll meet you over at the Ebar?"

Jet smiled and nodded. After purchasing coffee she selected a table for four in the mall concourse and sat down. Sipping her peppermint mocha she inhaled its minty aroma. Within ten minutes Barbara joined her, introducing Rita, a woman about the same size with bleached hair, tight pants and boots.

"How are you getting along without your mother?" Barbara popped the lid off her coffee and poured a couple packets of sweetener in it.

Jet explained that she and a friend had moved into the Sayre estate.

"Sayre?" Barbara frowned. "Relatives?"

"Cousins." Jet felt the overwhelming desire to shut down, smile and nod, allow the other two to chatter. However, that wouldn't accomplish anything.

"We really miss your mom. She knew how to have a good time." Barbara tore a bite off her lemon bread.

Jet grimaced. It depended on your definition of a good time. "Did you go to the parties she did?"

"We were her chaperones." Rita made a croaking sound vaguely resembling a laugh. She had the dried up skin of someone who drank and smoked too much plus a voice to match.

How much do they know, or even suspect? Much as she disliked the idea Jet needed to part with some data first. "Before she died Mom told me that Roger Thompson may not be my father."

"One of the last times I saw your mom she told me she needed to talk to you about that." Barb eyed her with a sympathetic expression.

Jet stared at her coffee cup. "Did she tell you the possibilities?"

Barb shook her head. "Mostly she talked about the fact she didn't know who one of them was."

"Do you know anything about him?" Was Jet's only hope of finding Mr. Unknown fading away?

"Although she wasn't aware at the time, it had been a joke on her and the guy. She was boozed up enough to be game for anything." Barb drowned another hunk of lemon bread.

"Were you there?"

"I'd been at the party. It was an after-work get-together for someone's promotion. I don't think I even knew the one who got promoted. Mona dragged me along for company."

"Did you meet the guy?"

"No, apparently another group at the bar from a different part of the government was celebrating someone's divorce. Some ruckus began between the two groups and they hooked up the loser with Mona. You knew your mom; she could be very charming if she wanted to be. I don't know what the deal was, but she ended up with the guy."

Jet swallowed her disgust and worked to keep her expression under control. "Were you there when she was with him?"

Barbara sighed, looking apologetic. "No, I left before it got that far. I tried to get her to go home too, but she was having a good time."

Jet took a deep breath. "You wouldn't have any idea who he was?"

"I don't, but," Barb raised a finger. "I know someone who might."

Jet was almost afraid to ask. "Would it be possible . . . ?"

Barbara put her hand on Jet's. "I can try to find out who it was, no promises."

❧

Considering his semi load of problems Kinsey commiserated with Atlas, feeling as if he balanced the earth on his shoulders. Would he have been so enthusiastic had he known the difficulties that would ambush him? That's a wimpy attitude. What did you expect? Your father had no reason for concern about the mansion's reputation and safety? Parkinson Sayre wasn't a coward or an alarmist. Kinsey didn't always agree with him but he did respect him.

Billy's disappearance made no sense. Kinsey wouldn't have been surprised to find him laying in the yard with a bullet in his body, but finding him gone, his car still in the garage didn't fit the evidence. The fact they found no body permitted a completely logical explanation. However, Kinsey's internal skeptic expected the worst.

A knock on the door of his suite gave him a jolt. He opened it ready for another visit from the Bad News Bear. Nathan shook his head in response to Kinsey's unasked question.

Kinsey waved his friend into the suite where Nathan dropped onto the sofa, locking his hands together behind his head. "I suppose Sarkis will check the hospitals."

"I imagine." Kinsey perched on the end of his bed and folded his arms across his chest. "Right now I'd sell you a castle cheap."

Nathan laughed. "You don't own a castle yet."

Kinsey moved to his sofa and propped his legs on the coffee table. "I never did know anything about Billy. I always thought it strange he showed up here out of the blue."

"Maybe that's where you should start checking. Maybe he didn't just show up out of the blue. Who knew you were renting out the place?"

"You and Dad, at Thanksgiving I told Evana and Jet. Jet told her friend Latte."

"I told Susannah, although she didn't act like she'd known Billy before."

"Did you mention it to anyone besides Susannah?"

Nathan stared at Kinsey's ceiling. "I told my mom, but I don't think I gave her any specifics or even the idea there'd be more room than just for me."

"I was considering taking another look in Billy's suite. Maybe there'd be clues keeping a low profile." Kinsey set his feet on the floor.

"Why not?" Nathan straightened. "How much trouble could you get into?"

Kinsey snorted. "Eternity in Hell."

"Where is Lieutenant Sarkis?" Nathan rose.

"He could be outside." Kinsey moved to the bay windows overlooking the lake. From there he could see forensic scientists combing the area. "I suppose I should talk to him first. Save on legal problems."

"Did you get anything out of Billy's relatives?"

Kinsey shook his head. "His mom was rude, said he had an uncle living on Veterans Drive. You want to help me try to find him?" Kinsey challenged his friend.

"Sure, I'm free for the afternoon."

Kinsey grabbed a waterproof jacket. "I'll meet you downstairs."

Veteran's Drive joined Gravelly Lake just beyond the estate. Heading west, they looked for the place described by Billy's mother.

"There." Kinsey pointed to the right, driving into the parking lot where they got out.

The austere four-plex possessed a set of mailboxes on the side of the entrance alcove. Kinsey examined the names on the boxes, locating one that said, "W. Krick."

Since the apartment was on the second floor Kinsey and Nathan climbed the open wooden stairs to knock on the door. Receiving no answer, they rang the bell and knocked again, still no response.

Kinsey grimaced. "I guess we can give the name and address to Sarkis."

Nathan pointed to a short medium built man moving toward one of the cars in the parking lot.

"I've seen someone like that before." Kinsey recalled his previous tailing job.

"Maybe it's our guy."

They made a speedy descent, but the man quickened his pace, leaped into a car and pealed out of the lot with a squeal of tires.

Chapter Twenty-two

Traversing the path to the house with Nathan, Kinsey noticed Lieutenant Sarkis heading to his truck. He hailed the lieutenant with an offer of coffee. Sarkis' suspicious expression told Kinsey he was in no twitter to spend more time at the castle chasing clues. He probably just wanted to go home and relax like anyone else. Nonetheless, Kinsey felt no great reluctance to pester him given that if the boot were on the other leg the man would have no mercy on him. He pointed the men to the library, continuing to the kitchen to fetch the coffee.

As Kinsey took the striped chair facing the bay windows the late afternoon sun, making its last stand beneath the layer of clouds struck him in the eye, blinding him for a minute with its beam of light. Without the sun in his eyes he was just about as blind regarding the mansion's mysteries. He switched on the chandelier and turned to the lieutenant who perched on the rose settee. Explaining his phone calls to the people on Billy's application he told the lieutenant about the trip to

Veterans Drive. Sarkis took down the name and address, plus the phone number of the mother.

Nathan leaned forward. "A man left in a flying hurry while we were there."

The lieutenant turned to him, arching a slim eyebrow.

"He looked like someone I saw the other night here on the property," Kinsey explained.

Lieutenant Sarkis focused on Kinsey over the rim of his spectacles. "You got a description?"

Kinsey pulled up the picture in his mind. "Short to medium height, in jeans and a leather coat. I only saw him from behind. He was wearing one of those caps golfers wear."

The lieutenant frowned at his coffee as if it were guilty of a faulty memory. Did the description mean something to him? He changed the subject. "It'll be morning before forensics has anything on those spots in your grounds."

With a glance Kinsey consulted Nathan. "We thought we'd do a search of Billy's room. Any problem with that?"

Davy Sarkis grimaced and heaved a sigh. "It's touchy, but if something has happened to him it would be better to find out sooner than later."

Kinsey stared at the sinking sun. Was that yes or no?

"Be judicious," the lieutenant warned.

Nathan cleared his throat, raised his eyebrows, and beckoned toward the stairs.

"I need to show you something," Kinsey addressed the lieutenant.

Sarkis looked as if Kinsey had just squelched his plans for an evening off.

The two men followed to the second floor where they entered the extra furniture room, greeted by the musty smell of a closed space and the pungent odor of old furniture. Moving a couple chairs and the miniature chest, Kinsey opened a pathway to the wooden table.

Apparently fascinated with the furniture collection, the lieutenant wandered along the periphery like an antique dealer examining a piece here and there.

Opening the table drawer, Kinsey called him away from his bargain hunting to point out the assortment of modules. "What do you think of that?"

Sarkis stared at the collection as if Kinsey had exposed a drawer full of kitchen utensils with which he expected the lieutenant to whip up something to go with coffee.

"Is this what caused all the light problems the other night?"

Lieutenant Sarkis grimaced. "Get me something to put these in. I'll take them with me and we'll see what it means."

Kinsey located a box into which they packed the modules.

The lieutenant tucked it under his arm. "Let me know if you hear anything from your renter."

When the lieutenant had gone, Kinsey asked Nathan if he was up for a look at Billy's room. Accepting Nathan's shrug as an affirmative, Kinsey started down the wrought iron staircase.

"What exactly are we looking for?" Nathan asked as they crossed to the main stairs.

"Something that would give us a place to find him, names, addresses of friends. We've checked relatives and that doesn't look promising."

After stopping in the library for keys Kinsey followed Nathan to Billy's room. The smallest one in the house and sparsely furnished it gave Kinsey a prick of guilt. He should have offered Billy some of the extra furniture.

The faint scent of shaving lotion clung to the air. The sea-green drapes had been pulled, pitching the room into total darkness. Kinsey flipped on the overhead light. Although the bed was unmade the room was reasonably tidy.

"Do you think he went to bed last night?" Nathan wandered to the closet. "There aren't any clothes lying around."

Kinsey headed for the night stand drawer hoping to find an address book. "Look in the bathroom. He may have left them there."

"There's a pile of clothes in the corner, but I don't see what he was wearing last night."

What was Billy wearing last night? "Check the closet. Maybe he put it away."

Poking through the items in the night stand, Kinsey concluded Billy had taken his wallet with him, leaving little clue to the room's occupant.

"Not in the closet," Nathan announced. "But there's a courier bag here."

"Let's take a look at that."

Kinsey flattened the purple bedspread and Nathan placed the bag there. Opening it, Nathan removed a clipboard with business forms attached and a couple delivery receipts. From the dates and times they appeared to have been accomplished late in the day and Billy had not returned to his office. An assortment of writing instruments, a notepad, a candy bar, and a calculator also occupied space in the bag. Nathan closed it then put it back where he found it.

"Let's go, there's nothing here I can see."

Nathan retired to his room across the hall. After returning the keys Kinsey stepped onto his deck overlooking the area where they had found the flashlight. What happened last night? Where was Billy? How could he find out? Undoubtedly a stupid concern, trouble never had any problem locating him. Any time now calamity could come charging in the door. If Billy had suffered some injury then the problems Kinsey faced relative to the house had migrated from the past to the present. Was his father correct after all? Something was wrong with Blast Castle? Did an evil spirit actually reside here?

✃

Crossing the rose garden heading for the house Jet pulled her coat tighter. A cold wind off the lake belied the brilliant sunset. Only mid-afternoon and already the sun was low in the sky. Glancing up at the mansion she noted a light in a window of Kinsey's suite. Otherwise the building was dark, almost foreboding.

Chilled from her walk, Jet switched on the lamps and gas fireplace as soon as she reached her room. No sign of the lieutenant made her wonder if Billy had been located. What would happen if he was never found? Would they search for another grave?

Since no dinner was served on Sunday evening, Jet trekked the hall to Latte's suite to inquire about her plans. She discovered her friend in the twin's room in front of the fireplace with a board game.

"I hadn't got that far," Latte confessed, moving her game piece with a flourish to the top of the board.

"How about I fix something and you guys can join me?"

Latte laughed as she rolled dice for another move. "How can I refuse an offer like that?"

Jet figured pasta and salad would be enough for the four of them. After fifteen minutes Latte joined Jet and took over making the salad.

"I made a DNA testing appointment for Roger and me." Jet took a stack of black and white plates from the cupboard to the table. "The only problem is it might take my mother's too."

Latte paused with a utensil in each hand as she tossed the salad sometimes in the bowl, sometimes not. "Maybe even if you don't have a really good sample, you'd have something that would work."

"Maybe," Jet considered the possibilities. "If I eliminate Roger, that's one down and three to go."

Latte snatched a piece of escaping lettuce and popped it into her mouth. "Are you afraid it's Mr. Unknown?"

"He is probably the least likely, a one night stand." Jet poured the pasta into a colander. "Park stayed for a while with Mom. I didn't ask her how often they . . ." Jet grimaced. "Do people never consider what their little larks could mean to their children?"

Latte put her hand on Jet's shoulder. "Most people aren't good at math, can't put two and two together."

Jet clenched her fists and waved one in the air. "I swear I'm not going to do that to my children."

Latte raised her eyebrows, glancing into the next room where the twins had moved their board game. "Stuff happens no matter what you do."

"Not so you don't know who their father is." Jet removed the bread from the oven, filling the room with its leavened scent. "It's going to be really awkward if I find out Park is my father." She beckoned to the other room and Latte went to get her boys.

Once they were seated and the food passed around, Latte asked, "You're okay about Kinsey?" She spoke gently. "You're not falling for him?" She glanced up from a fork wound full of spaghetti.

Jet felt a prick of conscience. "Most of the time he makes me mad, although I do care how bad things get for him. He's a nice guy; he doesn't deserve to be so set upon."

Latte cocked her head, stabbing Jet with a warning glance.

"Since he could be my brother, I'll steer clear," Jet assured her, bobbing her head. "Evana says mean things every time I'm around Kinsey that suggest . . . well."

"Kinsey has a thing for you?"

Jet rocked her shoulders. "I think he's just declaring his independence from her idea they're mutually miserable people who lost their loves."

Latte wiped a smear of pasta sauce off her sweatshirt. "My parents scheduled flights for us on Wednesday."

"Are you going to be gone just for Christmas or New Years too?"

Latte huffed. "Mom tried to get me to stay for New Years and hook up with George. I told her not to do that, but she did it anyway, so I paid the extra and changed our tickets."

Jet laughed, "She should give up her plans for you."

"When it snows in Hawaii," Latte growled. "Do you know your holiday plans yet?"

Jet shook her head. "I expect an invitation for Christmas dinner from Aunt Pat." She glanced at the boys quietly challenging each other over how much spaghetti they could get on their fork at one time. "Do you want to open your Christmas gifts before you go to California?"

The twins ceased their rivalry to observe the women.

"We could do our own little party here before we go." Latte suggested.

"Tomorrow night?" Jet lifted her eyebrows. "After dinner?"

Landon and Logan cheered their approval then went back to their pasta.

"Have you talked to Roger Thompson recently?"

Surprised by Latte's change of topic, Jet shook her head. "Have you seen him?"

"I thought I saw him out in the driveway this afternoon." She shrugged.

"What would he be doing here?" Jet lifted her palms. "It would simplify things if he were my father. I've lived with his benign neglect all my life."

"But wouldn't it be wonderful to find someone who was excited to be your father and willing to give you the care you deserve?" Latte's voice was full of excited anticipation.

"I don't know what I'd do with the attention. Park said he'd be happy to be my father, but he didn't look like happy about it."

"I'm not sure Park ever looks happy about anything." Latte rose from the table knocking her knife to the floor, bumping her head as she bent to pick it up. "Maybe it would cheer him up."

Jet laughed at her friend's misadventures. "I doubt it."

Chapter Twenty-three

Returning home from work Kinsey followed the taillights of Jet's roadster to the garages. Nathan was just closing the door on his muscle machine and headlights behind Kinsey warned him another resident was in line to put a car away. Jet, Nathan, Susannah, and Kinsey all walked along the path to the house together.

"Did you notice the black SUV sitting outside the main entrance?" Nathan wagged his head in the direction of Gravelly Lake Drive.

"What about it?" Kinsey had noted it but gave it no more thought.

"It's been there every night for the past week." Nathan's tone was suggestive.

Kinsey frowned at him.

"Usually a little farther north."

"What do you think it means?" Susannah, walking on the other side of Nathan, sounded excited.

Nathan snorted. "The police trying to catch us at a crime?"

"Or the Secret Service?" Jet put in.

"You don't think it's Sarkis' truck?" The possibilities were endless including the nosy press. Kinsey made up his mind; time to dig a hole in a wall and see what was there. After dinner, he made a trip to the basement and filled his pockets with wall-breaking tools.

Returning to the main floor, he continued to the kitchen from where the scent of butter and cinnamon enticed him. He found Latte, at the cluttered counter a measuring cup in each hand, pouring ingredients into the mixer bowl while it splattered its contents willy-nilly. Jet was crouched, searching the lower cabinets.

Standing over her, he asked, "What are you looking for?"

"Cookie sheets." She stood.

Kinsey pointed out the baking pans kept in the pantry.

She gathered a pile. "What are you doing?"

"Going to cut into walls," he huffed.

"Think you'll find anything?" She set the pans on the counter.

He waved a come on. "Let's go see."

From the solarium they climbed the circular staircase. Kinsey calculated the second floor room with all the furniture was his best bet. Since it would be a shame to cut into the walnut paneling he made his invasion close to the window, prying a section of the wood loose from the plaster beneath it. He used a handsaw to cut a square about the size of a letterhead.

Once he had made the opening he put his eye to it. All he got for his trouble was darkness. Reaching into his pocket he retrieved a small flashlight. This he put inside the hole.

Well, the girls were right again. He could see stairs coming from the floor above and ending on a landing in the middle of the space behind the wall. From there another set descended to the floor below. And if he wasn't mistaken, they even went farther.

Here was the equivalent of stairs from the third floor to the basement he felt had to be in the house. However, not the ones indicated on the house plans. What did that mean? Who knew about these and how did one get to them? Obtaining those answers leaped onto Kinsey's to-do list.

"Want to see?" He lent Jet the flashlight, but she was too short to reach it.

"Here," he said, "let me lift you up."

She eyed him with suspicion, reluctantly allowing him to hoist her up to the opening. "What do you think it means?"

"I don't know." Kinsey stuck the flashlight back in his pocket. "If this was the extra stairs from the main floor to the third why is it covered up? And why are the stairs on the plans located in a different spot?"

"Have you looked on the third floor?"

No time like this. "Let's go."

Taking the iron staircase again they reached the open balcony on three from which they went into the empty room. But the wall where the stairs would be was as flat and smooth as a Formica tabletop.

Jet sighed moving back to the balcony. "That guy I followed disappeared when he got this far." She studied the wall of the house. "What if he knew how to get into the stairway from here?"

Kinsey gestured at the masonry walls. "Do you see any way to do that?"

"What about where the stairs should be according to the plans?"

"Shall we take a look?" Kinsey motioned to the staircase. "You know these don't make any sense with the others right next to them, especially if those on the plans are there. At least one staircase is excessive."

When they reached the kitchen they found Latte with two large mixing bowls full of dough, an array of cookie sheets awaiting their turn in the oven, and racks of cooling cookies. The aroma alone would have converted an anti-sugar activist into a cookie-aholic.

Latte gave them a big smile from beneath her flower-covered nose. Her jeans and sweatshirt looked as if she'd been rolling in dough. "I got carried away." She laughed. "But I saw a freezer in the pantry."

"You should make some heart-shaped ones. We could use them for Valentines."

Latte gave Jet a tolerant grimace. "So what did you and Kinsey find?"

"You were right. There are stairs in that wall." Kinsey pointed to the laundry room.

The two climbed the backstairs to the second floor again. Kinsey immediately went to the wall where a door to the stairs on the plans should be. Turning to Jet he lifted his hands.

"Make a hole in that wall." She pointed. "That's where Susannah heard the noises. Maybe it's there after all."

Kinsey removed the tools from his back pockets and cut a hole. "Okay, you ready?"

Jet smiled at him. "You go first."

He put the flashlight to the opening and peered in. "Have a look." He handed the flashlight to her. This time he cut lower and Jet was able to see by standing on her tiptoes.

"It's there, just like the plans say."

Jet contemplated Kinsey as their eyes met. The dark hair falling over his forehead emphasized the bewilderment in his expression. "I really didn't believe they'd be here in spite of the logic." He switched off the flashlight and returned it to his pocket.

Jet made an exaggerated grimace. "No wild animals in the wall."

He snorted.

"What are you going to do now?"

He moved to the north end of the hall where he perched on the edge of the metal daybed and ran his hand through his hair. "I have to find out what's in the space we can't get to . . . without digging holes in walls."

"Maybe we missed something outside."

He stared at the floor as if any moment the answer would appear like writing on the wall.

She sat on the faded navy chair near him. "If what we heard on the stairs were footsteps then someone has to know."

"Ghosts?" Kinsey offered a twisted smile. "That's what Dad would say."

Jet made a face. "You don't buy that?"

He shook his head. "Even if more evidence in his favor shows up all the time." He sighed. "We've checked the first and second floors pretty thoroughly, haven't we?"

She mentally walked through the morning room and adjacent solarium, no access from either place. From where they sat on the second floor no visible way into the stairs. "What about the circular stairs? Could a passage be there? The other stairs must be pretty close."

He chewed his lip considering. "If someone is using these stairs or even secret panels, they'd have to live in the house or get in and out without being noticed."

"Latte mentioned seeing Roger Thompson here today."

Kinsey scowled.

"Would anyone notice him? People here just ignore him." She ran her finger along the groves in her French Provincial chair. "Although I can't figure what he'd want here." In spite of the fact he was a shirttail relative to the owners Roger seemed to have more to do with Blast Castle than Jet would have imagined possible.

Kinsey changed the subject. "I've been thinking about that SUV near the entrance tonight, wondering if Sarkis or the Secret Service is doing surveillance."

Jet noted his look of frustration. "Is it a problem?"

"Not really." Kinsey's eyes met hers. "It might be beneficial, especially if we knew who it was."

"You could send Susannah out to have a chat," Jet suggested. "She likes to talk to strangers, especially men."

He shot her an astonished glance. "I wasn't aware you had such a devious mind."

"That's not devious," she protested.

"I'm not sure I'd trust her to give us the straight scoop if she did find out something."

"Now who has the devious mind?"

He stared at Jet as if looking straight through her. Obviously his mind had left on a mission. She watched him contemplate, thinking she wouldn't mind being his sister. However, she realized the feelings Kinsey inspired weren't those she would have for a brother.

Shifting her gaze down the long hall with its bright white walls and twinkling candelabra bulbs she wondered what they would say if they could talk. Could they explain the mysteries haunting Blast Castle?

"There you are." Evana's perfect figure stood outlined in the doorway to the kitchen stairs. "What are you doing here?"

A twinge of guilt attacked Jet as she recalled how much Evana resented her association with Kinsey.

"I've been looking everywhere for you," she went on, hands on her hips. "Dad wants you to call him."

Kinsey's expression froze. "Like the other night?"

Evana opened her eyes wide.

"Okay, I'll call him," Kinsey dismissed her.

She remained standing in the doorway.

"I have my phone here." He removed it from his pocket and held it up.

Making a move, Jet murmured, "Maybe I'd better go help Latte."

"Just stay there," Kinsey ordered. "Is there something else you want?" he addressed Evana.

Flashing Jet an angry look, Evana turned on her heel and left.

Jet sighed. "She doesn't like me."

"I'm beginning to resent her interference."

"She doesn't want you mixed up with someone like my mother."

Kinsey's expression contained both amusement and frustration. "If you think you resemble your mother you need a reality check."

Jet didn't know whether to be complimented or insulted. She knew she did not have her mother's beauty. But she also didn't have her mother's reckless disregard for morality.

"Did I insult you?" Kinsey watched her assimilate his statement.

"I'm trying to decide." She smiled at him, moving her gaze to the black and white tile at her feet.

Kinsey took a deep breath. "Evana's problem has nothing to do with your mother."

Jet turned a questioning glance on him.

He huffed, "And I resent her trying to put me in her boat."

"Don't you think you'd better call your dad?" Jet wasn't sure she had understood the exchange between Kinsey and Evana.

"You think she was serious?" Kinsey tossed Jet a mocking glance.

She cocked her head and frowned at him. "Why wouldn't she be?"

He took out his cell phone and dialed his father. "Did you call?"

Chapter Twenty-four

The closer Christmas came, the less work got done at the office. Kinsey was buried in a review of the inventory process when Lieutenant Sarkis called.

"I need that information on who picked up Markovich's belongings."

"Let me make a phone call and get back to you." Kinsey dialed his father's number, wishing he could be the fly on Sarkis' shoulder. Would he learn something to resolve the mystery at the castle? On the other hand, what might he learn to further incriminate his father? With or without his personal knowledge, Kinsey had to fear what the lieutenant might find to point a finger at Park. Kinsey's own fear of what his father wasn't telling made him suspicious, what would the lieutenant do with it? Although Kinsey believed Park incapable of the crime with which he could be charged, he had insufficient information to convince the lieutenant.

Kinsey's father gave him a list of people with addresses and phone numbers. "I can't guarantee any of this is up to date."

"The lieutenant has sources we hardly suspect." At least, Park's attitude contained no apprehension, which eased Kinsey's mind.

With days so short he rarely had daylight hours at home. Allowing his employees off early, he decided to take extra time himself and drove home before the sun, making a late afternoon appearance, sank beyond the mountains and the sea.

Gravelly Lake Drive possessed a wide shoulder, as it passed the front of the estate. However, to his recollection rarely did anyone park there. Most residences had their own driveways, garages and parking spaces. No business occupied the area once a person got past the intersection with I-5.

Approaching the turn-off into the estate Kinsey noticed just what Nathan had described, an SUV, but not the lieutenant's, parked alongside the road opposite the castle driveway. Passing by to check it out, he went as far as Washington Boulevard, then turned around and returned to the truck. He stopped behind it and took note of the license plate number. Having noticed someone sitting in it, he got out and approached the driver.

The man rolled down the window of the Ford Escape and lifted his eyebrows expectantly.

"I'm Kinsey Sayre. I own the property there." He pointed. "Have you seen anyone coming or going?"

The black man with neatly clipped hair, a navy windbreaker and white shirt eyed Kinsey as if considering how to respond. "Only those cars that leave every morning and return at night."

"You have us under surveillance?"

The man removed a leather folder from inside his jacket and flipped it open for Kinsey to see, United States Treasury Agent.

"You're one of Elaney's men?"

"Apparently you have counterfeit money on your property."

"Had," Kinsey clarified.

It made little impression on the agent. Obviously he figured there's more where that came from. Kinsey sighed. Surveillance was okay, but who did the Treasury Department think was responsible for the hot money. Was it possible someone was manufacturing contraband cash at the estate? It might account for a lot of suspicious events.

Lieutenant Sarkis was unavailable when Kinsey returned his call so he left a message indicating he had the requested information. Since the lieutenant had not called again by the time Kinsey left work he forgot the matter until just before 5:00 pm. when descending the grand staircase he heard the door chime. A quick glance at the wall clock told him it was possible no one else was home yet.

When he opened the door Lieutenant Sarkis stood with his back to it gazing over the property. He turned to consider Kinsey over the edge of his spectacles. "You have those names?"

Kinsey held the door open. "In my briefcase." Sticking his hand into a side pocket he took out the note and handed it to Sarkis.

Glancing at it, the lieutenant said, "We found no usable prints on either those modules or the cages. Either the perp wore gloves or wiped them clean."

What had Kinsey hoped they would find? "Did you learn anything about the other body?"

"The two halves?" Sarkis' tone of voice questioned Kinsey's assumption.

He nodded, wondering if he had just been promoted to the suspect list.

"It's all one body, female, approximately the same age as the other. This one was shorter, larger boned."

"Shot too?"

The lieutenant shook his head. "Fractured skull."

Kinsey hesitated to ask. "Do you have any identification?"

"Not as such." The lieutenant's eagle eyes still scrutinized him. "We don't have much to go on except something found in the first hole the body occupied."

Kinsey raised his eyebrows, hoping the lieutenant would explain, but he just ignored him.

"Do you know any other missing persons?" Sarkis sounded as if he had just cast out his line hoping to reel in an admission.

"No. The other renter wasn't married, lived alone."

The investigator moved farther into the parlor looking around. Kinsey decided to give him something else to focus on. "Agent Elaney has this place under surveillance."

"The van by the entrance?"

Kinsey nodded.

"I'll have to see if he's learned anything."

Kinsey grimaced. This sure was fun, a nest of snakes under every rock.

❧

The Spirit of Christmas Present had captured the bank lobby with white poinsettias at every teller window and a silver-trimmed tree. The Christmas buffet would have warmed even the Grinch's cold heart. Although only a minimum of work got done, bridges of camaraderie were built.

Every holiday event, every scene became a reminder of the castle's Christmas party. Jet made a point to push it out of her mind, sensing the danger in reviewing the evening. She feared making more of the situation than it was, of creating expectations that would only bring pain. Even if he wasn't aware of it, she knew she needed to avoid a close relationship with Kinsey.

When she arrived home as she entered her suite her cell phone rang.

"This is Barb. I checked with the person I thought might know something about that night we discussed."

"Did you learn anything?" Jet moved to the switch for her fireplace.

"He remembered the incident and the guy, but he didn't know the man himself." Barbara sighed as if as disappointed as Jet. "He didn't work with the state government, but was only on a temporary assignment."

Jet wasn't ready to give up. "Did he know his name? Or which department he worked for?"

Barbara's voice was filled with apology. "The only thing he recalled was the guy worked for a law division of the federal government and they called him Sad-O. He thought the man's name rhymed with that and since he was divorced they were making a joke of it."

Jet perched on the heart-shaped stool in front of the fireplace.

"You can talk to him if you want. I'll give you his name and phone number."

Although she took down the information Jet was relatively certain she would not use it. Prying information out of people she knew had the answers was bad enough.

Shaking down a stranger on the off chance he would remember something was over the top. This person didn't sound particularly promising; not that she could blame him. She wasn't sure what she would have remembered thirty years after an event that really didn't concern her.

"I'm sorry, Jessica. I know this means a lot to you."

That was giving it a gentle spin. Until Barbara's call Jet failed to realize how intensely she counted on discovering a key to her paternity. Feeling utterly defeated, she slipped out of her coat and lay on her bed curled in a ball. Her thoughts returned to abandoning the project. Maybe she just needed to move on. However, she knew the question would reappear. She would never be able to get past it until she had an answer one way or the other. Regardless of her willful decisions to let go and put it out of her mind, or of how she assured herself of its unimportance, she would always wonder.

There should be a law against irresponsible conception. There probably was. What good did it do? Once again Jet resolved it would never happen to hers. Holding that thought she drifted into the land of the starry night.

కు

Waking to a knock at her door, Jet's return to reality took a moment. She recalled where she was and what day it was but hadn't made it to the hour when she opened the door.

Kinsey stood with his eyebrows raised. "Are you coming to dinner?"

"Oh," Jet glanced at her watch. "I'll be right there."

Although his expression held a question he simply nodded and left.

When she arrived in the dining room everyone looked up with the same question. "Fell asleep after work," she mumbled, taking her seat.

She filled her plate, inhaling the aroma of herb dressing and glancing around as she did so. Everyone was there except Billy, although his absence was less noticeable than the night before. In addition, his place was occupied by a guest. Park sat across the table between Latte and Nathan. Shooting Kinsey a questioning glance, Jet wondered what had occasioned his father's presence. However, Kinsey was occupied with a question from Nathan.

"So then we really are under surveillance?"

Kinsey grimaced. "By the Secret Service."

"What do they hope to see?" Evana huffed her annoyance.

"Someone sneaking out the gate with a bag of counterfeit money." Nathan wiggled his eyebrows and winked at Jet.

She noticed Park's attention playing hide and seek. What had brought him to the mansion?

Dinner topics moved away from the estate's problems as the guys went on to argue the merits of the local sports teams to which Susannah added a word here and there. When the meal was over, Kinsey, Park, and Nathan disappeared into the library. Jet followed Latte to her suite since they had decided on their own small party. She also needed to confirm arrangements for getting Latte's crew to the airport.

"Our flight is at 8:00 in the morning so we should be there by 6:00. I missed a flight once," Latte responded to Jet's raised eyebrows. "Are you staying in the house for Christmas?"

"I did get a note from Aunt Pat to join the family on Christmas Day. I should bring a gift. What would you suggest?"

"Cookies." Latte laughed.

"That's a good idea. Would you mind?"

Latte laughed again. "Are you kidding?"

"I can probably get some other goodies to add."

"You can drive the SUV if you want. I heard there's supposed to be snow here for Christmas."

Snow made rare appearances in the Pacific Northwest, even more rarely at Christmas. Since the unwelcome visitor tied traffic in knots Jet wouldn't be opposed to using Latte's four-wheel-drive, but she would miss her friend. Latte had become her family. "When are you coming back?"

"Just before New Years." Latte raised her eyebrows. "Evana cornered me last night. She was pumping me about your relationship with Kinsey."

"I don't have a relationship with Kinsey," Jet exploded.

Latte tipped her head and gave Jet a come-on-now look.

Jet sighed. "You know what I mean."

"But you're friends."

"Yes, but . . ."

"I think it's the yes that worries Evana." Latte opened her antique wardrobe and removed a stack of tee shirts. "You need to be careful."

Jet nodded, watching Latte set her pile on the bed and remove a roller bag from beneath it. "Kinsey told me his father was in love with the renter's wife that was killed here."

"Oooo, really?" Latte shot her a wide-eyed glance. "Does the lieutenant know?"

"I don't think so." But, Jet realized, he should have questioned that. "Although he may suspect since he found Park's name on the dead woman's cell phone."

Latte wagged her head solemnly. "No wonder Kinsey is worried."

"I can't believe Park is involved in her death." Jet sat on the lavender bench at the end of the bed.

Latte stopped to frown at her. "Could he be the cause someone else murdered her?"

"Like who?"

"Her husband?" Latte lifted her hands. "Someone else she was involved with, someone involved with Park?"

"Evana?" The name popped out of Jet's mouth before she thought.

"Oh-oh." Latte clapped her hand over her mouth. "We'd better wipe our brains or we'll suspect everyone around."

"I hadn't got as far as suspecting anyone, especially not in the house. But I did wonder if the things going on here are related to this business of dead bodies and counterfeit money."

Jet returned to her suite where she flipped the switch to her gas fireplace, prepared hot chocolate and a plate of Latte's cookies in anticipation of their gift exchange. She sat in the rose-colored chair next to the fire and put her feet on the footstool. As she soaked in the warmth nagging guilt from her conversation with Latte attacked her. Not only was Evana warning her away from her cousin, but so was Latte. She could ignore Evana, but not Latte. Was she in danger of a forbidden relationship with Kinsey? He didn't know the dangers. Would alerting him make it easier? But she had nothing to go on. How would he feel if she told him what she knew about Park's relationship with her mother? How would Park feel?

Then again, did it matter what Park thought? It wasn't as if Jet was to blame for what he and her mother had done. Somehow though, Jet was the one to pay the consequences. It didn't seem fair. The sooner she found out if he was her father the better. Maybe Roger would turn out to be the one and end her search.

Chapter Twenty-five

Surprised when his father showed up just before dinner, Kinsey okayed the extra guest with the cook then invited Park to join them. Given his negative perspective regarding the group at Blast Castle, allowing him an opportunity to observe them might give him a better feeling about it.

In the past few weeks Park had become a ghost of his former self. Was the discovery of Carmen Markovich's body the cause? If his father was in love with her then knowledge she was dead, leaving all hope gone, had to have been a blow.

Once the meal was over Kinsey secured his keys from the library and led his father on a tour of the staircases he had found. As they climbed the circular stairs, Park said, "You know, I think it's possible one of the renters requested permission to have this put in. He was frustrated having to go back to the grand staircase to get to the second and third floors."

When they returned to the library Nathan was sitting by the fireplace flipping through a magazine. Kinsey swiveled the desk chair around while Park arranged himself on the sofa.

"I just thought of something." Nathan closed his magazine and set it on the end table. "Remember that door in the brick wall on the south terrace?"

Kinsey nodded. "The one into the basement?"

"Right."

"Do you think there's a similar door on the north terrace?"

"With access to those stairs in the wall." Nathan sounded as if he ought to be congratulated on solving all the estate mysteries.

Kinsey shrugged. "It's worth a try." He glanced at the French doors where the sun had escaped leaving a black void on which was reflected the room's golden light. "In the daytime."

"Your lieutenant called today." Park ran his hand through his hair.

"My lieutenant?" I should be so lucky. What I couldn't do with a lieutenant of my own. Kinsey scowled at his father.

"He said they located Markovich's possessions. What hadn't been sold or disposed of."

"I have some questions about the people who received them and why." Lieutenant Sarkis spoke from the door like an apparition conjured up by the discussion. "Who would you leave your prize possessions with when you die?"

Nathan and Kinsey exchanged a startled glance.

"My family, probably," Kinsey wondered how the lieutenant got in without being noticed.

"Exactly." Lieutenant Sarkis stepped into the room. "Not your banker."

Nathan laughed. "If I left my stuff with my banker he'd send it back, charge me for the service, and dig me up to collect."

The lieutenant shot Nathan a disapproving glance.

"Did the banker have any other relationship with Markovich?" Maybe it was the man not the banker Markovich had trusted with his possessions.

Sarkis raised an eyebrow, but said nothing.

"What about the other body?" Eventually Kinsey would have to deal with that. "Have you got an identification?"

"Not yet?" The lieutenant raised both eyebrows. "Any ideas?"

"What about someone connected to Carmen Markovich?" Nathan put in.

The lieutenant helped himself to the purple chair. "So far no one connected to her is missing."

"Or her husband?" Kinsey figured he must fit in the deal somewhere.

Sarkis shook his head. "Him neither."

Kinsey sighed. "Is anyone missing who'd fit the remains?"

"Not that we know of."

Nathan rubbed his hands together. "Maybe someone got away with the perfect murder?"

The lieutenant scowled his disapproval. "We'll figure it out, don't you worry."

Kinsey couldn't say he was worried about it, except how the end result might affect him. He glanced at his father. Park looked like he expected another boot to drop.

Jet awoke with an idea born of the cookie baking Latte had done. She would take Roger a gift when they met for the DNA appointment. As soon as she was dressed she knocked on Latte's door.

She opened it still wearing her pajamas. "Sure," she agreed, brushing her hair away from her face. "Help yourself. Obviously I made enough." She laughed at her over-exuberance. "And good luck with Roger."

Rummaging in her closet Jet found a handled basket from the flowers at her mother's funeral. She took it to the kitchen where she used it to prepare a present for Roger wrapped in Christmas cellophane and ribbon.

When she stepped out the French doors to the south terrace, the bite in the air sent her back to put on a heavier jacket. The cloudless sky reflected in the puddles of water along the street made her feel light-hearted and hopeful. Raindrops still clung to the trees glittering in the sun's brilliance, belying the forecast promising snow later in the day. She noticed Roger's Mercedes in the medical center parking lot when she arrived, giving her an even greater amount of confidence.

After making the appointments and talking to the lab personnel she was able to arrange a solution regarding her mother's DNA that, although not the best, may at least be effective for her purposes.

Seated in an easy chair at the entrance Roger rose when she approached. "You ready to face the truth?" He smiled although his eyes held a question. She wished she could have a natural give and take relationship with him, even if he wasn't actually her father. Even if someone else turned out to be, it would not erase years of growing up believing Roger was.

"I'm not sure." Jet sighed. "Maybe it'll be good for you to know you have no responsibility for me."

"What makes you think I want no responsibility for you?" Roger's beady eyes twinkled.

Now that was a stupid question, but one for which Jet had no answer. "Do you know where the lab is?"

Roger pointed to her right. "Down that hall." He ushered her in the direction he indicated to a room to their left. It was a small waiting area with a large counter.

Jet located a sign-in sheet which she filled out then picked a seat next to a table filled with magazines. Roger sat at a right angle to her.

"What's going on at the mansion these days?" Roger tossed the question up nonchalantly.

"Getting ready for Christmas." Jet picked up a magazine with colorful holiday goodies on the cover.

"Is everyone staying there for the duration?"

"No. Susannah is going to Olympia to be with her family, Latte and her kids are going to California, Nathan will be at his mom's. I'm not sure about Evana and Kinsey."

"Isn't there another guy there?" Roger reached for a *Peoples* magazine he opened absentmindedly.

"Billy." Jet hesitated, unsure how much she should say. "He's been away since Sunday."

"Away?" Roger shot her a suspicious glance. "With his family?"

"I don't think so." Jet frowned, uncomfortable with the topic. "Kinsey tried to locate him from his mother, but she hadn't seen him."

"So you don't know where he is?" He mumbled then immediately changed the subject. "Did Kinsey go digging into those walls?"

"He found a couple sets of stairs." Jet explained Kinsey's discovery as she watched another couple enter and sign-in at the counter.

Roger sounded concerned. "Does he know how far it goes?"

Jet shook her head. "He just made a peep hole. He doesn't know how to get to the stairs from outside." She noted Roger's frown. "We're under surveillance by the Secret Service."

"How do you know?"

Wincing at his caustic tone, Jet described Kinsey's encounter with the SUV.

"What are they after?"

"You're aware the kids found counterfeit money on the grounds?"

Roger nodded.

"They've been around ever since trying to figure out where the money came from."

Roger took a deep breath, forcing a smile.

The inside door from the waiting room opened and a nurse appeared. "Jessica Sayre and Roger Thompson."

They followed her into the room adjacent where she pointed each of them to an old-fashioned schoolroom desk. She started with Jet, who concentrated on watching Roger while the nurse drew the blood sample, noting his jaw muscle tensing, testifying he was not so sanguine about the process as he made it appear. It took only a few moments then the nurse thanked and excused them.

The receptionist in the waiting room informed them the results would take at least a week. "You'll receive a letter when they're finished."

"Both of us?"

"That's right."

When they reached the hall, Roger turned to Jet. "You know, even if this turns out negative, you'll still seem like my daughter. You can always count on me if you need help."

Tears came to her eyes at his offer. "Thanks," she mumbled unable to trust her voice further.

Roger patted her shoulder.

She took a deep breath. "Would you come to the car with me?"

Roger's face registered surprise but he followed her to the roadster where she reached into the back seat for the Christmas basket she had prepared and handed it to him. "Merry Christmas."

A faint flush rushed up Roger's cheeks and his eyes became watery. "Thank you. I'm sure it's the best present I'll get for Christmas."

Chapter Twenty-six

Before Nathan could leave for work, Kinsey knocked at his suite. "You up for checking the north terrace for that door?"

"Sure." Dressed for work, Nathan grabbed his jacket and followed Kinsey to the solarium where they opened the French doors to the patio.

The sunshine played games with the frosty bite in the air, much more penetrating on the north side. Kinsey shivered as he considered the stone facade. "How did you find the other one?"

"By accident. I was running my hand along the bricks and there was an extra large space between a couple of them."

Kinsey eyed the wall looking for lack of symmetry in the arrangement of stone. Starting just below the windows for the second floor he moved his gaze across and down. Barely visible, the disparity was but a shadow along the line of masonry between the solarium and the laundry room windows. Nathan saw it at the same time and the two moved to the spot. Running his hand down to where the grout made a grove, Nathan located a notch allowing him to pull the door loose.

"There must be an easier way to get in than this."

Nathan stood back. "Are you ready see what's there?"

No way, Kinsey sighed. But hesitation wouldn't help. "Let's go."

Working together, they made the opening large enough to enter. This time Kinsey brought a flashlight and with it lit the darkness exposing the stairway down. He glanced back at Nathan. "Coming?"

"Maybe we should have a weapon or some means of self-defense."

"This is my house," Kinsey declared.

Nathan snorted. "You can die in your own house as well as someone else's."

At the bottom of the stairs they stopped to regard their surroundings.

"Empty." Nathan sounded disappointed.

Kinsey had many ideas of what he might find, but nothing was not among them.

In this spot the basement included an oblong room into which the stairway descended. Left of the stairs was a wide passage to another area. Moving that direction the guys looked at walls and floor. The next space was smaller but held a washer and dryer.

"What do you think this means?" Nathan wandered along the perimeter.

Kinsey lifted the washer lid. "It might be the reason Latte ran out of hot water." Making sure the temperature was set to hot, he turned the dial and water flowed into the tub. He tested and indeed the water was hot.

Nathan came to stand beside him. "Have you ever read how they make counterfeit money?"

Kinsey shook his head.

"A recent method is to take one dollar bills, bleach the ink out then reprint them in a larger denomination. They use a photocopier."

Kinsey opened the dryer and, crouching, peered inside, but saw nothing. He ran his hand around the interior and felt a rough edge. When he rubbed it he loosened a piece of paper about two by seven inches. He removed it and handed it to Nathan. "What do you think?"

"You'd better get your Secret Service guy here before you make so many fingerprints he thinks you're the one printing money."

Kinsey rose. "Why do you suppose there's nothing here?"

"Well," Nathan grimaced. "If they were in the house they might have realized you were getting close to discovering them."

"But how could they get everything out without someone noticing?" Kinsey struggled to prevent denial from making excuses for what he saw.

"No one is here most of the day."

"But the Secret Service is sitting at the gate watching," Kinsey protested.

"Maybe they're keeping what they see to themselves."

Kinsey considered. "You'd think though, if that were the case, they'd be nosing around the house too."

Nathan shot him a cheesy grin. "Maybe they are—when no one is here."

That aggravated Kinsey. "Wouldn't it be illegal?"

"Probably." Nathan shrugged. "Maybe they have a warrant in case they need it."

That does it, Kinsey thought, Agent Elaney was going to have to cough up some information.

Nathan had moved to the foot of the stairs. "Do you think we should go up and see what else is here?"

Kinsey followed as Nathan climbed three flights of stairs. When they reached the small landing at the top they found a pair of double six-panel doors opening into an oblong room with tall windows at the far end.

"It's not as clean here," Nathan observed, moving to the center of the room.

On the floor lay several mattresses each moved into one of the corners. A couple of them were accompanied by an antique night stand.

"Do you think they slept here?" Nathan continued to the windows facing east.

"Looks like it." Kinsey followed to the middle of the room where he noticed another section. Between was a door that opened into a bathroom where he found clumps of toothpaste still clinging to the sink. Evidence indicated toilet articles had occupied the medicine cabinet. "Maybe we should let Sarkis know. He could get his forensics in to check."

"Do you think these people are responsible for the murders?"

"I don't know who's responsible for anything." Kinsey barked. He wasn't ready to make any judgments. "But I don't want to overlook an opportunity to get hold of some evidence. I want this whole mess cleared up."

Here could be answers to account for mansion ghosts, the noises on the stairs, maybe even odd people on the grounds. Kinsey still wondered about the light phenomenon.

Walking from the garages to the mansion after work, Jet noted both the black Acura and SUV in the circular driveway. Auspicious, both the lieutenant and Secret Service Agent were in attendance at Blast Castle. What was up now? Approaching the south terrace she observed a glow from the library windows where she could see men gathered around the fireplace.

Jet felt at loose ends with Latte and the boys in California. Climbing the stairs to her suite she realized this had become an ideal solution for them. If Kinsey lost the house then they all would need to move again. She did not want that.

The thought of Anatuviak reminded her, with Latte gone, she was responsible for him. Grabbing her parka, scarf and gloves, she located him and headed out into the weather. Already large white flakes drifted to the ground, disintegrating at touchdown.

Anatuviak raced briskly along the edge of the driveway as they made their way toward Gravelly Lake Drive. He stopped occasionally to shake the flakes off his coat, looking at her as if encouraging her to move a little faster. Snow came more steadily now, pelting her cheeks and sticking to her eyelashes.

Jet wondered what new problem was making the scene. Even though Kinsey annoyed her at times she had come to appreciate their camaraderie. The level of empathy they had for one another she found compelling. Maybe that was what it was like to have a brother. She had no idea; no idea what it was like to have a father or a sibling. She wasn't even sure she knew what it was like to have a mother, although she certainly had one of those.

Roger's offer of assistance surprised and touched her, but she had failed to express her appreciation. Her next target was Park. Desire was growing to discover he was not her father, which made her all the more apprehensive that he was. And yet, her greatest fear convinced her it was Mr. Unknown and she would never know him.

As they reached the house she noticed the men had broken up their meeting and were standing in a group facing each other. She used the main entrance, stepping into the parlor as Susannah descended the stairs.

Noticing Jet, she waved a hand indicating the men. "What's that big confab about?"

Jet shook her head.

"Is Billy still gone?" Susannah's painted brows arched.

"As far as I know." Jet paused, removing her hat and gloves.

Susannah lowered her voice, glancing toward the library. "He kept asking me whether Kinsey found any more stairs."

"Did you ask why he wanted to know?"

"No." Susannah took a couple steps toward the dining room then turned back to Jet. "By the way did he find any?"

"Two sets, but what difference would that make to Billy?"

She shrugged. "He seemed more interested than just idle curiosity."

The men left the library advancing toward the girls. Jet noticed Kinsey's preoccupied expression. She also observed Agent Elaney staring at her. Had she become a prime suspect for counterfeiting?

He detoured around Davy Sarkis to approach her. "How is your friend whose boys found the money?"

That was it, Latte. "She's in California for Christmas with her parents." Jet took the first step on the staircase, putting her closer to eye-level with the man.

He lifted his eyebrows, continuing his stare. "I understand you're related to Roger Thompson."

Was he connecting Roger to the counterfeiting?

He gazed beyond her to the gallery wall where a series of portraits led the way upstairs. Susannah's comment about Agent Elaney being good looking flashed into Jet's mind. Beyond a polished professional appearance, he had thick dark hair and the eyes of a mysterious romantic. However, lines on his face and flecks of gray in his hair gave away his age.

"He was married to your mother, I understand." His gaze returned to Jet's face and remained there.

"Is that a crime?" It probably should be Jet thought bitterly.

The agent laughed. "No."

"He could be my father," Jet said, wondering why she gave out that information. Every time she opened her mouth she dug a hole into which she figured she would eventually tumble. How could her mother's marriage to Roger have anything to do with crimes at the mansion?

Agent Elaney opened his mouth then closed it. He appeared to consider an idea then discard it, arousing her curiosity. She contemplated asking what all the questions were for, but at that moment Lieutenant Sarkis addressed her.

"How much description could you give me of those you've seen around the property you didn't recognize?"

"Pretty vague." Jet grimaced "It was usually night and they were a fair distance away."

"How about a general physical description?" Sarkis approached the staircase.

Jet mounted the next step, but this didn't get her even close to eyelevel with the lieutenant. "The one I saw was a white male with dark hair, less than average height, and trim, who could have been any age from thirty to sixty."

"That fits with the man we saw at the apartment," Kinsey put in.

"The one I saw," Susannah approached, "was big." Her eyes widened with the word. "Ugly and mean."

Lieutenant Sarkis inventoried the faces around him. "It makes sense there were more than one."

☙

After dinner Kinsey stopped Jet with a hand on her shoulder. "Aunt Pat wanted to make sure you were coming for Christmas dinner."

Jet smiled, nodding. "I'm at loose ends with Latte and the kids gone."

"You'd be welcome Christmas Eve, too. In fact, consider this an invitation." He didn't need permission to invite someone to the home where he grew up. "We have dinner earlier in the evening then dessert. After that we go to the 11:00 candlelight service at church."

Doubt flickered across Jet's face, but she agreed. "What was the conference in the library about?"

Kinsey paused next to the grand piano. "Nathan and I found another entrance to the basement." Smiling at her, he leaned against the piano and explained their sojourn.

"So you figure there really was counterfeiting going on here?"

"Probably," he grumbled, assessing Jet's mood. "Agent Elaney had some questions about you."

She raised her eyebrows. "What kind of questions?"

"Do you take after your mother?"

"He wanted to know if I was a wanton scarlet woman?"

Kinsey laughed. "I don't think he was looking for a quick trick."

"Like anyone would." Jet blushed, her fair skin turning pinkish. "Did he know my mother?"

"I didn't get that impression."

Jet moved to the alcove behind the piano where tall windows looked toward the lake. "He asked me about my mother and Roger." She glanced at him from the corner of her eye. "I thought he was rather nosy."

Kinsey followed her. Snow in swirling flurries was sticking to the ground. "Maybe it was Roger he wanted to know about, not your mom."

"Maybe." Jet frowned at Kinsey. "Do you think I should leave Anatuviak outside?"

"Probably not." He considered the dog's predicament. "It's not usually so cold here."

"Where can I put him?"

"There's not much in the morning room." Kinsey headed to the library then stepped onto the terrace where Anatuviak lay on the mat in the front of the French doors.

Accompanying him, Jet moved to where the dog's leach was anchored at the edge of the terrace. Already a couple inches of snow had accumulated. "He's probably never seen snow before."

"Let him go. See what he does."

She frowned at Kinsey. "He'll be a mess."

"We can wipe him off."

She unhooked Anatuviak's leach. He stood for a moment uncertainly looking up at her. She pointed. "Go."

Then he was gone, galloping across the lawn burying his nose in the snow. Jet put her hand out to catch the flakes. Kinsey made a snowball he threw at Anatuviak who paused in his exploration to observe the missile sail past then headed for the front of the house. Jet and Kinsey moved to the west edge of the terrace from where they could watch the dog as he galloped in circles, some making no sense and others around objects like the yard lamp. He took a spin around the empty fountain. On the far side he paused to sniff, remaining there. Jet called to him. He raised his head to look at her then returned to his investigation.

"Did he find something?" Kinsey moved toward the paver encircled fountain.

Jet followed, stepping in Kinsey's footprints.

Anatuviak looked up and barked. Kinsey stopped. "Is that an invitation or a warning?"

"Maybe it's just a comment."

The closer they got the louder the dog barked. Kinsey stopped abruptly across from Anatuviak causing Jet to run into him.

"Sorry." She stepped back.

As she wobbled Kinsey put his hand on her arm to steady her. They both looked down at her Birkenstock sandals. "I wasn't intending to go walking in the snow."

"Shall I carry you?"

She scowled at him.

"Okay," he laughed, "I get the point."

Kinsey moved around the fountain to where Anatuviak was nosing a hole.

"What have you found, boy?" Kinsey crouched beside the dog, mumbling, "I'm not sure I want to know." Putting his hand in a hole next to the brick walkway he drew out a pistol. Looking up at Jet from his crouched position he grumbled, "What do you suppose this means?"

Jet removed the scarf from around her neck and handed it to him. "You'd better put it in this until we find out."

Chapter Twenty-seven

As soon as Jet, Anatuviak and the gun were safely in the house Kinsey called Lieutenant Sarkis who didn't answer, so he left a message.

He had no idea what the find meant. He had never been told what gun killed Carmen Markovich and could only guess he had found the weapon. The moment he saw what the dog uncovered his heart sank. He had hoped solutions to the mysteries would lead law enforcement away from the castle, disperse the rumors, and dispel the cloud hanging over it. He felt like a Whack-a-Mole, every time he stuck his head up he got slammed with another problem.

Kinsey figured he better inform Aunt Pat he had invited Jet for the evening. Although Pat wouldn't mind she would be unhappy if he didn't give her a heads up. Evana might be unhappy, but then it wasn't any of her business.

"Did you get her a gift?" Aunt Pat asked when Kinsey phoned.

Ughhh! He hadn't thought of that. "Should I get something from me or the whole family?"

Aunt Pat made a humming noise as she considered. "Best get her something from the family, or from Dan, you, and I."

"Any suggestions?"

"Let me tell you what not to get her," Pat said, "jewelry, cologne, or clothing. Get her something generic, or something related to her work, or something amusing, or all three."

"She's a bank officer."

"Then get her something for her desk at work."

That was a good idea.

A disagreeable thought seized him as he noted the brightness of the cloudy day. A quick glance out the window confirmed his premonition. Nature had dumped a load of snow. One thing his vintage BMW couldn't do was go in the snow. Its powerhouse rear wheel drive just dug a hole. Although the storm had ceased for the moment, the lead gray sky promised more. He could borrow Dan's SUV if he could get there. As he stared out the window debating his choices he noticed Jet bundled like a snow-bunny trudging across the front of the house heading toward the garages. Suddenly he recalled that she had Latte's SUV. If he could catch her, he might be able to get a ride.

Grabbing his parka and gloves he roared down the grand staircase and out the anteroom door. "Jet!" In the suspended stillness of the snow-bound day, his voice sounded like a blow-horn.

Jet stopped and turned.

Catching up to her, out of breath from fighting the deep snow, he puffed his request for a ride.

Her kaleidoscope eyes were the same color as the heavy clouds above them. A trace of uncertainty appeared. "Where are you going?"

He hesitated, realizing he wanted to be taken clear across town. "Aunt Pat's?"

She smiled at him. "You're not sure?"

"Yes. No. I'm not sure if you can take me that far."

"If I can take you anywhere I assume I can take you there."

Of course, she was the self-sufficient woman.

They trudged the rest of the way to the garages. Jet turned the key but Kinsey lifted the door before she had the chance. He received a frown for his trouble.

When they were belted in she asked, "Did you tell your dad about the gun?"

"I suppose I'll have to." Kinsey sighed. Yuk! Would his father have known anything about that? Doubts about his father's involvement in the mysteries washed over him again.

When she dropped him off he informed her of dinnertime. Noting a couple vehicles had left the garage previous to his arrival, he hoped the SUV would be available.

✌

Earlier Jet had confiscated some of Latte's cookies and wrapped them on a red plastic plate in Christmas decorated cellophane. After dropping Kinsey at his aunt's she proceeded to a strip mall where she purchased an assortment of gourmet coffees, a Belgian cocoa mix, flavored teas, Godiva chocolates, and a set of red and white snowflake mugs. She returned to the castle where she prepared a gift basket for the Barnes household.

Commiserating with Kinsey's shock and disappointment at Anatuviak's find, she realized it added another complication to his objective. Why she took on Kinsey's problems as if they were her own she had difficulty justifying. A hazy enchanted rhapsody floated somewhere within her emotions hinting at what prompted her interest, a melody that wouldn't let her go in spite of her dread of its significance. Determined to keep the lid on her emotional box she refused to consider what secrets resided there.

On her way down the grand staircase she heard the reverberation of the door chime. Realizing no one else may be home, she went to answer the door.

"Roger," she breathed. To her surprise he stood in the anteroom, snowflakes glistening on the shoulders of his pea coat. "Come in."

He removed his felt hat. "You home alone?" he asked, his beady eyes taking in the room.

"I don't know. Were you looking for someone in particular?"

"You." He smiled and handed her a bright red vinyl bag stuffed with green and white tissue paper. "Merry Christmas. I thought I'd act like a father while I still had the chance."

Blushing as tears came to her eyes, Jet opened her mouth but no words came out.

Roger put his hand on her shoulder. "It's not that wonderful."

Jet laughed as she reached into the bag and drew out a bottle of Versace cologne. Tears came to her eyes again. She brushed them away with her hand, murmuring her thanks.

Roger looked touched, almost regretful. "I guess I should have done the father thing sooner."

Jet took a deep breath recovering. "Would you like coffee or something?"

"If you have a minute."

"Sure. Sit down. I'll go see what's there."

She left him and went to the kitchen where she poured a couple cups, heated them, and raided Latte's stock of cookies.

Roger stood in front of the arched windows staring into the driveway where snow swirled around the fountain. Jet joined him, placing her tray of refreshments on a round occasional table.

"Has Kinsey solved any of his mysteries?"

"No. He just keeps getting hit with more."

Roger turned a frown on her.

"We found a gun near the fountain."

"A gun!" Alarm leaped into Roger's eyes. "What kind of gun?"

Jet shook her head. "I don't know anything about them."

"Have the police been here?"

"Kinsey couldn't get hold of the lieutenant."

Roger recovered his composure, giving her an indulgent smile as he took a seat. "Sounds like you and your landlord are pretty close."

Jet tensed defensively. "He could be my brother."

Raising a skeptical eyebrow, Roger studied her a moment. "I'm not sure emotions cooperate with intellect. I might have avoided your mother if that were the case." He took a cookie. "Has that Secret Service Agent been around lately?"

"They had a conference here the other night, he and Lieutenant Sarkis."

Roger grimaced.

"Kinsey and Nathan found a way into the basement area they couldn't get into before."

Choking on his cookie, Roger took a gulp of coffee. "What did they find?"

"Nothing much." Jet shrugged. "They figured someone could have been using the washer and dryer to launder money."

"That's not what laundering money means." Roger smiled. "Did they find any?"

Blushing at her ignorance Jet shook her head. "They also went to the third floor on stairs inside the walls."

"Did they find anything there?" Roger's gaze had drifted over Jet's shoulder.

"I don't think so." She sensed his apprehension. "Not to amount to anything. They still need the police to come in and examine it."

Jet observed Roger as he took another cookie, staring across the room with narrowed eyes. "Did you ever meet the renters who lived here?"

Roger lifted his eyebrows. "I met the guy that was killed one time. I don't even know why I was here, but I ran into him out on the driveway, not literally. Pompous chap, acted like I was spying on him."

"Did you meet his wife?"

"I saw her from a distance once, an attractive woman."

What brought Roger to the estate so often and why so concerned about Kinsey's finds?

As if reading her mind, Roger explained, "I knew the people on the property next to this. While their driveway was being refinished the only access was through here."

Jet managed her face to keep from looking skeptical. The only thing she remembered Kinsey mentioning was that one neighbor owned a Mercedes dealership. She decided to investigate what Roger said.

ᴄᴐ

Graciously allowing Kinsey use of his SUV, Uncle Dan added that it gave him a good excuse to stay home and not get caught in Aunt Pat's errands. A few moments out on the snow covered roads convinced Kinsey Jet was a better driver than he gave her credit for. Even with four-wheel drive it was tricky.

At Office Depot he found an elegant silver frame that held a collage of snapshots. After seeing her reaction to the one Evana had given her, he figured Jet would appreciate some photographs of the family they shared.

It was late afternoon by the time he accomplished his task. Evana came into the dining room as he finished wrapping the gift. Her intense expression warned him she was on the attack.

"Aunt Pat said Jet is coming tonight." Evana crossed her arms over her chest.

Kinsey stared at his sister, waiting for a shot from the other barrel.

"Does she need to be part of everything we do from now on?"

He taped his tag to the package. "She's part of the family."

Evana frowned. "Just the extended family. Isn't it enough that she comes tomorrow?"

Time had come to confront Evana. "Why is it such a big deal to you? Why do you dislike her so?"

"I don't dislike her," Evana's voice was painstakingly patient.

Kinsey shot her a convince-me-of-that look. "Then what is your problem?"

"I think you're becoming dangerously attached to her."

"Dangerously?" Kinsey almost laughed thinking of tiny Jet.

Evana opened her mouth then closed it again.

"If I had a thing for Jet it wouldn't be anyone else's business. Regardless of what you think I was never in love with Carol. She was a witch. I was well to be rid of her. Someday there'll be someone for me. I'll get married and have children like a normal person."

"You can't know that." Evana blasted him.

"Yes, I can, because that is what I intend to do." He flashed a "so there" look at her.

A smug smile played at her lips. "What if it doesn't work out?"

She was pushing Kinsey's buttons. She had always been good at that. "It won't be because I didn't try and it won't be because of you. I'm your brother Evana, nothing more, nothing less." He took a deep breath. "And for your information, Dad is your father, nothing more, nothing less."

"You're wrong about Carmen Markovich." Evana straightened her shoulders. "Dad was never in love with her."

"Go ask him yourself."

Evana's face flushed and her eyes flashed. Whirling on one foot she vaulted from the room.

Jet arrived just before the appointed dinner hour, carrying a gift basket. Her bouffant hair was held back with a red sparkle headband matching the sweater she wore with a short black skirt and boots. On the staircase as she came in, Kinsey noticed her pink cheeks and the melting snowflakes glistening in her hair. She looked like a wee fairy who could turn the room into a cloud of stars with a wave of her hand. She shot him a defiant glance as she noticed him staring at her.

Uncle Dan had answered the door and taken her coat before Kinsey reached the foyer. He accompanied her into the deserted living room where the Christmas tree sparkled with hundreds of miniature gold lights. A pile of decorated packages lay arranged beneath it.

Jet headed there and placed her basket next to the others. She stopped to admire a crystal angel standing on a lamp table across the room from the tree. "It's lovely. You can see the Christmas lights in the glass."

She was right, Kinsey observed. The angel changed color depending on the direction from which one observed it. "A little like life, you can look at it from different perspectives."

She stared at him with double lines between her eyes then touched the dainty harp the angel held. "If you can detach yourself from the outcome."

Aunt Pat stood in the doorway beckoning them to dinner. As soon as they entered the dining room she commandeered Jet, seating her beside herself across from Uncle Dan and Great Aunt Tansy. It briefly crossed Kinsey's mind his aunt was heading off trouble, which made him resentful of Evana who sat across the table from him.

What gave his sister the right to order his life around? He sighed. Was he letting her do that? Did he need to take a get-out-of-my-life stand? As peace-loving as his father, Kinsey didn't want to cause a family schism. Maybe Park could better address Evana's issues. He could defend himself regarding Carmen Markovich. Evana wasn't convinced by anything Kinsey said.

Chapter Twenty-eight

"Do you miss your mom," Aunt Pat asked, passing Jet the salad dressing.

"At the holidays?"

Pat nodded.

Jet sighed. "Christmas didn't mean much to Mom."

"We're pleased you could join us." Pat appeared embarrassed for having asked.

Jet looked down at her plate, mumbling her thanks. She wasn't buying, at least not everyone was glad. She noted the cold looks from Evana and Kinsey, facing his sister across the table, looked frustrated.

"Do you know my mother's sisters?" This might be a good time to locate them.

"They're traveling this year for Christmas, but maybe they'll be here New Years. That is if you are." Pat gazed at Jet with raised eyebrows.

Was that an invitation? Jet smiled, feeling uncertain how to respond. "What are they like?"

"A lot different from your mom." Pat laughed.

Jet grimaced. "The black sheep daughter."

Aunt Pat regarded Jet with sympathy in her eyes. "I think you'll like them. You're more like them than your mom."

"Thank you." Jet didn't know her aunts, but felt certain if they were unlike her mother Aunt Pat had given her a compliment.

"Your mom got caught up in the sixties feminism. She was rebellious to begin and that gave her a cause. She adopted the worst of the Counter Culture principles."

"Were there good ones?" Jet knew her mom but not much about the Counter Culture.

"Financial freedom allowed women to have credit, better paying jobs, more opportunity for education. It took away many of the professional limitations and prejudices." Aunt Pat hesitated. "Unfortunately I think your mom was interested in sexual freedom?"

"Sexual slavery," Great Aunt Tansy rasped, wagging her finger at Jet. "They said they didn't want to be treated like sex objects, then they went out and did everything they could to become objects of sex."

Uncle Dan covered his laugh with a cough.

Keeping her smile in check, Pat said, "Of course birth control came along so they could be promiscuous and not pay the consequences."

"They still pay the consequences," Aunt Tansy disagreed. "They just think they don't."

Jet stared at the little old lady with growing curiosity.

Aunt Tansy continued, "Women wanted love and security so they declared their independence from morality and now they get sex instead of love and the opportunity to provide their own security. Stupid!" She declared with a definitive bob of her head, "I'm glad to be an old lady."

Jet noted the merry twinkle in Uncle Dan's eyes.

Aunt Pat coughed nervously. "She's right. I'm still trying to figure out how it all happened."

"So there's no love anymore?" Jet asked.

Uncle Dan shook his head. "Men still fall in love like they always did, although often not with the one they have sex with."

Jet frowned. "Why is that?"

"The innate desire to pursue and win their love, not get her by default when she throws herself at him."

Jet wondered what her mother would have said to such an idea. Her gaze drifted down the table to Park. Obviously he had not been in love with available Mona, but according to Kinsey had fallen in love with out of reach Carmen Markovich.

When dinner was completed, Jordan's daughters helped Francine and Evana clear the table as everyone else retired to the living room and prepared to open gifts.

Jet felt intimidated by the prospect. When she was little, Mona had done the Santa Claus thing. They had put up a small tree with gifts beneath it and somewhere a stocking would be hung filled with small surprises. Thinking back Jet realized there had never been many gifts for Mona. Was that the crux of her issue with Christmas? It wasn't about her and she didn't know how to handle that.

When everyone had settled around the Christmas tree, Jordan's daughters handed out the gifts. Mary May handed Jet a shirt-sized box wrapped in foil and topped with an elaborate bow, indicating it came from Aunt Pat, Uncle Dan and Kinsey. It was heavier than an article of clothing would be and rattled. She glanced at Kinsey watching her with smiling encouragement.

She undid the bow then carefully slit the tape and removed the paper. Inside was a nine by fifteen silver frame containing a collage of pictures. Jet smiled at Kinsey then studied the pictures, recognizing most of the family. However, there were several people Jet did not remember.

All around the others laughed, cheered, squealed with pleasure at the various gifts they received. Kinsey opened a box containing an IPAD at which he seemed both pleased and surprised.

Time raced by and soon Park announced that it was time to leave for the church services.

℘

Kinsey indicated he would ride to church with Jet.

As they merged onto I-5, she asked, "Has your family gone to church always?"

"No. I don't think Uncle Dan went to church at all until he married Aunt Pat. She is lucky he was open to becoming a believer."

Jet frowned. "Why do you say that?"

"It's not good for a believer to marry someone who isn't." Although likely to land him in a corner, there was no sense dodging the issue. "Unbelievers tend to lead believers away from their faith."

"Couldn't it be the other way around?"

"Theoretically." Kinsey sighed. "But that's not usually what happens."

As the air grew colder the track in the street became an icy threat, and the church parking lot a hockey rink with cars for pucks.

Kinsey ushered Jet into the foyer behind Park, Evana, and Francine. Hanging back as they entered the softly lit sanctuary, Evana purposefully escorted Jet ahead of her then followed immediately, effectively sitting between Jet and Kinsey.

Evana's interference pushed Kinsey's frustration up the scale, making focusing on the service difficult. He no longer considered Evana's problem, which seemed obvious, but struggled with his personal chagrin. It wasn't inappropriate for Evana to sit between him and his cousin. He behaved if Jet were exactly what Evana accused her of being. A mental twinge sent naked truth in pursuit of denial. Kinsey's emotional radar detected an impending pitfall and flashed him a warning. His mind shifted to the service, which interspersed Bible passages depicting the birth of Christ with Christmas carols.

Two-thirds of the way through the service, ushers brought tapers to the head of each isle, lighting the first person's candle, who in turn lit the others in the pew, filling the church with the golden glow. Overhead lights were dimmed intensifying the Christmas tree's lights and prayers were whispered. A soloist sang *O Holy Night* with such reverence it sent chills up his spine. He found himself glancing at Jet to determine her reaction. However, Evana blocked his view.

Once the service was over he stepped into the isle and waited for the girls, forcing his sister out first. Kinsey fell in behind Jet. As Evana moved into the narthex toward Park and Dan, Kinsey whispered to Jet pointing to the side door, "Maybe we can beat the rush out of the parking lot."

"Are you going back to Aunt Pat's?" Jet asked when they were buckled into Latte's SUV.

"I think I'll stay at the castle. That should make it easier for you. I don't know what tomorrow's weather will be like. Maybe we could go to dinner at the Barnes together."

Although the automatic yard lights were on the house remained dark except for a dim glow over the door to the anteroom.

"I think we're probably the only ones around tonight."

Already past midnight the brightness of the snow reflecting the moon gave light to the parlor as it bounced off the crystal white and in through the windows. Something about the emptiness of the mansion and the night's chill made Kinsey reluctant to let go of Jet's company.

"How about hot chocolate and cookies?"

Jet laughed. "Are you cooking?"

"You think I can't?"

She shook her head then shrugged. "Sure."

They continued through the dining room where moonlight made the crystal pendants on the chandeliers shimmer. Kinsey flipped the switches that lit the ones in the kitchen.

"I can get cookies if you do the chocolate." Jet found a couple large green mugs and Christmas napkins. She placed them on the breakfast bar with a plate of cookies. "Will you explain now why someone who believes like you is in danger with someone who doesn't?"

Turning on the kettle Kinsey sighed. Give me the right words, his soul pleaded with God. "You know what sin is right?"

Jet frowned. "Doing something wrong?"

"Technically." To explain one thing always required explaining something else. Why was he reluctant to do this? Normally he would sail into the explanation without even waiting for an invitation. "But you need to understand what makes something wrong."

While Kinsey poured the hot chocolate, she perched on the stool facing him with her unreserved attention.

"When Eve ate the apple from the tree of forbidden fruit she failed God's test of obedience, trust and submission. She fell for Satan's temptation to pride. She wanted to be equal with God. Satan made her believe God was withholding something from her."

"Was He?"

"In a way. What she knew nothing about was evil. Her life was all goodness, harmony, and love. After they ate the apple what they learned was about sin and its consequences. They hadn't had to deal with that before. They hadn't disobeyed God so they had a perfect relationship with Him and each other. Now they had to deal with evil and all the pain, sorrow, illness, and death that come with it." Kinsey held Jet's regard for a moment. He took a deep breath and went on. "Adam and Eve started out perfect then they disobeyed God and became sinful. Now because of what they did, we all start out sinful and automatically don't want to obey God or believe in Him. It is only through faith with God's help that we can even want what is right."

Jet stirred hot water into her chocolate and reached for a cookie. "Because people want to be bad more than good it's hard to marry someone who doesn't believe?"

Kinsey grabbed a couple cookies. "People naturally don't believe, so any bad influence is stronger than good."

"So what makes someone a believer?"

Kinsey sipped his chocolate watching Jet's face. "Admitting that they sin against God and accepting Jesus as their savior."

"So where does Jesus come in?"

"When Adam and Eve sinned God had a plan to restore them to their perfection again. He sent Jesus, His son, to die in their place for the things they did wrong, allowing them back into their relationship with Him if they believe in Jesus and what He did."

She raised her eyebrows. "And all you have to do is believe?"

He nodded, taking a gulp of his chocolate.

Chapter Twenty-nine

Kinsey's words invaded Jet's dreams. Believing didn't seem that hard. Although confused about the sin thing she had no difficulty acknowledging she made mistakes. She could even deal with reverence and respect for God. But trust and submission? Life taught her to trust no one and a person didn't submit to someone she didn't trust.

Christmas morning brought a sun so bright it felt like flood lights. Her spirits lifted realizing the ice would melt and make traveling easier. Unsure when they were expected at the Barnes for dinner, Jet stepped across the hall and knocked on Kinsey's door. Receiving no answer she recalled her responsibility for Anatuviak. Putting on her parka she headed downstairs for the dog. On the main floor the smell of coffee drew her into the kitchen where she found Nathan making breakfast.

"I thought you were gone for the week."

"I am, sort of." He sprinkled cheese on eggs in the frying pan. "I came by to get a few things and decided it would be easier to fix something here than find a place to buy it."

"Doesn't your mom fix breakfast on Christmas?" Not that Jet's ever did.

"Not until lunchtime." He grabbed the English muffins from the toaster.

Jet zipped her jacket. "Have you seen Kinsey?"

Nathan shook his head. "Is he here?"

"He was last night." A twinge of discomfort attacked her at Nathan's inquisitive glance. "We came back here after the eleven o'clock church service." Nathan's raised eyebrows made an unfounded accusation. Jet added, "He was down here when I went upstairs last night."

"I'd like to see him myself." Nathan slid his eggs onto a plate and poured a cup of coffee. "I saw someone who looked like Billy Monk."

"Where?" Jet eyed his coffee thinking it was a good idea.

"Crossing the street where my mom lives." Nathan lifted his shoulders. "But I didn't know what he'd be doing there or why he doesn't come to the house."

"Was he alright?"

Nathan paused to think. "Basically. He looked okay, but he walked carefully, if you know what I mean."

"Like someone who had surgery?"

Nathan pointed his fork at her. "Precisely."

"You should have followed him."

"I did," Nathan said, "for a while. But it was difficult since he was on foot and I was in the car."

A noise near the back door was Kinsey, entering the room wearing a parka, knit hat, and gloves. "What inspired the powwow?"

"Hunger," Nathan answered.

"I'm taking Anatuviak for a walk. Nathan thinks he may have seen Billy."

Kinsey turned to Nathan who explained what he had told Jet.

"That's odd." Kinsey removed his hat leaving his hair standing on end. "His family lives on this side of town."

"Maybe he's avoiding his family," Jet suggested.

"Couldn't blame him."

Nathan dusted the crumbs off his hands. "Thanks to whoever made coffee this morning."

"You're welcome," Kinsey gave him an exaggerated grin then turned to Jet. "What time were you heading to the Barnes?"

She had no idea when dinner was. "Eleven?"

"Sounds good." Kinsey poured himself a cup of coffee then grabbed the creamer from the refrigerator. "I have to talk to Dad about that gun."

"Maybe he can guess who it belongs to."

Kinsey grimaced. "I can't decide if it would be better for him to know or be totally in the dark."

"Are you afraid he's mixed up in this business?" Nathan asked.

"I know he's mixed up in it. I'm afraid of how." Kinsey dropped a couple pieces of bread into the toaster. "Where did you see Billy?"

"If it was him," Nathan cautioned. "Near the pharmacy on Pearl and 21st."

Kinsey turned to Jet. "Why don't we cruise through there on the way to dinner?"

Jet nodded then left to fetch Anatuviak from the morning room.

A few minutes after eleven she descended the stairs to the grand parlor wearing a short grey dress with black piping and black leggings. Kinsey waited for her seated on the piano bench, his blue plaid sweater emphasizing the intense blue of his eyes. They stared at each other for a moment, before she broke the silence asking if he were ready to go. He grabbed his wool dress coat from the bench beside him.

"Do you think it was Billy Nathan saw?" Jet asked as they headed out the French doors to the garage.

Kinsey sighed. "Who lives over there?"

She unlocked her garage. "Roger Thompson."

"Him again." Kinsey lifted the door.

Roads were either clear or had a well-dried track courtesy the brilliant sun. Jet chose Bridgeport Way. Constructing a map of northwest Tacoma in her head she made a left at Pearl then continuing to 26th where she made another left. In a few blocks 26th became Narrows Drive. Just beyond she turned onto a dead end street and stopped the SUV across from Roger's story and half brick home and pointed it out to Kinsey.

"Could we come up with an excuse to visit him?"

Jet sighed. "Unfortunately I've already delivered his Christmas present."

"Bummer." Kinsey grinned. "You gave him a Christmas present?"

"For the time being he's the only father I know."

Kinsey frowned. "The only father you know?"

Perceiving a pitfall, she changed focus. "What would you hope to accomplish?"

"See if Billy is there." Kinsey leaned forward to stare at the house. "I wish I had binoculars."

Jet opened the console and drew out a small pair of field glasses she handed him. "Latte is a bird watcher. She's always spotting some flying creature she wants a better look at."

Directing them at the house, Kinsey stared for a few moments. "Someone's there. It's hard to tell but it definitely could be Billy." He handed the pair to Jet.

She gazed through the enlarged vision, locating a person by the window. Definitely male, husky build, and floppy dark hair, he was turned to the side and bending. "It looks enough like him to make one think."

❧

As Jet continued to the Barnes house Kinsey wondered why Roger Thompson turned up at every corner. Was he harboring Billy Monk? And if so, why?

The day's brilliance made Commencement Bay sparkle like a tinsel-covered Christmas tree. After parking in the long driveway behind Jordan's Land Cruiser they entered the house.

Kinsey felt Jet tense as Evana stepped out of his father's study to greet them. He also noted Evana's grimace.

"Merry Christmas," she greeted them with forced cheerfulness. "Everyone's in the living room." Crossing the foyer she disappeared into the kitchen.

Noting how intimidated Jet appeared, Kinsey put his hand on her shoulder. When they reached the living room, crowded with people, he noticed her great aunt Jane Sayre, conversing with Aunt Tansy.

"You want to meet your Aunt?" He beckoned in the direction of the two elderly ladies.

Jet froze in place.

"I doubt she'll bite." Putting his hand in the middle of Jet's back he pushed her in their direction.

His aunt frowned at him but addressed Jet with a kindly, "How are you, Jessica?"

The old lady next to her adjusted her spectacles to peer at Jet with her near-sighted gray eyes. "Jessica?"

"Jane," Kinsey said, "this is Jessica Sayre."

"Mona's daughter?"

"That's right," Jet said as if challenging her to object.

"She doesn't look like her mother," Jane Sayre observed.

Tansy squinted at Jet. "I believe you're right. She must take after her father."

Kinsey considered Jet's features noting her embarrassment. If he wasn't mistaken she had the same gray eyes as her great aunt.

"Are Aunt Teresa and Aunt Ethel here?" Jet asked.

"No," Jane huffed. "They decided to spend the holidays gallivanting around Europe."

"I have some things my mother left all of you." Jet spoke as if she had rounded up all her courage to face the giant. "I didn't know how to get hold of anyone."

"Why don't you give me a call and we'll all have lunch when they get back." Jane took a slip of paper from her handbag, wrote a telephone number on it then handed it to Jet. "How are you getting along without your mother?"

"I'm fine." Jet glanced at the paper then put it away in her wallet.

"Good." Jane nodded. "I doubt your mother was much help anyway."

Jet smiled, lightening up a little. Kinsey set a chair for her next to her aunt then left to greet his father who had just entered the room.

The apprehensive frown on Park's face charged Kinsey with foreboding. Before he could say a word, his father addressed him. "I need to talk to you after dinner."

It was so atypical that all through the Christmas feast Kinsey wondered what he could want. Had he learned something new? Was Park upon the point of confessing his part in the debacle at the estate? Or had he devised another reason to squelch the deal he had made with Kinsey for the property?

When the meal was over Park beckoned Kinsey with a nod toward his study. Consumed with anxiety, Kinsey perched on the edge of an easy chair and faced his father. Instead of taking his usual chair behind the library-table desk, Park chose one next to Kinsey and focused his gaze on his hands. "This is not something I ever wanted to do."

Kinsey's internal organs flinched. How could he head him off? What could he offer in his defense?

However, Park's beginning confused him. "Remember our conversation when you jumped to the conclusion I'd had an affair with Carmen Markovich?"

Kinsey frowned.

"I didn't have an affair with Carmen, but with someone else I had . . ." Park grimaced. "Not an affair really." He sighed. "But an . . . interlude."

Tensing, Kinsey struggled to control his facial expressions, apprehensive of where the conversation headed.

Park took a deep breath and blurted out, "I spent some time after your mother died with Mona Thompson."

Kinsey scowled. What did that mean? He glanced at his father's expression, noting the remorse. "You're not serious. You didn't have an affair with Mona?"

"I spent a couple weeks with her and . . ." Park's voice trailed off as he observed Kinsey's expression.

Words escaped him. Denial was battling acceptance for control.

"I'm sorry, son. I'd rather leave it in the past like other stupid mistakes I've made."

A bell rang in Kinsey's head. "Why are you telling me?"

Park sighed. "You're aunt and I have observed your affection for Jessica."

Kinsey crossed his arms over his chest. "What has Jet got to do with it?"

"From a conversation with her recently I learned that . . ." Park ran his hand through his hair. "It's a matter of timing."

"Timing what?" Kinsey stared at his father while comprehension and doubt played hide and seek in his mind.

Leaning back in his chair, Park contemplated the ceiling over Kinsey's head. "She could be your sister."

"My *sister*?"

Park's agonized gaze returned to Kinsey's face. "Mona told Jessica I could be her father. I didn't want you to get involved not knowing the danger."

Kinsey felt as if he'd taken a one-two punch to the abdomen. What difference did it make if she were his cousin or his sister? He couldn't answer the question, but he knew it made a difference. His gaze moved to the window where daylight was fading. "How does Jet feel about this?"

"She asked if I'd give her a DNA sample so she could have a paternity test done."

"Have you done that?"

Park turned startled eyes to him. "Not yet."

"Why not?" Kinsey snapped. What was the matter with his father?

"No reason." Park shook his head. "Just haven't gotten around to it."

"Then you'd better get around to it." Kinsey spit out the words.

Kinsey stared at the pale green drapes on the window of his father's study. Park remained silent, painful regret occupying his face. So many emotions battled for Kinsey's attention he couldn't process them.

Remembering the pistol, Kinsey recalled his father's attention. "We found a gun."

"A gun?" Park sounded as if he had never heard of such a thing.

"Right. A 9mm SigSauer." Kinsey explained Anatuviak's find "Would you know anything about that?"

Park shook his head. "Lots of people have guns, especially if they have a lot of valuables or live somewhere remote." His father sounded like a mealy-mouthed politician.

"Buried in the yard?"

Park appeared confused.

"You never had a gun there?"

"Me?" Park looked as if Kinsey had accused him of watching dancing videos on YouTube. "What would I be doing with a gun there?"

Heaven knows, Kinsey thought. His father was involved in a lot of things of which he had no idea. "This is going to cause trouble you know."

"Why?"

Was Park that obtuse? "I didn't get the impression Lieutenant Sarkis thinks you're about ready to sprout wings and a halo."

"What would he think I'm guilty of?"

"Let's see," Kinsey licked the end of his forefinger. "Murdering Carmen Markovich or her husband, or some

264

other unknown person, burying people in various places around the property."

"Then playing hide and seek with their bodies?" Park sighed. "Son, do you really think I'm a suspect?"

"Dad, do you really think you're not?" What sand pile was his father's nose stuck in? "You have more motives than anyone I can think of and more opportunity."

Park studied Kinsey as if he couldn't figure out how he managed to materialize in front of him, exhaling so deeply Kinsey feared he'd pass out. "No matter how things look, I'm not guilty of any crime or even thinking of one. I can't see anything to tie me to any of it."

"That's the problem, Dad, there's nothing to tie anyone to any of it. Eventually the police will have to find someone to pin something on."

"It's not like these people died yesterday. For all we know the killer is dead too. Maybe you need to think of someone besides me who could have motive and opportunity."

Kinsey redirected his gaze to the alabaster vase sitting on the bookshelf behind his father. Was he unnecessarily accusing his father? Had he failed to consider other possibilities for fear of what Sarkis might pin on Park? Had the time come to go on the offensive? "Can you think of anyone with motive or opportunity?"

Park shifted his gaze to the window where darkness still advanced across the sound. Only the snow's brightness gave more than the usual light to the late afternoon. As they sat in silence Kinsey searched his mind for another person to hold up to the lieutenant for suspicion.

"What about the guy who picked up Markovich's things?" Park tossed out.

"If we were talking about Matt's body being found that would be worth considering."

"Would the Secret Service Agent's counterfeiters be the ones who killed at least one of the bodies?"

"Possible I suppose. What about Roger Thompson?"

Park frowned at Kinsey. "You think he has something to do with your problems?"

Funny how it had become Kinsey's problems, not his estate, but his problems. "He keeps showing up at unusual times."

"I could see him involved with counterfeiting, but not murder."

Kinsey had to agree.

Evana appeared at the door to Park's study. "Dessert is being served." Her gaze moved to Kinsey and remained there a moment.

"We'll be right there," he dismissed her.

Evana turned on her heel and left, but not before she shot him a daggered glance.

Kinsey turned back to his father. "You need to set Evana straight about people being in love."

Park lifted one of his winged eyebrows.

"You need to tell her about your relationship with Carmen." Kinsey shrugged. "Not that she'd believe you. She thinks Mom is the only person you have or ever would love."

Park sighed. "I thought she'd have guessed about Carmen. Women are more intuitive about things like that and she talked with Carmen a few times."

"I'm not sure Evana is intuitive. She's caught up in denial."

Chapter Thirty

Jet stood by the wooden plant stand across the hall from Park's study wondering what Kinsey and his father could have discussed for such a long time. When they emerged neither of them looked like a Merry Christmas. Kinsey indicated they should leave for the castle before sundown turned the streets to a sheet of ice so she waited, Latte's keys in hand, for him to be ready to go.

He stood with Jordan at the entrance to the living room while little Aunt Tansy shook her finger at them.

Evana had disappeared with Francine as soon as dessert was finished and Jet had not seen her again. Not that she wanted to. Park was back in his study alone working on the computer and Pat was in the kitchen. Most of the guests had left earlier.

Kinsey approached Jet with such an expression of doom on his face she wondered what disaster had befallen him.

"You ready to go?"

Standing by the door with her coat on and keys in her hand wasn't enough to make it obvious? She led the way to the SUV.

Insulated in silence they negotiated the streets back to the arterial. Ice was forming again. Christmas lights twinkled in the darkness providing new landmarks to guide them.

To fill the quiet Jet chattered about the visit with her great aunt. Kinsey remained encased in gloom, his silence finally inducing her to join him.

Approaching the estate she noted the SUV still sat at the gate. "Agent Elaney's men must still be on the job?"

Kinsey sat up straighter to observe the van.

Jet passed the vehicle to enter the lake road to the garages. "I wonder if they've seen anything."

"It'd be a good time for illegal activities with everyone gone."

After putting the truck away they walked the path together through the garden where snow-covered roses shimmered in the light from the motion detecting yard lamp.

"I have to take Anatuviak for a walk," she said as they approached the south terrace.

"Why don't you let me do that? I need to check things out before I quit for the night."

"What are you looking for?" Had Park said something about the estate that worried him?

"With the snow I should be able to tell if someone's been here." Kinsey unlocked the door to the library for Jet then went to get Anatuviak's leash.

Jet headed to her suite where she removed her outer garments then switched on the fireplace. Although darkness was complete the hour was not late. In her miniature kitchen she put on the teakettle, wondering if there had been activity on the estate while they were celebrating Christmas. She heard a knock on the door.

Kinsey was there. Although he had removed his coat snow still glistened in his hair.

"Cup of tea?" Jet offered.

"Hot chocolate?"

"Sure." She held the door open for him. "Have a seat." She motioned to the striped sofa facing the fireplace then went to the kitchen. She put the teakettle, cups, hot chocolate, tea and a plate of Latte's cookies on a tray and returned to the sitting area where she set it on the mahogany table in front of Kinsey. "Did you find anything?"

He ran his hand through his wet hair. "Lots of footprints. Lots and lots of footprints."

Jet sat on the other end of the sofa. "What do you think that means?"

"Someone's been here." Kinsey looked beaten, dispirited. Was the prospect of clearing Blast Castle's reputation getting the best of him? His expression was the same as Anatuviak when she scolded him. "Most of them were around and in the herb garden just outside the kitchen door. In the morning I'll go and see what's there." He took a cup, filled it with chocolate mix then poured hot water into it.

Leaning back against the sofa arm, Jet gazed into the fireplace flame. "Do you think they got into the hidden staircases from somewhere near the herb garden?"

Stirring the mixture in his cup, Kinsey also stared into the fire. "Possibly."

Jet wondered again what plagued him. "What did your father have to say?"

Kinsey concentrated on stirring his chocolate. "I asked him about that gun but he didn't seem to know anything about it."

Silence drifted between them. The fire had taken the chill from Jet's body and she relaxed.

Inhaling deeply, Kinsey spoke. "Dad told me about his affair with your mother."

Jet cringed. "You sound like it's my fault." She felt a stab of anger accompanied by irrational guilt.

"You could be my sister." Kinsey shot her a reproachful glance.

Jet stared into her teacup. "Would that be so awful?"

He fired anther question, "Did you know?"

"My mother told me just before she died." Jet watched frustration fill his expression.

"You could have warned me," he grumbled.

"So you could avoid me?" Jet murmured.

"That might have helped," he snapped.

"Helped what?" She felt hurt. He didn't need to be so nasty.

"Prevent me from falling in love with you."

Jet snorted her disdain, opening her mouth to protest, but the look on Kinsey's face stopped her. She stared into his pain-filled eyes. "You're kidding, right?"

He shook his head. "I wish I were."

Tears flooded Jet's eyes. "I tried to keep you away, to make you realize I'm not a good person to spend time with."

"You are so wrong." The words sprung from him.

Jet bowed her head, tears falling into her lap. Dragging a tissue out of her pocket she dabbed her eyes.

Kinsey reached for her hand. "I'm sorry. I don't mean to hurt you. It's just that I never saw it coming. It's bad enough to wonder if you would ever care for me, but to know it's impossible no matter what . . ." Kinsey shook the hair off his forehead. "I just don't know how to handle it.

You're such an impossible creature. I wish I never had to see you again. Then I wish I could put you in my pocket and keep you forever." Kinsey put his head in his hands.

"I don't think I'd care for either of those options." Jet wadded her tissue into a ball.

He lifted an eyebrow, gazing at her without raising his head. "Who asked you?"

For Jet the world had become surreal, a place of dreams and irrational hope. "It's not definite . . . that I'm your sister." *You shouldn't tell him that*, her conscience pricked her, *keep him away*. "There are other possibilities."

"Possibilities?" He emphasized the plural.

"My mother told me about four."

"Four!" Kinsey gaped. "Who are the others?"

"Besides Roger Thompson and your father, Susannah's father, Jesse McFadden, and someone else." Jet watched incredulity succumb to reason on Kinsey's face.

"Who else?"

Jet shrugged. "I haven't been able to find out."

"You've been trying?"

She explained what her mother had told her.

Kinsey stared into the fire. His frown lines had eased and the gloomy look on his face had disappeared.

"Roger and I had DNA samples taken. He could still turn out to be the one."

"I can make sure Dad does his part," Kinsey declared. "What about McFadden?"

Jet sighed. "It's really hard to approach someone about something like this."

"No kidding." He shot her a sympathetic glance. "What have you done to find out who the other one is?"

Jet explained her chat with Barbara Baker.

Kinsey stirred his hot chocolate again, staring into the cup.

"You're going to wear a hole in that cup if you don't quit stirring and drink it."

Kinsey rolled his eyes and took a sip. "It wouldn't matter who your father is if we could find out that my dad isn't."

"It matters to me."

"I'm sorry." Kinsey gave her a sheepish glance. "I didn't mean that."

Stunned, Jet was unable to process. Her emotional computer had gone off-line. She was tempted to giddiness one minute and tears the next. Instead she sat very still watching him, wondering what was next.

❧

The day after Christmas, before Kinsey finished breakfast, Lieutenant Sarkis rang the chimes and demanded to know what they had found.

"Coffee, lieutenant?"

Sarkis scowled but followed him into the kitchen. Kinsey poured two cups while the lieutenant perched on one of the stools. After shoving the milk and sugar his direction, Kinsey took the other stool.

"I found two hidden sets of stairs, a couple rooms accessible only from those stairs, and a gun." Kinsey explained the search.

"Let's see where you found the gun."

First he showed the weapon to the lieutenant then took him to where they found it. A hefty eight inches of snow had fallen in the yard, covering the place where Anatuviak dug it up. After clearing a swath round the fountain, Kinsey succeeded in uncovering the brick and demonstrating the process of discovery.

The lieutenant seemed mystified. "Am I going to find your fingerprints on it?"

"Probably. I didn't have gloves on. Jet gave me her scarf to keep it in."

Lieutenant Sarkis frowned.

"Were you around here yesterday? Or one of your crew?"

Pinning Kinsey with his bright eyes the lieutenant shook his head.

"Is it possible Elaney was?"

"I wouldn't think so. You got a problem?"

Doubtful of the consequences Kinsey explained the proliferation of footprints near the kitchen door.

"Let's go," the lieutenant said.

Instead of tracking through the interior Kinsey led Sarkis around the north end of the house to the herb garden. In spite of the additional snow indentations remained from the previous prints.

The lieutenant stopped at the edge of the house to observe. "That door goes into your kitchen?"

Kinsey nodded.

"Are there any other doors on this side of the house?"

"Not to my knowledge. Although I'm to the point of believing another one exists whether I know about it or not." Kinsey pulled his stocking hat down over his ears. "There's access to part of the basement from the north terrace."

The layer of snow made the terracing more pronounced. "Did you check if the kitchen door was locked when you got home last night?"

"Yes, I did." Kinsey turned his collar up. Snow flurries had begun again. "No footprints going to the kitchen door and nothing on the stoop."

Looking to where the greatest number of footprints congregated, Kinsey wondered if whatever they sought lay in the herb garden. Small rosemary shrubs, spikes of chive, and mounds of thyme were heaped with snow. Closer to the foundation a couple rows of mint and oregano bent under their heavy load. The night before there may have been evidence of disturbance, but another several inches of snow had obliterated any sign.

Poking around, the lieutenant managed to stay on the gravel paths in spite of the fact they were barely discernible.

Kinsey stood on the lawn near the wall to the garden staring at the house's façade. Something caught his attention, a pair of windows beneath the fifteen-foot bay that held the grand staircase. Mentally walking through the house, Kinsey wondered where they appeared on the interior. As the lieutenant continued his examination, Kinsey moved to the windows. He could see nothing to determine where in the house they opened.

Something else caught his attention. The lever normally on the inside to open the window was on the outside. Kinsey moved it down and the window clicked open like a door. "Lieutenant."

Sarkis moved his direction. "What did you find?"

"An entrance to the basement."

Cautiously they descended into a narrow hall running parallel to Kinsey's storage area, but separately walled off. They followed it north to where it turned a corner and continued to another running parallel. It put the storage area in the middle of two inaccessible halls. When they reached the second one they turned to a door at the right.

"Open it," Lieutenant Sarkis instructed.

Kinsey opened the door into a very small space the size of a closet.

"How come you didn't find this last week?"

When they stepped into the room Kinsey had previously explored they could see why it had not been noticed. Visible was a wall of cupboards accessible through bi-fold doors. Opening them allowed view of the shelves. It would take careful observation to notice they were set with slightly different spacing, allowing the door which was nearly invisible to open without smashing the shelves together. The doorknob was neatly tucked under one and invisible to the casual observer.

The lieutenant shot Kinsey a peremptory glance. "You might want to give Elaney a heads up. This is more down his lane."

Kinsey grimaced.

"We have a tentative identification of the second body," Lieutenant Sarkis informed him as they returned to the circular driveway and his truck.

"How did you do that?" Hadn't he said no missing persons matched?

The lieutenant eyed Kinsey as if he thought his expression would give something away. "We found an engraved ring in the original grave. The name was Judy Severson."

Kinsey shrugged. "So who was she?"

"Worked for the State of Washington." Lieutenant Sarkis kept his eye on Kinsey as he opened the door to his truck. "Equal Opportunity Division."

"Never heard of her." Kinsey turned his back against the bite of blowing snow. "What would she have to do with this place?"

"I thought you could tell me." The lieutenant lifted an eyebrow. "Ask around and see if anyone knows the name?"

"No problem." He hoped he wasn't headed for another nasty surprise from his father. "I'd like to know what you find out about that gun."

The lieutenant climbed into his SUV. "Give me a call in a couple days."

Kinsey hoped it would be at least a couple days before he saw the lieutenant again. Before he gave Elaney a heads-up he needed to call his father and get him on the ball.

❧

Jet found it difficult keeping her mind on the loan papers in front of her. Lost in recollection of the past day's events she gazed into the dazzling white scene outside her window. Chastising herself for failure to concentrate she made an effort to focus her wandering mind, but landed again lost in her memories. She shied away from her conversation with Kinsey, unwilling to tackle that. Every time his image materialized she diverted her attention. Whose gun had they found? Had there been someone around the mansion while they were gone? Were there really counterfeiters using the hidden parts of the house? And why had Kinsey said he loved her?

Who was her father and why had Roger suddenly decided to take an interest in her? Did he have something to do with the mysteries at the castle? Had it actually been Billy they saw in the window of his house? If so, why?

She had come to wish Roger was her father. However, things never worked out that easily. Her brain ran in circles neither accomplishing her work nor answering her questions. She renewed her effort to concentrate on the loan papers.

At 11:00 Park called, taking Jet by surprise.

"Are you free for lunch?" he asked.

Dumbfounded, she hesitated. "Yes, okay."

"I can pick you up at noon."

She set the phone down. Misgivings paraded onto her mental stage with questions and accusations as she recalled the extended interval Kinsey and Park had spent secluded in his office. Foreboding built a wall of apprehension. By the time Park appeared in the bank foyer Jet had wound herself into such a state of dread she felt she might suffocate from anxiety.

"How is it going?" He approached her desk as she put away her paperwork.

"Fine." How could she explain her feelings? Noting his relaxed, confident expression, she wondered what she had expected him to look like, the judge and executioner.

He ushered her to his dark sedan and opened the door for her. She was too dazed to object. They chatted about the weather, road conditions and incompetent drivers while he drove the short distance to an upscale restaurant on Gravelly. The hostess ushered them to a table for four near the windows and left them with menus.

Too distracted to concentrate, Jet picked out something that caught her eye to avoid being put under pressure by the waitress who was approaching their table with two glasses of water.

"You asked me about DNA testing," Park began when the waitress had left with their orders.

Jet nodded. "Roger Thompson and I had testing done last week." Which reminded her, they should be getting the results.

"Where did you do that?"

It took courage on her part to meet Park's eyes. "The lab at the medical center in Lakewood." She noted his straightforward gaze, which held no resentment or condemnation.

"Presumably I could do the same thing." He raised his eyebrows, the same expressive, winged eyebrows as Kinsey. "I imagine if your DNA results are on file all I'd have to do is have the blood test and they could compare them."

"Probably." Jet took a deep breath, hastening to add, "You might want to wait until after I hear the results on the tests Roger and I took."

"You'll let me know?" Park asked.

As the waitress returned with their orders Jet wondered why he was suddenly so interested in determining her paternity.

He must have read her mind for when the waitress had gone he said, "Kinsey was anxious I get this done for you."

Jet couldn't bring herself to meet his eyes. Was he aware of what Kinsey had told her?

Still anticipating her questions, Park said, "I've noticed his growing interest in you."

"I've tried to discourage him." Jet rushed out the words.

He shook his head, smiling. "It's useless to try to discourage him. We always fall for the most impossible people."

Jet frowned. That's not fair. I'm not impossible.

"Love is a ridiculous emotion, totally unaccountable and uncontrollable."

Upon the point of protesting, Jet realized he was speaking of his own emotions. She recalled what Kinsey had said about Carmen Markovich. Watching Park stir his soup, she felt an empathetic sympathy for him.

"I'd hate to see Kinsey hurt again." Park's gaze held a challenge. "I realize you can't help it if you're his sister."

But, Jet's mind finished his sentence, *if you're just leading him on.* What could she say? How could a boyish twit like she was lead someone on? She stared at her soup. A question occurred to her. "Do you know the Mercedes dealer on the other side of the mansion?"

Park raised a surprised eyebrow. "Slightly, they've lived there ever since I can remember."

Having successfully changed the subject, Jet rushed on. "Did they have work done on their property making it necessary for people to go through the estate to get to their place?"

Park frowned.

"Roger said he had to come through the estate to see them during the time the man who was killed lived there."

"I don't remember that." Park frowned at his plate. "Why do you ask?"

"He shows up at the estate and seems to know a lot about what's going on all the time." Questioning Roger's behavior made Jet feel like a traitor.

"I've never given it much thought, but he's always been around a lot," Park conceded. "You'd think he was my cousin."

"What does he do for a living?" Jet had never known for certain. Roger lived an upscale life style, always had plenty of money, but never seemed to work.

"His family owned that big chain of furniture stores in the area."

Jet nodded. That much she knew. "Mom said he'd gotten into trouble with the business after his father died."

"I think that's the case, although somehow he pulled himself out." Park grimaced. "When I've talked with him his big passion is the stock market, although that's a bust these days too."

Jet still found no reason he should hang around Blast Castle.

On the drive home from work the inevitable and unwelcome question she had dodged since the previous day sprung before her eyes like a billboard. *Was she in love with Kinsey?* I can't be! I won't be! It's not fair!

Moments after Jet arrived chimes echoed through the empty parlor. Setting her handbag on the piano bench she went to the door where she was surprised to find Agent Elaney. She had to reign in her frustration to keep from verbally attacking him.

"I'm meeting Mr. Sayre here," he explained his presence, stepping into the parlor.

Jet sighed. "Kinsey should be here shortly." She took a step toward the piano.

"I met your mother once."

She turned back to him. "Really. Where?"

"At a bar."

Figures. "She spent a lot of time in bars."

He moved to the large painting occupying the north wall. "I didn't."

"Is that why you remember her?" Jet's gaze followed him as he bent to study the signature on the Flemish landscape painting. Did he suspect them of counterfeit art too?

"Partly, I guess." He abandoned the painting and moved toward the piano. "She was very attractive."

"Something she didn't pass on." Jet said then regretted it. Why did she have to open her mouth?

"Do you have brothers or sisters?"

"Only cousins." Not that it was any of his business Jet thought uncharitably.

Kinsey appeared at the library door, rescuing Jet from the agent's inquisition.

Chapter Thirty-one

All through his workday Jet's image invaded Kinsey's conscious. His emotional processor sprang to life, parading across his mental screen snapshots of his war within. Ambushed by feelings he never realized he had and confronted simultaneously by his father's confession, he found himself submerged in a sea of vulnerability.

First he challenged his feelings, arguing against the conclusion he was in love with her. However, he couldn't rid himself of the perception that what he felt for Jet was something he had never felt for anyone before. He wanted to be with her, understand her, and protect her. All this in spite of the fact she would as soon spit in his eye as accept anything from him. A passionate excitement raced through his blood stream making him feel as if all his nerve endings hung loose. At the same time his head ached with the knowledge she might be his sister. He actually felt like bawling.

All of a sudden the day ended. Elaney's Acura sat in the driveway with a light frosting of snow when Kinsey came from the rose garden. What kind of hassle was this going to be? The man stood speaking to Jet when Kinsey crossed through the library into the parlor. His heart quickened at the sight of her while noting the perplexed expression on her face. Elaney had that interrogator look on his which brought out Kinsey's protective nature.

Sifting through the mail as he approached, Kinsey accosted him, "On the trail again, Elaney?" He handed Jet several envelopes.

The man raised an inquisitive eyebrow. "You had something to show me?"

"This way." Kinsey led the agent through the kitchen outside to the window he had found beneath the staircase. Opening it, he ushered him into the basement. There Kinsey took the lead again, pulling strings on bare light bulbs to illuminate their way as he led his companion through the hall and out the back of the closet to where the laundry equipment sat. When they arrived Kinsey paused, allowing the agent time to appreciate the full effect.

Elaney wandered around the room, into the adjacent area and then stood at the bottom of the hidden staircase. "Where does this go?"

"Third floor." Kinsey waved his hand to encourage the man up the stairs.

Once there the agent asked, "How much monkeying around in here have you done?"

"It's Christmas. No one has been here."

"Have you ever heard of someone named Desmond Clark?" Elaney moved to the window overlooking the back yard. "Good looking wiry little guy with a big ego?" Agent Elaney turned slightly, looking over his shoulder at Kinsey.

Something in his move, the tilt of his head with his thick dark hair and chiseled features reminded Kinsey of someone. "Not to my knowledge. Who is he?"

"He fits the description Jessica gave of someone she saw around here at times." The agent turned his back on the window to study the room where eggshell walls were turning yellow with age.

Was that what Elaney wanted from Jet? Kinsey frowned. "Who is he?"

"A plate-maker, an expert at producing currency plates."

Where exactly would one become an expert at manufacturing money? "Did he work for the government?"

The man moved to the marble fireplace. "I think he learned the trade from someone else who had worked for the government." He continued to stare where the fire would be as if something could have been burned there.

Approaching, Kinsey saw nothing but an empty grate and charred walls.

"Okay," Elaney said as if he had seen enough.

Kinsey reopened the door to the stairway and they headed back to the basement. At the bottom Elaney paused. Kinsey nearly collided with him.

"Does anyone in your house know about this besides you?" Agent Elaney waved a hand to indicate the basement room and stairs.

"Jet and Nathan."

"Were you well acquainted with Jessica's mother?"

Perplexed, Kinsey stopped. "No, she was more of a legend than an actual part of the family."

"What about her father?" Nosey Parker continued.

Kinsey flashed a suspicious glance at the agent. "She doesn't know who her father is."

That stopped Elaney's questions while they climbed out of the basement and headed back to the kitchen door.

Just before reaching it Elaney stopped him. "Does anyone know who Jessica's father is?"

Kinsey shivered in the cold. "Not to my knowledge. Why do you ask?"

Elaney shrugged. "She reminds me of someone," he mumbled.

"Do you have any link for the counterfeiters with the estate other than the money found here?" Kinsey felt the Secret Service was operating on a thin thread. Maybe it was time to send them on their way, if he could.

"All the activity centers on this location. Even what you showed me tonight supports that."

"So you think they're operating from here and making money in the basement?"

"Don't you?" Elaney challenged Kinsey with a look.

Kinsey sighed. "Maybe there's a more logical explanation."

"You can give it to me when you come up with it."

Elaney was sinking his ship. How was he ever going to get the monster off his back if they just kept chasing ghosts?

જ

Grabbing her handbag, Jet started up the stairs as Kinsey invited the Secret Service Agent to join him outdoors.

Two of her envelopes were Christmas cards; the third was from a medical laboratory. Suddenly she realized it could be results of the DNA tests. She waited until she reached her suite to open it. In fact, once there she hesitated, wondering if she really wanted to know.

She tore open the envelope and unfolded the sheet of paper. The first word her eyes fell on was negative. She felt a thud of disappointment. Returning to the top she read the letter, which spelled out her lack of relationship to Roger Thompson. She wondered if he had received his and how he would feel about it.

Jet had come to welcome his fatherhood. Would he utterly abandon her now? She almost regretted having the test done. In addition, it increased the possibility Park Sayre was her father. Life seemed so unfair at times.

Worn out and depressed she dropped onto her striped sofa and promptly fell asleep.

සිය

When Elaney had gone, Kinsey retired to his suite where he made a sandwich from the grab-bag of deli meats and cheeses he found in his refrigerator. Once finished, he wasn't sure he wanted to eat it. However, Aunt Pat's maternal voice in his head recited a litany of rebukes regarding his health. Taking the sandwich with him he pushed open the French doors to his deck, which took some effort with all the snow. The round table and wrought iron chairs looked like cupcakes piled with white frosting.

What had happened to him in the last month? Had his brain taken an extended holiday, leaving his emotions home alone? How could he have fallen in love with Jet? *How could you let this happen to me?* he addressed his Maker. It wasn't fair. He took an angry bite of his sandwich then struggled to swallow it.

The door that closed when his father told him about his relationship with Mona reopened when Jet explained her father possibilities. What were the odds his father wasn't also her father? If he were a betting man what would he risk? His pessimistic side assured him whatever was the worst that could be, would be. But hope wouldn't let go of him.

Moving to the east edge of his terrace, he could see between the trees the sliver of moon dancing its beams across the lake. Longing filled him with a spirit of excitement, while his brain argued with his heart. Every nerve in his body was on alert. He had never felt so alive, yet so vulnerable to emotional death.

Through the open French doors he heard the sound of his door buzzer. Frowning he reentered his dinette, closing the doors behind him. The buzzer sounded again. He jerked the door open to a startled Jet.

She motioned behind her. "I saw someone in the yard from my window. I thought we should see who it is." The alarm in her eyes looked more like regret for disturbing him than apprehension of who was outside.

"Okay, let's go."

As they hurried through the hall and down the stairs Kinsey asked, "Where did you see him?"

"Coming from the garages."

"It wasn't Nathan?"

"He was heavier than Nathan."

Just as they reached the anteroom door, it opened and Billy walked in.

Jet and Kinsey stood together shocked. "Billy."

From the look on his face, he was as surprised as they were.

"Where have you been?" Kinsey was torn between relief and anger.

"Home for Christmas." Billy's appearance was not nearly as light-hearted as his tone of voice.

Kinsey glanced at Jet wondering if she was as skeptical as he was. She returned his glance with raised eyebrows.

"You didn't take your car."

"Mom came and got me."

Likely story, Kinsey thought. He had talked to Billy's mom. "We've been worried about you."

Billy's expression was doubtful.

"We heard shots and found blood on the lawn. When we couldn't find you we thought maybe you'd been shot."

"Shot?" Billy's voice squeaked. He laughed half-heartedly as if the idea was absurd. Beckoning to the stairs, he asked, "Is it okay if I go to my room?"

"Sure." Jet and Kinsey moved out of his way.

Kinsey turned to observe as Billy climbed the stairs. Although never streak and steam Billy's movement seemed more restricted than in the past.

"What do you think?" Jet followed his gaze.

"Sounded like hooey-booey to me."

She walked toward the stairs. "Do you think we'll ever find out what's been going on around here?"

Kinsey followed. "I have to or else." He stopped. "By the way, the lieutenant was here this morning. He said they identified the other skeleton. Someone named Judy Severson, worked for the Equal Opportunity Department for the State."

"Severson?"

Kinsey caught the tone in her voice. "Someone you know?"

She shook her head. "But I think Mom did. I've heard the name before."

That sounded promising. "Can you ask someone about her?"

Jet took a deep breath. "Maybe Barb would know. I'll call her in the morning." She started up the stairs.

"Don't go." Kinsey sought a way to keep her there, ignoring the inadvisability. "Would you mind going over the renter agreements. Maybe we can find something helpful."

Frowning her skepticism, she followed him to the library where he turned on the fireplace then went for the files. She stood at the mantel looking into the flames. Kinsey watched wondering what was on her mind, amazed how short the time it took for her to infiltrate his life to the point he could no longer imagine it without her.

What would the options be? If she really was his sister, what could be done to deal with the passion he had for her? He loved her, but not like a sister. Did he have the courage and character to give her up? On the other hand would it even be his choice? She gave no sign she cared for him.

Caught staring as she turned to him, he lowered his gaze to the paperwork he held. "Here, take a look at these."

She held out her hand with a puzzled expression. Suddenly it occurred to him that she didn't believe him. He had declared his love, but she didn't believe it. Possibly he could let go of her, of any hope of being together, but not without her believing he cared. If she didn't love him, that was one thing. But if she was unwilling to risk that he cared for her; that was another.

She sat in the purple chair, concentrating on the forms, her childish build lost in the huge bold print. Kinsey sat at the desk, staring at the window where a spray of moisture caught his attention. It had begun to rain, like tears falling from long pent up emotion.

After allowing her time to peruse the applications, he spun his chair around and moved next to where she sat. "You don't believe me, do you?"

She scowled at him.

"You don't believe I love you."

Her eyes widened at the challenge, then shifted to the flames. "I'm not sure anyone has ever loved me," she murmured.

"What about your mother?"

Jet sighed. "She didn't have room in her life for anyone but herself. She didn't quite approve of me." Jet smiled at him with a rueful twist of her lips.

"Did you love her?"

"I think so." Jet lifted her gaze to the wrought iron sconces above the mantel. "I cared about her, appreciated her for the good things, accepted the bad. Although I wished she would change I still cared for her the way she was. I even miss her."

Kinsey was bewildered. "But you don't think she cared for you?"

Jet shrugged. "She always tried to change me into what she wanted."

Studying the small forlorn figure in the big chair, Kinsey tried to imagine what her life was like. "Did she tell you she loved you?"

Jet laughed. "All the time. But what she did made the words meaningless."

"I'm sorry."

She looked darts at him. "Why are you sorry?"

Kinsey took a deep breath. "Because it makes it hard to tell you I love you and have you believe me."

"Why would you love me?"

What a question! "I don't know. Believe me. It's not like I want to, you're such a hard headed little spitfire."

Jet scrutinized him as if he were transparent enough to see through. He wondered what she saw. She smiled then frowned again. "I got the DNA test results from when Roger and I went."

Kinsey held his breath.

"He's not my father."

Kinsey sighed. Figures.

Chapter Thirty-two

Having forgotten to set her alarm, Jet woke with a start at the sound of her cell phone. Dawn was apparent in the gray light beyond her windows. A glance at the clock sent her into a panic. She was due at the office in half an hour. She flew into the shower and grabbed the first thing she saw in her closet to wear, totally forgetting the cell phone. Seated at her desk she realized she had neglected to see who called. She found she had missed a call from Park, which both surprised and concerned her. Checking her messages she found one informing her he had the DNA test. She should expect to receive a copy of the results in three to five days.

She wasn't ready to think about Kinsey. His renewed expression of love only left her more bewildered. She parried the emotions assailing her when his face escaped her guard to appear in her conscious. However, she did recall Judy Severson's corpse and her intention of talking to Barbara Baker.

As soon as she had managed the morning routine, taking care of urgencies that arose over Christmas break she fingered in Barbara's number.

"Jessica, sweetie, how are you?"

"Fine," she dispensed with the embarrassing preliminaries. "I have a couple questions. Could you meet me for coffee?"

"I'll be in Tacoma for a meeting. It should be over around 3:30 if that would work for you. I have to drop something off in Dupont. We could have coffee at the Forza."

"Great. I can do that." Relieved at her quick success, Jet spent a minute recalling what her mother had said about Judy Severson. The picture Jet retrieved was the look of chagrin on Mona's face as she uttered the name. However, that said nothing about Judy nor gave any clue to why the woman's skeleton should be found on the castle grounds.

Working on loan papers, Jet considered Agent Elaney's odd questions. When had the agent met her mother? Would he know who the other father possibility was? Maybe she should muster up her courage and ask. She had little doubt she would see him again.

Working through lunch allowed her to leave in time for her appointment. Just like everything else in Dupont the Forza coffee shop was brand new. In addition to espresso beverages and sandwiches it served Italian gelato. With the frozen ground covered in patches of snow and a cold drizzle in the air gelato sound like cruel and unusual punishment. Jet ordered an extra-hot mocha and found a table toward the back away from the door.

Inhaling the aroma of her mocha she noticed a small sedan park across the street. She recognized Barbara immediately. Entering the coffee shop she came directly to Jet's table. "Traffic was a nightmare." She set her handbag on the extra chair and drew her wallet out. "How are you?"

"Good." Jet made an effort to mobilize her thoughts while Barbara ordered coffee.

"You'll never believe who I ran into yesterday." Barbara set her cup and a stack of sweeteners on the table then pulled her chair out. "Roger Thompson." She flipped the lid off her coffee. "In Olympia of all places."

Jet wasn't sure what made that so extraordinary, but the fact Barb thought it was seemed significant.

"He said something about seeing you." She raised her overly darkened eyebrows. "Did you ever find out for certain if he was your father?"

"He's not." Jet grimaced.

Barbara placed her hand over Jet's, "I'm sorry. Not that he made the best father in the world." Her gaze drifted out the window. "I've spent more time thinking about that night trying to figure out if there was anything more I could tell you."

"Do you remember what the man looked like?"

Barbara narrowed her eyes. "Medium height, dark, good looking."

"Dark hair or dark skin?"

"Both. He looked Oriental, or Indian, or Hispanic."

Or African, or Arabian or something else helpful, Jet thought ruefully. She wondered if Mona could have given a better description. It almost made her ill to think her mother probably didn't know what the man looked like either.

Barbara sipped her coffee, focusing her attention on Jet. "So what can I do for you?"

"Did you know Judy Severson?"

Barbara's eyebrows shot up. "Oh, yes, I knew Judy."

That sounded ominous. "What did she have to do with my mother?"

Barbara stared at Jet with something akin to pity. "They were competitors. She was one of the managers in EOD."

"How did they compete?" Jet wasn't sure what she needed to know.

"Judy was single too. So of course they competed for male attention. They competed for promotions and accolades." Barbara sighed. "Mona usually won out with the opposite sex, but Judy generally beat her when it came to promotions and rewards."

"One of the skeletons found at the estate was identified as Judy Severson."

"You're kidding!" Barbara's eyes opened wide.

Jet shook her head. "I can't figure out how she would have ended up there."

Barbara shook her head. "She left one day on vacation and no one ever saw her again. I heard she resigned and took a position somewhere else."

"Where?"

Barbara lifted her shoulders.

"Would it be possible to find out?"

"There should be a record of her resignation." Barbara tipped her head. "I could check that."

"Would you?"

"Sure, sweetie, but what difference does it make?"

Jet took a deep breath. "We're trying to clear up some mysteries on the estate."

"You're helping out that cousin of yours?" Barbara gave her a knowing glance and patted her hand encouragingly.

❦

No black SUV, no Acura sat in the driveway when Jet returned to the mansion. However, when she entered the house it was full of chatter and activity. Everyone had returned from the holidays except Latte and the kids who were due on a flight later that evening.

Nathan was sprawled on the sofa in front of the fireplace. Next to him Billy, perched in the corner propped up with both back and arm, laughed at something Nathan said with obvious restraint. Evana, at the piano, played tinkling classical music with romantic sensitivity. Susannah stood at the bottom of the stairs apparently hunting for someone in particular. The only one missing was Kinsey.

On her way upstairs to put away her briefcase and handbag, Jet met him on the landing at the bend in the stairs. He smiled uncertainly, gazing into her eyes. She mustered her mental resources and told him about her meeting with Barbara.

He frowned. "I can't see anything in that to connect her to the castle. Why don't you ask Susannah if she's ever heard of her?"

Jet nodded, continuing to her suite where she left her jacket, gloves and bag. When she returned to the parlor it appeared dinner had been called for no one was there. At the dining room she stopped in the doorway. The group was still getting settled. She noticed Nathan signal Kinsey with a glance over the door. Kinsey raised his eyebrows. When Jet looked back at Nathan he had cocked his head in admonition. Suddenly Kinsey put his hands on her shoulders. She looked at him in surprise.

"You need to be careful of doorways around here," he said then bent and kissed her.

Although his kiss was quick and gentle, Jet backed up as if she'd been shot, blood rushing to her face.

"Kinsey, why don't you sit down and behave yourself," Evana voiced a sharp reproof.

Noting Nathan's thumbs up as she moved to her chair, Jet sat quickly, concentrating on her salad with her nose so close she could smell the onions.

Conversation took up the weather, work and what had everyone done over the holiday. Gradually Jet regained her composure sufficiently to lift her gaze and glance around the table. Kinsey watched her with evident concern. Evana eyed him like a mother for her misbehaving child. Susannah's expression held a new look of respect, hovering between astonishment and fascination, which reminded Jet of the question she was supposed to ask.

"Have you ever heard your father mention Judy Severson?"

Susannah raised her eyebrows. "Yeah, she gave him headaches, always making some demand or complaint. I don't think he liked her much." The list of Judy-be-gone candidates continued to grow. "I haven't heard anything about her for a long time, years."

Jet passed her salad plate to the end of the table to be picked up by the cook. "Do you think your father would know what happened to her? Why she quit working for the state?"

"I can ask him."

The rest of the meal proceeded without incident, reducing Jet's discomfort. Since Latte was expecting Jet to pick her up she decided to leave early and wait in the cell phone lot.

Stepping into the hall putting on her jacket, Jet encountered Kinsey. His expression shifted from concern to embarrassment then back to concern.

"Are you okay with . . . ?" his eyebrows hovered anxiously.

"Being attacked in the dining room?"

"You had a chance to move out of the way." Even in the dim light of the hall sconce the flush in his face was evident.

Jet took a step back. "If I'd known I was in the way."

"You were warned."

"About the mistletoe?"

His voice softened, "And that I love you."

She took another step back. "Do I need to be armed?"

"Was it that awful?"

She looked into the depths of his dark blue eyes and shook her head. "But you do need to stay away."

"Temptation got the best of me," he grumbled.

She zipped her jacket and pulled on her gloves. "I need to go."

The sky couldn't make up its mind, dropping fat snowflakes one minute, rain the next. The SUV skidded in a couple places as Jet made her way to the freeway, but she managed to stay in control. The airport appeared surprisingly quiet when she turned off at the cell phone exit.

Alone with her thoughts Jet found she lacked the strength to fight them off. As if taking advantage of her unguarded moment they rushed her like shoppers for an early Christmas bargain. *You're in love with him, admit it. Stay away from him, he's your brother. He doesn't really care for you, how could he?* Overwhelmed, Jet suddenly found herself sobbing. After a few moments she dried the tears and repaired her makeup.

Was she in love with Kinsey? Or was it just infatuation, a physical attraction? She did care for him. Could she refuse to be in love? She was afraid of being hurt, of believing in something that didn't exist or never could be. She had wanted her mother's attention and a father who cared for her. But they were all illusions. She was alone, always had been.

However, no matter how rational her thought process, the one thing she couldn't seem to extinguish was the tiny flame of emotion residing inside her. The best she could do was ignore it.

Her cell phone began its jingling tune.

"We're here," Latte announced breathlessly.

By the time Jet had lined up for the terminal Latte and the kids were waiting for her. After a flurry of hugs and greetings, the luggage was stowed and everyone buckled in, Jet asked about her trip.

Latte heaved a sigh. "We managed to get out of Dodge before I had to spend time with George."

"You did see him?"

She nodded. "Briefly. He returned from his parents a couple days ago and spent a day with the kids, which I thought was appropriate."

No matter how flighty Latte seemed at times, she was a consistently conscientious mother. "Was it hard for them?"

"Everything is hard. It's hard if they see him. It's hard if they don't. What are you going to do?" She lifted a palm. "I don't want to bad mouth their father to them. They need to feel okay about him. They wouldn't understand the problems now. But I don't want to get sucked into my mother's plans for reconciliation. I can't understand what she's thinking."

"Does she realize he's chronically unfaithful?" Jet couldn't figure Latte's mother either.

"She's met his "other" women when he was with them." Latte's voice rose an octave. She sighed. "How was your Christmas?"

Jet struggled to come up with an answer.

"That bad?"

She amended the impression she had given. "Just complicated."

"So give me all the gory details."

Jet described the snowstorm, Christmas with the Barnes, Billy's reappearance, the Secret Service surveillance, and the DNA testing. "Roger is not my father."

Latte cast a sideways glance at her. "Is that good news or bad?"

"Bad." Jet grimaced.

After few miles riding in silence, Latte asked, "What is it you're not telling me? You've carefully avoided mentioning Kinsey."

"Oh," Jet said enthusiastically, "I thought you'd realize he was at the Barnes. Since the weather was bad and neither his car nor mine are any good in the snow we used your SUV."

"That's not what I meant." Latte shot her an admonishing look. "I have the feeling something happened between you two."

"What is it with you? Mental telepathy?"

"Spit it out woman. I'll find out eventually."

Sighing, Jet resigned herself to the truth of Latte's claim. "Kinsey told me he loved me."

"Do you think that's a big secret? It's written all over him every time he's around you." Latte laughed. "You're probably the last one to know."

Blushing, Jet shifted her thoughts to the driving rain.

"And," Latte demanded Jet's attention, "just for your information, you're in love with him, too."

She opened her mouth to protest then closed it. What could she say?

"I'm sorry, Jet. Denial won't make it any easier. At least it never worked for me."

She was counting on denial for protection. "I'm not going to do what my mother did," she declared vehemently. "I'm not."

"Do you think what your mother did was because of love?" Latte admonished. "It was pure self-centeredness. It was all about her. With you, it's never been all about you, especially where Kinsey is concerned."

Fighting back tears that threatened to surface, Jet took a deep breath and concentrated on the lights drifting by as they cruised I-5.

Latte touched her arm. "I'm sorry, Jet. I know this is a struggle for you. Things will work out. You'll be okay."

Jet snorted her disdain.

❧

Kinsey remained in the hall where Jet left him, his gaze following her small figure down the stairs. Was she always so in control? Or did she simply not care for him? She certainly hadn't responded positively to his declaration of love.

His heart fought the idea she simply didn't care. She's fighting it, afraid to love, afraid of being hurt. He couldn't blame her, but he could change that, show her she was wrong; but not if she was his sister.

Voices on the stairs made him turn as Nathan and Billy approached.

"What's with Evana?" Nathan asked. "If looks threw sparks she'd set your hair on fire."

"I'll see you later." Billy moved to the stairs. "I've got some work to do."

Nathan and Kinsey watched him climb, favoring his right side.

"Has he said anything about what happened while he was gone?" Kinsey moved to the door of his suite.

"I saw him popping pills at dinner, but I couldn't get him to talk about it." Nathan ran his hand through his bright hair. "I could try bumping into him and see what he does."

Kinsey cringed.

Susannah, arriving from the parlor, accosted the pair, "Where's Jet?" The dim light of the hall softened the heavy makeup she wore.

"Went to pick up Latte."

Susannah spun around with a flip of her short skirt. "Tell her I found out some things about that Severson woman." She headed toward her suite.

"What did you find out?" Kinsey stopped her.

Looking back over her shoulder, Susannah paused. "Apparently just before she wasn't back to work she'd gotten a promotion Jet's mother fought hard for."

"You think Mona bopped her over the head because she beat her out of a promotion?" Nathan asked.

"Don't be silly." Susannah flung him a black look. "My dad said Judy got the promotion the same week she disappeared."

"That makes it even more likely Mona bopped her on the head." Kinsey declared.

Susannah's expression implied he had moon cheese for brains.

"But it's not unreasonable to think the promotion had something to do with her going missing or even ending up dead. Did your dad say what the position was?"

Taking a step toward him, Susannah softened her attitude with a coquettish look. "Making certain all the

302

minorities got their rights, filing the suits when they didn't, pursuing the out of compliance organizations and businesses."

He took a step back. "That leaves lots of openings for some rankled person who wanted more recompense than he got, or revenge."

"But your problem," Susannah countered, batting her eyelashes, "is how and why she ended up in your garden."

Chapter Thirty-three

Heading to work Wednesday morning Jet noted the melting snow, unmasking sidewalks and landscaping. As soon as she got there she called Roger's cell phone and left a message.

He returned the call he inviting her to lunch again. After agreeing she wondered if this would be their farewell. When Roger arrived, his hair blacker than usual, wearing a dark business suit he had such a solemn expression on his face it gave Jet a prick of apprehension. "Would it be a problem if we took extra time and went to the waterfront?" he asked.

Noting all the employees in place, she said, "Let me give the other officer a heads-up."

On their way Roger asked, "You received the DNA test results?"

"Yes," Jet murmured.

"You sound disappointed." He gave her a sideways glance.

"I am." She met his gaze. "I got used to your benign neglect. Now I'm an orphan again."

"I'm sorry about that." He even sounded sincere. "I'm perfectly willing to be your stand-in father. I'd gotten used to having a daughter, even enjoyed it."

Tears rose to Jet's eyes. "Thank you." She smiled, her spirits lifting.

In The Lobster Shop the hostess led them to a table by the windows. The sun sparkled on the sound like a bowl of crystal bobbles. Vashon Island and Dash Point in their deep green appeared newly painted.

While receiving menus and making lunch choices Jet wondered why Roger invited her out. She voiced her question when the waiter had gone.

He tipped his head considering her. "I needed to see how you were taking the results of the test."

His hesitation raised Jet's doubts. "I can't say I'm happy about it," she admitted. "By the way did you know one of mom's fellow workers? A Judy Severson?"

Roger's expression froze in position. Only his beady eyes moved as they glanced at her then away. "Why do you ask?" His voice had dropped to a hoarse rasp.

"That's the name of the second body they discovered at the estate."

He cleared his throat. "How did they figure that out?"

"Apparently from a ring they found in the spot where the body was first buried."

A slow flush crept up his face. He took a deep breath. "I believe I met her once or twice at Mona's office. Your mom didn't have much use for her."

"What was she like?"

Roger frowned in his effort to recall. "Short, a little on the plump side, dark hair."

"I mean what was she like as a person?"

He focused his gaze in the distance. "According to Mona competitive and sneaky."

"Sneaky?"

"She'd snoop in people's files and belongings, talk behind their back, manipulate circumstances and bad mouth those she thought might get ahead of her." He paused then added, "Nothing worth dying for."

The waiter brought their lunches. When he had gone Roger took control of the conversation. "I understand the Secret Service has the mansion under surveillance." He appeared concerned. "Have they discovered anything?"

She shook her head, savoring a bite of her spicy tomato bisque.

"Have you heard from the other guy living at the castle?" He tossed out the question with studied nonchalance.

"Billy came back Sunday night."

Roger's eyebrows shot up. "Did he say where he'd been?"

"Home for Christmas," Jet replied with a touch of sarcasm.

"You don't believe him?" Roger cocked his head, eying her. He pulled the tail off his shrimp. "You thought he might be injured."

Jet shrugged. "He seems okay—maybe a little stiff."

"But he's not saying anything?"

She shook her head.

Roger's gaze drifted out across the shimmering sound. Jet tried to decide if he was relieved, concerned or calculating.

⌘

For the first time in more than a week the whole crew had gathered for the evening meal, chattering boisterously. The candlelight quality of the chandeliers, the scent of herb roasted chicken with garlic pasta sauce, and warmth of the fire in the dining room made it feel festive, almost romantic. Kinsey glanced down the table at Jet whose small face was barely visible from beneath her bubble of dark hair. Her glasses sat on the edge of her nose as she listened to Latte across the table from her. Something in her posture reminded Kinsey of someone else he had seen lately, leaving a vague impression that passed through his senses but never quite reached his conscious.

Watching Billy, he detected restriction to the young man's movements. His eyes met Nathan's who nodded as if thinking the same thing. As he glanced around the table he caught Evana's eyes on him. He smiled but she dropped her gaze to her plate, obviously still put out. He couldn't help it. She wasn't going to engage him in her negative fantasy.

Susannah chatted with Billy and Nathan, each trying to top the other's story. "What are we going to do for New Years Eve?" she addressed Kinsey.

"How about another party?" Nathan added.

"Something low key. I don't need any New Years Eve bash here." Realizing he had the perfect place for an extravaganza, he also had enough trouble to last through the coming year without including the aftermath of New Year's Eve. Their end of the table broke into a discussion of party ideas.

When dinner was over Kinsey followed Jet, informing her, "I asked Dad about Judy Severson. He didn't know anything about her."

"It doesn't make any sense." Jet turned back to him. "And it must make sense somehow." She was adamant.

"Her body didn't split in half and drop into holes in the yard by magic."

"You're certain?" Kinsey raised his eyebrows. He wasn't sure of anything anymore. For all he knew skeletons were circling the mansion at the very moment looking for a good place to rest.

She stopped, looking as if she suspected him of a sarcastic remark.

He moved in the direction of the alcove overlooking the lake where they sat on the upholstered window seat.

"What do we know for certain?" Kinsey watched Billy climb the stairs.

"The twins found counterfeit money on the grounds. There is concealed space here that could have been used for counterfeiting. They've traced the bad money back to Lakewood." Jet summarized, ticking off items on her fingers.

Kinsey turned a sharp glance on her. "Did Elaney say that?"

She nodded.

Frowning, Kinsey asked, "Do you think Billy is involved in that?"

"Or can he be linked to the corpses?" She crossed her arms over her small bosom. "Maybe he's connected to Judy Severson."

He hadn't thought of that.

"Maybe she was competing with my mom on another front." Jet watched his face for the reaction.

"Like?"

"How many fatherless children she could have." She shot him a crooked grin. "Maybe he's her long lost son."

Kinsey frowned at Jet's humor. "You do have a point," he conceded. "We haven't looked at all the possibilities."

"Did you hear anything on that gun we found?"

"No, but I think I'll give the lieutenant a call tomorrow." Kinsey wished the lieutenant would just offer the information.

Nathan approached the pair and stood leaning against the cherry paneling. "I did get something out of Billy."

Kinsey lifted an eyebrow.

"He muttered something about not drinking at the party because it wouldn't work with his medications." Nathan flashed Kinsey a wide grin. "He said and I quote 'I got hit in the side with a stray bullet.'"

"Stray?"

Nathan wiggled his eyebrows. "I asked if it was here on the property. He mumbled about it happening up in the north end of Tacoma."

"That makes even less sense."

"You and I know that, but I didn't want to put him on the defensive." Nathan perched on the parlor chair nearby. "But he wouldn't have been on the north end without his truck, would he?"

Kinsey shook his head. Why would Billy tell such a goofy story?

Jet interrupted. "You should ask Nathan if he knew Judy Severson."

Nathan raised an eyebrow. Jet explained and Kinsey suggested he ask Billy about her.

Nathan slid back in his chair. "I'll tell you what I think. He knows nothing about her. Maybe she had something to do with the counterfeiting?" Nathan shot Kinsey a cheesy grin. "Or you can hook her up to your last renters."

Kinsey sighed. He was tired of the whole mess.

Chapter Thirty-four

The sun was sneaking up behind Mount Rainier as Kinsey drove to work considering his idea of getting more information out of Lieutenant Sarkis. By now he should know whether the gun they found was the murder weapon.

When he reached his desk he made a list of things he wanted to know. Before he could embark on it Latte called. She had taken the week between Christmas and New Years off since her kids were out of school.

"Did you have workers coming out here?" Her voice contained a trace of alarm. "I saw a couple men crossing the lawn a little while ago."

Racing through the possibilities, Kinsey found her anxiety contagious. "I've not arranged anything. Were they Lieutenant Sarkis' men?"

"They didn't look like police. Although I suppose that doesn't mean anything if they were undercover."

"I don't know what the police would be doing undercover on my property," Kinsey mumbled. "Where exactly did you see them?"

"Coming from Gravelly Lake Drive, cutting across the lawn toward the garden where the fountain is and . . . they were carrying something."

Horrible images attacked Kinsey. Another body? That was all he needed to make life a perfect dream.

"Each of them had a medium size box of some sort."

He sighed, probably not a body unless they cut it in half like the last one. "I'll give Elaney and Sarkis a heads up." Were the counterfeiters moving back onto the property? "If you see anything else let me know."

He had put both the lieutenant's and the agent's phone numbers in his cell phone directory. He called Elaney first. When the man answered in his articulate voice Kinsey asked, "Do you still have your surveillance crew outside the entrance to my property?"

"No. We pulled them off after you showed me the group left." Elaney's inflexion betrayed his curiosity.

Kinsey explained his call from Latte.

"You're sure she didn't recognize them?"

"She'd know if it were Nathan, Billy or I."

"Okay," the treasury agent agreed, "I'll see what I can do."

When Kinsey ended that call he went to Lieutenant Sarkis' number, receiving the lieutenant's customary growl in response. Kinsey explained the call from Latte and his conversation with Agent Elaney.

"Okay, I'll give him a call later." It sounded like a dismissal.

Kinsey refused to be put off. "Did you find out about that gun?"

Sarkis hesitated like the dog caught with the cat dangling from his jaw.

"Whose gun is it?" Kinsey wasn't putting up with a brush-off.

The lieutenant sighed. "It was registered to Matt Markovich." Sarkis cleared his throat. "It appears to be the weapon used to kill his wife."

"Does that mean she was killed on the property?" Was it ever possible she'd been killed somewhere else? "Maybe her husband killed her." To Kinsey's knowledge they were the only two living on the estate at the time. "Is there anything to say she died after he did?"

The lieutenant inhaled audibly. "That's a point worth considering." He sounded as if Kinsey had just informed him the earth was round.

Obviously Kinsey wasn't the first to have considered the idea. "Were there any fingerprints?"

"It had been wiped clean." Sarkis' tone had become scrupulously patient.

"Have you learned anything more about the other body, Judy Severson?" The lieutenant could snap, condescend or evade, Kinsey wasn't letting up.

However, this time Sarkis became the interrogator firing a question. "Do you know something about her?"

Kinsey explained what he had learned from Susannah and Jet.

"Did you find out where she went for her vacation?"

"Nowhere."

"Nowhere?" Kinsey's voice squeaked. "What does that mean?"

"You tell me. We found nothing to indicate she went anywhere on vacation or had any such plans." The lieutenant sounded as if he thought Kinsey had given him false information.

"Was she actually on vacation?"

"Apparently she arranged time off," Sarkis said, then asked, "Do you happen to know the name of the person Ms. Sayre spoke to about her?"

When Kinsey ended the call he figured he had sicced the lieutenant on both Susannah's father and Jet, not to mention Jet's friend, Barbara. That ought to raise him in the popularity poll.

Ploughing into inventory issues and budgeting, Kinsey was still spinning figures when he realized everyone had left for the day. Stuffing the work into his briefcase, he grabbed his coat and headed for the parking lot.

Contemplating where he had gotten in his plan to free the estate from its bad reputation, he felt worse off than when he started. Perhaps he had false expectations. Obviously if the mansion had become known as Blast Castle it wasn't just the media tossing words around. The challenge was real.

At the entrance to the estate he noted the surveillance SUV back in position and in the circular driveway Elaney's Acura. He found the agent talking to Nathan in the parlor and immediately joined them. As they conversed Jet came through the door from the anteroom. Casting a glance their direction she continued to the stairs. Elaney's gaze followed her, which infused Kinsey with an irrational twinge of protectiveness.

With a sudden decisive movement, the agent moved to intercept her. As Kinsey watched he struck with an idea, but immediately cast it aside. It was too far-fetched.

❧

Entering the house through the anteroom, Jet noted Kinsey and the Secret Service Agent near the windows overlooking the lake. She wondered if they had made any progress, but wasn't about to stop and ask. However, as she reached the stairs, Agent Elaney approached.

"You haven't seen Roger Thompson here today?"

Frowning, Jet shook her head. "I haven't been here. You can ask Latte."

The agent continued to stare as though she had tucked Roger in her handbag.

She continued to her room where she changed from her skirt into a pair of slacks. As she descended the grand staircase she noticed Latte near the piano with Agent Elaney.

"It wasn't Roger Thompson," Jet heard Latte tell the agent.

His back was to Jet so she couldn't hear what he said, but Latte continued to talk about Roger.

There was another question from Agent Elaney that Jet couldn't hear, then Latte nodded.

The dining room doors opened, indicating dinner was ready. Jet wondered if Agent Elaney was joining them, but he made his apologies and exited through the anteroom door.

When everyone had been served, Kinsey brought up the fact someone had seen a stranger on the property.

"I heard noises in the wall again," Susannah offered.

"In your suite?" Kinsey frowned at her.

She nodded.

He glanced at Jet who lifted her eyebrows.

"Maybe we're getting a re-infestation of counterfeiters," Nathan suggested.

That was the most logical conclusion Jet figured. But why move out, which apparently they had, then move back in?

What conclusion had Agent Elaney drawn from his discussion with Latte? He seemed more interested in Roger Thompson than counterfeiters. Suddenly Jet realized the obvious. She had been avoiding any connection between Roger and the counterfeiting, which might explain his continual presence around the estate. Just having the thought made her feel sad.

Evana spoke up. "When I came home I met a dark green van on the lake road heading toward Gravelly Lake Drive."

"Has anyone else ever seen someone across the road to the west of the rhododendron garden?" Kinsey tossed the question out to the group.

There was a jumble of conversation as the question went around the table.

"Where the kids found the money would make some sense if the counterfeiters were traipsing to the house through the rhodies," Nathan put in.

"I'll have to check it out." Kinsey said. "Did anyone say anything to Agent Elaney about it?"

No one responded.

"There's been a suspicious absence of that sheriff's lieutenant," Nathan pointed out, insinuation in the tone of his voice.

All eyes turned to him as if he had announced the government officially cancelled tax refunds. The group looked as if they hoped Nathan and his ideas would go away.

Chapter Thirty-five

When Kinsey reached work he called his father who informed him he had spoken to Carmen Markovich's sister. He learned two things. Number one, the 9mm SigSauer was Carmen's gun and two, Matt had another gun of his own, a 357 magnum.

"Apparently Matt bought Carmen a gun after they started seeing strangers on the property," Park said. "Since Carmen was often there alone at night."

"And the other gun?"

"That was part of the inventory taken from the house after Matt died."

Kinsey ended the call undecided where that information got him. As soon as he did his cell phone chirped again.

This is Latte." She sounded upset, her voice coming in a rush. "Strange things are going on around here again."

Again? More like still. "What exactly?"

"Footsteps on the stairs behind the laundry room and Susannah heard some again near her suite." Latte sounded as if she had been elected the Bad News Bear and wasn't happy about it.

Kinsey sighed. "When did this start?"

"After lunch." Latte took a deep breath sounding relieved Kinsey hadn't attacked the messenger. "The kids saw that green van again on the road by the lake."

Kinsey grimaced. "I'll give Elaney a call." The moment the phone was answered it switched him to the answering service where he left a message for the treasury agent.

Returning to the inventory and budget, Kinsey worked until noon then closed up the office. After putting his car in the garage he noticed Jet's roadster arriving. He waited for her and they walked toward the house together while he explained his call from Latte.

"Are you going to let Lieutenant Sarkis know?"

"This appears to be counterfeiters not murderers."

"And you know the difference?" Jet peered at him over the edge of her glasses.

"Point." Kinsey made an invisible slash in the air with his finger.

Just as they reached the terrace his cell phone rang. "This is Agent Elaney."

Kinsey explained Latte's call.

"Okay." The agent sounded harassed. "I'm working on something right now that may take some time. I'll see you out there as soon as I get through.

The moment Jet and Kinsey entered the grand parlor Logan and Landon came running. "We found a mouse," Landon declared.

Kinsey peered at them through narrowed eyes. "Where?"

"In the kitchen." Landon pointed.

Kinsey glanced at Jet with his brows drawn together. "Probably coming in from the cold."

Wishful thinking, she figured.

"Where is it?" he asked the boys.

Logan stood up taller. "Mom threw it outside."

Kinsey gave Jet an exaggerated wide-eyed look.

She laughed. "Latte deals with the wild things in life. She doesn't put up with guff, not even from a mouse."

"Where's your mom?" Kinsey asked the twins.

"In the laundry room."

"Where else?" Jet laughed again heading there.

Latte stood at the stainless steel sink running water, testing it with her hand. "Water's cold." Her tone suggested someone was purposely thwarting her plans.

On hearing Latte's comment Kinsey headed immediately for the basement door. When he opened it a little white mouse zipped into the room then suddenly froze. Grabbing the creature by the tail, he declared, "This is suspicious." He waved the dangling rodent. "This is a lab mouse."

Jet and Latte stared at him wordless.

"Get me something to put him in."

Glancing around the kitchen, Jet spotted a three pound coffee can on the counter. Lifting the lid she observed it was only one-third full. Latte opened the cupboard and handed her a bowl into which Jet poured the remaining coffee. Then she handed the can to Kinsey who dropped the mouse in, slapped the lid on, and with a knife from the block on the counter put air holes in it.

She could hear the mouse running in circles inside the can.

"Caffeine high." He flashed her a grin then turned back to the basement door. "I'm going to check on the hot water."

As she searched for a better receptacle for the remaining coffee Evana came into the kitchen wearing a heavy sweater she clutched together. "Isn't it cold in here?"

Jet checked the thermostat on the kitchen wall. "Sixty-six."

"That's what it's set at?" Evana shivered.

"No, it's set at seventy."

Kinsey came from the basement carrying two more white mice he dropped in the coffee can.

"What's going on?" Evana shuddered.

"She says her suite is cold and it isn't that warm in here either," Jet informed him.

"Let's go take a look." He waved a come-on to Evana.

"I'm going to check on a couple things," Jet said and left Latte with her laundry.

In the parlor she investigated the heat registers. All of them were cold. The parlor was worse than the kitchen; the morning room and solarium were frigid. By the time she finished the main floor rooms, Kinsey was returning on the grand staircase.

"I checked Evana's register and it's on full, but no heat. I checked my suite and it's the same thing." Kinsey ran his hand through his hair. "I'm going back to the basement and see what's going on."

Noting the invading darkness as the sun sank to the edge of the horizon, Jet moved through the parlor turning on lamps. She could hear Anatuviak and went to the library French doors. The dog stood at the terrace edge, barking in the direction of the formal gardens. When she opened the door and called to him he turned to look at her, then turned back and continued the noise.

Jet returned to the kitchen. "Anatuviak is barking at something."

"He's been doing that off and on all day." Latte was perched on a stool leafing through a magazine. "I even took a walk in the yard to that fountain, but I didn't see anything."

Jet heard footsteps in the butler's pantry and Nathan entered the room, stopping when he saw the girls.

"What's going on?" He brushed his hair with his hand. "Did you rearrange the furniture in the music room?" He glanced from one girl to the other.

They stared as if he spoke a foreign language.

"That peach loveseat was up against the French doors with the round ottoman in front of it."

"I was just in there," Jet said. "Everything was the way it always is." She cocked her head and gave Nathan a scolding glance.

"I'm not kidding. Come see for yourself." He headed for the door.

Jet and Latte followed. As they did so Jet paid attention to where furniture was placed. Although she didn't totally accept what Nathan said, she felt a twinge of doubt. It wasn't beyond the scope of what had been happening.

In the music room the furniture was placed just as Jet remembered. Nathan stood in the middle of the floor turning in a circle. "I'll swear that loveseat," he pointed to the silk covered settee, "was in front of that door."

Latte smirked.

"I'm not losing my mind." He scowled at her.

Jet stared at the Chinese rug. Near one of the settee's wooden feet was an indentation the exact size of its leg. She moved the settee slightly so that the foot nearest the indentation was placed right in the middle. It fit perfectly. The indentation left when she moved the settee was barely an impression.

"You know what Nathan, I believe you."

He turned to Jet surprised. She showed him her discovery.

Nathan rubbed his chin. "What do you think it means?"

"Strange things are happening around here," she explained.

"Another invasion of the birds?"

"Mice."

Jet and Latte took turns explaining. "We'd better let Kinsey know." Jet felt sad since he was already beset beyond endurance.

౭౩

In the basement, Kinsey checked the two water heaters. One was a household heater for the water supply to the kitchen, main floor baths, laundry room, and butler's pantry. The other, considerably larger, supplied water for heating the house. Neither was operating. Checking he found both pilot lights out. Sniffing to determine if gas was escaping into the air, he wondered if it had been shut off.

In the kitchen, he tried the gas stove, which lit when he turned the knob. He grabbed fireplace matches from the morning room and took them back to the basement. Cautiously he relit the pilot lights. While waiting to make sure they did not go out again, he wandered the periphery of the area checking the small foundation windows to determine if they were the cause. He found nothing except another white mouse hiding in the shadow of one.

He took the mouse to the coffee can thinking at this rate he would have enough to supply the university laboratory.

As he finished Nathan, Latte and Jet returned to fill him in on the moving furniture. Perching on one of the kitchen stools, he stared at the dark window over the sink. What was going on?

"Is anybody hungry?" Nathan asked opening the refrigerator. "Whoa, look at this."

"Leave it alone," Jet warned him.

"It's for the party," Latte explained.

"What are you doing for dinner?" Nathan addressed Kinsey.

He shrugged, noticing Jet and Latte exchange a glance.

"Why don't you guys join us in my suite? We can make spaghetti." Jet offered.

"Hey, thanks," Nathan spoke for both of them.

"I'll go get things started while you get your load set up," Jet told Latte.

When she had gone Kinsey asked Nathan, "Do you really think someone moved the furniture?"

Nathan raised his right hand. "I swear that settee was blocking the door to the music room when I got home."

"But you've seen no one around?" Kinsey narrowed his eyes.

"No one that doesn't belong here." Nathan grimaced.

Kinsey wished he could believe the whole thing was simply a prank, but he had run out of somebodies to be playing tricks.

"I haven't checked on Billy recently," Nathan suggested.

"Why don't you see what he's been up to? Invite him to Jet's if you need to."

"Gotcha," Nathan said heading out the door.

How the heck was he supposed to find out what was going on, Kinsey wondered? What should he say to Agent Elaney when he did show up? For the group to go on a wild goose chase was one thing; to send the Secret Service on one was another. He wasn't hot to get locked up for aiding and abetting.

As he proceeded to Jet's room something struck him as out of place. However, intent on his destination it remained only an impression in the back of his mind.

Opening the door to his knock, Jet invited him in. He followed her through the pink tinted bedroom into the kitchen.

"You're the first one here," she declared, "so you can set the table."

Crossing his arms, he raised his eyebrows.

She looked like the judge and he had refused to take the oath.

"Your honor," he raised his hands, "where are the dishes?"

Her eyebrows drew together as she shot him a frustrated glance, but she pointed to the cupboard nearest the table.

While counting people and plates Kinsey found uninvited pictures of doing this regularly entered his mind. Temptation beckoned his thoughts to greater detail. He felt more than saw her small figure moving about as she turned the heat on the water, stirred the sauce, and worked on a salad.

Something occurred to him. "Do you have a plan for checking out Susannah's father? You said he may be your father."

"I was hoping I wouldn't have to go that far."

Kinsey cast a sidelong glance, noting the look of dread on her face. "Maybe I could help."

"How?" She pronounced the word as if daring him to try. "For some reason my mother was particularly protective of Jesse McFadden; which doesn't make any sense if you knew my mother. She was proud of her conquests."

Suddenly what struck Kinsey as he headed to Jet's suite flashed before his eyes. "I just realized that big antique clock on the wall next to the stairs was moved. It's sitting in the hall next to my suite."

"You're kidding." Jet set down the knife she was using to cut cucumber. "I'm going to look."

Kinsey followed her to the hall where she checked his statement. Turning back to him she shook her head. "It's where it always is."

Stepping out of the room he verified her word. The clock was back where it normally hung. Had he imagined it? He couldn't have. He knew what he saw. Looking at her, he shrugged.

"Where have you and Nathan been?" She shot him a twisted grin. "You're having hallucinations."

As they returned to the kitchen, Kinsey said, "I can live with hallucinations, but what if we're not?"

Hearing a brief knock at the door, Kinsey stepped into the bedroom as it opened for Latte, the twins and Nathan.

"Who moved the clock?" Nathan asked as he followed Latte into the room.

With long strides Kinsey headed to the hall door where he noted the clock now stood against the wall next to his suite. "Jet, come and look at this."

She came from the kitchen with a reproving expression.

"Look, that's where it was when I came."

She frowned.

"Tell Nathan where it was the last time you saw it.

"Kinsey and I just looked a few minutes ago. It was at the end where it always is."

Stepping into the hall, Kinsey approached the instrument. Nathan wandered to the spot it usually occupied. With a quick look of understanding the two guys made a run for the stairs then scrambled up them to the room at the south end of the third floor.

"Did you find Billy?" Kinsey asked when they had reached the top.

"Yep, he was in bed." Nathan moved toward the hall. "It took him a couple minutes to open the door. He looked like he had been asleep. His hair was all over the place and his shirt all crumpled up. I asked if he wanted something to eat, but he said he wasn't feeling well."

At the entrance to the hallway they stood for a moment looking around.

"There's nowhere here for anyone to hide," Nathan observed.

"Did you lock your suite?"

Nathan nodded, trying the knob. They wandered along the passage looking in crannies and opening linen closet doors.

"Nothing." Nathan shook his head.

"Okay, let's go back to Jet's."

೦⁊

"What's with those guys?" Latte asked, pitching in to help Jet finish the meal.

She explained Kinsey's clock encounter.

"It's odd." Latte said, wiping spaghetti sauce off the stove.

Jet motioned to her to wipe it off her nose.

"I'm worse than the kids."

"What can I say?" Jet grinned at her. "You're worse than the kids." She drained the pasta and poured it into a bowl.

"It's been strange around here all day." Latte removed the salad dressing from the refrigerator. "I keep thinking I hear strange noises. But when I stop to listen it quits."

The door into the hall opened as Nathan and Kinsey returned.

"What did you find?" Jet asked.

"Not a dang thing." Kinsey sounded frustrated.

"Except, the clock actually was moved," Nathan added.

"Dinner's ready," Latte announced.

Jet motioned to the twins who sat on the floor playing with a puzzle and followed Kinsey and Nathan into the dinette. After a short discussion of where to sit, they commenced to dish up.

"All we're missing is the light show and birds," Nathan wiggled his eyebrows.

"Don't hold your breath, the night's not over." Kinsey stabbed a piece of bread.

"That reminds me," Nathan said. "I think Billy is hiding out in his room. When I knocked, he asked who it was. When I told him, I heard him unbolt the deadlocks."

"Maybe he always locks himself in," Latte suggested.

"Always is the operative word." Nathan gave her a big grin. "He didn't do it before. I've knocked on his door in the past and it was never even locked. He'd just yell 'come in'."

Jet turned to Kinsey for his opinion.

"Maybe he knows something we don't."

"Like who is moving the furniture?" Nathan huffed.

"Or turning off the water heaters," Latte added.

"And dropping off mice," Kinsey mumbled.

"Do you think it would help to ask him?" Jet suggested.

Nathan shook his head. "He's into denial. Denying anything is going on or that he knows anything about it. I already tried that."

"Can we catch the furniture movers?" Jet asked.

Nathan narrowed his eyes. "Whenever something is moved out of place, as soon as it's noticed it's moved back again."

"What if we find something moved and keep an eye on it? We might see it put back." Kinsey took a deep breath then went on, "What do we do when we catch them?"

Nathan made a breaking arm gesture.

Kinsey scowled at him. "I'd probably lose an appendage in that transaction."

"Should we call Lieutenant Sarkis," Jet suggested.

"I'd rather find out first if we have anything to report."

Logan piped up, "I heard the door."

Everyone was quiet. The door buzzed again.

When Jet opened it, Susannah and Evana rushed into the bedroom.

"Something funny is going on," Evana reported.

"It's giving me the willies." Susannah wrapped her arms around herself, shivering. "And it's cold everywhere."

Kinsey came into the room behind Jet. Even in her agitation Evana managed to give him a disapproving frown.

"Do you want to join us? We're having something to eat and trying to figure out how to handle the problems."

"Sounds good to me," Susannah immediately accepted.

Evana looked like she couldn't decide but followed the rest to the kitchen. Jet brought the footstool from near the fireplace and one of the parlor chairs from her bedroom and they squeezed the extra girls around the table.

"If someone is actually moving furniture where are they when it's not being moved?" Latte raised her eyebrows looking from Kinsey to Nathan.

"What are you guys talking about?" Evana sounded exasperated.

Kinsey explained the moving furniture.

"That explains it," Susannah burst out with enthusiasm. "There's a wooden settee I hadn't noticed before in front of that window to the left of the staircase."

Thinking about the spot Susannah indicated, Jet didn't recall seeing furniture in that small alcove.

"If we're going to have anything to give Elaney or Sarkis we need to catch them in the act," Kinsey declared.

"How would you suggest we do that?" Latte demanded.

"What if we stake out all the hiding places?" Nathan suggested.

"What places are we talking about?" Kinsey eyed his friend.

"The closet at the top of the grand staircase."

"There's another closet on the other side of my suite," Susannah added.

"Someone should be at the top of the third floor stairs," Nathan pointed his fork that direction.

Kinsey gazed around the table. "Volunteers?"

"I'll do the top of the stairs," Nathan said. "That's a fairly large area to cover."

"Why don't you girls pair up?" Kinsey suggested.

"Evana and I can take the closet on the other side of my suite," Susannah volunteered.

"That leaves the Christmas decorations closet for Latte and I," Jet said.

"What about us?" Logan asked.

"Yeah," Landon joined.

"You're to guard this suite from intruders," Latte said. "Make sure no one gets in except one of the people here."

Jet mentally applauded Latte's strategy.

Chapter Thirty-six

"It's dark in there," Latte said when Jet opened the closet door. "I'll get a flashlight."

Hesitant to settle in the closet alone, Jet left the door cracked. Pushing a Christmas box into the corner under the lowest shelf, she observed enough space for them with room to spare. Shelves were located at the back and the bottom one was thirty inches from the floor.

Latte knocked softly then slipped in, turning on the flashlight. "Do you think they're watching us?"

"Probably," Jet huffed. "But the plan might work anyway."

She pointed to the open space. "Why don't we get under those shelves? Then if someone looks in they won't see us right away."

"Are you kidding?" Latte snorted. "We're not invisible."

"We could cover ourselves with a sheet."

Taking one off the shelf Latte put it over her head. "We need something to cut holes with," she complained. "I can't see anything."

"Put it on like the Arabs dress." Jet wrapped a sheet around herself, over her head and across the bridge of her nose. "It's dark in here so no one should see our eyes anyway."

Latte imitated Jet's management of the sheet. "I can imagine the whites of my eyes glowing like candles in the dark."

"Overactive imagination." Jet settled into one of the corners.

"This whole thing is overactive imagination." Latte managed to get her covering arranged. "How long do you think we'll be here?"

"You sound like your kids."

"I feel like my kids." She sighed then declared in a whisper, "You know we did this wrong,"

"What do you mean?"

She laughed. "You and Kinsey should have been in the closet."

"Latteee," Jet warned. "If you're not careful I'll see that you end up in a closet with Nathan." Latte's quiet made Jet wonder if she had hit upon an idea. "It sounds as if you wouldn't mind that."

"He's actually a lot of fun."

"I forgot to ask, how was your trip to the Pantages?"

Latte squirmed into a different position. "We had a good time."

"He seems to enjoy the kids."

"What's even better, they enjoy him."

Jet could just distinguish her form beneath the sheet with the light from the hall squeezing under the door. "Are you in love with him?" When Latte didn't answer, Jet wondered if she didn't know either. However, Jet recalled when Latte got married. "You were in love with George weren't you?"

"I was," she conceded. "But being in love isn't an answer to anything, it's just a beginning."

"To heartache, misery, mistreatment . . ." Jet recalled how things had been when Latte learned of George's unfaithfulness.

She cleared her throat. "I know people who fall in love and are happy forever."

"Kinsey said that about Aunt Pat and Uncle Dan, about his mother and father, even about Evana and her husband. So what makes the difference?"

"Some of it has to do with what happens afterward." Latte sighed. "Falling in love is a kind of emotional reaction to someone. You can fall for someone who is totally unsuitable or unavailable or impossible to live with."

"Was George one of those?"

"No." Latte shook her sheet. "George was in love with George. As long as he felt I adored and approved of him he was happy. In fact, he was always happy. He was also unfaithful because just one woman to love and appreciate him wasn't enough."

"Do you still love him?"

Latte remained quiet a few moments. "There's a difference between attraction to someone and really loving that person. I love the George I believed in, but that one doesn't really exist. I don't wish him any harm but I don't want to be with him either."

"So" Jet challenged her friend, "what happened to being in love?"

Latte stretched her legs. "It can help you get to know someone well enough to commit for life and a wonderful long relationship, or," she paused, "it can fizzle out from lack of real love."

"I don't think I loved Brad."

"When you go right to a physical relationship there's little chance to develop real love, which is more a gradual getting to know someone deeper and deeper. Going directly to the physical short circuits all that. You become sexually intimate and never develop true intimacy."

Impressed by Latte's wisdom, Jet's mind traveled to her mother's relationships. Mulling over what Latte said Jet stared at the strip of light below the closet door. Suddenly the strip went black making darkness complete.

"What happened?" Latte squeaked.

"I don't know."

❧

Kinsey and Nathan climbed to the top of the third floor stairs and performed another reconnaissance along the hall to Evana's suite.

"Nothing." Nathan dropped onto the striped sofa at the end of the hall and placed his feet in the wicker chair opposite. "What now?"

Kinsey perched on the window seat. He was clueless. He only knew the outcome he wanted. "I'm surprised Elaney hasn't come yet."

The lights flickered. Nathan's feet hit the floor as the two exchanged a glance.

Flickering lights didn't mean anything . . . necessarily.

"Someone should be on the first floor. They could be loading a U-haul with the furniture while we're stashed up here."

Kinsey grimaced. "We could stake out the music room stairs."

"I'll do that." Nathan was on his feet.

When he had gone, Kinsey turned to the window facing the garages. Since the terrace off his room was directly below he could see nothing close to the house. While he strained to see beyond it the cell phone in his pocket alerted him with a text message. "Someones here cant c, do?"

Kinsey texted Nathan back, "Sty pt I comn."

Calculating the best path there, Kinsey descended to the second floor and moved to the grand staircase.

From the lowest landing on the stairs he would be able to glimpse the room unobserved. Descending carefully, hoping to avoid making noise, he reached a vantage spot then flattened himself against the wall and listened.

Near him the standing clock ticked, the radiator clanked, floors creaked both above and below, but only randomly, not as if someone walked there. Lighting was dim, coming only from the arabesque sconces in the parlor. The double doors to the dining room were closed. His ears strained for a sound he could not identify. Nothing, all was quiet. Was Nathan mistaken?

Just as he was about to descend the remaining steps, a voice nearby hissed, "What the hell do you think you're doing?"

Kinsey's heart took off on an out of body experience leaving him frozen in place. If he could have moved he would have answered the question, but shock saved him from speech.

A voice farther away answered in a disgusted tone. "Just what you told me to do."

Holding his breath, Kinsey listened to determine their location. One was just below where he stood, next to the clock. The other sounded as if he were across the room. All of a sudden the absurdity of the situation occurred to him. Here he was, the owner of the property, hiding in the shadows for fear of a couple of intruders. Who the heck did they think they were anyway?

Next to where he stood were a row of switches controlling the parlor lights and outlets. With the broad side of his hand he flipped all the switches at once. Nothing happened. His heart, having deigned to return, took off again. He felt like a prisoner in his own house. What did the wall switches control? For one thing the outlets in the parlor into which the lamps were plugged. It was barely possible the lamps had been switched off. Some of the switches had already been in the up position. They could have been for the sconces. One by one he flipped the switches down. The lights near the fireplace went out briefly before suddenly every lamp in the room flared bright. Kinsey glanced at the row of switches. He had only gotten to two of them. There were four. He moved the third one. Nothing happened. Nothing lit, no light went out. He could think of no object besides lights the switch might operate. As he reached for the fourth all the lights went out together. This time he had not touched anything. A racket across the room sounded like someone bumping into the fireplace irons.

Before Kinsey's eyes adjusted to the darkness he could see a band of light from beneath the doors to the dining room. Was someone there or had one of those in the parlor made it that far? In the shadows against the wall on the staircase he still felt like a plucked goose with the light from the second floor hall shining down on him. Realizing the fourth switch must be for those, he flipped it and the lights above were extinguished.

"What was that?" the voice near him sounded alarmed. "Did you do the lights on the next floor?"

From across the room a voice hissed, "I've done nothing."

Would it be better to make it to where Nathan was or the kitchen? Could he make it either direction? Kinsey figured he knew his way around the house better than the intruders. If he got all the lights out at once and the guy near the clock to move he could probably make it to the music room without being seen.

After removing his shoes he retrieved a pen from his shirt pocket. Observing the position of the switches, he pushed three of them the opposite direction which turned on all the main floor lamps, but did nothing to the sconces. However, he had mentally planned his route to the music room. He switched all the lights off and tossed a pen toward the dining room doors. He heard it strike the piano then hit the floor. He could hear the person just below him move across in front of the stairs. As soon as he had passed, Kinsey quickly descended, made an abrupt left and followed along the east wall of the parlor. When he had passed the Chesterfield he turned right and continued until he could see the yard light through the music room window. Just as he entered the room and made the right turn toward the stairs the lights in the parlor came on again. Opening the door he jumped into the stairway.

Nathan was flattened against the wall defensively. "What's going on?"

"What did you see?" Kinsey closed the door except for a crack.

"I heard someone come in through the sliders and a couple of them talking. They had something with them that rattled." Nathan sat on one of the steps. "Metal."

"Do you think they're letting loose a bunch of birds again?"

"Could be, but I'm thinking it's something different. One guy said, 'This should scare the devil out of them'."

"Seagulls are annoying but not scary." Kinsey peered with greater concentration through the crack. "What about mice."

"If he was talking about scaring women that would make sense."

Kinsey joined him on the stairs, wishing Elaney would get there. With his luck the whole mess would be over before the treasury agent arrived.

Nathan moved restlessly to the door. "Shouldn't we do something?"

"Probably." The manage-the-lighting trick no longer alarmed Kinsey. To what other activities might the criminals resort to discourage his renters. Once he caught the problem makers and cleared the mansion's reputation he didn't need renters any more, but he certainly didn't want anything to happen to one of them, particularly *One* of them.

What complications would they face if he and Nathan swept through the house on raiding party? All things considered it was namby pamby stupid to be hiding in a stairwell in his own house.

"Come on." Kinsey pushed the door open. The music room was lit by a table lamp near the settee. No one was there. "Let's go."

The two exited the stairway closet. The double doors to the parlor were open. They each took a position behind one of them and peered into the parlor. Once again only the wall sconces provided light. From Kinsey's position he could see the base of the grand staircase, the furniture in front of the fireplace, the piano, and one of the doors to the dining room. He spent a few moments searching his visual space for an individual.

At that moment the door chime reverberated through the main floor.

"Elaney." Kinsey took a deep breath. "It's time to quit sneaking around."

Nathan followed Kinsey into the parlor.

The door chime reverberated again.

Kinsey pulled the front door open and Agent Elaney stepped in.

Chapter Thirty-seven

Agent Elaney wore a harassed expression, his lips set in a grim line, creases in his forehead. "So what's up?"

Kinsey and Nathan took turns explaining. Concentrating on the discussion Kinsey didn't notice the four girls descend the stairs until Latte let out a horrific shriek. When he turned she was pointing to the floor beneath the piano.

"Snake!" Evana squealed.

"There's another one!" Susannah backed up the stairs pointing to a striped reptile slithering along the edge of the room next to the dining room doors.

By this time the three guys had come to the foot of the stairs. Kinsey peered at the intruder. "Garter snake." He picked it up by the tail. "Harmless."

Nathan grabbed one from under the piano. "What do we do with them?"

Kinsey glanced at Jet with raised eyebrows. "Could you get the garbage can from outside the kitchen door?"

She glanced at her feet then at the pathway to the dining room as if preparing to cross the swollen Puyallup

River. Stepping high and light, watching the space around her she made it to the dining room doors. In a couple minutes she trotted back, her eyes on another slithering creature just ahead of her. Tiptoeing a wide swath around it, she dropped the garbage can near the guys and stumbled over the first step as she hopped onto the bottom of the staircase, pointing to a new arrival wiggling its way toward the piano.

Kinsey lifted the garbage lid and dropped the snake he held into it.

While Nathan deposited his, Kinsey grabbed the new intruder. Evana, Susannah and Latte still perched several steps from the floor looking as if they figured snakes couldn't climb stairs.

"Did you see anyone back there?" The agent addressed Jet, beckoning toward the dining room.

A stab of alarm struck Kinsey as Jet shook her head. "If you mean people not snakes."

"I'll get hold of Sarkis. We might need his people." Elaney took out his cell phone.

"I'll take our buddies out." Kinsey picked up the can of snakes. "By the way, I also have a tin of mice in the kitchen."

Elaney crinkled his dark eyebrows.

Jet retreated up the steps with the other girls. "Is there something you'd want us to do?"

Agent Elaney contemplated her with a distracted look and spoke to Kinsey, "You've made certain no one is in that end of the house?" He waved his hand toward the library and music room.

"I'll take care of it." Nathan took off.

As Kinsey moved toward the solarium and north terrace he heard Agent Elaney tell Jet, "I'd like you girls to stay here. That would limit the area we need to cover."

He moved through the dining room, patrolling the oak floors and oriental rugs for additional reptile visitors. He spied another traveling from the direction he was headed. When he opened the door to the morning room he confronted a swarm of giant gummy worms, making his heart lurch. Shuddering, he conquered his squeamishness, grabbing every creature he found and depositing it in the garbage can. Entering the solarium he found even more.

What was the deal? Obviously the snakes had been turned loose in the solarium. Had that been the intruder's intention? Or had they been interrupted, dropping them there to duck out? Had the arrival of the treasury agent ended their sojourn in the house?

In the solarium Kinsey locked and bolted the French doors and windows then did the same in the morning room. In the dining room he turned the knob on the billiard parlor door, located at one end, figuring it was locked. However, the door opened easily, triggering a prick of suspicion. Slowly pushing it farther he observed the portion of the room available to his range of vision.

With no illumination from the windows and no light on it was difficult to see. Reaching around the door, Kinsey flipped the switch, igniting sconces on the non-windowed walls. The deep emerald paint, absorbing the light, left the room barely discernible. A billiard table occupied the center, with an assortment of wood-framed chairs scattered about. The powder room door was closed. Something caught his eye, resting on the corner of the pool table, a soft-sided attaché.

Was someone in the powder room?

He took out his cell phone and sent a text message to Nathan.

In a couple minutes Nathan appeared with Agent Elaney.

Kinsey backed up a couple paces and explained what he had found.

"Shall I get the bag," Nathan moved toward the room.

Raising a hand to stop him, Elaney removed the pistol from his holster and took a defensive posture.

Nathan stepped into the room retrieved the case then backed out and handed it to Kinsey.

"Can we see what's in it?" Nathan leaned over Kinsey's shoulder.

Elaney shot him an admonishing glance.

Undaunted, Nathan raised his eyebrows. "We might learn something."

Kinsey undid the buckles and opened the bag.

"Money!" Nathan squealed.

"One dollar bills," Kinsey snorted.

"Must be coming not going," Elaney took a bill out and examined it.

Kinsey noted Elaney's troubled expression as the door chimes echoed through the house. Then he saw the knob turn on the powder room door. "Someone's there."

Resuming his defensive position, the treasury agent directed his pistol at the opening door.

Kinsey turned as Lieutenant Sarkis entered, his eyes focused on Elaney's gun. His brows rose in a question. Kinsey pointed into the billiard room. "We have intruders again."

"Who do we think it is?"

"Counterfeiters."

Four cats at the mouse hole watched the door as a small, wiry man stepped out. His glance went directly to where the bag had resided.

"This belong to you?" Agent Elaney waged his head toward the case Kinsey held, keeping his weapon leveled at the man.

His alarm escalated as he noted the pistol. His hands sprung into the air as if lever activated. Kinsey could see him calculate, seeking an answer to the question. He shifted his gaze momentarily from the gun to the unarmed men.

"Never saw it before."

Kinsey's jaw dropped at the blatant lie.

"Step out here," Lieutenant Sarkis commanded.

The man, his hands still in the air, moved into the dining room.

"What are you doing here?" Agent Elaney continued covering him while the lieutenant stepped forward to frisk the man.

"There've been problems with the lights in the area. We came to check them." The man's small eyes darted back and forth between the two officers.

The lieutenant shot Kinsey a glance. "Are you having light problems?"

"Sort of," Kinsey conceded, "but we didn't call anyone."

"Who told you to come here?" The lieutenant towered over the intruder, looking down his nose at him.

The small man inhaled, standing as tall as he could. "We're from City of Tacoma Power."

"This is Lakewood," Nathan informed him.

The man frowned, glancing at Kinsey as if appealing for help.

"What's your name?" Agent Elaney demanded.

The man glanced around as if searching for a suggestion. "Desi Clark."

Recalling the earlier incidents, Kinsey asked, "Where are the others?"

Mr. Clark produced a blank expression. "What others?"

"You said 'we'," Agent Elaney reminded him.

"In the neighborhood. This isn't the only residence with problems."

Lieutenant Sarkis eyed Kinsey who shook his head.

"I have a patrol car behind me. We'll have them keep an eye on this guy while we sort this out." The lieutenant beckoned toward the billiard room. "How many ways in and out of there?"

"Only one, unless someone uses a window."

Elaney waved his pistol directing the man into the billiard room. Permitted to lower his hands Desi Clark backed toward the table.

Lieutenant Sarkis made a cell phone call after which the doorbell rang again. At the door to the dining room Jet appeared with two patrol officers. The lieutenant instructed them to keep Mr. Clark safe then beckoned Kinsey and Nathan to join him in the parlor. After a moment Agent Elaney also joined the group.

༼༽

Shocked by what she had seen in the dining room, Jet returned to the parlor. Who was that man and what did the gun mean?

Standing at the arched windows, Latte turned to her with raised eyebrows. "You look like you just saw Darth Vader in the kitchen."

Just then the men came from the dining room.

Lieutenant Sarkis scowled at Kinsey. "What's this about a lighting problem?"

Kinsey explained what happened before the lieutenant arrived.

His gaze consulted Agent Elaney. "What do you think is going on here?"

"Counterfeiting." Agent Elaney met the lieutenant's gaze. "They must have moved their operation out then back again."

"Okay," the lieutenant sounded resigned, "I'll get one of my officers and we can make a search." He turned to Kinsey.

"I'd say the best bet is to check the closed off area."

"You mean that basement of yours." Lieutenant Sarkis scowled.

"Or the third floor." the agent suggested.

"What do you want us to do?" Nathan asked the lieutenant's back.

"Stay here and out of the way," he barked.

"Together, in this area," Elaney added with more courtesy.

"Sayre, you come with us." The lieutenant beckoned to Kinsey. "We don't need to get lost in this labyrinth of a house."

Kinsey waved toward the dining room. The lieutenant tramped off in that direction with the Secret Service Agent behind him.

Nathan surveyed his harem. "So what are we going to do, girls?"

"We could get ready for the New Years Eve party," Susannah suggested.

"Capital idea."

Jet was grateful for Nathan's leadership, figuring it would help to keep everyone calm. Some anxiety for Kinsey haunted her, which she realized was a danger sign.

Was she in love with him as Latte surmised? She didn't want to be in love. She thought perhaps she didn't ever want to be in love.

However, as the swell of emotion bubbled inside she realized the hopelessness of controlling her feelings. Want it or not, admit it or not, believe it or not, she was in love with Kinsey Sayre.

She jerked with a start when Latte touched her shoulder. "Lost in space?"

Jet sighed.

For what seemed the hundredth time that evening the door bell chimed. Both Latte and Jet turned to Nathan.

"Better see who it is," he said.

Jet went to the front door. "Roger."

"I thought I'd wish you a Happy New Year in person."

She backed up, noting his beady eyes survey the room as he entered the parlor. Here he was again, flashed into her mind, with something unusual happening.

"I noticed a patrol car." He nodded toward the driveway. "You called the police?" It sounded like an accusation.

"Lieutenant Sarkis called in some of his officers. Agent Elaney is here too."

At this Roger looked even more concerned, pinching the end of his nose. "Where are they?"

Jet took a deep breath, frowning at him. "You seem to show up every time we have intruders."

Roger lifted his brows with an expression of interest. "You have intruders?"

Although Jet couldn't say why she believed he knew before he came about their unwanted guests. She felt hurt and disappointed at the thought, but realized fooling herself was not going to help. She wanted Roger to be the good guy, but in all probability he was not. The only thing she doubted was whether his involvement was with counterfeiters or murderers.

ᕔ

When Kinsey, Agent Elaney, and Lieutenant Sarkis left the parlor they stopped by the billiard room where the lieutenant summoned one of the officers to join them. Kinsey led the group through the dining room, butler's pantry, and kitchen. He found only one sign of trespassers, an electrical module plugged into a wall.

After completing their perusal, he led them out the back door through the herb garden to the window beneath the grand staircase. He brought the lever up, opened the glass door, and ushered the group into the passageway. Lieutenant Sarkis led the way through the maze to the door through the back of the closet. All along Kinsey looked for signs someone had been there, but found none. Once the four had climbed through the closet, the three carrying weapons drew them and advanced. Lieutenant Sarkis and his officer led the way past the closets and cupboards into the room where the laundry equipment sat, clearing the area. Kinsey examined the washer and dryer. Had they been used since he last looked at them? Concern about leading a wild goose chase returned to his mind. Where in the house could the interlopers have gone? Did they know reinforcements had arrived? Kinsey presumed the culprits had a tighter fix on the law than the law had on them.

Finding no clue in the laundry appliances and none in any of the basement rooms, Kinsey started up the stairs to the third floor sanctuary.

"Sayre," Lieutenant Sarkis stopped him.

Kinsey turned.

"You follow us."

Keeping their weapons ready, the uniformed officer began the flight of stairs with Sarkis following and Elaney behind him. Kinsey brought up the rear. Emotionally worn out from the stress, he sincerely hoped this would end the adventure. He had no idea where to go if no one was in the room at the top. The intruders could have escaped from the house, but could they escape and not leave anything behind such as whatever Latte had seen them carrying?

When the four reached the top the officer stood at the double doors with Lieutenant Sarkis beside him. The officer opened the door with a quiet click. No sound issued from within. With his foot he pushed the door farther open maintaining his ready to fire position and stepped inside with Lieutenant Sarkis and Agent Elaney following. When Kinsey stepped into the room and glanced around he realized it looked the same as when he had taken the agent to see it. The law officers still moved with guns leveled as they cleared the space. A moment of panic seized Kinsey as he realized his fears may be real. No one was there. Stepping to the middle of the room he scrambled through his brain seeking an avenue for their escape.

The lieutenant returned to where Kinsey stood.

At that moment Kinsey spotted one of the modules plugged into an outlet. He pointed to the place on the wall.

Sarkis turned to observe it. "You think that wasn't here before?"

"I know it wasn't." Kinsey squelched his doubt, certain he would have noticed it when he and Agent Elaney were there.

"He's right," the agent supported Kinsey's declaration. "That wasn't here when I went through."

"You think they were here and gone?"

Agent Elaney shrugged.

It was up to Kinsey to convince them. Two possibilities occurred to him. The intruders had not come up this far and were still somewhere in the house or they had escaped somehow. Was there another way out of this room? While Elaney and Sarkis discussed the module Kinsey moved along the walls, considering possibilities. One was the location where the staircase from the kitchen to the second floor would have continued to the third. Moving there, he ran his hand along the wall to determine if any irregularity indicated a way to move the wall, but nothing doing. It was as smooth as a baby's butt.

Suddenly he recalled the other stairway beside the one hidden in the wall and the kitchen one—the circular staircase. He mentally calculated its position relative to the arrangement of the room they occupied, which formed a lopsided H with a protrusion in the middle from each end. One of these Kinsey figured was where the official staircase should be. The other was a bathroom into which Kinsey wandered. It was a small room with a single vanity and sink, a toilet and shower, no bathtub. He followed along the wall looking for a way through one of the walls, realizing in the process the best bet was the shower. However, it appeared to be single piece fiberglass put in the room intact. Kinsey took pains to investigate the decorative groves and bumps. One of them appeared disconnected from the fiberglass. Kinsey pushed on it. With a click it unlatched, allowing a portion of the shower wall to move. Kinsey pried it open and there were the circular stairs.

"Lieutenant," he called.

Sarkis and Elaney appeared at the door. It took seconds for them to realize the possibilities and go charging through the opening onto the wrought iron staircase. Following to the second floor, Kinsey mentally raced ahead of them. If they simply continued down they would be in the morning room where they had begun the search. Was there a chance the intruders took cover on the second floor? Or were the officers on a merry chase through the house with the interlopers escaping right ahead of them? As the men charged down, Kinsey stopped and used his cell phone to text Nathan, "Ck mrning rm & prsnr. Crful!"

When the lieutenant reached the second floor he stopped.

"What's here?" Agent Elaney took a step away from the stairs.

"A small anteroom and another room full of furniture."

"That's all?" The lieutenant sounded disappointed.

"You can't get from here to the rest of the second floor."

Lieutenant Sarkis shot Kinsey a skeptical look. "Are you sure?"

What could he say? He had been unsuccessful in the past. Kinsey lifted his shoulders.

The lieutenant peered into the space beyond. A quick glance told Kinsey no intruders occupied this space. The only other option was the excess furniture room. What were the chances?

At that moment his cell phone grumbled, "Droid". Kinsey checked for the text from Nathan. "AOK here.? up?"

Kinsey made a quick return text. "Wrn Offcr & be rdy. Watch crcl strs."

Lieutenant Sarkis and Agent Elaney had each taken a side of the door to the closed room. With his weapon ready, the officer turned the knob and kicked the door open. At that moment two men charged out, pushing the officer back. Agent Elaney grabbed one of them as the other made for the stairs.

"Hold it right there!" Lieutenant Sarkis demanded.

However, the other man dived for the stairway and slid out of sight on his stomach.

In three quick steps the lieutenant was on the stairs after him. Kinsey turned to Agent Elaney who aided by the police officer had the other man's hands secured behind him. The intruder was nearly as tall as the officer, but broader. It took both men to overcome him. The agent pushed the man ahead of him as they also headed for the stairs.

Chapter Thirty-eight

Nathan approached Roger. "You come to join the party?"

"You having a party?" Roger turned to Nathan.

"It's New Years Eve."

"So I've heard."

A faint technical alert sounded. Taking out his phone, Nathan observed the face. "Duty calls." He gave Jet a quick gleeful glance and headed for the dining room doors.

What did that mean? He looked like he had been tagged to play quarterback.

"Something wrong?" Roger asked.

"No heat, no hot water." Jet shrugged. "The furniture has been playing hide and seek."

Roger frowned at her. "Where's Kinsey?"

"Upstairs with Lieutenant Sarkis and Agent Elaney." Turning to observe Roger's face, Jet explained the evening's events, wondering at his concern, convinced his presence was not a coincidence.

A flicker of surprise skipped across his face, but he recovered. "You don't think I should take care of you?"

Jet wasn't buying. "Kinsey and Nathan believe you have something to do with what's going on."

Roger grimaced. "I think I'll go see where your friend went." He moved toward the dining room.

Jet hesitated only a moment before following into the morning room, arriving just in time to see a man scrambling to stand at the bottom of the stairs. He glanced around, a wild look on his face. Lieutenant Sarkis was right behind him. Nathan stood near the door to the butler's pantry, the officer guarding the prisoner occupied the door to the billiard room while Jet and Roger paused at the dining room doors, leaving the only escape route through the solarium. However, before he could move that direction, Lieutenant Sarkis had his gun in the man's back.

"Don't move," the lieutenant warned.

The man, who came barely to the top of Lieutenant Sarkis' shoulder, stopped abruptly and threw his hands in the air.

Another bigger man with his hands cuffed behind him was being escorted down the stairs between Agent Elaney and the other officer. Kinsey brought up the rear.

"In there," the lieutenant bobbed his head in the direction of the billiard room.

As the two additional prisoners were conducted there Jet noticed Roger give them a hard warning stare. She studied him carefully to make sure. Intent on communicating with the two men he didn't notice her. In that moment she knew he was connected to the counterfeiters. Although she tried to reserve judgment her heart sank in disappointment.

As soon as Kinsey reached the bottom of the stairs he beckoned to her. "Could you do something for me?" he asked. "Check the room with the extra furniture and see if there's anything there you don't remember seeing before. Something those guys could have brought in the boxes Latte saw."

On reaching the second floor Jet glanced around for any sign of what Kinsey suspected. The room was as empty as before. She turned the knob of the room next to it. What immediately caught her eye were a couple computer printers resting on the stack of end tables she and Latte had previously raided. Was that what Kinsey meant? They certainly hadn't been there the last time she was in the room.

After walking through looking for other items she returned to the morning room. Kinsey and Nathan stood with Roger watching as the law officers escorted the intruders out of the house.

Kinsey raised his eyebrows when she reached him.

She nodded. "Printers."

He called to the lieutenant. "There's something you need to see." Kinsey pointed toward the stairs.

Lieutenant Sarkis heaved a sigh, but followed Kinsey back up the circular staircase.

Nathan, Jet and Roger moved into the parlor where a dance tune drifted toward them. Jet could see the Chinese carpet had been rolled away again. Beneath the painting left of the anteroom the sideboard had been set with an array of hors d'oeuvres and beverages. Susannah had stationed her collection of candles throughout, producing a romantic glow.

"Too bad the trespassers can't stay for the party." Nathan winked at Jet.

She turned to Roger, "Do you want to join us for New Years Eve?"

A look of honest regret passed over his face, but he shook his head. "I have a previous engagement."

∽

When Lieutenant Sarkis saw the printers he grumbled, "Lock up this room, I'll send someone to get them."

"You want the snakes and mice too?" Kinsey wasn't hot to entertain them for New Years Eve.

The lieutenant made a face and sighed. "As soon as we deliver the prisoners someone will be around to get them." He marched ahead of Kinsey back down the stairs, through the dining room and out the anteroom door.

After breathing in enough air to calm his nerves Kinsey joined Jet, Nathan and Roger.

"Are we rid of the invaders now?" Nathan twitched his eyebrows.

Kinsey shrugged. "I wouldn't bet on anything at the moment. Other than a couple printers upstairs there's nothing here to connect them to anything but breaking and entering and I'm not sure the police could make that stick." He turned to Roger. "You joining us for the party?"

Roger shook his head.

Something about his quick response and averted gaze made Kinsey suspicious. Since he made no move to leave, Kinsey suggested a New Years Eve toast.

Roger inclined his head and the group moved to the refreshment table where Nathan nabbed a beer and Kinsey poured wine for the others. He lifted his glass. "Here's to a new beginning, no more counterfeiters, no more dead bodies, no more nasty rumors."

Nathan held up his bottle. "To security and tranquility."

The anteroom door opened and Lieutenant Sarkis stepped in.

"So much for tranquility," Nathan mumbled as the lieutenant joined the group in a few long strides.

"I'd like you to take a ride downtown with me," the lieutenant addressed Roger.

Roger's dark brows crinkled in alarm. "I guess I'll have to toast the New Year later."

"What do you think that means?" Nathan asked when the two had exited the parlor.

Jet sighed. "He knows those counterfeiters. I saw him trying to warn them as they were being taken out."

Kinsey noted the disappointment in her expression.

"You said he shows up every time something is happening." She straightened her shoulders. "I don't think it's a coincidence."

"Maybe he's the ringleader," Nathan suggested.

Kinsey struggled to believe Roger manufactured funny money.

The three moved to the sofas in front of the fireplace where Latte was on the floor with her boys and a board game.

"Who's winning?" Nathan asked.

"Mom always wins," Landon grumbled.

Nathan shot her a hairy eyeball. "You never let your kids win?"

"What would that teach them?" She grinned at Nathan.

"Life isn't impossible?"

"Are you sure it's not?" Kinsey wouldn't have put money on that.

Just then Susannah ran shrieking from the music room, stepping like a prancer, eliciting a burst of laughter from Kinsey and Nathan.

She ran to the easy chair next to them and pulled her feet off the floor. "That's not funny." She scowled. "There's another one of those snakes in there."

"We need to do a purge," Kinsey said to Nathan. "Let's get everyone in here and we'll start on the third floor and work our way down. Where's Evana?"

"Here." She came out of the library with a handful of CDs.

Kinsey explained to the group what they needed to do, check the heaters to be certain they were on, that all the suites had hot water, look for the modules that affected the lights, and keep an eye out for animal intruders. He told the girls they just needed to let him or Nathan know if they found a mouse or a snake.

It took a couple hours to accomplish the task. When they met back in the parlor and counted up the findings there were six more mice, four snakes, and half a dozen modules. The heat and water problem seemed to have been solved. Lieutenant Sarkis still had not come to collect so Kinsey and Nathan put the reptiles and rodents in the basement.

In the parlor the girls had returned to sit by the fire, each with a glass of wine and a plate of hors d'oeuvres.

"Has anyone checked on Billy lately?" Jet asked.

Kinsey had forgotten him. He glanced at Nathan. "Why don't you invite him to come down?"

"Sure." Nathan took off for the stairs.

"Would you like a glass of wine?" Jet offered.

Kinsey followed her to the sideboard where he made a sandwich out of cocktail bread and cold cuts.

Noise on the stairs made them turn as Nathan and Billy came down. While Jet poured Billy a soda Nathan spoke under his breath to Kinsey. "He wouldn't come out of his suite until I convinced him the intruders had been taken away by the police."

"What do you think that means?"

"If you ask me," Nathan glanced at Billy, "he's scared of those guys for some reason."

"Maybe they shot him." Kinsey watched Jet and Billy cross the parlor to join the group around the fireplace.

As Nathan and Kinsey moved toward the gathering, Susannah rose and went to the music room where she turned on the stereo loud enough to be heard in the parlor. At the door she called to them, "Time to dance the New Year in."

"Come on, Latte." Nathan offered his hand to help her up.

"One more move." She picked up her game piece and changed its location with a flourish. "I win."

The boys groaned.

"You go dance," Logan suggested as they waved her away.

Latte heaved an exaggerated sigh. "Sore losers." She accepted Nathan's assistance and they moved to the music room.

Susannah offered her hand to Kinsey who glanced briefly at Evana then accepted Susannah's invitation. Although he wasn't hot to get tangled in Susannah's clutches he figured it would disperse some of the Evana's daggers.

Joining in the up-tempo piece Kinsey found Susannah a fair dancer, able to follow him without hesitation.

She turned a glowing smile on him with a seductive look from beneath her dark eyelashes. "My dad said he thought something funny was going on between Jet's mom and that Judy whose body was found here."

"Like what?"

Susannah shook her head. Kinsey narrowed his eyes. Would Jet have any idea what she was talking about?

⌘

After collecting plates and taking them to the kitchen, Jet joined the twins on the floor. She felt a twinge of envy when she saw Kinsey dancing with Susannah, then chastised herself. You can't go through life being jealous of every woman near him. Life was a perpetual parade of painful emotions.

Any time now she should hear whether or not Park was her father, which brought her thoughts to Roger. What would happen to him? She didn't want him in trouble.

"Do you want to play with us?" Landon asked.

Before she could answer a voice behind her said, "She's going to dance with me."

She turned to Kinsey who held out his hand. "Maybe later." She smiled at the twins.

As they moved toward the music room Kinsey said, "I have to apologize."

"For what?"

"After sending you for the garbage can I realized I could have sent you into harm's way." He gave her a sheepish smile as he spun her into the open position.

Jet laughed. "I was more worried about snakes than intruders."

As the next tune began, a longing ballad by Air Supply, Kinsey took her in his arms. Holding her close he said, "I really need to find you a father that's not mine." After a time dancing in silence, he asked, "Would it make a difference?"

Jet felt as if she had electric wires for veins, with volts of current pulsating through them. Periodic surges numbed her brain and made her feel as if every nerve ending had an antenna on it. How would she be able to deal with it if Kinsey were her brother? She would have to go away somewhere she wouldn't see him every day.

"What are you thinking about?" his deep voice invaded her thoughts. He held her at arm's length to observe her expression. She tried to avoid his eyes, but the temptation was too great. She felt pulled into his gaze. His deep blue eyes searched as if he could read her mind. "I still love you," he said.

"I love you." The words escaped as if they had a life of their own. Even as they left her mouth she tried to pull them back, closing her lips and pressing them together. What other disclosures might escape? What other secrets was her subconscious ready to fling into circulation the moment her guard was down.

With an elaborate spin, Kinsey moved them toward the windows to the south terrace bending to kiss her cheek. "We'll get through this," he whispered in her ear.

As Air Supply crooned the last note, he paused. "I think I heard the door chime."

"Maybe the lieutenant finally sent someone to pick up those animals."

"Let's go."

"Happy New Year," Park greeted his son when he opened the door.

"Dad," Kinsey's voice squeaked in surprise. "What are you doing here?"

"I came to wish you a Happy New Year." Park looked from Kinsey to Jet. "You look like you were expecting someone else."

"I was," Kinsey confessed. "One of Lieutenant Sarkis' officers."

Park's winged eyebrows crinkled.

"It's going to take some explaining." Kinsey backed up a few steps. "Maybe we should go to the library. It might be quieter."

Jet stopped when they reached the fireplace to address Evana who gazed at her with narrowed eyes and thin lips. "Why don't you come help explain things to your father about tonight?"

Although Evana's eyes propelled daggers she rose and followed.

In the library, Kinsey took the office chair, Park the purple chair and the girls each one end of the settee. Kinsey recapitulated the day's events, giving Park a rundown of the phenomenon that had alerted the group to problems, their call for assistance and the final capture of the invaders.

"Are they responsible for Carmen's death?" Park didn't sound convinced.

Kinsey grimaced. "I doubt it."

"Lieutenant Sarkis took Roger Thompson, too." Jet watched Park's reaction.

"Roger?" He sounded as incredulous as Kinsey had. "I've known Roger for more than thirty years." Park sounded skeptical. "He's no boy scout, but he's no crook either."

The more apparent Roger's involvement became the more distressed Jet felt about it. In spite of the evidence she couldn't believe he was actually part of a criminal gang, undoubtedly denial and wishful thinking.

"Why don't we have something to toast the New Year?" Kinsey rose.

"I need to talk to Jessica a moment. Fix me something and I'll be there in a minute."

Kinsey frowned, but beckoned to Evana. "Come on, Sis."

Apprehension seized Jet as Park leaned forward clasping his hands together.

"I got the DNA test results." He appeared to be watching for her reaction.

Anxiety crept up her spine and doubt made her numb. Here was the moment of truth. Could she refuse to listen, fade into oblivion?

"Did you receive your letter?" He raised his eyebrows.

Jet shook her head. "I don't think anyone got the mail today. Too much has been going on."

Park gave her a sympathetic look. "I don't know if it's good news or bad, Jessica, but I'm not your father."

Jet sat perfectly still. Technically she didn't know if it was good or bad either. Her emotions told her it was wonderful news, so wonderful she was afraid to believe it. "You're sure?"

"The letter said results with my DNA was negative. I suppose that's what it meant." Park shrugged.

Tears flooded her eyes and tumbled down her cheeks. She felt ridiculous. It certainly wasn't something to cry about.

Park's expression became alarmed. "Even if you're not my daughter, we're still family. I'd be happy to treat you as a daughter."

Jet shook her head, dragging a tissue from her pocket and dabbing her eyes.

"I suspect my son wants you to be my daughter-in-law."

Her tears started up again. "What am I going to do?"

Park frowned. "If you don't love him, you don't have to accept."

"I do love him, but . . ." She opened her hands in a vague expression of uncertainty. "Are you going to tell him?"

"You don't want me to?"

Jet took a deep breath. "Not for a little while." She brushed her hair away from her face. "I need some time to think."

"He won't let me alone about it for too long. And he won't forgive me if I keep it from him." Park bit his lip. "But I can give you a couple days. Maybe you should tell him."

Jet felt like her logic and sense had left for a walk in the park.

Chapter Thirty-nine

New Years Day was so subdued, the whole world seemed hung-over, hoping to eradicate the headache. Rain fell steadily from a gray sky, dripping from the eaves and making puddles in the circular driveway. Precipitation was so heavy the houses across the lake had disappeared abandoning Blast Castle on an island in a misty sea. It left Kinsey with a feeling of deep melancholy for which he sought a cause. However, nothing explained it. The removal of the counterfeiters left him with hope of clearing up at least one of the estate mysteries.

Jet accompanied him to church wrapped in a blanket of silence. He felt no rancor or resistance, only withdrawal. When he asked about her conversation with his father she only shrugged and said it wasn't important. Although Kinsey wasn't buying he figured he would just cause more trouble pestering her.

After returning as they stood in the hall between their suites, Jet asked, "How do you know there is really a God and Jesus died for your sins?"

"Faith," Kinsey responded, surprised by her question.

"What does that mean?" Her question sounded sincere rather than skeptical.

"You accept what God says in the Bible as the truth."

She drew her eyebrows together. "You mean you just believe it?"

"Right."

She sighed. "What if you can't just believe it?" Her gray eyes appeared clouded in the gloomy hall.

Kinsey ran his hand through his hair. "You realize that's a ridiculous statement."

"Why?"

"Because everything you believe, you just believe. You decide for some reason you're going to believe it and that's it."

She eyed him with suspicion.

"Actually," Kinsey added, "God helps people believe it. The only thing people can do well is refuse to believe."

"What if you're wrong?" She crossed her arms over her chest.

"About believing God?" Kinsey widened his eyes. "The unbeliever has more to lose than I do. God could have made it so no one had to have faith, everything was plain to see, but he wants people to have faith."

"Why?"

"How do I know, I'm not God."

Jet shot him a look that made him feel like the ultimate flimflam man then left him in the hall wondering what that was all about.

After fixing a sandwich he relaxed on his sofa to watch the football game on television. Hours later he awoke. The football recap was in progress and the game over. He flipped on the fireplace and took out his briefcase intending to work, but found he was unable to concentrate. Speculation hinted at possibilities for Jet's questions. His gaze kept drifting to the fireplace where he saw her face as he reiterated his declaration of love. She had said she loved him but looked as if the words were rung from her against her will. At the moment he had been elated, but now wondered if she had been captured by the moment and regretted her confession? He wanted to believe she loved him, but he couldn't feel confident, which left an ache within.

The next day, although the official New Year's holiday, Kinsey was awakened before 8:00 with a call from Lieutenant Sarkis informing him crews were arriving at the estate to do more checking. For the time being, the lieutenant added, they were concentrating outside.

Expecting them back in the tree and rhododendron gardens, he was surprised when he stepped onto his terrace. The formal garden, balustrade and main entrance to the property were overrun with uniformed police and forensic scientists. What were they looking for?

He met Jet in running shoes carrying her jacket when he opened his door. "What's going on?"

Kinsey explained the lieutenant's call as they continued to the kitchen where Nathan was cooking eggs.

"I thought you were the one who didn't want a kitchen," Kinsey accosted him.

Nathan shrugged. "Hunger forces the chef out in all of us."

Kinsey snorted. Jet smiled at Nathan and headed out the back door.

"I can't figure out what they're doing there." Kinsey uncovered the toaster and hunted for bread in the refrigerator.

"Did they ever determine where that renter's wife was shot?"

Kinsey scowled at his friend. "You think that's it?"

Nathan slid his eggs onto a plate. "They could have gotten some information from those intruders of yours."

Now the counterfeiters belonged to Kinsey, how generous of him. Undoubtedly Lieutenant Sarkis and Agent Elaney would be just as magnanimous. "You think one of them killed her?"

"Or they could have seen who did. After all, apparently they were living here, too."

Nathan had a point. Kinsey tried to recall if anything had been said about where Carmen Markovich was killed. So consumed with the discovery of her body on his property he hadn't considered where she was before that. However, that was the important issue.

"The bullet in the grave came from the SigSaeur Jet and I found. Her sister said the gun belonged to Carmen."

"Maybe she shot herself." Nathan wiggled his eyebrows.

Kinsey's toast popped up. Nathan waved a couple slices of bread questioning the toaster's availability.

"Go ahead." Hearing a noise by the butler's pantry, Kinsey turned to see Lieutenant Sarkis standing in the doorway.

"Just in time for breakfast," Nathan chirped.

The lieutenant's gaze darted around the kitchen. "I'd take coffee if you have any."

"Sure." Kinsey grabbed the pot from its perch near the toaster. "Nathan?" He poured three cups of coffee then moved the milk and sugar within the lieutenant's reach.

"We're speculating on your investigation this morning." Nathan sat on the stool next to his plate.

Lieutenant Sarkis' bright eyes looked down his slender nose at Nathan. "What did you decide?"

"That you're trying to locate where Carmen Markovich was killed."

"Not bad," the lieutenant nodded, perching on a stool. "Your intruders were here the night she was killed. They said Markovich was shooting at them."

A picture flashed into Kinsey's mind. He recalled what his father had said about the night he was supposed to meet Carmen near the formal garden.

Lieutenant Sarkis took a small object out of his jacket and set on the counter.

"A bullet?" Nathan identified it.

"Where did you find that?"

"Stuck in the side of one of those pots in your garden." The lieutenant lifted an eyebrow. "I'd make a bet it's from that SigSaeur you found."

"Carmen's gun?"

Sarkis bobbed his head. "That small 9mm isn't so accurate at that distance."

Kinsey took a deep breath. "You think Markovich killed his wife by accident?"

"It would fit the evidence."

It would also mean that Kinsey's father could have been killed instead. In addition, his father could have been the reason Carmen was where she could be killed. That knowledge would devastate Park.

A noise at the back door drew their attention as Jet entered the kitchen.

"When will you know if that bullet is from the gun we found?" Kinsey asked the lieutenant.

He shrugged. "Tomorrow."

"You're sure she wasn't shot by one of the intruders?" What made them jump to the conclusion it was Matt?

"According to them they weren't carrying any weapons." Lieutenant Sarkis gulped the last of his coffee.

"How did she get into the grave in the tree garden?" Nathan stacked his cup on his plate and rose.

"The theory is her husband found her, realized what he had done and buried her himself." The lieutenant took his cup to the sink. "The counterfeiters had no reason to do it and neither would anyone else."

Kinsey wasn't sure he bought that. "Have you any theories on the other body?"

"Not a one." Lieutenant Sarkis headed for the front door.

What would be the next surprise coming down the pike? "Would you let us know about the bullet when you find out?"

"Sure," The lieutenant tossed over his shoulder.

ॐ

Jet stood for a moment as Kinsey and Nathan tidied the kitchen. Her cell phone played its tune, indicating a call from Roger.

"Can you do me a favor?" he said when she answered. "Get something at my house and bring it here?"

"Where is here?"

"The police station." His tone of voice contained a grimace. "You remember the envelope you gave me from your mom?"

"Yes." Apprehension gave Jet a jolt.

"Would you get that? It's locked in a drawer in my desk." He explained where to find it, how to get the key for the drawer and the house, then how to disarm and rearm the security system.

"Why are you at the police station?"

"They think they ought to pin a murder on me." Jet could hear the frustration in his voice.

"Murder? Who? How?" Anxiety elevated to alarm.

"Bring that envelope and I'll tell you the story. Don't worry, I didn't kill anyone."

Jet pushed the end button on her phone and dropped it in her pocket.

"What was that about?" Kinsey squinted at her.

She shrugged. "I'm not sure. It didn't make a lot of sense."

Kinsey frowned. "He's still at the police station?"

Jet nodded then continued upstairs where she put on a pair of slacks and grabbed a raincoat. Moisture dangled in the air, fluffing her hair as she walked to the garage. She had suspended her thinking regarding Roger. In fact she had difficulty thinking period. She kept running into dead ends. Roger was not her father, nor was Park. She was back to Mr. Unknown. Could Kinsey really help with that? And what was she going to do about him? She needed to process, but everything kept moving too fast.

Roger's house, perched on a dead-end street, overlooked the entrance to the Narrows with a magnificent view of the bridge. Jet breathed a sigh of relief when she found the key and succeeded in disarming the alarm system.

According to Roger his study was off the central foyer to the right. It turned out to be a cozy room with a gas fireplace, built-in bookcases and a huge walnut desk. An unobtrusive drawer built into the desk's decorative trim opened with a key she found in the middle drawer.

There she located a number of envelopes among them the one from her mother she had given him weeks before. How could that clear him of a murder charge? Another prick of doubt seized her as she considered the possibilities. Had her mother been involved in something worse than what Jet already knew? Undoubtedly, she thought bitterly.

Closing the house, she rearmed the security system then took her roadster and headed for the police station. After parking she managed to get through security where in the hall she came face to face with Agent Elaney.

He stared at her as if she were an apparition. "What brings you here?"

"Roger Thompson asked me to bring him something." Jet held her handbag close to her body lest he demand she turn over the envelope.

He raised his eyebrows, but asked, "How's the search for your father coming?"

Jet eyed him with suspicion. "Zero for two."

"You have other possibilities?"

"I have one I know about and one I don't. I guess if I eliminate the one the other one would have to be my father." Jet lifted her shoulders.

The look in Agent Elaney's dark eyes contained sympathetic comprehension, which made her rebel inside. She didn't need his pity.

"Why do they have Roger here?" Jet thought for a moment he would refuse to answer as a painful grimace crossed his face.

"He's involved with the counterfeiters."

"How?" Might as well find out the worst.

The agent shook his head. "We are still working on that."

"Who do I ask to be able to see him?" She glanced at the doors in the hall. They all looked the same.

"Let me help you." Agent Elaney escorted her into the Sheriff's office where he arranged for her to meet Roger in one of the interrogation rooms. He removed a business card from his wallet and handed it to her. "If you learn something helpful, why don't you let me know?" He wrote a phone number on the back. "That's my cell number."

Jet felt trapped in the small windowless room as she waited for Roger, reading the agent's card. "Asado Elaney, United States Treasury, Secret Service Agent." It flickered through her mind to wonder why he would have given it to her. Did he really think she would tattle on Roger?

In less than five minutes the door opened and a uniformed officer escorted Roger in. He appeared weary and deflated, although not unkempt. He gave her a twisted smile. "Sorry about this."

She removed the envelope from her handbag.

Roger beckoned toward the table and chairs. "Why don't you sit down? This might take a while."

"Agent Elaney said you were connected to those counterfeiters." Jet sat down and put the envelope on the table.

Roger took it and removed a sheet of paper. "First read this, it'll explain a lot." He slid it across the table to her.

She unfolded the paper, instantly recognizing Mona's fluid handwriting, and read.

To Whom It May Concern:

I, Mona Sayre Thompson, swear that this is a true and accurate account of the death of Judy Severson on June 30, 2009.

Shocked, Jet glanced up from the paper to observe Roger's small dark eyes fixed on her face. He nodded for her to continue.

Judy and I worked for the Equal Opportunity Department of the State of Washington in Olympia. We were very competitive regarding our positions and work. In her efforts to outdo and pass by me in position and authority, she interfered with my work by confiscating paperwork placed on my desk. She snooped in my files, listened to my phone calls and questioned other workers about what I did. She was not in a position of authority over me and had no right to even look at work I was doing. Her nosiness and interference made me very angry and I tried to keep her from spying on me. On June 30 when I returned to my office after a meeting at the end of the day, I found Judy in my office, at my desk, with a leather portfolio in her hands. I decided I would not let her leave with any of my paperwork. I asked her to show me what was in the portfolio. I accused her of stealing and spying on my files. She refused to allow me to look in the bag. I tried to take it from her and had gotten a good hold on it, when she swung around, wrenching the bag from my hands and also losing her balance. She fell hitting the corner of a glass table in my office. She broke the table in her fall and it punctured her head as she hit it. Afterward she did not move. I thought she was knocked out and tried to get her to wake up, but she was dead. I panicked. The offices were all closed; the workers in my department had all gone home. I called my ex-husband, Roger Thompson, who came and helped me move the body. He was familiar with and had access to a deserted estate with a large landscape and gardens. He helped me bury the body at the estate.

I write this to explain my guilt in the situation, to tell you that Judy Severson died by accident and that Roger Thompson's only involvement was after the fact in helping to conceal the body.

This is most certainly true,
Mona Sayre Thompson

Stunned speechless, Jet stared at Roger, attempting to mentally arrange the information. Roger watched with sympathetic concern. "So that's why her body was at the castle?"

He nodded. "But there's more."

Jet took a deep breath preparing for the next blow.

"What I didn't know the night we buried Judy was that those counterfeiters were on the property. As far as I knew the estate was deserted."

"And they saw you?" Jet surmised.

"Apparently. At least they knew what I'd done. I couldn't figure it out any other way. They also learned I was involved in finance. They wanted help circulating money and threatened to turn me over to the police if I didn't help them."

"Does that mean you're the one who introduced the counterfeit money to the marketplace?" Jet was still putting two and two together.

"More or less." Roger rocked his shoulders.

She gave him an admonishing glance. "How could they implicate you without giving themselves away?"

Roger's face colored slightly. "They didn't act like that was a concern. I could see their story getting out of hand and accusing me of murder."

"Like now?" Jet grimaced.

With a deep sigh, Roger said, "There are some things I can't explain."

"Like?"

"The bag your mother fought with Judy over didn't contain any papers belonging to Mona, it had money in it." Roger sounded vexed.

"Counterfeit?"

He shrugged. "I don't think so, but I don't know."

"What did she do with the bag?"

"I still have it."

Jet frowned at him. "Why didn't you have me bring that too?"

"I don't know if they'll believe this much." He put his hands on the table and folded them. "It's true, but that doesn't mean they'll accept it. I didn't want what I don't know about that bag and what's in it to color the decision."

Jet fastened her gaze on the papers in front of them. "What's going to happen to you?"

Roger huffed, "It depends on whether they believe I'm guilty of murder or not."

"Are you going to give this to them?"

"Not yet." He folded the papers again. "I want you to take and have them copied. Then take a couple copies to my attorney and have him give one to the police. I don't want to lose track of the original."

The uniformed officer opened the door. "Time's up."

Roger pushed the envelope back to Jet after writing the name and phone number of his attorney on it. They stood and Roger said, "I'm sorry."

Jet hugged him. "We'll hope for the best. Mom didn't do anyone any favors."

"She let you live. With her attitude she might not have done that."

Chapter Forty

When Jet and the lieutenant had gone, Kinsey returned to his suite and called his father. Given it was still the New Year's Holiday and no dinner would be served at the castle, Kinsey accepted the invitation to join his family, wondering briefly if Evana would be there.

"Why don't you bring her along?" His father suggested when he mentioned it.

"She doesn't have much use for me these days."

"All the more reason to invite her."

Kinsey wasn't sure he saw it that way, but acquiesced. While they drove to the Barnes house he considered Jet's concern for Roger Thompson. Her mysteries remained unsolved, reminding him he needed to contact Jesse McFadden. What excuse could he use to pry information loose? Even if he had to be crass he would hit the guy up with what he knew, realizing Jet would disapprove. Maybe he could figure out a better approach. A wild idea tumbled through his conscious from time to time presenting a possibility he would prefer to check out before tackling McFadden, but he had no clue how to proceed there either.

Jet's admission of love left him in a twilight zone of doubt his emotions hanging on a thread of hopefulness. Could he convince her his love was real and he would not abandon her? Would that make a difference?

Wondering if Park had found out yet about his DNA test, Kinsey determined to bring it up. It was also time to finalize his deal for the estate.

One by one they were closing in on the mysteries. The counterfeiters had been evicted, their fun and games having caused most of the unusual phenomenon, especially what had engendered the tag "Blast Castle". The death of the renter and his wife had a reasonable explanation, leaving out such things as ghosts and electrical blasts. The deaths before the Markovichs would probably be forgotten in the logical explanation of the others since they had been deemed natural causes in the beginning. It left only the second female body and her death. A charge of excitement surged through Kinsey's veins as he considered the realization of his dreams. If only he could share it with Jet.

Evana had been quiet while they made their way to the freeway. Then she asked, "You really think Dad was in love with Carmen Markovich?"

"It's not what I think, Evana, it's what Dad told me."

She folded her hands in her lap and stared at them. "Are you in love with Jet?"

Kinsey sighed, might as well get it over with. "Yes, I'm in love with Jet."

Abandoning her usual tirade Evana said no more. With emotions alternating between jigs of excitement and apprehensive apoplexy Kinsey had enough on his mind without questioning her attitude.

"I'm going to see Aunt Pat," Evana announced when they reached the house. Kinsey went immediately in search of his father, locating him in his study.

"I need to talk to you, Dad," he declared dropping into one of the fern printed easy chairs.

Park stood by the bookcase searching for a volume. He turned to his son with a frown.

"Have you heard from Lieutenant Sarkis?"

"No, I haven't," Park's tone indicated he could happily live forever without hearing from the lieutenant.

"He was at the estate this morning with a forensics crew. They found bullets from the same type of gun that killed Carmen," Kinsey explained.

"So now you think you're successful at clearing the estate?"

"Nearly," Kinsey replied. "There's still the other body to account for, but we're closing in. And for your information it involved no ghosts, rats, or supernatural phenomenon."

Park eyed him with a twisted grin. "I suppose you want me to sign the deed over to you."

Kinsey flashed him a big smile. "That would be good." He took a deep breath gathering his fortitude. "There is something else, Dad."

Park froze, a volume of European history in his hand.

"The counterfeiters told the police Markovich was shooting at them one night." Kinsey paused to be sure his father's attention hadn't drifted into space. "Apparently it was the night you were to meet Carmen. Evidently she was shot by her husband."

"What?" A flush swept up Park's face, reddening the rims of his eyes.

"I'm sorry, Dad, I realize what it means." After a time in agonized silence, Kinsey said, "I didn't want you to hear it from the police or the media."

Park took a deep breath and exhaled. "You're sure?"

"Not absolutely. They have to determine if the bullets came from the same gun. But, Dad, it all fits. If Markovich shot his wife by accident then found her body and became frightened, he could easily bury her with the trees and have no one the wiser."

At least for a time," Park mumbled, shaking his head. "Eventually someone would want to know where she was. I for one wouldn't have let him alone about it." He pressed his lips together, his eyes blazing.

"If he hadn't electrocuted himself the next day." Kinsey realized he had lost his father who perched on the chair by his computer and stared out the window. Park had not only lost the woman he loved but would now have to deal with guilt for his part in it. "You couldn't have known, Dad."

Park ran his hand through his hair. "I've done some stupid things in my life."

"Which reminds me, did you find out anything on your DNA test?"

Park lifted a winged eyebrow. "I promised Jet I'd give her a little time before telling you."

Kinsey scowled. "When did you tell her that?"

"Sunday."

"Okay," Kinsey declared, "you gave her some time."

Park studied his son. "The test was negative."

"You're not her father." The thrill that shot through Kinsey almost lifted him from his seat.

Park shook his head. "You're in love with her?"

"The real question is," said Kinsey, nodding, "is she in love with me?"

"You don't know?"

"She said she is and I want to believe her." Kinsey sighed. "But she's still fighting it."

"You should let her tell you about the test."

"Keep you out of trouble?" Kinsey cocked his head and raised his eyebrows.

A trace of a smile flickered across his father's face. "It'll give her a chance to be prepared."

❧

Aunt Pat appeared at the door to Park's study informing them dinner was ready. After nodding to her, Park shot Kinsey a reproving glance. "I hope someday you'll bring good news."

Kinsey commiserated. "Me, too."

During dinner Kinsey explained recent events at the castle to Pat and Daniel, figuring even Evana was unaware of some of it. He refrained from mentioning the significance as far as Park was concerned, but did grin over his success in clearing the castle mysteries sufficiently to claim ownership of it. Leaving Jet out of the conversation, he noted that Evana even managed to smile.

When the meal was over she approached Park with a whispered question and they departed. Pat declared she would serve coffee and dessert for Daniel and Kinsey in the living room. They settled in front of the fireplace where Pat joined them with a plate of chocolate frosted brownies. Pouring coffee she asked, "Have you noticed a change in Evana?"

"She was pretty subdued when we drove over here." Kinsey studied his aunt wondering what she was getting at.

"She's struggling to accept a change in her ideas. Her whole world has been turned upside down."

They sipped coffee, chatting about Pat and Dan's acquaintances until Evana and Park joined them.

"We need to get home," Kinsey said to Evana.

She nodded. On their way back to the mansion, she said, "I'm sorry I've been such a pill lately."

Her apology surprised Kinsey. "Believe me, Sis, I understand. Nothing has been easy for you for a long time."

"It's no reason to take it out on you."

"I never saw it that way. All I saw was someone trying to make sense out of the disasters in her life and find a way to live with them. However," he shot her a sideways glance, "the position you took would make it harder for you in the end."

"And no one was going to join me in the deal."

Kinsey grinned. "Sorry about that."

Evana laughed. "I haven't got it together yet, but I'll let you off the hook."

"And Jet?"

"I'll try."

When they reached the mansion Kinsey drove up the main driveway to drop Evana at the front door, noting the lights on in Jet's suite. Once he had put the car away and dropped his coat off, he went to Jet's door and knocked. Her eyes widened when she saw him, but she stepped back, allowing him to enter.

"I just got back from Dad's." Kinsey noted the fire was going and a book lay on the sofa.

Closing the door behind him, she asked, "How did he take the news?"

"I'm sure he realized the implication, but he seemed okay." Kinsey sighed. "How about you, what did you find out at the police station?"

Jet beckoned to the sofa. "Sit down." She tucked herself into the corner of the davenport. "Roger had me bring him a letter from my mother I'd given him some time ago."

"Your mother?" Kinsey was confused.

Jet explained the letter and what Roger had said.

"Wow." Kinsey ran his hand through his hair. "I'd never have figured that out, although I was beginning to suspect Roger was involved."

"He was blackmailed into helping those counterfeiters."

Kinsey noticed that she watched his face with apprehension. "Plus he didn't want anyone digging up another body."

Her eyebrows drew together. "What do you think will happen to him?"

Kinsey considered. "I suppose he'll have to do some time for the counterfeiting at least. But he should be okay where the death was concerned, maybe a suspended sentence. You'd really need to ask Agent Elaney that."

"So that solves all of your mysteries?"

"Just about. Dad said he'd sign over the deed to Blast Castle."

"We should celebrate." She smiled.

He shook his head. "I'd rather wait until we get your mysteries solved, too."

"That might never happen." Jet's expression became melancholy as her gaze moved to the fire.

Kinsey wondered how to bring up the subject of his father's paternity. He realized it would be better if she brought it up, but would she? He watched the gas flame flicker across the logs.

"I still have no idea who Mr. Unknown is," she murmured. "I realize Jesse McFadden could be my father, but . . ."

Kinsey leaped on the implication. "Does that mean you've found out my father is not?"

Jet looked as if she had given away something unintended. She sighed. "He told me Sunday night that his test was negative."

Kinsey held his breath. This should be the moment they threw their arms around each other and pledged their love. But from the look on her face he figured that wasn't going to happen. What was he supposed to do, get down on his knees and beg? No problem. He could do that. Moving from his seat on the sofa he dropped to his knees in front of Jet. As he took her hand, he noticed with alarm that her eyes filled with tears.

But even as the tears ran down her cheeks, she laughed. "What am I supposed to do with you?"

"Marry me, what else?"

She rolled her eyes heavenward. "Don't you have to marry a Christian?"

"You're not a believer?" He looked into her eyes.

Jet's gaze drifted back to the fire. "I don't know. I haven't come to terms with that either." She sighed. "I really think it would be better if I find out who my father is first."

"Do you think that makes a difference to me?"

"It makes a difference to me." She met his gaze.

"You did say 'first' right?" Kinsey wasn't going to let hope pass him by. "Does that mean you will marry me when we get things straightened out?"

The look in her eyes was almost regret. "I do love you." Then her eyes lit with an impish sparkle. "Since I refuse to be like my mom, I guess I'll have to."

"You really don't give a guy much encouragement." Keeping her hand, Kinsey moved to sit beside her. "I guess I'll have to get busy and find you a father."

Chapter Forty-one

Kinsey awoke elated, all out of proportion to the circumstances. Even the threat of sleet and snow didn't daunt his exhilaration as he drove to work in January's darkness. He had a mission he was determined to see through, whatever it took. Although he admitted he had no clue how to go about it.

He spent the morning putting together the financial reports for the business, while allowing his subconscious to consider his mission. By eleven he had decided on a direct approach. To begin he had a few questions for Agent Elaney in order to put to bed the mysteries at his castle. He called his number for the agent who actually sounded pleased to hear from him. Elaney indicated he was on his way to Seattle and would prefer to meet him at the Starbucks on 320th in Federal Way.

The coffee shop was hushed when Kinsey arrived. Only a couple preoccupied laptop users engaged tables. He ordered a latte and parked in one of the easy chairs by the windows where he could watch for the agent's arrival. Shortly he noticed the black Acura pulling into the parking lot. After securing his beverage the treasury agent took the chair next to Kinsey who took a deep breath and plunged into his questions. "You've cleared up the counterfeiter problem?"

Agent Elaney's eyebrows drew together, making Kinsey think he expected a different question. "As far as it goes," he responded. "We've not been able to track all the connections to the marketplace, but we're a lot closer than we were."

"What about Billy Monk? Was he involved?"

"He is William Krick's nephew. Krick masterminded the whole operation. However, Monk was just a plant to keep an eye on you people. Apparently he became too attached to your group and the counterfeiters became suspicious he'd sell them out. They planned to scare him off, wounding him instead. Monk used his cell phone to call Thompson who rescued him and kept him at his home until Monk could get around on his own. The forgers aren't admitting to the shooting, although Monk doesn't appear to be involved, beyond knowing about the operation."

"So you're not prosecuting him?"

Elaney shook his head. "We reserve the right if new information surfaces." His gaze drifted out the window. "How is Jet taking Thompson's involvement?"

"She's disappointed, doesn't seem to have any relation who hasn't turned out to be a scumbag." Kinsey took a deep breath. "I wanted to talk to you about that."

Agent Elaney turned his dark eyes on Kinsey with a guarded expression.

"You seem to have a big interest in Jet's relationships."

The agent took so long to respond Kinsey wondered if he was ignoring him.

"She told me she doesn't even have a name for one possibility for her father."

Kinsey frowned. "That's right."

"Do you know anything about that person?" Elaney met his eyes. "Does she?"

"From what she told me her mother had a one night stand with someone she met at a bar celebrating his divorce. His friends hooked him up with Mona."

Agent Elaney grimaced and stared out the window. "Does Jet really want to know who her father is?" He returned his gaze to Kinsey, adding, "Regardless of who that may be?"

Kinsey cocked his head. "Are you kidding? I want to marry her, but nothing will work until she can lay this mystery to bed."

"The first time I saw her she reminded me of someone, but I had to do some research. I remembered a picture I had often seen as a child. Jet reminded me of that. At Christmas when I was home with my family I looked it up." Elaney cast an apprehensive glance at Kinsey then went on. "It was of my mother when she was a young woman. Jet is a carbon copy of that picture."

Kinsey was amazed. "You mean you think she's related to your mother?"

"She's my daughter."

Although the thought had entered Kinsey's mind, he shied away from it now. "You think she's your daughter?"

"I know she is. I knew she was having DNA tests done, so I had mine compared to hers. I'm her father."

"You're Mona Thompson's one night stand?"

Elaney bowed his head in acknowledgement. "I'm not a one night stand kind of guy. I don't think I've ever done that before or after, but I was drunk and angry and my mind was messed up. It just never occurred to me that . . ."

"Do you have other children?"

The agent shook his head. "My wife then didn't want children. We fought about that, among other things." He grimaced. "When I remarried, my wife was past the age."

For a time they sat in silence, sipping their beverages. How would Jet feel about this? Would Agent Elaney let her know? Or would he just hurt her more?

"Are you going to tell her?"

"Should I?" The agent's expression was anxious.

"It wouldn't be fair to keep it from her. This means so much to her." Kinsey didn't add how much it meant to him also. "What about you? She doesn't need another ambivalent, disinterested parent."

"I do what I do." Elaney ran his hand through his hair. "But I wouldn't be disinterested, or ambivalent. I even think my wife would be happy about her."

"I can't say how she'll react." Kinsey sighed. "She's an unpredictable feisty character."

"And now you want to take care of her." Elaney eyed Kinsey as if assessing his son-in-law suitability."

"Don't get carried away," Kinsey warned.

Agent Elaney laughed. "How should we handle it?"

"Let me feel her out. I'll tell her if that's what seems best, or let you. But at least I can prepare her."

"I have to be in Seattle the rest of today and won't be back until this evening."

"I'll call you," Kinsey said.

☙

Tuesday morning arrived too promptly to suit Jet. A glance at the gray dome with fat rain falling did nothing to infuse her with energy. However a glance at the clock charged her with enough momentum to get dressed and out to work. As she plunged into it she found the day went quickly. Suddenly it was growing dark again. Sloppy snowflakes still plopped on her windshield as she returned to the castle where she overtook Kinsey in the rose garden making a dash to the house. He ran alongside as they made for the covered patio outside the library. As he removed his keys and opened the French doors Jet sensed a suppressed excitement in him.

"I had coffee with Agent Elaney today. He filled me in on another couple details. I can safely say we've solved the mysteries, which will eventually clear the mansion's reputation. Dad should be satisfied."

"Are you going to keep renting suites here?"

"I don't feel I can turn anyone out. I enjoy the company. Besides it helps pay the bills." He grinned at her. "You're safe, you can stay."

The castle residents were gathering for dinner when Jet and Kinsey entered the parlor.

"I need to talk to you later," he said as they continued to the dining room.

Dinner was a lively affair with a full post mortem on the weekend events and their conclusion. Kinsey reiterated his decision to retain his tenants and they gave him a cheer. Billy was unusually loquacious, full of lively jokes, keeping Susannah amused with his chattering stream. The change was so dramatic Jet wouldn't have known him. Latte and Nathan carried on a silent conversation across the table with each other. Evana spoke to Jet, even smiled at her. She was upon the point of assuming she'd shown up at the wrong dining table, everything had altered so much. Wondering if she was as different, she put it to Latte as they left.

"I hadn't thought about it, but yes, you are."

"How?"

"You've quit behaving as if you're a tank firing a round of ammunition every time a man asks you to do something."

Jet opened her mouth to protest then changed her mind. "Was I really that bad?"

Latte laughed, "Not really. But you've changed and in a very nice way. I honestly think you've given up trying to be what your mother wanted you to be and become who you really are. You were never cut out to be a belligerent feminist." Latte patted her shoulder. "You're a brave-hearted sweetie, Jet. We all love you like that."

Not knowing how to take her, Jet said, "I have to go. Kinsey wanted to see me."

While Latte shooed her boys upstairs, Jet looked for Kinsey who stood at the bottom of the stairs gazing at her. She went to him, "Okay?"

"I'll come to your suite in a minute or two."

Continuing upstairs behind Latte, Jet was torn between curiosity and apprehension. She had already agreed to marry him, someday. Did he want to withdraw his offer? Press her to get married sooner?

She strolled to the windows overlooking the front driveway. The day's clouds and rain had disappeared, leaving a star-filled sky. Perhaps he wanted to talk about whether or not she believed in God. She recalled how she had felt about Pastor Ansgreth when she met him leaving her mother's room. She realized she had come to associate the compassionate concern in his eyes with God. He had cared enough to convince her mother to confess. Was that how God cared? Maybe the real test would be if God answered her prayer and helped her find her father.

She had ceased to object to the idea of God. In fact, she even welcomed the knowledge of His existence.

Opening the door to Kinsey's knock, she allowed him to enter. For a moment they gazed at each other as if taking stock of the enemy.

"You look like you think I'm going to bite." Kinsey laughed.

She shrugged "Maybe you will. You look like you think I'll shatter into a thousand pieces."

Kinsey took a deep breath. "What I need to know is whether you're serious about wanting to know who your father is."

Cocking her head, Jet eyed him with suspicion.

"Sometimes we think we want something, but what we really want is to have it a certain way."

"What does that mean?" She scowled at him.

"Do you have expectations where your father is concerned?" Kinsey lifted his eyebrows.

"Like?"

"What kind of person he is, what he does, where he lives, how he'd feel about you?"

"I expect he's an irresponsible, selfish scumbag, especially if he is the one night stand my mother had."

"That doesn't necessarily follow." Kinsey gave her a warning frown.

She narrowed her eyes. "Do you know who my father is?"

Kinsey sighed. "Actually I do. But in all fairness to him, I'm not sure I should let you know unless you're willing to hear his side without prejudgment."

Jet was offended. "You can't keep it from me, that wouldn't be fair." After all their talk and effort that he should take this attitude. She crossed her arms.

Waving a come on, Kinsey opened the door. "Let's go face your nemesis."

Torn between apprehension and excitement Jet hurried to join him. They took the grand staircase then continued to the library. The door stood open. Jet saw Agent Elaney standing by the fireplace. As they entered the room she glanced around expecting to see her father. She frowned at Kinsey wondering what was up.

The treasury agent appeared nervous, his face slightly flushed, noticeable even with his tanned complexion. He didn't seem to know what to do with his hands. Jet had to bite her tongue to keep from asking what he was doing there. Perhaps he was the one who found her father. Maybe that was why he had asked all the questions.

Suddenly pictures in her mind came together. She recalled his business card. Asado Elaney it had said. Her mother remembered the name of the one night stand as someone named Otto Lane. Jet's eyes went to his face as she suddenly realized she possessed the same bushy dark hair, thin expressive eyebrows, and fine features. She opened her mouth then closed it.

Kinsey put his hand on her shoulder. "Let me introduce you to your father." He motioned toward the agent.

"You?" She was stunned. "You're my father?" Tears filled her eyes but she fought them back.

Elaney nodded apprehensively.

Jet was frozen to the spot where she stood. Agent Elaney began explaining the situation the night he met

Mona. "My wife divorced me, something I didn't want. That day the judge declared it final. My friends took me out to celebrate, which wasn't how I felt about it. I was mourning, not celebrating, but I got drunk, not quite incapacitated I guess, but willing to do things I wouldn't have under other circumstances. I never saw your mother again. I had no idea there was a child. In fact, if someone had suggested the possibility I'd have argued it given the state I was in."

"How did you know?" Jet was still numb with surprise.

"The first time I saw you, you reminded me of a picture of my mother. I heard in conversations here that you were looking for your father and having DNA tests done. I had mine tested and compared to yours."

"So there's no doubt?"

Agent Elaney shook his head. "I'm your father." He grimaced. "For better or worse." He held out his hand. "I'm sorry. I'd never have left you to grow up with no father if I'd known."

Suddenly tears came roaring to the surface and rolling down Jet's cheeks. She backed up embarrassed by the emotional traitor inside. Kinsey, stopped her, moving her toward Elaney who took her hands.

"I can't make up for all the years I wasn't around, but I'm happy to know you're my daughter. I think my wife will be too."

In his eyes Jet saw the concern, which made the tears come faster. Accepting the handkerchief Kinsey offered, she asked, "She wouldn't be upset?"

Agent Elaney shook his head. "I think she'd be glad to have a daughter, just as I am." The agent beckoned toward Kinsey. "And if you marry this guy, it would give us a couple we could call our kids. Maybe even have grandkids."

Jet took another step back. "You guys are moving too fast for me."

Kinsey caught her by the shoulders. "We can give you time to get used to the idea, just as long as you don't forget the plan."

She was overwhelmed. All she could do was laugh and cry at the same time.